NEVER THE CRIME

a Charlie-316 novel

Colin Conway | Frank Zafiro

Never the Crime: A Charlie-316 Novel

Cover design by Zach McCain

ISBN: 978-1-7368543-8-9

Original Ink Press, an imprint of High Speed Creative, LLC
1521 N. Argonne Road, #C-205
Spokane Valley, WA 99212

For my mom, Bonnie Louise Conway.
—Colin Conway

This is for a certain K-9 crew from back in the day: Dave Overhoff, Kevin King, Shawn Kendall, Danny Lesser, Craig Hamilton, Paul Gorman, Dan Waters, and Keith Cler. They know why. Molon Labe, my brothers.
—"Lieutenant" Frank Zafiro

NEVER THE
CRIME

Men in general judge more from
Appearances than from reality.
All men have eyes,
but few have the gift of penetration.
—Niccolo Machiavelli, political philosopher

TUESDAY

Justice delayed is justice denied.
—William Gladstone, former Prime Minister of Great Britain

Chapter 1

Spokane Police Officer Gary Stone pulled into an *Emergency Vehicles Only* stall outside city hall. From where he parked, he could see a gathering near the front entrance of the building. He checked his Apple watch. It was barely eight a.m. That could only mean one thing—a press briefing.

He climbed out of his unmarked patrol car and stood behind the opened driver's door. After glancing around to ensure that no one was watching, he tucked his shirt in, his hands moving expertly around his belt, being careful not to jam his fingers against the badge and gun on his left hip. He then straightened the knot on his tie and smoothed the length of its tail. He took off his sunglasses and tossed them onto the dashboard.

He leaned back into the car and grabbed his personal cell phone. For a moment, he thought about bringing his department-issued cell phone, too, but decided against it. He hated carrying both, so he forwarded his department number and emails to his personal one. Usually, the only time he carried the department phone was around the brass. The chief and captains wanted to see him with the appropriate equipment. Besides, the department-issued one was a Blackberry and who carried those anymore?

Stone then grabbed his portable radio, slammed the car door, and stepped to the sidewalk. The early morning sun was up, and the air felt crisp. Spring was Stone's favorite season as it always filled him with hope.

He approached city hall slowly, his eyes scanning the small crowd of journalists and protestors as they stood in the morning shade. A couple of security guards positioned themselves nearby, but no uniformed officers were present.

That meant the briefing was unscheduled and they didn't expect any hostility. Stone knew why the press was gathered. He'd read the morning newspaper. He would have expected at least one uniformed officer to be present and would have made that recommendation if asked.

City Councilman Justin Buckner stood behind a lectern. At thirty-nine years old, he was in his second term representing the third district. Recently divorced, he had two children, ages four and two. Normally genial, Buckner's face was twisted with barely disguised anger.

"What I did was not wrong," he said. His hands tightly gripped the edges of the lectern.

"Can you confirm the girl was eighteen years old?" Kelly Davis yelled. She was a reporter for the *Spokesman-Review* and a regular at city hall briefings.

Buckner's jaw tightened. "She's nineteen."

A murmur went through the crowd.

"I'm a man. She's a woman." Buckner's finger tapped the lectern, emphasizing each point. "That's all that matters."

One reporter hollered above the crowd's rumbling, "You're twenty years older than her."

"What does age have to do with this?" Buckner said, throwing his hands in the air. "She's an adult. So am I, for that matter. This reeks of ageism."

Someone yelled, "She was the babysitter!"

Stone studied the faces of the crowd. No one present appeared to be supportive of Buckner. No way for the councilman to win this argument. Even if what he'd done was legally okay, it *seemed* wrong.

Politically, Buckner should have known better. He'd been around long enough to understand how it would play in the public eye. Stone watched Buckner for another moment. He looked like a man juggling water and doing a bad job of it.

Shaking his head, Stone moved past the crowd, nodded at the two security guards, and walked into the building. As he stood near the elevator, an elderly woman approached. She had a knitted shawl wrapped around her shoulders and a sun hat on.

"Excuse me?" she said.

"Yes?"

"Where do I find the parks and recreation department?"

Stone smiled politely. "I'm sorry, ma'am. I don't know. You'll have to ask the security desk." He pointed to a booth where a guard sat.

"Oh, I thought you worked here."

"No, ma'am. I'm a police officer."

"You don't look like one," she said with kindly smile. "You're dressed so nicely."

Stone's smile remained. "Thank you. The security guard should be able to help."

The elevator dinged and Stone stepped in. He turned to watch the woman walk away. As the doors slid shut, he shook his head. It frustrated him that people confused him with city hall security.

The doors opened on the recently renovated seventh floor, where the mayor's office was now located. The new carpet smell still hung in the air.

As he stepped out of the elevator, Charlene Mapes, the mayor's latest assistant, made eye contact with him. She sat behind a monstrosity of a central hub. Anyone stepping off the elevator would not get past her without a greeting of some sort, even a silent one.

"Gary," she said flatly before turning her attention back to her computer.

Charlene was in her mid-forties and slightly heavy. Her short brown hair was tucked behind her ears.

"New haircut?" Stone asked.

Charlene's eyes shifted back to him suspiciously. "Why?"

"I was going to say it looked nice."

"Okay," she said, her voice flat. Again, her attention returned to her computer.

Stone waited for her to glance his way, hoping for a smile or at least some recognition for the compliment. When she didn't look up, Stone took it in stride. His goal was to make friends with everyone in city hall. Charlene had yet to smile at him, but he wouldn't give up.

As he walked away from the receptionist's desk, Stone noticed Mayor Andrew Sikes talking in hushed tones with Councilwoman Margaret Patterson. The two of them leaned close together. When the mayor noticed Stone, he flashed a grin and raised his hand in a perfunctory wave.

Stone nodded in response but continued toward his office.

"Gary!" the mayor called.

He stopped then and turned.

Sikes ambled over. "Hey, when you have some time, let's get together. I'd like to bounce some ideas off you. Maybe catch up on how things are going in your world."

"Sure," Stone said. "That sounds great, Mr. Mayor."

Sikes patted his arm. "I'll have Charlene set it up." He turned and hurried back to where the councilwoman was waiting. She studied Stone with intense interest.

He nodded once toward her then headed to the mailstop, where both internal and external correspondence was delivered each day. There were several items waiting for him, including an interoffice envelope.

His small office at the far end of the floor had a mahogany desk, a laptop, and a filing cabinet. No pictures hung on the walls.

I should decorate this soon.

He'd been in this assignment for almost a year and the seventh-floor remodel had only been finished for about sixty days. Everyone else on the floor had made their offices presentable, like little homes away from home, so Stone was now looking like the odd man out.

Soon.

Prior to the move, he'd worked out of a cubicle near Charlene's old desk. There was never an opportunity to decorate that. Stone half expected someone to take this office away from him and move him back into a cubicle on a lower floor.

His first order of business was his mail. There were two letters addressed to him. One was from a local volunteer organization that supported the police department. They were asking him to participate on their board. He set it to the side. It was something to consider. He might even run it by the chief to get his thoughts on it.

The second letter was the police union announcing that their annual meeting was set for next month. Union President Dale Thomas smiled in a photo in the upper left corner. Even in the black-and-white picture, his sport coat looked ill-fitting and tie knot too large. Why the union bothered to still use printed mail escaped him. He crumpled the announcement and threw it away.

He picked up the interoffice envelope then, unwound the string fastener, and opened it. He removed a letter with a Post-it attached to it.

Handwritten on the little yellow note was *I think this is for you—Jean.*

Stone removed a letter addressed to Councilman Dennis Hahn. The handwriting was shaky, and the thought process was incoherent. The author, Lyle Bunney, accused the councilman of being a pawn of the Russian government, conspiring with the FDA to withhold a cure for cancer, and poisoning the aquifer with fluoride. The letter rambled for three pages of tightly spaced printing.

Part of Stone's city hall assignment was to provide threat assessments when necessary. That was a fancy way of saying he needed to respond whenever wingnuts wrote threatening letters and emails to city hall employees. Most often, he would review a letter and quickly determine that further action wasn't necessary.

In this case, however, Lyle Bunney earned himself extra attention with the final line of his letter. He wrote:

To Stone, even with the spelling errors, the letter looked like a threat to kill. It would require a response.

He grabbed the letter, headed to the stairs, and walked down to the sixth floor where the city council offices were located. Due to the recent remodel, the mayor's office was now above the council members'. No one missed the significance of that fact.

Everything was a power struggle within these walls.

He pushed open the door and stepped onto the sixth floor. There were nine city council members and each had their own assistant. The council members had separate offices while the assistants sat in front in a wide-open area. He headed toward Jean's desk and she smiled as he approached.

"Hey, boy-o, snazzy tie."

"Where are the others?" he asked, thumbing toward the vacant assistant desks.

"What am I? Chopped liver? They went to get coffee."

Stone did a head count. Only three council members were in their offices. The rest were vacant.

He leaned in and whispered, "You see what was going on downstairs?"

Jean leaned forward. "I know. Crazy, isn't it?"

"Why is Buckner making such a big stink about this?"

Jean's eyes swept the offices before she answered, her voice low. "He's stupid."

"He should shut up and hide out. Let this whole thing blow over."

"No! He should resign is what he should do."

Stone's eyes widened. "Resign?"

"He's having sex with the babysitter, Gary. That's political suicide. He should pack it in."

"Isn't he divorced?"

"So what, it's gross. Women aren't going to vote for him again."

"Did you know about this? I mean before it happened."

Jean smirked. "What do you think?"

"I think you knew."

"We assistants, we're like the CIA. We know, but we don't tell."

"So you're telling me you know where the bodies are buried?"

"You said it, not me."

"Remind me not to cross you."

"I'll remind you, Gary Stone. Never doubt that."

"So, Miss CIA, do you think this is going to get worse?"

"Oh, it's going to get much worse."

"Wait. What else did Buckner do?"

Jean pulled back.

"What's wrong?"

"Nothing."

"Did he do something worse than the babysitter? Is something else going on?"

Before she could answer, Councilwoman Patterson walked into the office. Jean noticed her and said, "Councilwoman, good morning."

Patterson stopped at Jean's desk. "Jean, when is Dennis coming in?"

"Councilman Hahn will be in shortly, ma'am. He had an appointment this morning."

"When he arrives, will you have him see me?"

"Yes, ma'am. I'll let him know."

Patterson then turned her attention to Stone. Her eyes flicked to his shoes, then quickly ran his length. "To what do we owe this pleasure, Officer Stone?"

"Following up on a letter."

"Letter?" Patterson asked.

"A threat against Councilman Hahn."

"Is this anything the rest of us need to be worried about?"

"Not sure yet. I'm going to check it out now."

Patterson's gaze moved between Stone and Jean. "Well, then, don't let us hold you up." She turned and strode into her office.

Jean leaned forward and, in her best impression of Patterson said, "Well, then, don't let us hold you up."

Stone gave a small wave goodbye and headed toward the elevators.

Chapter 2

Officer Ray Zielinski drummed his fingers on the top of his mobile data computer (MDC), his eyes scanning the street. He'd been on scene for five minutes, waiting for Gary Stone to show up, and he was already tired of this call.

Chief's Bitch probably got lost on the way.

Zielinski grunted at the thought. "Ol' Charlie Bravo," he muttered. He was mildly surprised that the chief's favorite pet ever left city hall unless it was to drive to the police station to huddle in the chief's office. Zielinski didn't know what the two of them talked about in those meetings, but he knew one thing—he'd been on the job twenty-one years, and he'd been in the chief's office exactly once and that had been to get his ass chewed for lipping off to a lieutenant at roll call. Outside of that, he'd spoken to the chief of police less in his entire career than Gary Stone probably did in a week.

Now he had to sit here, up the block from some nutbar's house, and wait for the guy like he was the crown prince of the police department. It was bull. Stone was a patrol officer, just like Zielinski.

What does the chief see in that guy?

He had to give it to Baumgartner, though. The man always seemed fair. He was old school enough to believe that you either got a reprimand letter in your file or you got an ass-chewing, but never both. As unpleasant as it had been that time to stand tall in the chief's office getting bawled out, at least when it was over, it was over. And less than two months later, the chief was in the same roll call room where Zielinski had mouthed off, handing him his fifteen-year pin and offering sincere congratulations in front of the same lieutenant he'd smart-assed.

Baumgartner was a cop's cop, which Zielinski respected. It was also why he didn't understand the whole Stone thing.

Whatever, he finally decided. He had bigger problems these days than wondering about Charlie Bravo. The newest IA complaint, for starters, filed by some whiny civilian who obviously thought Zielinski should kiss his ass. And there were the constant money issues.

As if on cue, his phone buzzed. He glanced down and saw it was a text from ex-wife number two. He didn't even have to open the message to know what it would be about. Her favorite word since the divorce was *alimony*. Zielinski called it ali*money*, which ticked her off to no end. The close of the two-year window requiring him to pay it was just two months away, but he had a sneaking suspicion she was going to take him back to court to get it extended. On what grounds, he had no clue, but her scumbag lawyer would manufacture something.

He glanced up the street again, then checked his rearview mirror.

Where the hell was Stone?

The phone buzzed again, but this time it continued, letting him know it was a call, not a text.

Zielinski thought about not answering, but she was persistent. There was a fifty-fifty chance she'd keep calling over and over until he either answered or shut off his phone. He could say what he wanted about Amber, but she would not be ignored.

He answered the call. Before he could utter a greeting, she snapped, "What the hell, Ray?"

"I know."

"You know? If you know, then why am I looking at a bank transfer that's short?"

"Some expenses came up."

"How is that my problem? You need to pay me as agreed, or there'll be consequences."

"You sound like a loan shark or something."

"If I could send some thug to break your legs, I would. Believe me."

"Nice. My lawyer might be able to convince the judge that's a threat you just made."

She scoffed. "Your lawyer couldn't convince the judge that there's no Santa Claus."

Zielinski didn't argue, mostly because she was right about how lousy his attorney had been. "Look," he said. "Jody has to get braces. I had to make a down payment to the orthodontist for what the insurance doesn't cover. That's why I was short this month."

"So once again, the first wife comes first. You know, if that hadn't been the case the entire time we were married, we'd probably still be together. But you always picked her over me."

"That's crap," Zielinski said, clenching his jaw. "I'm not picking her over you. I'm picking my kid, who needs braces."

"Her teeth are fine. Little Miss Priss is just using Jody as a tool. She's trying to carve more money out of you, like always."

And you're not?

"I didn't know you were a dentist now," Zielinski said.

"It wouldn't matter. You always choose her over me."

"Like I already said, I'm choosing to pay for my kid's braces over paying ali*money* to a full-grown woman who can work."

"I do work!"

"Ten hours a week? Spare me."

"Screw you, Ray. Let's see how smart you are when I take you back to court. You'll be paying alimony for another two years or paying that numb nuts lawyer the same amount in legal fees to stop it. Either way, it's money out of your pocket, smart ass."

Zielinski suppressed a sigh. "Chill out," he said. "I'll get some extra duty work between now and next payday, and I'll get you the rest of your money, all right? Just cut me some slack for once?"

"For *once*? Our entire marriage was me cutting you slack."

"Well, then you should be good at it by now."

"Go to hell, Ray."

"Already there, sister," Zielinski replied, but halfway through his retort, he heard the click of a severed connection. As usual, she'd hung up on him. Amber was hell on hanging up on people. Him, at least.

He dropped the phone onto the passenger seat. When he glanced up, he saw a brand-new unmarked police car glide to a stop in front of the target address.

"The hits just keep on coming," he grumbled.

Zielinski pulled the keys from the ignition and exited his patrol car. In no particular hurry, he sauntered toward Officer Gary Stone, who waited at the end of the sidewalk leading to the small house. He was smoothing his tie as Zielinski approached. When he was near, Stone greeted him with a warm grin.

"How's it going, Ray?"

Zielinski grunted and nodded upwards once with his chin. He pointed to Stone's Impala. "Nice ride. I mean, it's a little small, but nice. New?"

Stone shrugged. "I've had it about six months."

"No, I mean it's new. This year's model."

"Yeah, maybe." Stone thought for a second. "Or last year's. I never really thought about it."

What a jerk.

The patrol car Zielinski was driving today was at least eight years old, with plenty of hard miles on it. Based upon his seniority, he was able to grab one of the better vehicles available in the motor pool, but it was still junk compared to Stone's ride.

"I like how you parked it," Zielinski said, barely containing a sneer. "Charlie Bravo style."

Stone's eyes narrowed in confusion. "Charlie Bravo?"

He doesn't know what they call him. That warmed his heart.

"Charlie Bravo style is right in front of the target address," he said to Stone, motioning up the sidewalk.

"Damn." Stone at least had the decency to look sheepish. "Thank God I'm not in the probation car, right?"

Zielinski just stared at him.

After an awkward moment, Stone raised his eyebrows. "Shall we?"

Zielinski stepped to the side and waved him forward.

Stone took the hint and led the way up the sidewalk. Zielinski strode behind him, shaking his head. He'd spent his entire career in patrol and didn't have much use for any of the cake-eaters outside of the division, except maybe a few detectives. When they weren't shopping on duty, they at least solved a case or two. Most of them had the sense not to park in front of the house they were contacting.

"You want to clue me in here?" Zielinski asked as they approached the door. "All dispatch said was to back you on a citizen contact."

"Sure," Stone said, without turning around. He stopped at a ramp leading up to the porch and waited for Zielinski to catch up. Then he said, "Guy's name is Lyle Bunney. He wrote a letter to a city council member that contained a threat. I need to talk to him and see if he's a credible danger or not."

"So he's crazy?"

Stone frowned. "He might have some mental health issues."

"Great," Zielinski groused. "From one crazy right to another one."

"Did you just handle a similar call before this?"

"Something like that." Zielinski sidestepped the ramp and mounted the steps, taking up a position to the side of the door. "Go ahead and knock."

Stone took the ramp to the small porch and stood on the opposite side of the door. Zielinski was glad for that. Any cop who didn't know not to stand in the fatal funnel directly in front of the door was too dim to safely be around.

The first two polite knocks Stone gave the door went unanswered. Stone waited patiently with a smile. He turned his hand over and examined his cuticles.

"What are you doing?" Zielinski asked.

"What?"

"I'm not standing around here while you check your manicure."

Stone dropped his hand and his smile. "Maybe he's not home."

"Did you schedule an appointment?"

"What?"

Zielinski rolled his eyes then pounded loudly on the door with a balled fist. Years of graveyard and power shifts had honed his feel for the right kind of loud to wake the drunks or convince the reluctant that it was time to immediately come to the door, because the cops weren't going away anytime soon.

"I'm coming already!" The muffled voice from within sounded agitated. When the door swung open, an angry man in a wheelchair stared out at them. "What do you want?"

"Good morning, sir," Stone began, his voice calm, but direct. "Are you Lyle Bunney?"

"Who's asking?"

"I'm Officer Gary Stone, Spokane Police. This is Officer Zielinski."

Zielinski gave Lyle a nod, his eyes sweeping over the man.

Lyle Bunney's eyes had a slightly frantic quality to them, but Zielinski noticed that his hair was combed and he was recently shaven. He was also better dressed than some detectives Zielinski had seen.

"The hell do you want?" Lyle demanded.

"Can we talk inside?" Stone asked, his tone genial, but still in control.

"Here's just fine."

Stone smiled, and he lowered his voice slightly. "I figured you might not want the neighbors listening in on your private conversations."

Lyle's scowl softened while he considered. He glanced to the left at the house next door, nodding slowly. "Yeah, okay. You can come inside, but don't touch anything."

Lyle reversed his wheelchair to allow them entry. Zielinski followed Stone inside. He had to give the officer some credit. He'd read into Lyle's possible paranoia and played on it to get them invited inside the house.

Zielinski took up a position away from Lyle and off to the side while Stone talked.

"Mr. Bunney," Stone said, "do you know why I'm here?"

"To harass me," Lyle said. "Or arrest me for no reason and hold me without bail. I know how SPD operates."

"I'm not planning to arrest you," Stone said. "But I am concerned about a letter you wrote to Councilman Hahn."

Lyle didn't reply. He stared at Stone with deep suspicion.

While the two of them spoke, Zielinski alternated between watching Lyle's hands and scanning the interior of the home. At first, it struck him as a mess, but as he looked more closely, he determined that while it was cluttered, the house itself was clean. There were no stray dishes in the living room, or discarded clothing. No dog or cat waste, which Zielinski saw—and smelled—all too often. He gazed beyond the living room and into the kitchen, noticing the counters were mostly bare and the sink empty.

"Stop looking around!" Lyle snapped at Zielinski.

Zielinski motioned toward Stone. "I'm just standing here."

"You can't look at my stuff without a warrant."

"I can't stand here with my eyes closed, either, pal." He pointed at Stone. "Mind your business with him. Things will go faster."

Lyle glanced back and forth between Zielinski and Stone. "You two trying to trick me?"

"No, sir," Stone said, "but we do need to talk about a few things."

"So talk!" Lyle lifted his arms and dropped them in frustration.

Unruffled, Stone began to ask him some general questions.

Zielinski eyed the clutter more closely. It consisted mostly of newspapers, magazines, and composition notebooks. He picked up one of the notebooks and flipped it open to a random page. The shaky, condensed handwriting revealed Lyle's thoughts on the connection between the assassinations of both Kennedy brothers and Martin Luther King, Jr. In the short paragraph he read, Zielinski got the sense that it was the CIA who had been responsible in all three cases, using patsies to accomplish their ends. Lyle's multi-pronged analysis concluded that the remaining Kennedy brother was allowed to live because he forswore running for the presidency.

Zielinski frowned. Didn't Ted Kennedy make a run one year? He couldn't remember. Maybe he was thinking of Gary Hart.

Lyle spotted him holding the notebook. "I said don't touch anything!" he yelled, pointing a finger. "That's a violation, right there. That's a lawsuit."

"Mr. Bunney—" Stone tried to placate him, but Lyle ignored him.

"I'm suing you!" he shouted at Zielinski.

"Yeah?" Zielinski said, unmoved. "Well, the line forms to the right."

Lyle blinked, not sure what to make of the reply. Even Stone looked at him like he was unsure of how to take Zielinski's response.

He put the notebook down and lifted his hands in a *there you go* gesture to both Lyle and Stone. "All better?"

Lyle pressed his lips together. "Leave my stuff alone."

Zielinski didn't answer him. Instead, he stood in place and waited for Stone to resume his conversation with the man.

"Mr. Bunney," Stone continued, "your letter made some interesting allegations."

"They're not allegations. They're true."

"That may be, but there was one thing that concerned me."

Zielinski waited until Lyle was fully engaged with Stone again before he slowly moved around to the other side of the living room. As he passed the coffee table, he noticed several stamped letters stacked there.

"What concerned me," Stone said, "was how you ended your letter. Do you remember what you wrote?"

"I remember everything."

Stone pulled out his phone and tapped the screen. "Well, I don't, so I took a picture of it. You wrote, 'Stop your terrorist ways, councilman, or I'll stop them for you. Permanently.' Do you remember writing that?"

"I just told you I remember everything. The chem trails haven't affected me yet. That's because I stay inside most of the time."

"Chem trails?"

"Don't act like you don't know what I'm talking about. They issue you people pills to counteract the effects."

"Okay," Stone said amiably. "But what you wrote, Mr. Bunney, it sounds like a threat. At least, you can see why someone might construe it that way, right?"

"I wrote that letter to Councilman Dennis Hahn of the fourth city district. It was strictly intended for his eyes only. You're violating federal law by intercepting private correspondence."

"Councilman Hahn gave me the letter, Mr. Bunney. I didn't intercept it."

"So you say."

"What you wrote worried the councilman."

"It should," Lyle said.

Zielinski lifted the sealed envelopes and glanced at the addresses. "There's one here to the mayor," he said, thumbing through the small stack. "And two state senators. Oh, and this last one is to the chief of police."

"Put those down!" Lyle shouted at him. "You're touching my stuff!"

Zielinski let them fall to the coffee table. The thick envelopes thudded against the wood. "Were you going to send these, too, Lyle?"

"No."

"Then why are they stamped?"

"I can send letters to whoever I want! It's my first amendment right. Freedom of speech. And freedom of the press."

"You're a journalist?" Zielinski said, doubtful.

"Yes."

Zielinski gave him a skeptical look. "What news outlet?"

"I'm an independent."

"Of course you are," Zielinski said. For a second, he wondered if he was pushing his luck with this guy. He was clearly a little crazy, but crazy didn't keep people from calling Internal Affairs. One demeanor complaint hanging over his head was enough.

"How's that work?" Stone interjected, drawing Lyle's attention back to him.

Lyle stared at him for a moment without answering. Then he said in a low tone, "I have a blog."

Stone's eyebrows went up. "Really? What's it called?"

"*Piercing the Veil*," Lyle answered, his voice a mixture of pride and irritation.

"That's a cool name," Stone said. "What kind of journalism do you focus on?"

"The kind that sheds the truth on all the lies in our society today."

"Like what?"

Lyle's eyes bugged out at Stone. "Like what? There's literally hundreds."

"Which lies are you most concerned with?"

Lyle proceeded to tell him. Zielinski tuned out the conversation, listening only to the tone of Lyle's voice to monitor it for danger. He wandered into the kitchen and glanced around, seeing nothing of interest. When he turned to the hallway that led to the back of the house, though, he spotted a rifle leaning against the wall.

Immediately, a small flare of adrenaline flashed in his stomach. Being crazy with some conspiracy theory issues was one thing. Being crazy with some conspiracy theory issues and a gun was a little different.

Zielinski made his way to the hallway with his hand on his pistol. After peeking into the bedroom to make sure no one else was there, he picked up the rifle. It was a .22 caliber with a bolt action and open sights. A small clip fed the bullets into the loading assembly. Zielinski pressed the magazine release and removed the mag. Empty. He worked the bolt to check the chamber and found it empty as well.

Well, he's not shooting anyone with an empty gun.

Still, getting bullets and loading the rifle would be easy enough. He wondered if Lyle had it in him. He doubted it. Half the time, the crazy bastard probably forgot it was his gun and thought it was the CIA planting evidence to make him a patsy for the next assassination.

When he returned to the living room, Lyle was telling Stone about the nefarious purpose of fluoride in the city water.

"What's with the gun?" Zielinski interrupted.

Lyle stopped mid-sentence and turned to look at him. "Are you searching my house?" he asked. "Where's your warrant?"

Zielinski ignored him. "He's got a .22 rifle leaning against the wall in the hallway," he told Stone. "It isn't loaded."

"You touched my stuff! That's another violation!" Lyle said. "That's another charge in my lawsuit."

"Good luck with that," Zielinski said. "You can't get blood from a turnip." He glanced at Stone. "Or a stone, for that matter."

"You can't search my house," Lyle persisted. "I know my rights."

"I didn't search. I saw."

"It's the same thing!"

"No, it's not." Zielinski looked at Stone. "We about done here?"

Stone frowned at him but shrugged. "I think so." He turned to Lyle. "Mr. Bunney, you can write all the letters you want—"

"I know I can. I know my rights."

"That's fine. But what you can't do is threaten people. Especially public officials. It's a crime, and you can be charged for doing so."

"That sounds like persecution to me."

"It's the law. Now, tell me: what did you mean when you wrote about stopping Councilman Hahn's terrorist ways permanently?"

Lyle stared at him, his jaw clenched and working. Stone waited, his expression neutral and open. Zielinski watched them both, feeling his patience slipping.

Finally, Lyle gritted out his reply. "I meant getting him thrown out of office. Or not reelected."

Stone eyed him closely. "How?"

"Through my blog. And voting."

"But not hurting him somehow?"

"No."

"You're sure?"

"I just said it, didn't I?"

"I'm double-checking."

"Well, double-check your ass next time. Or get your hearing examined."

Zielinski let out a small sigh. "C'mon, man, it sounds like we're done. This guy is no threat."

"I could be a threat!" Lyle protested. "You think just because I'm in a wheelchair—"

Zielinski turned to him, interrupting. "Really? You could be a threat? Because if so, we've got to take you to jail, right now. Directly. Do not pass go."

Lyle stared at him, stunned.

"Is that really what you want? I'll get to touch all your stuff then."

Lyle looked from Zielinski to Stone. "I'm not a threat," he muttered.

"What?" Zielinski asked, leaning forward.

"I'm not a threat," Lyle repeated, still barely above a whisper.

"I didn't think so." Zielinski looked to Stone for confirmation that they were finished.

Stone hesitated, as if he wanted to pursue the interview further, but after a moment, he nodded. "I'm going to believe you, Mr. Bunney, but please consider how you phrase your letters in the future."

Lyle scowled, muttering about freedom of the press under his breath.

"Thanks for taking the time to speak with us today," Stone said, removing a business card from his pocket and putting it on the table near Bunny. Then he glanced at Zielinski and headed out the door. Zielinski followed. When the front door closed behind him, he heard Lyle turning the deadbolt lock.

Once they reached Stone's car, Zielinski shook his head. "That guy's a complete one-oh-five."

Stone gave him a confused look. "What's that?"

"Old radio code for mentals."

"One-oh-five," Stone repeated. His phone buzzed, and he checked his text. Then he glanced up at Zielinski. "Sorry, I don't mean to be rude. That was Marilyn."

"Your girlfriend?"

"What? No. Marilyn. The chief's secretary?"

You little name-dropping prick.

"The chief wants me back at the department ASAP. I gotta go."

"Charlie Bravo time, huh?"

Stone scowled. "What's with the Charlie Bravo bit? Is that another old radio code?"

"Something like that." Zielinski turned to go, then stopped. "Wait. You're not expecting me to cut paper on this, are you? Or is this a One-David call?"

One-David was the clearance code for a contact without a report. This call merited at least a brief report, though. Zielinski wondered if Stone was going to try to dump it on him, using the chief's summons as an excuse.

Stone shook his head. "No, I've got it. Thanks for the help."

Zielinski grunted a reply and walked back to his own car without looking back. Somehow, he didn't think watching the chief's little minion scurry away in his new car would improve his mood. It was only after he closed the car door and started the engine that another thought occurred to him.

I should've made nice with the kid. He could've helped me out with this demeanor complaint in IA. Put in a good word with his pal, the chief.

Zielinski shrugged. It didn't matter. The complaint was bull, anyway.

He cleared the call with the disposition code of Two-David, an assist with no report. Then he made the notation *CB to file report*. He laughed at the note, wondering if any of the other guys would notice it.

He pulled away from the curb. Before he made it a block, the dispatcher sent him another call for service.

Back to the grind.

Chapter 3

This is ugly, Captain Dana Hatcher thought.

The latest batch of crime statistics from the FBI were about to be released to the public and she sat at her desk, staring at an advance copy. No matter which way she turned the page, the numbers sucked.

The FBI comparison report provided an in-depth look at specific crimes within each jurisdiction and ranked each jurisdiction in comparison to similar-sized communities throughout the country. Spokane made the top ten in several categories, which wasn't a good thing.

She wished she could take some solace in the fact that the report lagged by six months, but the internal reports from the department's own crime analysis unit showed a continued steady increase in several categories. Things weren't getting better, they were getting worse. The city was bleeding, and as the captain of patrol, a lot of the responsibility to stop the flow of blood fell right on Hatcher's shoulders. Hatcher pushed the report away and rubbed her eyes.

"The extra bar getting to you already?"

Hatcher opened her eyes to see Captain Tom Farrell settling into the seat across from her desk. He hadn't knocked, just walked right in. For a moment, she wondered why. Did he still think of her as a lieutenant?

Or is it because I'm a woman?

She dismissed the second thought. Farrell was senior to her, that was all.

"I won't lie," she said. "Things were easier when I was a lieutenant."

Farrell pointed to the captain's bars on his collar. "Double the bars, triple the headaches. That's executive leadership."

"I've been finding that out."

"It's been three months now, so your feet should be pretty wet."

"It's not my feet I'm worried about. It's more like the water is up to my neck." She pointed at the report on her desk. "The NIBRS report gets released to the public next month. When people see these numbers, it's going to be brutal. And city hall has this advance report, too, so you know they'll be ready when people start clamoring."

Farrell nodded sympathetically. "Yeah, I saw it. We're getting absolutely raped on stolen vehicles and burglaries."

Raped? Are you kidding me? Hatcher clenched her jaw, letting the description begrudgingly pass without comment. "Fraud is up, too. All property crime, really."

"The UCRs are six months old, though."

Hatcher frowned. The FBI report was previously called the Uniform Crime Report (UCR), but that changed years ago to NIBRS, the National Incident-Based Reporting System. It was far more precise and covered many more categories than its predecessor. She knew Farrell only used the term UCR out of habit, but the fact still mildly irritated her.

"You shouldn't frown like that," Farrell said. "It makes you look angry."

Her frown deepened. That comment was *definitely* because she was a woman. "I *am* angry, Tom. Our own analytics for the last two months show crime up, too. We've got to do something about it."

"Like what?"

"That's what I'm trying to figure out."

Farrell nodded slowly, then shrugged. "These things are cyclical, Dana. Crime goes up in the summer when it's warm, and it hibernates a little in the winter. You're seeing an uptick from the winter numbers now that spring is here."

Hatcher shook her head. "Property crime is much higher compared to this same time period last year. The overall trend line is sharply up. I'd say we have to get ahead of this, but I think the truth is that we're already behind."

"We're always behind the curve. It's the nature of police work."

"Maybe," she conceded, "but we're falling further behind, and I'm worried."

"Worried about what, exactly?"

"About how bad it might get," Hatcher said. "Tom, we have to put our heads together on this. You're in charge of Investigations, I'm in charge of Patrol. Between the two of us, we've got to be proactive. If we don't, these numbers are only going to get worse, and it's going to start to look like a full-fledged crime epidemic. One we'll get blamed for."

Farrell sighed. "We'll take the hit, for sure. And it won't matter that your patrol cops are running from one call to the next, or that my detectives are carrying bigger caseloads than ever before. We'll get blamed, just like we get credit when crime goes down. But let me tell you something I've learned. The crime rate is a lot like the economy. It's too big and has too many moving parts for anyone, including us, to have a major impact on it. Sure, we can do some things, and maybe after we do them, the crime rate will drop, but does that mean we actually caused it? I mean, any more than a tax cut or a tax increase has any significant impact on the economy?"

Hatcher stared at him in mild surprise. "Are you really trying to say that the police don't have an impact on the crime rate?"

"No. I'm saying we greatly overestimate how much of one we have. A big snowstorm or a new Costco opening has more of an impact than we do."

Hatcher shook her head. "I don't believe that. I *can't* believe that."

"Either way, it doesn't matter," Farrell said. "We're expected to make a concerted effort, so we have to do whatever we can, and take whatever victories we can get."

Hatcher wondered if Farrell should think about retiring. His philosophy reeked of cynicism.

"It all comes back to drugs, when you think about it," Farrell said. "Mostly meth, but heroin, a lot more now that marijuana has been legalized."

Hatcher nodded in agreement. She knew this.

Farrell continued, explaining anyway. "Users need money for their dope, so they break into houses and cars, or just steal the cars to sell or use as meth taxis. They write bad checks, shoplift, scam old people, the whole gamut."

"I know."

"It's not going to stop unless people stop being addicted to drugs."

"Isn't your narcotics unit supposed to be working on that?"

Farrell chuckled. "Touché. But their mandate isn't to focus on the user level. They're working on the supply side of things, targeting mid-level dealers. The idea is to take away the supply and make it harder for dopers to get their dope."

"The problem with that concept is when less dope is available, it costs more, so these people have to steal more stuff to get enough money to pay for their fix. That drives up the theft stats. Less available product actually makes things worse."

"In the short term, yes."

Hatcher raised the NIBRS report from her desk. "These numbers are six months old. I'd say we're edging into mid-to-long-term territory."

"You're the new kid on the block, command-wise," Farrell continued. "You always had good ideas as a lieutenant. What's your idea here?"

Hatcher took a deep breath and leaned back in her chair. "You say that the crime rate is hard to impact in the same way the economy does, right?"

Farrell nodded.

"Well," she said, "some things have a disproportionate impact. Have you heard of the Pareto Principle?"

Farrell squinted. "No."

"Sometimes it's called the eighty/twenty rule."

His eyes registered recognition. "Oh, sure. It's a leadership thing. You'll spend eighty percent of your time dealing with twenty percent of your people, right?"

"Right, but it has a broader scope than that. The principle says that eighty percent of your outcomes result from twenty percent of your causes." She waited for a moment for Farrell to catch on, but he kept watching her and waiting, so she continued. "If we apply this to our crime here in Spokane, how does that look?"

Farrell considered. "Twenty percent of our criminals are doing eighty percent of the crime."

"Exactly. Our twenty percent is probably those same dopers you were just talking about. I think it's a considerably smaller percentage than twenty, but I'll have to get crime analysis to run those numbers to be sure."

"So you want to target the twenty percent?"

"Makes sense, doesn't it?"

"Of course," Farrell said. "It's not a new idea. You arrest a high-profile offender, you get more bang for your buck."

"So what if we created a team that did nothing but target those high-profile offenders?" Hatcher said. "We untether a few hard-charging patrol cops from the radio so they don't have to answer calls, and send them out hunting for the most active criminals. Plus, we add a detective to the team to handle search warrants and routine follow-up and to coordinate with the prosecutor." She made a fist and dropped it onto her desk with a thud. "We could crush a lot of crime that way."

Farrell thought about it. "Sort of a search and destroy team, huh?"

"Exactly."

"And you have the staffing for this?"

"No, but I'm willing to pull a few bodies from answering the radio. If that means a few lower priority calls for service have to wait longer or simply get dumped, I think the tradeoff is worth it."

"That'll make the citizens who placed those calls angry," he warned.

"More people are going to be angry about bigger issues if we don't deal with this situation."

"True," Farrell agreed. He thought about it some more before answering. "It could work," he said. "And if nothing else, no one could say we sat on our hands doing nothing while the crime rate continued to climb, right?"

"Maybe we'll even make a dent."

Farrell nodded. "It's a good idea, Dana. You should take the lead on it."

Hatcher blinked. It had never occurred to her to do otherwise. She was the patrol captain, and the team would be largely comprised of patrol officers. Besides, it was her idea.

"Okay," she said. "I will."

"I'll assign you a detective when you're up and running."

"Thanks."

"You got a name for your team yet?"

She shook her head. "I hadn't even thought about that. I was focused on how it will work."

"Think of something sexy. It'll make the chief more likely to approve it."

Hatcher frowned. "You think I need permission for this? I'm supposed to be the captain of patrol. I'm trying to solve a problem here."

"You could just do it and beg forgiveness later," Farrell said. "But I think we all know how that would go over with the chief. Besides, you're not just talking about patrol here. You want a detective and I wouldn't be surprised if the prosecutor ends up wanting to funnel all the cases to one attorney, so what you've got is multi-divisional, multi-agency collaboration. If I were you, I'd at least plan on advising the chief of your plan, even if you aren't necessarily saying mother-may-I."

Hatcher considered his words. "All right. Thanks, Tom."

He smiled at her and stood. At the door, he stopped and said, "The bars look good on you, by the way. I'm glad you got promoted."

After Farrell left, Hatcher touched the twin bars on her collar. Then she reached for a legal pad and started making notes.

Chapter 4

Chief Robert Baumgartner slid the letter across his desk toward Gary Stone, then waited while his Special Police Problems officer read it. He remembered when he first came across Stone while attending the police academy graduation to give a few remarks. During the informal milling around that occurred afterwards, he found himself standing next to Stone. At first, he was put off by how little of the high-speed, low-drag alpha-hunter persona the new officer seemed to have. Frankly, he had wondered if Stone was the kind of kid who had his milk money taken from him by bullies every day at school. Or whatever bullies did nowadays. Maybe they reprogrammed his iPod, or something.

It only took a little while to see that while Stone wasn't cut from the cloth of the hyper-aggressive, meat-eater mold that Baumgartner preferred in his frontline cops, he also wasn't intimidated by much. He carried on a conversation that was respectful of the chief's position, but without the awe or the sycophancy that he sometimes experienced from those supposedly tougher cops.

And he seemed smart.

Afterwards, he talked to the academy commander and looked through Stone's file. A picture soon emerged of a different kind of cop, with a different set of skills. Baumgartner saw the value in those skills, and although it took a few years for him to find the right way to exploit them, he had Stone correctly positioned now.

Stone glanced up from the letter. "This is a pretty serious accusation Miss Rabe is making."

"It is," the chief agreed.

"The press will freak when they get wind of it. A married city councilman accused of having sex with a seventeen-year-old?"

"Sixteen is the age of consent," Baumgartner said.

"Really? What about a teacher sleeping with a high school student? Aren't the students sometimes older than sixteen?"

Baumgartner waved his hand. "That's a supervisory relationship, but you're complicating the issue. Like I said, sixteen is the age to worry about here and since that's the case, Hahn shouldn't be in jeopardy with the law."

"Maybe not," Stone said. "The sharks will smell blood in the water, either way. Of course, Councilman Buckner will be thrilled. This is way worse than him and the babysitter. It'll take the heat off him in a heartbeat."

"Let's not worry about that right now," the chief said. "This information isn't in the public domain just yet."

"I see," Stone said. "Because it's an ongoing investigation, you mean?"

"In a way, yes."

"In a way?"

Baumgartner pointed at the letter in Stone's grasp. "I want you to look into this, Gary." Stone was one of the few patrol officers the chief addressed by first name. "And I want you to be discreet about it."

Stone looked surprised. "Wait. Shouldn't a sexual assault detective investigate?"

"Under normal circumstances," Baumgartner agreed, "but these aren't normal circumstances. We've got the Buckner situation, for one thing. As you pointed out, the accused is another council member. That makes things…volatile."

"I see your point." Stone glanced down at the letter with a look of uncertainty. "Her letter *is* a little vague, sir. I mean, she's clear about being seventeen, and she's clear about having sex with Councilman Hahn, but she sort of hints at a later sexual assault."

"That's the number one reason I want *you* looking into this instead of a detective. If it is a political scandal but not a police matter, I don't want the department getting dragged into someone else's garbage. If it actually turns out to be a criminal matter, we can turn your investigation over to the sex crimes unit for follow-up."

Stone stared at him for a moment, saying nothing.

"Gary?" Baumgartner asked.

"Just making sure I understand. You want this to stay quiet unless there's a crime?"

Baumgartner gave a small shrug. "Not exactly. I want to know what we're dealing with before anyone else is aware of the situation. It could go a number of different ways, and doing what's right for the department depends on knowing as far in advance as possible which way it's going to go."

"And Miss Rabe?"

"If you determine she's a victim, we'll do right by her, of course."

Baumgartner didn't mention to Stone that he'd already had Michelle Tremblay in crime analysis pull a history on Betty Rabe. From what he'd seen, he doubted she'd turn out to be the victim of an actual crime. In fact, he had his doubts about whether she was even telling the truth about the sexual liaison with Councilman Hahn. He decided not to let Stone in on his thoughts. He didn't want to bias the officer.

"This is sensitive, Gary," Baumgartner continued. "The letter was sent to the mayor's office, and he handed it over to me personally. We want this contained until you get whatever happened sorted out. So don't talk to other officers about it."

"Understood. What about my sergeant?"

Baumgartner waved his question away. "He's your sergeant for payroll and logistical purposes only. For all intents and purposes, you work directly for me. Investigate this letter and report back with whatever you find, but do it all discreetly."

"Yes, sir."

"And don't enter the report into the system, either."

"What?" Stone looked surprised. "Why not?

"I want a chance to review it before I decide if it needs to be an official report or not."

"Okay…" Stone's expression seemed stuck mid-way between confusion and reluctance.

"Do what I ask," Baumgartner said, putting a slight edge of command in his words. "Either write it up by hand or type it out, but I don't want a digital record of this. At least, not yet."

"Use a typewriter?"

"Exactly."

"I don't know where one even exists these days."

"Then use a pen," Baumgartner snapped. "I'm assuming you know how to use one of those."

"Yes, sir." Stone looked troubled.

"What's the matter?" Baumgartner asked.

"It seems a little…irregular."

Baumgartner scratched this chin. "It's not. It just seems like it is because this is where politics and policing converge. We're not taking some guy to jail for smacking his wife or arresting some mope for stealing a TV. This is about navigating dangerous waters in a way that keeps the department and the officers on the street safe. It's not checkers, it's three-dimensional chess."

Stone nodded, but his expression remained vexed. "Why me, though? I'm just a patrol officer."

"No, you're not."

"I'm not?"

"Listen, Gary, you're different. I knew that the moment I met you. From the day you walked into this department it was clear you didn't fit the normal mold. Most of these guys, they're cut from the same cloth. They're hunters who want to chase bad guys like dogs want to chase cats. Catch 'em, spit 'em out, and do it again tomorrow. It's all about the chase, and the chase makes them happy. You, though, you don't fit that. You're something different. Then I figured out how to use your talents, and we entrusted you with city hall. You like it there?"

Stone nodded. "I do."

"And you're good at it."

"I think so," Stone said.

"That's because you're a round peg in a round hole in that position. It fits you. You're a politician with a gun, Gary."

Baumgartner watched Stone's face as he seemed to process his words, and then a slight smile tugged at the corners of the officer's mouth.

Good. He's happy with what he is. People always performed better when that was the case.

Baumgartner took the opportunity to ratchet things up a notch. "But I need more from you. Lately, you haven't exactly been funneling much in the way of intel into this office. That's why you're at city hall—to be my eyes and ears."

Stone swallowed and cleared his throat. "I apologize."

"Don't apologize. Just give me something I can use."

"It's been kind of quiet over there, Chief. Since the mayor's reelection, the remodel has been the only big thing going on."

"And the expansion of the city council to nine members," Baumgartner added.

"Yeah," Stone said. "Oh, *yeah*. I did hear something interesting happen this morning from Jean Carter. She's Councilman Hahn's personal assis—"

"I know who she is. What happened?"

"She'd given me a threatening letter addressed to Hahn. You know, the run-of-the-mill crazy stuff." Baumgartner nodded and Stone continued. "Anyway, we chatted for a second about Councilman Buckner's problems and she said it was about to get much worse. When I asked her what she meant, she suddenly got quiet. At the time, I thought she was talking about Buckner, but now I'm starting to wonder if she meant Hahn."

"You think she knows about this letter?"

Stone looked down at Betty Rabe's letter in his hands. "I don't know, but maybe."

Baumgartner leaned forward and gave Stone a hard look. "Well, you better find out."

Time to earn your stripes, kid.

Chapter 5

Betty Rabe lived in a quiet, north Spokane neighborhood known as Indian Trails. An early 2000s red Toyota coupe was parked in the driveway.

It was shortly after three p.m. when Gary Stone pulled up outside her house. He'd driven to that location based upon the return address listed on the letter sent to Councilman Hahn.

At first, Stone parked directly in front of the yellow two-story, but remembered Ray Zielinski's earlier admonition. He knew better than to park in front of a contact's house. He had never done it while on patrol. However, the past year working in city hall had allowed some bad habits and sloppy thinking to creep into his professional routine. The hard work and studying that he did during the academy and probationary period seemed to be atrophying.

Stone put his car into reverse and backed up several houses before parking again. How many previous contacts had he gone on where he parked directly in front of a residence? How many fellow officers failed to say anything about the safety concern? It bothered Stone that a senior officer like Ray Zielinski had to point out his failures to him. Perceptions mattered to Stone, and now Ray had a tainted opinion of him. Stone made a mental note to work on Ray. He seemed like a decent guy despite his outward gruffness and would be a good person to get to know better within the department. Someone with twenty years of experience had to know how the system worked.

He tapped the screen of his mobile data computer, calling it to life. Then he typed in Betty Rabe's name, but his finger hovered over the Enter key.

He had no other information to go on. He should have run her name before leaving the department, but Stone was bothered by Chief Baumgartner's request.

Keeping the interview quiet was unsettling for Stone. They were the police. They shouldn't be afraid to be open and transparent. The only times they should be quiet was for officer safety or legitimate privacy laws, such as medical information. They should only use trickery when trying to solve a crime. None of those applied to this situation.

Stone stared at Betty Rabe's name on the screen. He was tasked with investigating a possible sexual assault against an underage woman, but not being allowed to enter his findings into the system. Maybe he should have talked with his sergeant about the matter.

However, the chief expressly told him not to do so. Stone looked up to the chief and didn't want to cross him.

Maybe he should talk with Dale Thomas, the union president. Stone pinched his lips together at the thought. Dale was a tool. He had only talked with Stone once and that was when he asked him to pass along a message to the chief. He would never ask Dale for advice.

His finger continued to hover over the Enter key. If he pressed it, there would be a record of him running Betty Rabe's name. How would he explain that to the chief if asked? Or to someone else, if they came asking?

Jeez, he was over thinking things.

Stone's eyes drifted to the red Toyota in the driveway. He quickly cleared the screen and called up the Department of Licensing screen. Stone entered the car's license plate. It came back to Donald Rabe at the same address. Perhaps her father? Stone mused. That was good enough to confirm the address.

He pressed the status button on the computer and the screen changed again. He was about to put himself out at the address for a "contact citizen" call, but he remembered another of Baumgartner's directions. He wasn't to let anyone know what he was doing. Therefore, he left his status unchanged and available. Besides, radio never sent him calls anyway.

He got out of the car, leaving his portable radio on the front seat.

She opened the door for Stone before he ever made it to the small porch.

"Is everything okay?" she asked.

The girl was small, bordering on frail. Her clothing and appearance were in stark contrast to her frame, though. She had jet black hair and black lipstick. She wore a black top that read *In This Moment* and had on a red plaid skirt. Her black stockings had large holes in them and her combat boots were not laced, the tongues hanging out like her boots were about to vomit.

"Excuse me?"

"I saw you sitting outside, then you came up here. Is everything okay? I tried calling my mom, but no one answered."

"Everything is fine."

"But you're a cop, right? That means something bad has happened."

"Are you Betty Rabe?"

"Yeah," she said, drawing out the word. "Thanks for not calling me Bethany."

"When are your parents supposed to be home?"

Betty stood inside the door and shrugged. "I dunno." A flash of curiosity appeared in her eyes. "How did you know it was Betty?"

"I was hoping one of your parents would be here."

"My mom, she'll probably be home about six. My dad, you can never tell with him. If he's not working late, he's probably at the bar with his friends."

Stone looked around the neighborhood.

"Back to my name," Betty said. "How'd you know?"

"What's the problem? You're Betty, right?"

"I am now."

"What?"

"Everybody calls me Beth and I *hate* it. Sounds like a librarian or worse, an old lady. I wanna be a Betty."

"Betty's cool," Stone said easily.

"And popular."

"Okay."

"That's what I'm talking about. Only my friend, Alex, calls me Betty. You're not my friend. So how did you know?"

Stone pulled the letter from his back pocket. "You sent this to city hall. Your name was right here."

"Oh." The interested look in her eyes faded. "That."

"Can we talk?"

"If we must."

"You sent it to the mayor. He figured you'd want to talk with someone."

"I wanted to talk with *him*."

Stone nodded. "I understand, but that's not how it works. The mayor has people. I'm one of them."

Betty pushed the door fully opened and walked away. Dejectedly, she said, "C'mon in."

Stone stepped inside and closed the door behind him. As he followed her into the living room, he passed a wall full of pictures. He stopped and studied the various pictures of Betty and her family. In each picture, she had brown hair and her face was bright with smiles. Not a single picture had the dark hair or dark look.

She sat on the edge of the couch, her knees clasped together, her elbows on her knees. A book was on the couch next to her, opened in the middle. Stone couldn't see the title.

"Your family looks nice."

"Looks can be deceiving."

"Meaning?"

Betty shook her head. "Nothing."

"Is everything okay?"

"It's fine."

"You sure?"

She glanced up. "My parents, they don't like my new look."

"When did it change?"

"This week."

"Why the change?"

"I was tired of being walked on. I thought maybe I should toughen up some. Maybe people would take me serious."

"Has it worked?"

"I don't know. Maybe. I feel tougher."

"That's something."

"I think so."

Stone sat on the edge of recliner. He leaned toward Betty. "Tell me about Councilman Hahn."

Betty looked away.

"If you want, I can call a counselor to be with us while we talk about it, about what happened."

Betty glanced at the letter in Stone's hand, then looked away. "I wish I had never sent that."

"Why not?"

"Because of this. Because I want to move on from what happened, but now I can't. You're here. Someone will always be here because of it, right?"

"It's something we have to respond to," Stone told her. "You had to know that."

Betty stared past Stone at the wall behind him. "Don't talk like you know me. You sound like my parents when you do that."

"All right. But what made you send the letter, Betty?"

She shrugged. "A lot of men are getting called on their behavior these days. You've seen the news, right?"

"I've seen bad behavior being reported more openly," he said. "And people more willing to listen than before."

"Exactly. The whole thing has its own momentum, something I'm a part of now. And he shouldn't get away with it, you know?"

"Get away with what?" Stone tucked the letter back into his pocket. "Can you tell me what happened?"

She set her jaw and looked directly at Stone. "He attacked me."

"He attacked you?" Stone quickly thought about the letter. He wanted to pull it back out of his pocket and refresh his memory. She had been vague about the assault, but he wanted to remember her precise words. Unfortunately, he couldn't recall them correctly.

"Yes. He attacked me. He was aggressive and forceful." As an afterthought, she said, "And handsy."

"Handsy?"

"His hands were all over me," she said softly.

"Let's step back, okay? Where did you meet him?"

"At church. He's part of the youth group's leadership."

"Is that where he attacked you? Church?"

"No. He attacked me in my car."

"Hahn was in your car? The little red one out front?"

"Yeah."

"How did he get in your car?"

Sadness passed over her face. "He was in my car a lot."

"For youth group stuff?"

"Sometimes, yeah."

"What about the other times?"

"We were just talking at first."

"Then what happened?"

"You know."

"No, I don't."

"We made it."

"You had sex."

"Sort of. I mostly did stuff to him."

"Were you ever in his car?"

"Yeah."

"Same thing? Talking and then…"

"Exactly."

"How long was this going on for?"

Betty shrugged. "I don't know. Couple months, maybe."

"Every day?"

Her face scrunched. "What? No."

Stone held up a hand in defense. "I apologize. I'm trying to understand."

Betty picked at the seam of her skirt.

"Was this ever at someone's house?"

"Here. A couple times. That's when we finally, well, you know."

"What about his house?"

"Oh no. We couldn't do it there."

"Why?"

She looked at Stone like he was stupid.

"Did you ever," Stone paused, "at the church?"

"No! What the hell?"

"Again, I'm only trying to understand."

"You're not doing a very good job at it."

Stone nodded, made a couple entries in his notebook, then lifted his eyes to her. "When did he attack you?"

She shrugged and looked away.

"Betty, when did he attack you?"

"I don't know."

"You don't know *when*?"

"No."

"All right. How about where? Where did he attack you?"

"I don't know."

Stone lowered his notebook and pen and gave her a plaintive look. "I'm trying to help, Betty. Did he say anything when he attacked you? Did you say anything to him before the attack?"

She shook her head, still not looking at him.

"Betty, please. You were in a relationship with him, right? You guys were…" Stone struggled for the right words before continuing, then chose hers. "You were doing stuff, somewhat regularly, right? Then he attacked you. Something happened. Tell me what that was."

She turned back to him, a look of resolve on her face.
"Maybe I'm remembering it wrong."

Stone was taken aback. "How can you remember it wrong?
You sent a letter to the mayor implying that he attacked you.
It took time to write that letter. To address it, stamp it, and mail
it. Which, by the way, why not send it by email?"

"I hate computers."

"You hate computers?"

"Uh-huh. I only use one when the school makes me."

"You don't have a social media account?"

"That's for losers and posers who can't live their own life,
so they present a fake front to their friends."

Stone found himself immediately thinking about his own
social media accounts. For a second, he wondered if the
teenager had a valid point.

Betty brought him back to the moment. "I sent the letter
because…it doesn't matter."

"It does matter."

Her eyes softened.

"Did you make it up?"

Again, she looked at Stone like he was stupid.

"You made it up."

She returned to picking at her skirt.

"Why? Why would you do that?"

"He wanted to stop."

"He wanted to stop seeing you?"

She refused to look at him.

"And you didn't want that."

"No."

"Because you liked him?"

She looked up. Tears filled her eyes.

"Why write the letter then?" Stone asked. "Why say he
attacked you?"

"He can't throw me away."

"Did you tell him that?"

"It didn't matter."

"Why say he attacked you?"

"I wanted him to lose his job."

"That's not how it works. The mayor can't fire him, but if he hurt you, really hurt you, I can do something about it. I can take him to jail."

When she wiped tears from her eyes, her black mascara smeared across her cheeks. "I don't want to hurt him that way. I don't want to hurt his family, either."

"Betty, did he attack you?"

She sat quietly for a moment before nodding. "I don't think he meant to."

"So he did? Where did it happen?"

She shook her head.

"Betty, talk to me."

"No. You need to go."

"Please."

"Go!"

Stone stood and closed his notebook. He noticed the title of the book lying open faced on the couch—*Thirteen Reasons Why*. He removed a business card from his wallet and offered it to her. Betty refused to look at him. He gently placed it on the couch next to the book.

When he walked out of the house, he looked up and down the street, before walking to his car. Stone wondered if anyone noticed his car parked there.

Chapter 6

Margaret Patterson held up her hand until she caught the attention of the bartender. When the handsome guy with the fauxhawk looked her way, she lifted two fingers, then made a circle, and pointed at her table. He lifted his chin and turned to the back bar.

"As I was saying," Patterson said, "Justin Buckner is a complete moron, both literally and figuratively."

Dana Hatcher smiled as she leaned her head back against the black vinyl booth.

They were seated in the upstairs portion of Durkin's Liquor Bar. It was shortly after four p.m. and the after-work crowd had not descended, yet the small restaurant was already packed.

"The guy can't get out of his own way," Patterson continued. "Seriously. I mean, he barely won his first election before his wife divorced him. Listen, I'm not a fan of the man, but the wife, she's a real winner, you know what I'm saying?"

Hatcher lifted a copper mug and drank the remaining portion of her Moscow Mule.

"She was mad at him for being on the council and the amount of time it took away from the family. I mean, if you don't want to be married to the guy, then leave, but don't keep kicking him in the balls for it."

"If you don't like the guy, why do you care what she's doing to his balls?"

Patterson smirked. "Seriously?"

"Seriously. Why do you care?"

"Because he's actually good at what he does, and I don't want him moping around the office. Just makes me sad and hurts our efficiency. After their divorce he was like a sad puppy all the time. *Oh, look at me, my wife is gone, and now I have to make my own sandwiches. Boo-hoo.*" She mimed rubbing her fists into her eyes like a crying child. "Just ridiculous. Then he starts running around with the babysitter and the guy looked like he was on top of the world. Man, he was full of ideas and energy again."

"But he was stupid."

"He *was* stupid." Patterson lifted her empty glass, shook the remaining ice cubes in it, and put it back down. "I don't care about what he did. She might have been the babysitter, but the woman was of legal age."

"Legal, yes."

"Listen, Captain…" Patterson stopped, leaned forward, and smiled at Hatcher. "Oh, man, that still sounds cool, doesn't it?"

Hatcher smiled. "Yeah, I like it. The bars look good, too."

"Hell yeah, they look good and you deserve it."

"Thanks."

"So, as I was saying, *Captain*, I get there's a difference between something being legal and something being right. What Justin is doing isn't right. He should go bury his head in the sand somewhere instead of standing in front of city hall making a big stink about it. He should let the press get excited until they run out of steam. Everybody's got skeletons in their closets, but he thinks if he comes out and fights the press that they'll go away. The guy is a moron."

The bartender came over with their drinks. He placed another copper mug in front of Hatcher and a Grey Goose and tonic near Patterson. As the bartender walked away, Patterson watched him with a smile.

"Geez, Maggie, be obvious, will ya?"

Patterson kept her eyes on the bartender's gait and gave a slow, appreciative whistle. "If I had that swing in my backyard…"

Hatcher laughed. "Keep it in your pants, Councilwoman. There are people watching."

Patterson's eyes swept the bar. "Hell with 'em. Most of these folks don't know who I am, and if they do, they didn't vote for me. Not my district." She clinked her glass against the side of Hatcher's copper mug and raised her glass in a silent toast.

Hatcher raised her drink and sipped. "Speaking of districts, how are things with the recent expansion to nine seats?"

"Better than expected. I thought the public would care, but they don't. I mean, it just made sense to prepare for the future with how fast the city is growing. Seattle has nine seats…well, you already knew that, right?"

"We're not Seattle."

"Thank God, but that doesn't mean we shouldn't be forward thinking. For too long we've been stuck in the mindset of keeping us as a small town. We need to abandon that thinking. Let's be something special."

"You're preaching."

Patterson smiled. "I'm campaigning."

"The election just ended, and your seat wasn't even up."

Patterson sipped her drink. "Yeah, I'm glad I wasn't running, though. Brutal cycle. Man, did Sikes ever savage Lofton."

"He took his share of shots, too."

"That's what I'm saying," Patterson said. "Brutal. I thought the pretty boy could actually beat the mad king."

Hatcher nodded. "A lot of us did."

"I mean, he was the mayor's chief of staff, right? Got him through the entire situation with Garrett, and that disaster went national." Patterson lifted her hands in disbelief. "You'd think that kind of insider information would give him an advantage."

"It was a close election," Hatcher said.

"Voters are stupid."

Hatcher's eyes widened, and she glanced around. "What?"

"Aren't you worried someone will hear you?"

"We're in a bar."

"Someone could be recording us."

Patterson leaned out of the booth and looked around. When she resettled herself, she shook her head. "These people are too immersed in their own worlds to worry about what we're talking about."

"It's your career, not mine."

"Oh no, it's your career, too, sister."

Hatcher had lifted her mug for another sip but paused. "What do you mean?"

"My fortunes are your fortunes."

Hatcher thought about the statement, then took her sip.

"So, Sikes gets reelected," Patterson began.

"Barely."

"Yes, barely," Patterson agreed. "No sooner is the county auditor finished counting votes, and what's the first thing he starts chirping about?"

Hatcher shrugged.

"Term limits. He thinks it's unfair that he can only be in office for two terms."

"Yeesh."

"My point. He's trying to get us to rework the city charter. He's found a sympathetic ear with the council president."

"Who is also limited to two consecutive terms, right?"

"Exactly," Patterson said, raising her glass in emphasis.

"How are the rest of the council members leaning?"

"The new guys are just happy to be in office. They love Sikes, which is totally freaking me out. The sycophants. Blech."

Hatcher smiled. "You're on a roll, Big City."

"I told you before, Pittsburgh ain't that much bigger than Spokane. People just think it is because we have actual sports teams."

"Whatever."

"Besides, I haven't lived there in twenty years since I came out here for law school. That makes me a local girl just like you."

"You're a transplant, Maggie. You don't fool me. I can still pick out that Midwest accent of yours whenever you get riled up." Dana smiled. "Just like now."

"Screw you and your west coast ears. I'm only riled up because of the jagoffs I work around. Don't tell me you love the people you work with. I've heard you spout off plenty of times."

"The department has its problems," Hatcher admitted.

"Things are better since you got the promotion?"

"I think so. People seem to be taking me more serious."

"They should have taken you serious from the get-go."

"They are now, so that's what matters."

"What matters is how we go about getting the fat boy out of there."

"The fat boy?"

"Baumgartner."

"He's *big*," Hatcher said, "but he's not fat."

"He's fat. It's just that he's tall so you can't tell how much."

"I would never call him that."

Patterson thumbed toward the bartender. "Compared to that, Baumgartner's fat."

Dana appraised the man behind the bar. "Compared to that, they're all fat."

"Yeah," Patterson agreed, casting another longing glance at the bartender.

"Why do you want to get rid of Baumgartner?"

Patterson turned her attention back to her friend. "Have you seen his approval numbers?"

"No."

"He's the most popular leader in the city. Way more popular than the mayor. None of us council members have any name recognition. I bet if he walked in here, most people would know him, even without his uniform. I could walk in naked and no one would notice."

"I think they would notice that."

Patterson smiled wickedly. "Probably, yeah."

Hatcher rolled her eyes.

"Sikes wants him to take a fall," Patterson told her.

"Who? Baumgartner?

"He won't come out and say it, but he wants it. I mean, he hints at it like a schoolboy trying to get in a girl's pants. It's pitiful."

"Why?"

"Crime stats are horrible. He's getting beat up over them. He needs someone to take the heat. It's a slaughter of expediency."

"Crime isn't due just to police efficiency," Hatcher said, thinking about her earlier conversation with Captain Farrell. "There are other factors."

"Those factors don't matter. Only votes matter. Even to a guy who is in his second term. *Especially* to a guy in his second term who is angling to rewrite the rules and get a third. He's going to find a way to sacrifice Baumgartner to get every council member a little more name recognition."

"And you're okay with that?"

"Why wouldn't I be?"

"Baumgartner's done a good job."

"He's done a *great* job," Patterson said.

"But you're talking about laying him on the altar of public opinion."

"And? You can't tell me you're that naïve about this game. Listen, here's how it works. If he did his job and did it well, but did it in the background, he would be of no value. Where would the gain be? But if he was a screw up as a leader? Then he's valuable."

"He's valuable if he's bad at his job?" Hatcher shook her head. "That makes no sense."

"Sure it does. Let's say the department disliked him. We could sacrifice him to gain their trust. It would look to the public like the mayor was taking strong action to address the crime problem."

"Well, he's liked," Hatcher said. "A lot."

"I know. He also has a lot of recognition. He seems untouchable. There's an air to him that people in the city just gravitate toward. Even Sikes has to be careful around him. But…" She raised a finger and lowered her voice a little. "If you kill the king, you become the king."

"The king is dead. Long live the king?"

"Exactly. Sikes will be the king. I mean, technically he is the king, it's just that he'll be a more popular king. A more popular mad king." Patterson looked at her drink. "What's in this drink? Is the kid making me doubles?"

"You think the other council members will benefit, too?"

"Definitely. Especially the ones who don't have their own problems to deal with."

"Like Buckner?"

Patterson laughed. "Like Buckner. Geesh, if he just would have kept his mouth shut, he could have kept banging the babysitter."

"It sounds like you're condoning it."

Patterson leaned forward. "Sister, have you seen my babysitter? Eighteen-year-old stud muffin. My kids adore him. My ex-husband *hates* him. I love having him around. Good Lord, I *love* having him around. I'd gamble on the fall-out with his mother if she wasn't my campaign manager. I just can't risk it, know what I mean? Now, drink up. I've gotta be out of here in thirty minutes, so I can make a neighborhood council meeting and I wanna get another drink inside me. I can't go to another one of those sober."

Chapter 7

Gary Stone parked in his favorite space at city hall, the one marked for *Emergency Vehicles Only* that was furthest from the building. He slid out of his car, slammed the door, and jogged toward the front entrance. It was almost five and he wasn't sure if he would make it before the council offices closed.

The elevator seemed to take forever. When it opened, he had to wait as several people exited. One of them was Jean Carter.

"Hey, boy-o," she said, with a big smile. "Want to bounce for a drink? I'm thinking about skipping my spin class."

"Is Hahn still upstairs?" he asked, his expression tight.

Jean's smile slipped. "You still working?"

"Yeah."

"Oh, in that case, yeah, he's just finishing something up before he leaves. He'll be down in a few minutes. Everything all right?"

Stone relaxed slightly. "I've got to talk with him before he leaves."

"What about? Maybe I can help."

He was about to say she couldn't when he remembered the chief's orders.

You better find out.

Stone shifted gears, secure that he'd arrived in time to meet with Hahn and focused on Jean. "Hey, you know when we were talking about Buckner before?"

"How he's an idiot for calling a press conference, you mean?"

"You said something about how things were going to get worse. Remember?"

What remained of Jean's smile fell away. "Why?"

"What did you mean? It wasn't about Buckner, was it?"

Jean swallowed. "Gary, I…"

"I'm trying to be prepared for whatever might happen down here at city hall," he said, surprised at how easy the lie came. "Whatever you tell me stays between us."

"I…" Jean shook her head. "No, I can't. But you don't have to worry. It doesn't concern you."

Stone gave her a long look. He couldn't decide if he was more disappointed in her for not confiding in him or with himself for lying to try to get her to do so. He turned away and walked toward the elevator, punching the up button again. The doors opened almost immediately.

"Why do you need to talk to Hahn?" Jean asked from behind him.

Stone stepped into the empty elevator and hit the button for the sixth floor. When he looked back at his friend, he said, "Sorry, Jean, it doesn't concern you."

Jean stared at him as the doors closed.

When the doors opened, Councilman Dennis Hahn was standing at the elevator, waiting. He was a tall man in a tailored blue suit. The shirt was checkered and the tie solid yellow. His eyes were bright behind tortoise-shell framed glasses. Even at the end of the day, his short hair was still perfectly coiffed in the front.

"Councilman, got a minute?"

"Mister Stone, good to see you. I'm on my way to my car," Hahn said and stepped into the elevator. "Let's walk and talk."

"Yes, sir, definitely."

With his free hand, Hahn pressed the button for the lobby. In his right hand was a worn leather satchel. It appeared to be nearly empty.

"How are things, Gary?"

"They're good."

"The upstairs remodel ended up fairly nice, don't you think?"

"Yes, sir."

"If you ever want to move down to our floor, we'd make room for you. I hope you know that."

Stone smiled. "I appreciate that, sir, but I go where the chief tells me."

"But where do you want to be, Gary?"

"I don't know if it matters as long as I'm in city hall. I like it here."

Hahn winked. "Okay then, we'll talk with the chief about it. See if we can make it happen. Was there something you wanted to talk about?"

The lobby doors opened, and Hahn stepped out, not bothering to wait for Stone or to even see if he was following. Stone hurried behind him.

"Yes, sir. We received a letter."

"Jean mentioned that. Another threatening one. Anything to it?"

"No, sir. Everything was fine with that, but we received a different letter. One of a personal matter."

"Oh?" Hahn asked while striding toward the north exit of city hall. "Something personal?"

"Yes, sir. It was from Betty Rabe."

Hahn shoved the door open, banging it against the outside wall. It was then that the name registered with him. He turned to Stone. "Who?"

"Betty Rabe."

"Betty? You mean Beth? Beth Rabe?"

"Yes, sir. The same."

Hahn straightened, looked around the entrance and nearby parking lot, then said, "What did she want?"

"She said you assaulted her."

"*What?*"

"Yes, sir. Sexually. That's what she said."

"I did no such thing. I wouldn't. Never. No."

"Okay, well, that's what I'm trying to find out."

"I wouldn't. You believe me, right? Who did she send this letter to?"

"The mayor."

"The mayor? Why would she send it to him? He gave it to you?"

"He gave it to the chief who gave it to me."

"The chief knows about this, too?" Hahn stepped close to Gary and whispered, "Listen, Gary, I'm just a guy, like you. I'm not perfect. You probably know I was messing around with her, but I realized it was wrong and I stopped it. That's why she wrote the letter. You can see that, right? She wasn't happy about me breaking it off. She begged me not to do it. Maybe this is her way of getting back at me. I don't know, but I would never hurt her."

"You never assaulted her?"

"No, never. I mean, what else am I going to say, right? But you know me, Gary. I'm not the kind of guy who is going to hit a woman, much less force myself on her. Yeah, okay, I had an inappropriate relationship with her, but so what? Life goes on."

Stone raised his eyebrows.

Hahn noticed his reaction. "I don't mean to sound so cavalier about it," he stammered. "But she's young, she'll get over it. It was pretty obvious I wasn't her first."

"She's only seventeen."

"She's above the age of consent."

"Doesn't matter in the eyes of the public. Just ask Councilman Bucker."

Hahn stepped back. "Do you really want to go down this road?"

"I only want to find the truth."

"Listen, I have no idea why she would write a letter like that, but if you want to discuss this further, set an appointment with Jean and we can talk tomorrow." The councilman trotted toward his car.

Stone let him go. For a moment, he stood on the sidewalk replaying the conversation in his head. Then he pulled his cell phone from his pocket and texted Jean.

sorry for what I said. It was rude.

A couple seconds later, his phone dinged. Jean had responded. *It's cool. See U tomorrow.*

"Officer Gary Stone," a woman's voice said.

Councilwoman Margaret Patterson was heading toward him. She wore a dark green pantsuit and her purse was slung over her left shoulder.

"Ma'am?" Gary asked, tucking his cell phone into his pocket.

"Ma'am? Do I look like my mother? It's after five and we're all alone. You can call me Margaret."

"I don't think that would be appropriate."

"You're right," she said. "Too formal. Call me Maggie."

It was then he could smell alcohol on her breath. "Okay," Stone said, elongating the two syllables.

"What were you and Councilman Hahn talking about?"

"Nothing. We just walked out together."

"Don't lie to me, Gary Stone. He was tucked in tight on you. He only does that when he's sharing secrets. I know how he is."

"No secrets, ma'am. I promise."

"Okay, fine. If you don't want to play, then I'm leaving." She jangled her car keys and turned toward the parking lot.

"Ma'am? Councilwoman?"

She turned back to him. "Yes, Gary?"

"Have you been drinking?"

"As a matter of fact, that's none of your business."

"Are you okay to drive?"

The councilwoman smiled. "Are you offering to give me a ride, Gary?"

"No, ma'am. I would call you a cab, though."

She jangled her keys once more, then grabbed them, silencing them. "I don't get you, Stone." She spun on her heel and walked into the parking lot.

Chapter 8

Spokane Police Officer Tyler Garrett stood in front of the granite headstone. The setting sun still provided enough light to read the inscription.

Delmar Everett Oakley

"I'm back," Garrett said. "We never did resolve those differences."

A Nissan with a loud muffler raced by on Government Way. Garrett lifted his gaze and watched the car speed northbound.

"Kids," he said. "They don't appreciate the sanctity of this area."

He was at Lilac Memorial Cemetery, among a cluster of graveyards along the stretch of road.

Garrett's microphone chirped on his shoulder and he listened to the dispatcher send a unit to investigate a two-vehicle collision.

"You know, I should have gone to your funeral," Garrett said, "but I didn't think it was right with how things ended for us. Mom asked if I went, asked if I talked with you before you died. I lied and said I did. She didn't need to know about our bad blood. She was sad you passed. I'm not sure I told you this before, but you two should have gotten together, Oak. I could have used you in my life more."

Garrett shoved his hands into his pockets.

"I've said it before, but I'm still sorry for letting you down. It was hard living up to your expectations."

Another vehicle raced by the cemetery, its stereo blaring some heavy metal music. Garrett watched the beat-up truck with disdain.

"You were always too black-and-white for me, but I still loved you. I hope you know that. Even when you stopped loving me, I kept loving you."

Garrett's patrol car rolled toward the exit gate and triggered the sensor, causing it to slowly open. He had contacted the cemetery's office a few months ago. The managers were happy to give him the passcode. He explained that he wanted to visit the grave of a friend, but it wasn't always conducive for him to do so during regular hours. They were happy to have an officer drive-through the property whenever he wanted.

After his car passed through the gate, it slowly closed behind him.

Garrett waited to turn onto Government Way and resume his patrol shift. He was going to turn south and could see in the distance a gray car alongside the road. Due to the number of southbound cars, he couldn't turn into the flow of traffic.

A white BMW zoomed by heading north. The driver was looking at her phone as she drove. She never noticed she had just sped past a police officer.

He turned his steering wheel, accelerated into the northbound lane, activated his emergency lights, and followed the white car. It took her some time to realize Garrett was there with his red-and-blue lights whirring, then a little more time to realize the lights were meant for her. When she did, her brake lights flashed, and she pulled over.

Garrett pressed the button on the car's microphone. "Charlie three sixteen, a traffic stop."

"Charlie three sixteen, go ahead," dispatch responded.

"A white BMW M3," Garrett said, then recited the license plate number. "Government Way and Fort George Wright Drive. Code four."

"Copy. Code four."

Garrett exited his car and walked confidently to the white sedan. The driver, an attractive woman with brown eyes, red lips, and a short afro, looked up at him.

"Ma'am, I'm Officer Garrett with the Spokane Police Department. Do you know why I stopped you?"

"I was speeding."

"Do you know how fast?"

"I don't know. Forty-five, maybe?"

"Do you know the speed limit along here?"

The woman looked back over her shoulder. "No."

"It's thirty-five."

She glanced up to Garrett. "Really?"

"You were also texting."

Her brow furrowed. "No, I wasn't."

"You were doing something with your phone when you drove by me."

She lowered her eyes, then nodded. "I was looking up directions."

"There you go."

"Am I getting a ticket?"

Garrett held out his left hand. "License, registration, and proof of insurance, please."

"So, that's a yes?"

Garrett tilted his head. "Why don't we start with the paperwork first?"

She quickly removed her driver's license from her purse and handed it to him. Then she dug through her glove box to find the registration and proof of insurance. When she found the papers, she returned to her seated position and handed them to Garrett.

"Wait here," he said and headed back to his car.

He ran her name through DOL.

Tiana Madison Kennedy.

Her driver's license was current, but she'd had two speeding tickets in the past three years. Thirty-two years old.

Her address was in downtown. Garrett thought about it for a moment, then realized it must be a condo.

He checked her insurance certificate and it was current. He put it to the side.

Then he ran her license plate through DOL. It was also current.

He put his hand on the edge of his mobile data computer and thought for a moment, weighing the options. When he made his decision, he grabbed her license and registration and exited the car. As he walked, he pulled out his business card and put it underneath the paperwork.

"Mrs. Kennedy," he said.

She turned to look at him. "It's Miss."

"Miss Kennedy, I'm going to let you off with a warning tonight." He handed her back her paperwork. "But do me a favor and slow down through here, okay?"

"Thank you, Officer. I will. I promise." She tossed her license back into her purse. Then she noticed his business card. "Tyler Garrett," she read.

"Yes, ma'am."

"You're the officer that was in that shooting a while back."

"That's right."

"The city treated you horribly. I mean, really bad."

Garrett stared at her.

"Until the settlement, right?" She smiled a little. "That kind of money wouldn't suck. I read about you in the paper. The whole thing, what a mess."

"Do you have any questions about the warning?"

"No."

"If you do, you give me a call, okay?"

She nodded.

Garrett tapped the edge of her door. "Drive safe, Miss Kennedy."

He walked back to his car.

Chapter 9

Detective Wardell Clint sat in his unmarked police car. Most of his vehicle was obscured by a roadside billboard sign hawking the nearby Northern Quest Casino. The billboard itself was periodically lit up with something that Clint assumed was supposed to approximate the Vegas feel the Indian tribe was going for. He didn't care. Most gambling was a tax on people who were bad at math, and most advertising was barely concealed manipulation to trick people into spending money on things they didn't need. He had no use for any of it.

The way the sign lit up gave him a strategic advantage when he parked behind it. The flashing lights created a curtain of light that kept him hidden from the casual eye, and difficult to see even if someone was looking.

And Clint was pretty sure Officer Tyler Garrett was always looking.

Piece of human garbage that he is.

Clint's stomach burned with acid. Without taking his eyes off the cemetery entrance, he reached into the glove box and removed a bottle of antacid tablets. He chewed several of them, the chalky, processed fruit flavor barely registering anymore. He put the bottle back in its place and closed the glove box.

Glove box. What a stupid name for the passenger side container. Clint knew where the name came from. Early cars were mostly convertibles and the weather, along with the rough nature of the vehicle design and the barely improved roads, necessitated driving gloves. Gloves were like anything else—they needed a place to be stored. So manufacturers created a compartment for them. It made perfect sense to him, but it was an anachronism now, and no longer accurate. He understood, and almost accepted, that the world was a messy place, but it still irked him when things were wrong or in disorder when they didn't need to be.

People were incapable or unwilling to change their preconceived perceptions, that's what it was, as far as Clint was concerned. It was easier to go on calling it a glove box than change the paradigm, even if it was for the better. He'd seen that same tendency in a lot of cops and especially detectives, and it always resulted in substandard results.

But it was the perception people had of Officer Tyler Garrett that had him chewing antacids these days. Clint knew the man was dirty—*knew it!*—but the officer was slippery and had managed to avoid getting caught, so far.

Officer. It pained him to even use the word to describe Garrett. The son of a bitch not only provided protection to a drug dealer, siphoning off money to do so, he killed two detectives in the process. That both Butch Talbott and Justin Pomeroy were dirty did little to assuage Clint's outrage. No one publicly admitted to either fact. Talbott got a hero's funeral, and Pomeroy's suicide was quietly acknowledged as a tragic consequence of the weight a police career brings. But Clint knew the truth. Any man who dishonored the badge the way they did deserved to be called a lot of things, but not officer. That word had a long, proud history with only a few unfortunate tarnishes to it. It didn't belong to men like Talbott or Pomeroy, and especially not to Garrett.

That wasn't what most of the world thought, Clint knew. They saw a model police officer—handsome, fit, and smiling. The public ate that up, the politicians loved it, and the department exploited it. Garrett being black was a bonus.

For Clint, Garrett's race added to the betrayal. He played the race card to cover his dirty deeds, and for the most part, it worked. In the face of questionable evidence and strong public opinion, the city cut its losses. The investigation—Clint's investigation—was halted, all charges were dropped, and Garrett was reinstated. The city even paid an undisclosed settlement to him.

Undisclosed, Clint thought ruefully, but big.

Clint ground the heels of his palms into his eyes, trying to fend off sleep. Then he half rubbed, half scratched his afro. He noticed the usually tight cut was getting a little long. He jotted a note on his pad to see a barber sometime tomorrow.

Haircuts. Just another in a list of benign concerns that most people worried about. They were soft. Cake-eaters, all of them. Clint envied them their blissful ignorance. They got to look at Garrett and see a hero, a hard charger. He knew better.

Most cops weren't cake-eaters. They were meat-eaters. Clint was all right with that fact. The job frequently dictated the need for that kind of mentality. But Garrett wasn't just a meat-eater. He was like a dog that had gone rabid, but everyone still reached out to pet him, unaware that he'd contracted the disease.

When Clint looked back at the cemetery entrance, the gate remained closed. Even at this distance, he could see the small red light indicating the access pad that provided some measure of security to the facility in the evening hours. This had been no obstacle for Garrett, so Clint surmised the dirty officer must have the gate code. How he got it was a mystery, but Clint was reasonably certain he could find out without any difficulty. He imagined Garrett approaching the manager or the groundskeeper, all confidence and sincerity, with some contrived story about who was buried there and how hard it was to get in to pay his respects since he worked power shift. If the employee was black, Garrett might even throw in a strategic *brother* to help seal the deal.

The thought of it burned Clint to no end. Garrett wasn't just a dirty cop, he was a charlatan. And yet, that wasn't what people saw.

For now, he assured himself. Someday, they'd see the truth, and he'd be the one to bring that bad karma back around.

The only other person who really knew the truth about Garrett was Captain Tom Farrell. Clint had overcome his natural and well-reasoned distrust of the brass where Farrell was concerned. They both shared the same desire to see Garrett brought to justice someday, somehow. Despite his feelings about the brass, most of which hadn't changed, Clint knew having some air cover was good strategy, if he was going to bring the man down.

But Tyler Garrett remained the golden child of the department, and the city. If anything, the so-perceived wrongful treatment in the aftermath of his officer-involved shooting only served to enhance that image with a healthy dose of martyrdom. Garrett played that piece well, too, not showing any rancor or bitterness, or giving anyone reason to doubt him. "I'm just glad to be back to work to serve my community," he'd said in one of the few interviews with any media.

Over the last twenty-one months, he seemed to be doing more than just playing a role. The guy was toeing the line, as far as Clint could tell. There was no way to be certain, because Clint couldn't keep him under surveillance twenty-four seven, but he dedicated every spare hour to watching Garrett and waiting for him to show his true colors. So far, since the shooting and all that followed, Clint had nothing.

Nothing.

Clint clenched and unclenched his jaw. If he wasn't absolutely one hundred percent certain of Garrett's guilt, logic would have forced him to abandon this…what was this? A crusade? An obsession? It didn't matter, because Clint knew the truth, so he had no choice but to keep at it.

As far as who Garrett was visiting at the cemetery, that part was easy. Garrett's father was interred elsewhere, but his longtime mentor and friend, Delmar Oakley, was buried there. About once a week, Garrett stopped to pay his respects. Clint wondered if those respects were legitimate or if it was one more charade Garrett played.

Before he could decide, the cemetery gate opened, and a marked police cruiser edged out. A few moments later, Garrett's lights activated, and he zipped into northbound traffic. Clint stayed where he was, but turned up the volume on his radio, which was set to the south channel.

Garrett's smooth, professional voice came over the airway. "Charlie three sixteen, a traffic stop."

"Charlie three sixteen, go ahead," came the dispatcher's reply.

"A white BMW M3," Garrett reported, reciting the license plate number. "Government Way and Fort George Wright Drive. Code four."

"Copy. Code four."

Clint had to adjust his position behind the sign to get a bead on the traffic stop location. Through his binoculars, he watched Garrett exit his patrol car and walk confidently to the offender's car, where he spoke briefly and retrieved the driver's paperwork before returning to his car. Clint switched his radio to the data channel to see if Garrett ran the driver's name with the dispatcher but heard nothing. That meant Garrett was using his mobile data computer, just like he was supposed to. The perfect patrol officer, following policy.

Clint smirked. He wished he had that setup in his detective's vehicle, but the system was expensive and strictly for patrol use.

He made a note of the time of the stop and the license plate. He could run Garrett's unit history tomorrow from the station and fill in the gaps.

Garrett returned to the car he'd stopped and handed the driver her paperwork. After a brief conversation, he walked back to his patrol car. The BMW crept carefully back onto the road and drove away. Garrett made a U-turn and headed south, turning off his overhead lights as soon as the maneuver was complete.

"Charlie three sixteen, I'm clear of that stop. One-David."

Clint recognized the disposition code. Officer contact, no report. He wrote *No ticket* on his notepad. He waited until Garrett was almost up to the bend in the long straightaway, before leaving his hiding place and following southbound.

It only took another minute for the dispatcher to send Garrett and another unit on a domestic violence call in East Central. That was Garrett's assigned beat within the district, but Clint knew no one would say a word to him about being temporarily out of his beat. Being the model officer had its perks.

Clint cruised slowly toward the DV call, parking in the lot of a nearby park when he arrived. The swimming pools weren't open yet, so the lot was mostly empty. He sat and listened to the occasional radio traffic from Garrett or his partner. This time, since they were inside the house, they had to utilize the data dispatcher to check both names, and a third with a different last name. Clint could have guessed at the dynamics happening, but he didn't care. Garrett was his concern.

They eventually arrested one of the males, and it was Garrett who transported the prisoner for domestic violence assault. Clint paralleled Garrett's trip to jail and watched from the middle of the crowded employee parking lot as the officer pulled into the sally port of the booking area.

Clint checked his watch. If he went home now, he'd get four, maybe five hours of sleep. He needed it, too. He'd been burning the proverbial candle at both ends for twenty-one long months, and the strain took a toll. And for all his trouble, Tyler Garrett seemed to have gone straight.

No way. Clint didn't buy it. But isn't that what he should want? For Garrett to be legit?

No, he decided. That was what the mayor wanted, what the public expected, and what the department needed. Even if they once suspected Garrett had been everything that his worst accusers said he was, all they wanted now was for him to be exactly what Clint was seeing—a model officer.

Clint wanted something else.

He wanted justice.

Suppressing a yawn, Clint pulled out of the parking lot and headed home. He wasn't giving up, but he needed to snatch a few hours of sleep. Shadowing Garrett was a priority, but he had cases to work, too.

Justice was going to have to wait at least another day.

WEDNESDAY

It is a very trying task for deceitful people,
always to have to cover up their lack of sincerity
and to repair the breaking of their word.
—Madeleine de Souvre, French writer

Chapter 10

Gary Stone woke before his alarm sounded. It wasn't hard since he'd slept horribly. He'd called it a night after eleven and slipped out of bed shortly after four. He trundled out to his kitchen and started a pot of coffee. He then turned around and stared at his closed laptop. He leaned back against the counter and thought about last night.

When he returned home following the interview with Councilman Hahn, he was prepared to write his report.

Chief Baumgartner had instructed him to file the report by hand, but that was old-school and unproductive. The department still kept a few of the blank forms around for emergency use, but it was a throwback to another time—an era before the online reporting system. Now officers entered their reports directly into the system, thereby reducing the time for follow-up by detectives and other agencies. Once it had been entered and approved by a supervisor, anyone with system clearance had access to it. It was a vast improvement over yesteryear.

Before leaving the department, Stone grabbed a couple of the blank forms. He now considered them with disdain. Stone figured he could create the report the way *he* wanted. The chief would see the light, he thought. Baumgartner always did. He was a smart man and would listen to reason.

Stone sat at his kitchen table, pushed the blank report forms to the side and opened his laptop. He called up Microsoft Word. He stared at the blank screen for several moments. The department's new reporting system was so much better than even Word, he thought.

Stone set about creating a report heading on the blank screen. He listed several categories across the top of the page: date, address, incident type, report number.

Report number.

It was then that he began to consider the implications and consequences of a report with no incident number. He leaned back in his chair and crossed his arms. Since he never called it in, no report number had been assigned. Without a number, there would never be an official record for Betty Rabe's claim of Councilman Hahn's potential assault.

Even if he checked out on the call with dispatch yet cleared the call as One-David—officer contact with no report—an incident number would still be generated, creating some record of his time with Betty Rabe. As it was, there was no record of him ever being there. For all purposes, his interviews with both Rabe and Hahn did not exist.

That's what this was about.

He got up from the table and walked around.

The mayor sent the letter to the chief who then told him to keep it out of the system while he determined the validity of the claim.

They wanted it kept quiet.

Why?

Why would they do that?

Were Sikes and Baumgartner actually helping Hahn?

Were they helping him get away with something?

Stone considered the idea for a moment, then rejected it. No, that didn't seem like either of them.

He wasn't thinking about this correctly. Stone stopped walking in circles and stared at his computer. He wasn't seeing it like the mayor, nor was he thinking about it like the chief.

Stone liked the mayor. More than that, he liked *and* respected the chief. He thought Hahn was a douche bag. Hahn didn't deserve a break and if he did something wrong, he should be pinned to the wall.

If Sikes and Baumgartner wanted it kept quiet, then should he just shut up and do it?

Or was he betraying himself by not doing what he thought was right?

What was *the right thing?*

Maybe it was just writing the report by hand and delivering it to the chief.

Stone continued to stare at the blank computer screen for several minutes until he walked over and closed the laptop. Then he headed to the kitchen, looking for something to eat.

The coffee pot gurgled, bringing Stone's attention back to the present. He turned around and noticed the empty box of Ritz crackers and the half-empty jar of peanut butter. Next to them was the empty half-gallon of milk. He frowned.

He poured himself a cup of black coffee and sat at his kitchen table.

Last night, he'd thrown his diet completely out of whack by nervous eating. He hadn't done that since college when he overate before every final exam. The social aspect of higher education had initially been easy, but the studying, geez, the studying had gotten him fat. Then the social aspect got harder. Stone's parents paid for him to see a therapist to regulate his nervousness. He had to work extra hard to control himself, keeping everything in check whenever life's pressure got to be too much.

By the time he went through the academy and the training car, he thought he could handle stress like a pro. Nothing tripped him up in his three-year career until this.

It didn't feel right, but how was he to know if it was *actually* wrong? *Life isn't black-and-white,* he thought. It is a rainbow of grays. Maybe this fell into a darker gray, but who was he to tell the chief of police that he was wrong?

Stone finally settled onto one calming thought. His job was to follow directions and that's what he was going to do.

He sat at the kitchen table and pulled one of the blank forms to him. With his pen, he began filling in the empty boxes.

When he came to the one labeled *Report Number*, he left it blank.

Chapter 11

Breakfast used to be Chief Robert Baumgartner's favorite meal. Nothing beat an omelet stuffed with bacon, sausage, and onions along with a side of hash browns. Wash it down with coffee, and he had enough fuel to get him to dinner if he had to. As busy as the chief's position tended to be, that happened more often than he liked.

Since the Tyler Garrett incident twenty-one months ago, breakfast was ruined for him. He still ate, and heartily, if he was being honest, but he didn't enjoy it as much. The reason for that was simple. Several times a week, he met with the mayor for breakfast. Listening to Mayor Sikes didn't exactly do much for his appetite.

"Can you believe that idiot Buckner?" Sikes asked him, shaking his head.

Baumgartner grunted, shoveling a bite of waffle into his mouth. The Safari Room at the Davenport Hotel made passable waffles, but they were nothing compared to the blue-collar beauty of Waffles n' More up on Monroe. He missed the days when he could drop in there on his way into work. Most times, graveyard officers would just be finishing up their own end-of-shift breakfasts and it gave him a chance to connect with one or two. If he was lucky, he'd hear a war story from the preceding shift, though these days, officers were cautious about what they said in public, or to him. Even if he missed the graveyard cops, he still got one hell of a waffle and some great conversation from the owner of the place, unlike Sikes and his garbage.

"The guy has no political instinct," Sikes continued. "I mean, if he just shut his mouth and laid low, stopped tapping the babysitter for a little while, this would run through a news cycle or two and be over. Instead, he calls a news conference?" The mayor shook his head again. "Idiot."

Baumgartner cut another piece of waffle. Before he could eat it, Sikes spoke.

"You don't have an opinion on this?"

Baumgartner thought about it for a second. "Sure," he said, "but Buckner is neutral on police issues, at best. Half the time, he's a negative vote. I don't really care if he torches himself."

"You know what? I agree. I don't care, either, but I love watching him twist, especially since he's doing it to himself." Sikes smiled malevolently. "It's about time someone else got ravaged by those media jackals."

"You should be happy," Baumgartner said. "You got reelected."

"Barely. That little traitor Lofton made a game of it."

"Win by an inch, or win by a mile, it's still a win."

"Everyone remembers the landslides. Optics matter, and an overwhelming victory gives you a mandate."

"History remembers the winners," Baumgartner said. "It's about results."

"Easy for you to say." The mayor's tone had an underlying sharpness to it. "You're more popular than Santa Claus."

"No one's more popular than Santa."

Sikes wasn't hearing any of it. "It's not fair. I get blamed for every damn pothole, burnt out streetlight, and traffic jam, because I'm elected. But you're a cop, and you've been around forever, so you get a pass. It's all about popularity."

Baumgartner snorted and reached for his coffee. "We both know how fast public opinion can change."

Just look at the whole Garrett incident. First a hero, then a villain, then a hero again.

He wondered if Sikes was thinking the same thing, but he couldn't tell. He knew the mayor resented his standing in the community, but he wasn't going to apologize for it. He worked hard to build those bridges, and he put in a lot of years coming up through the ranks to earn his position. Sikes might be a rarity in Spokane—a two-term mayor—but as far as Baumgartner was concerned, Sikes still had a way to go before he could say he'd paid his dues like the chief had.

"As long as we're on the topic of changing public opinion," Sikes said, "let's talk about the crime stats. Have you read through the FBI report?"

"Of course." Baumgartner wondered if Sikes knew that the FBI compiled the NIBRS report from the data the individual police agencies sent to Quantico. It wasn't like any of the numbers were a surprise to him. Besides, he was the one who forwarded the report to the mayor and the council.

"Property crime is up," Sikes said, his tone clipped. "Sharply, I might add."

"The NIBRS numbers are six months old," Baumgartner reminded him.

"Are your current numbers any different?"

Baumgartner shrugged. "They're different, but the trend is the same. Property crime is up here, just like most of the country."

"See, that's a problem," Sikes said, jabbing his finger toward the table for emphasis "It sabotages things."

"Yeah?" Baumgartner took a long drink of his coffee, preparing himself for another lecture from Professor Mayor. At least the java here beat out Waffles 'n More's. He hated to admit it, but sometimes fancier was better.

"The economy is up," Sikes explained, in full sage mode. "The housing market is way up, better than anyone expected when it crashed. Those are supposed to be good things."

Baumgartner took advantage of Sikes's monologue to take a bite of bacon.

"But you know what drives the housing market?"

"People buying and selling houses?"

Sikes scowled. "Don't be simple." He paused, then shrugged. "But yeah, that's pretty much it. They say location is the number one factor to most home sales, but the thing about location is that people are looking at more than just a nice view. They're looking hard at the school system and what the sustained property value will be. The school system is mostly out of your realm, but property value isn't."

Baumgartner swallowed. "The crime rate impacts property value. That's what you're saying?"

"Don't say it like it's a theory or something. We both know it's one hundred percent true."

"It is," Baumgartner said. "But the crime pattern seems to be—"

Sikes held up a hand. "The crime pattern is an upward trend line, that's what it is. All of these burglaries and stolen cars are going to negate the positive economic growth soon. Not to mention, it will lead to violent crime, and once that kicks in…well, forget it. We might as well be Detroit."

Baumgartner wiped his mouth with a cloth napkin. "I get why you're concerned," he said. "But let's be clear about something here. Most of this property crime is being driven by drug use. Dopers are stealing things to supply their habit. These aren't career criminals on a trajectory to committing murder at some point. What we've got are people scrambling around for twenty bucks so they can get their fix for the day."

"How long before they turn to robbing convenience stores for that?"

"Robbery is down. In fact, most violent crimes are down."

"Not domestic violence," the mayor countered. "That's up, what? Two percent?"

Someone's been doing his homework.

Baumgartner took another drink of coffee and gave the mayor a placid look. "First off, that's an historically normal variance. Second, you tell me what I'm supposed to do to stop people who live together from arguing and hitting each other?"

"I don't know. Maybe work closer with social services?" The light sneer in the mayor's voice was unmistakable now.

"We already do, but we are never going to completely eradicate domestic violence, only mitigate it and respond to it when it happens."

"Sounds defeatist to me."

"It's realistic, is what it is."

"The murder rate is up, too," Sikes persisted. "Substantially. What do you say to that?"

"I say you're looking at the percentage there, and not the raw numbers. Last year, there were eighteen murders in Spokane. That was a ten-year low. During the NIBRS reporting period, there were twelve murders, which puts us on pace for twenty-four. That's roughly average since about 2000 or so, but the percentage reads as a thirty-three percent increase. Raw numbers this low skew how the percentages look."

"I'm sure the families of all twenty-four victims would be comforted by your convenient math," Sikes said.

"All due respect, sir, what's your deal this morning?"

"My deal? My *deal* is that I want to know what you're going to do about these crime rates, Chief?" He stared hard at Baumgartner. "Do I need to remind you that you work for me?"

"I know the chain of command," Baumgartner growled.

"Good. Are you starting to get a picture of how bad the optics on this are?"

Baumgartner didn't answer right away. He wasn't going to be outright insubordinate to Sikes. The man was his boss, after all, and Baumgartner respected that, but he'd never kissed anyone's ass in his career, and he wasn't going to start now. "I understand why you don't like the way it looks," he finally said, diplomatically.

"It *looks* like dog puke. Those stats are your work results, Chief." Sikes gave him a humorless smile. "Since you're so focused on results over optics."

Baumgartner stared back at him flatly. He'd seen Sikes like this a few times over his term, though the mayor had rarely directed this attitude toward him. Other staff members were more frequent recipients.

"I am working on it," he said. "It takes some coordination."

"I expect positive results, and soon. You can count on that."

Baumgartner tapped a meaty finger on the table. "As long as we're counting, let's not forget that sexual assault and serious assault are both down significantly."

"Sexual assault *and* serious assault?" The mayor gave him a look like he'd just watched the chief step on a landmine and the loud click still rang in the air. "So sexual assault isn't serious?"

Baumgartner shook his head dismissively. "Come on, don't play semantics with me, Mister Mayor. Of course sexual assaults are serious. The two crimes are catalogued as separate categories, that's all."

Sikes stared at him for a long moment, then he let what passed for a genuine smile spread across his face. "Well, good. I think we fully understand each other. You have my full confidence, Robert. I know you'll reverse this trend. It's too important."

It never failed to amaze Baumgartner how quickly the mayor could shift gears and change his persona. The sheer artifice of it disgusted him. He preferred to know where he stood with people, and to make sure they knew the same. But in his own way, the mayor was being very clear. Fix the crime statistics, or else. He didn't know how big the mayor's balls were when it came to the *or else* part, but he didn't want to risk finding out. Besides, fighting crime was his job, so it wasn't like he needed coaxing to get on it.

"Speaking of sexual assault," Sikes said, his tone amiable again, "what did you do with Hahn's letter?"

"I gave it to Stone. He's investigating it."

"Quietly?"

"Of course."

"Is there anything to it?" Sikes looked left and right, then lowered his voice slightly. "Did he rape her?"

"I haven't got a report back yet. I'll brief you when I know."

"Make sure you do. If it's bad, I need to know first. I want to distance myself from that kind of trouble."

Of course you do. Distance yourself and leave me holding the bag.

Baumgartner popped the remainder of his bacon strip into his mouth.

I don't think so.

"I understand," he said, around his food. "I'll let you know."

"I've already gotta distance myself from Buckner and all I did was let that idiot support me. Don't want to be in bed with another one who's accused of running around with an underage girl. What's gotten into these guys? Can't they find some desperate housewife to consort with? I mean, it's not rocket science." The mayor wiped his mouth and motioned toward Baumgartner's plate. "How's your breakfast?"

"It's good."

Sikes looked around the posh restaurant. "Best place in town for breakfast, am I right?"

Baumgartner grunted and finished off his coffee, leaving the remainder of his waffle uneaten.

Chapter 12

Detective Wardell Clint stared at the open case file, trying to concentrate, but his tired, bleary eyes could barely focus. So far, all he could make out of the case was that it was an assault, possibly a robbery. The unreliable victim "maybe" knew his assailant and was in that part of downtown where drugs were sold for "no reason" and couldn't remember if anything was taken from him. The whole thing was shaping up to be a fight over a dope deal instead of an actual legitimate robbery, which was barely worth Clint's time, in his considered opinion. The only reason the case even got assigned probably had to do with the partial license plate. It was a potential lead, but one that would be tedious to follow-up. He had four digits out of six, so he'd need to run all the possible configurations of the last two digits, looking for possible matches to the vague vehicle description. Then he had to run all the registered owners for possible suspects. All that work for someone who probably got jacked in the eye for trying to underpay a dealer. No one would have looked twice at the report if the punch hadn't been hard enough to break the orbital bone.

He wondered if Michelle in Crime Analysis could run some sort of search to speed up the process…

"Ward?"

"Don't call me that," Clint responded automatically. He looked up to see Lieutenant Dan Flowers standing next to his desk. "It's Wardell. You know this, Lieutenant."

"Oh, yeah." Flowers shrugged. "Forgot."

"Sure you did."

Flowers frowned. "I did."

"Uh-huh." As Clint saw it, either Flowers was being honest, and he had legitimately forgotten, in which case the unit commander's lack of attention to something as basic as a person's name was questionable leadership. Or Flowers called him by the shortened version of Clint's name on purpose, in which case…well, that was questionable leadership, too. Maybe it was some latent racism. Clint wasn't sure. In the grand scheme of all the crooked things going on in the world, the first name thing wasn't a big deal, but it still rubbed Clint the wrong way. "What do you want, Lieutenant?"

Flowers didn't hide his exasperation.

"What's going on with the Ainsley case?"

Clint let out a slow, controlled exhale. "It came to me as a push-in home invasion robbery, but that's a load of crap, no question. The girlfriend refused to be interviewed, said she couldn't remember. The boyfriend told some obviously contrived story about a couple of unidentified males forcing in through the door when he opened it."

Black males, Clint thought, but decided not to mention. Funny how it was always a black man, though, wasn't it?

"So…?"

"So, either it's a domestic violence situation and they're covering up, or it's about drugs." He held up his newest case file. "Like this ridiculous caper right here."

Flowers ignored the reference. "How about the Nylander case?"

Nylander was the suicide he'd been called out for three days ago. "He's still dead," Clint said.

Flowers gave him a stern look. "No kidding, he's still dead. I mean, did you get anywhere yet with—"

"Where exactly am I supposed to get on that case, Lieutenant?" Clint interrupted. "I conducted a thorough investigation. All the evidence clearly indicated that he purposefully hung himself. He even left a note, which is far less common than people think. There was no evidence of foul play. My report wasn't at all ambiguous about this."

"Look, *Detective*," Flowers responded, an edge creeping into his tone. "Don't patronize me."

"I wasn't patronizing you. I was answering your question."

"I wasn't asking you about your finding. I was asking you if you had any luck locating the next of kin."

Clint held up a finger. "First off, you didn't specify that. And second—"

It was Flowers's turn to interrupt Clint. "I didn't get a chance. You jumped right in the middle of my question."

Clint paused. Then he shrugged. "That is factually correct," he admitted.

Flowers waited, as if he expected more. Probably an apology, Clint figured, but he wasn't going to give him the satisfaction.

Learn my first name, ofay, and maybe I'll consider it.

Besides, he'd already conceded that Flowers had been correct. That should be sufficient. How much ego stroking or hand holding did a grown man need?

Flowers sighed, which Clint took as a sign that the matter was settled. He turned back to his case file, ignoring the lieutenant. When Flowers didn't walk away after fifteen seconds, he glanced back up. "What is it?"

"The Nylander case? What was the second thing?"

"Oh, that's right. The second thing is that locating the next of kin is not my job. I'm a detective, not a funeral director."

Flowers scowled. "I know it's not a normal part of your duty, but you could do it."

"Of course, I *could*. But it isn't my job, and it's a clear misuse of my time, especially with my case load being so high."

"Everyone's case load is high."

"Mine is nine percent higher than anyone else's," he told Flowers. "I've done the math."

"You've got time for that kind of math, but you can't run down a next of kin?"

"Managing my case load is part of my job."

"No, it's *my* job," Flower said.

"With that kind of variance, something is obviously going on with the way you do your job, Lieutenant."

"*Damn* it," Flowers growled. "Why are you always so impossible?"

Clint just stared at him.

"Look," Flowers explained, "we lost a lot of experience when Talbott and Pomeroy went down, okay?"

Clint didn't answer, but his jaw clenched. Even when he wasn't following Garrett around, the officer's actions invaded his life. Talbott and Pomeroy were Garrett's partners in the dirty he was up to, and Clint was supposed to mourn their passing?

"The new detectives take a little time to spin up from property crimes investigations to major crimes level work," Flowers continued. "I have to balance the case load accordingly."

Clint almost exploded. After everything else, now Garrett's actions caused him more work, too?

Flowers seemed to sense Clint's fury, even if he didn't know its origin. A look of concern crossed his face. "You all right, Ward...ell?"

"I'm fine," Clint gritted.

"Things'll get better soon," Flowers said. "Marty Hill is back on light duty from his knee surgery, so he'll pick up cases and the new detectives are just about up to speed. Everything will even out over time, as far as the case load goes."

"I'm sure."

"All right." Flowers nodded, and his expression shifted to something that looked to Clint like he thought they just had a 'good talk.' "So you'll follow-up on Nylander, then?"

Clint thought for a moment. Then he asked, "The chaplain gets paid, right?"

"Yeah."

"Let him do it, then." Clint turned back to his file. This time, after a few seconds, Flowers shook his head and walked away.

Good.

He read through the remainder of the new assault case and put it near the back of his case load rack. The rack used to be organized by report number and date, with the most recent case in the front, but Clint had adapted his thinking on that. Now he organized his cases by priority. Important cases, especially homicides, were near the front. Wastes of time like this latest robbery/assault case were near the back. Finding next of kin didn't even make the rack.

And Garrett?

The Garrett file was an unofficial collection of his notes that he kept in a small locked file box, and he kept *that* secured in the trunk of his car when he wasn't in the field working the case. At night, he brought the file box into his house, just in case Garrett ever got wise to him and tried to steal it out of his trunk. His aged Crown Victoria was still a department-issue vehicle, and Clint wouldn't put it past Garrett to con a universal "cheater" key out of some mechanic at the city garage so that he could get into Clint's car.

If he knew he was being watched, that is.

Clint figured Garrett had to know he was watched at first, right after everything that went down. Did he wonder if that tailed off and eventually ended? Clint wouldn't fault him for thinking so. Twenty-one months was an absurd amount of time to keep up an investigation that wasn't bearing any fruit. But Clint knew the truth, and there was no way he was letting go.

"Wardell?"

Clint pressed his lips together in irritation and looked up to see Captain Tom Farrell at his desk.

Farrell frowned in concern. "Something wrong?"

"Except for the brass parade to my desk while I'm trying to work important crimes? No, Captain. Not a thing."

Farrell's frown changed to irritation. "Don't treat me like I'm the enemy."

You're the brass. The brass is the enemy.

"I'm only checking on you."

Checking up *on me, you mean.*

"I don't need checking on," Clint said. "And if I do, my mama will be the one to do it."

Farrell looked a little closer at him. "You're looking rough, Wardell. You want to take a day off or something?"

"No. Do *you* want to take a day off?"

"No," Farrell said.

"Then that's settled. How about we both get back to what we were doing. *I* was working."

Unlike Flowers, Farrell didn't rise to the bait. "All right, but let's get coffee soon and talk about things."

Clint whipped backward in his chair, leaning away. "You know what?" he whispered harshly. "You ain't doing no one any good coming by here and looking all friendly with me. Why don't you just let me do my job and I'll let you know when there's something you need to know, huh?"

A momentary anger flashed behind Farrell's eyes, but he didn't respond right away. He appeared to be studying Clint, and that was not something Clint liked or approved of. He didn't know if he could continue to trust Farrell or if the man was still as on board as he had been in the aftermath of Garrett's crime spree, but he did know that he didn't need a daddy.

"Wardell—"

"I've got to pee," Clint said, standing. He turned and walked away from Farrell and down the hall. When he reached the bathrooms, he kept on walking until he was out the west doors and felt the brisk wind on his face. He hesitated there, wanting to enjoy the sensation, but the odds were too high that Farrell would follow him and try to have the same conversation here as at Clint's desk. He couldn't go back, and he couldn't stay here.

Might as well do something productive.

Clint walked to his car, stopping to remove his file from the trunk before heading south. Garrett wasn't due to work for several hours yet, but there were things Clint could check on.

Chapter 13

Gary Stone sat in the small lobby outside the chief's office. Marilyn, the chief's assistant, ignored him as she worked on her computer, her fingernails clicking the keyboard annoyingly loud.

Marilyn was in her early fifties with short curly hair, lightly applied makeup, and a conservative polyester blouse. She had been in the position for almost twenty years surviving through three different chiefs. Marilyn held a certain amount of status within the department for the secrets she held, not to mention the access she controlled. No one dared cross her.

The lobby was set back from the harshly illuminated hallway and was lit by decorative lamps instead of overhead lighting. A perk that someone close to the chief could get. Photos of forests hung on the walls. Near Stone's chair, a noise machine played rain sounds. He wondered its purpose. Was it for ambiance or to hide voices from inside the chief's office?

Stone glanced at his watch. It was fifteen minutes after the hour. The chief was rarely late, but this was now going on ridiculous.

"Marilyn?"

"He said he was on the way," she said without glancing at him.

Stone nodded. He was silent for a moment, then turned to face Marilyn. He opened his mouth to ask another question, but she quickly turned to face him, irritated by the interruption. Stone saw the look in her eyes and remained quiet.

"He said for you to wait. I don't know how to be any clearer than that, Officer Stone."

He nodded even though Marilyn had already turned back toward her computer. Stone leaned forward, his elbows resting on his knees. In his hands was a file containing the handwritten report on Betty Rabe's accusation against Councilman Hahn.

He opened the folder and reread his work. The missing report number continued to bother him. If this report was lost, technically there would never be a record of his interview.

Technically.

"Marilyn," the chief's voice boomed. Stone sat upright, even though the chief was still not visible to him.

"Good morning, sir," Marilyn said.

"Has Officer—never mind." The chief rounded the corner and now stood directly in front of Stone. His eyes focused on the manila folder in the officer's hands. "Is that the report?"

"Yes, sir."

The chief did not appear to be in a good mood. "Let's go," he said and walked into his office.

Stone looked to Marilyn for a show of support, but her focus remained on her computer. He turned and followed the chief.

With his foot, Baumgartner pushed his chair away from his desk, banging it against a credenza. He turned around and dropped into the chair. "Get straight to the point, Stone."

"Well, sir, yesterday morning, after talking with you, I drove out to meet with—"

"Stone!"

"Sir?" It did not go unnoticed by Stone that the chief was not calling him by his first name.

"Did he do it or not?"

"It's not that cut and dried, sir. If I can explain—"

Baumgartner slapped his hand on the edge of his desk. "Gimme the file."

Stone stepped forward and handed the folder to the chief. Baumgartner pulled the papers from it then tossed the file to the desk. He leaned back in his chair and read the report. It was three pages long. Baumgartner's scowl never lessened as his eyes scanned the papers.

From the corner of his eye, Stone noticed Marilyn was slowly closing the door to the chief's office.

Since he hadn't been invited to sit down, Stone remained standing. He crossed his arms over his chest, inhaled once, and let the breath slowly out. His eyes then wandered around the office. There were various commendations, photos, and police memorabilia on the wall. Baumgartner had a long and distinguished career, and it was obvious he liked showing it off as well as remembering it.

The chief slowly lowered the report and lifted his eyes. Stone returned the chief's gaze and smiled hesitantly. The big man studied Stone's appearance and shook his head in disgust. When Baumgartner's eyes returned to the page, Stone realized how he was standing. He corrected his position and placed his hands behind his back while straightening. He stared directly forward, his face passive.

The chief finished the report, returned to the beginning, and reread it a second time, albeit quicker. When he was done, he laid the report on the desk and studied Stone. He nodded a couple of times, then said, "At ease, Gary."

"Thank you, sir."

"Is this the only copy?"

He'd been prepared for the question and confidently answered, "Yes." Even though he was prepared for the answer, it still made his stomach hurt, and he wanted to use the restroom.

"Good. That's good. Did you talk with anybody about this?"

"No, sir."

Baumgartner studied him. "Not even your sergeant?"

"No."

"Girlfriend?"

Stone shook his head. "No, sir."

"No copies, right? Right. You already said that. What about notes? Anything in your notebook?"

His stomach felt like it was doing flip-flops and he needed to get to the bathroom. Stone pulled his small notebook from his back pocket and opened it. He flipped through it, found the two pages of notes from the Betty Rabe and Councilman Hahn interviews. He ripped them out and put them on the chief's desk. Stone returned to his position of standing at ease.

Baumgartner picked up the report again along with the notebook pages. "How'd you clear your contact?" Baumgartner asked. "One-David?"

Stone swallowed. "I…I actually didn't check out on the call."

Baumgartner peered at him. "So no record in CAD, either?"

"No," Stone said. Then he added, "I don't always check out with radio. Only when there's an officer safety concern."

Baumgartner considered, then looked back down at the report. "Good work, Gary," he said, without looking up. "I mean it. You did good. Dismissed."

Stone turned as smoothly as he could and left the office. He walked by Marilyn without saying goodbye. When he was in the hallway, he hurried toward the restroom.

Chapter 14

Captain Dana Hatcher refilled her coffee cup from the oversized pot in the detectives' division. The coffee oasis was located just up the hall from her office. Tom Farrell told her about it when she was first promoted. He called it one the most important resources within the department, and membership was a steal at a few bucks a month per person.

He was right about that this morning. This was her fourth cup so far, and while the caffeine had done some of the work cutting through the hangover fog she had when she first rolled into the office, it didn't do much for the headache or acid stomach.

She shuffled back down the hallway, ignoring the sideways glance one of the detectives gave her. He probably thought she was mooching the coffee instead of being a paying member of the coffee club.

I'm never drinking hard liquor on a work night again.

It was a weak promise, though, and she knew it. There was an old saying: "The danger past, and God forgotten." She figured it worked with booze and hangovers, too. Besides, Margaret Patterson was fun to be around, and she'd become a good friend.

Friends were hard to come by for cops. A slew of weird social dynamics got in the way, as well as the attitude that some cops developed in response to what they experienced. Hatcher had come into the career with a wide circle of friends from the neighborhood, from school, from her jobs at the grocery store and doing loss prevention at JC Penney. Slowly, though, that circle tightened, as the natural progression of life conspired with her status as a cop to push many of them out.

Sometimes it was the other person, but she knew sometimes it was her.

How does someone go to a barbecue with a bunch of people who ask about work when her last shift ended with a call involving a dead child? It's not like she could ever explain it to them. Trying to do so would come out as gruesome, and they'd resent her for pouring that kind of poison out where everybody could see. Yet, keeping it to herself made her response seem secretive and fake, reinforcing the cop stereotype. Not to mention that the poison ate up her insides.

So she did what most cops do. She socialized with other cops, where she could speak shorthand if work came up. Where she could tell jokes only cops would get. And where sharing that dead child call was met with understanding and empathy.

Slowly, most of her old friends gravitated away. Or she did. Everyone had their lives and careers, but none of them operated with the same round-the-clock hours that Hatcher did. As her career progressed, her social life became steadily more insular. Her time with good friends outside of law enforcement dwindled, until one day she realized that almost everyone she knew was a cop.

At her desk, Hatcher popped a couple of aspirin and sipped the coffee. Then she closed her eyes and grimaced.

Those Moscow Mules kick like their name.

The silence of her office was welcome, but it was lonely, too. The terrible irony of the police experience was that it involved a devious bait and switch. After surrounding herself almost exclusively with police officers and dispatchers and other department members, she took a promotional exam and made sergeant. Immediately, she noticed a shift. She was a sergeant, and that seemed to create a distance. Cops she knew well suddenly treated her differently. Not quite at an arm's length, but with a small measure of caution. People she was only acquainted with never seemed to get past the formality that came with rank.

She overcame that distance by developing strong relationships with everyone she led on her squad. All her team's officers came to trust and respect her, and she worked hard to earn that every day. Each year, regardless of the personnel on her squad, she created something akin to a family.

It wasn't lost on her that her circle had gotten smaller.

Later, when she became a lieutenant in charge of an entire shift, she lost that ability to build a tight-knit team and to be a part of that group. One of the loneliest moments of her career came shortly after she got her gold bar and was assigned to graveyard. She ran roll call, then sent the shift out into the night. Standing in the empty roll call room, she realized how separated she really was from the people that used to be her support system. She was part of the brass now, and that gold bar was all most cops saw, just like her old friends who only saw the badge.

This was that terrible irony, the bait and switch. Because of her job, she'd grown apart from most of her old friends, replacing them with her police family. Now her rank was separating her from most of that same police family, leaving her more and more alone.

Fortunately, that was about the time she met Councilor Margaret Patterson at a neighborhood watch meeting. The two of them talked and Hatcher realized right away that Maggie was in much the same place she was. The two women had a lot in common, and it didn't take long before an easy friendship began.

Easy, Hatcher mused, except for these occasional mornings after.

"Captain?"

Hatcher opened her eyes to see Ray Zielinski standing in her open doorway. "Hey, Ray."

"Am I interrupting?"

"No," she said, setting down her coffee. "Just thinking about some things. Come in, sit down."

Zielinski took the seat in front of her.

"How are you?"

He shrugged. "Fine, I guess."

Hatcher waited for him to continue. She'd been Zielinski's sergeant when he went through his first divorce, and it had been an ugly one. They'd had more than a few cups of coffee during that period, some to talk about the divorce and some to keep him from thinking about it. Of course, since he was a man and she was a woman, a few rumors circulated, but Hatcher ignored them. She did the same thing when the inevitable lesbian rumors swirled around her, too, something every female cop of her generation seemed to get hit with at some point. People couldn't seem to decide if she liked women or liked sleeping with her subordinates. The rumor mill was nothing if not inconsistent.

"You always do that," Zielinski said.

"What?"

"Wait. You let the silence sit."

Hatcher smiled. He was right. It was a common enough interview tactic, though it seemed difficult for some cops to master. The approach worked because of the natural human desire to fill the silence. The problem was, it worked on the interviewer as much as the person being interviewed.

"See? You're still doing it." Zielinski's voice didn't sound irritated, though. If anything, Hatcher heard some affection or nostalgia there.

"I'm just surprised to see you," she said. It wasn't often a patrol officer stopped in to visit the patrol captain. She was four full steps up his chain of command.

"I figured I should check on you," Zielinski said. "Make sure you haven't forgotten your roots."

She spread her hands. "I remain well grounded."

"Good." He fell silent for a moment.

Hatcher knew about Zielinski's second divorce, too, though none of the details, only that it had happened. She'd been divorced once herself, and she remembered feeling like a complete loser, like she failed the marriage test. She wondered if Zielinski was feeling the compounded sting of being twice divorced.

"Look, I'm sorry to bother you," Zielinski said.

"It's no bother."

"It's just that…well, you were one of the best sergeants I ever had, and I thought you were pretty damn good as a lieutenant, too."

"Thanks." A flush of pride washed over Hatcher. Zielinski's words were clearly sincere, and welcome ones.

"I'm sure you'll do good as a captain, though why you'd want to hang out with brass all day long is beyond me." He gave her a rueful grin, but it had a distracted quality to it. "Anyway, I know it's been a while since we had one of our talks, but…"

"You can always come talk to me, Ray. You know that."

"I wasn't sure. You're a captain now."

"Close the door," she said.

"Huh?"

She flicked a finger toward her open office door. "Close it."

Zielinski stood and did as she asked. Then he sat down again.

"Turn off your portable," Hatcher said.

He looked confused but snapped off his patrol radio.

"There," Hatcher said. "Now it isn't Captain Hatcher and Senior Patrol Officer Zielinski anymore. It's just Dana and Ray, okay?"

Zielinski gave her an appreciative nod. "Thanks, Sarge," he said meaningfully.

She laughed. "Close enough. What's on your mind?"

He took a deep breath. "You know Amber and I split up, right?"

"I heard. I'm sorry."

"I'm more sorry that the judge decided to give her max alimony for the full two years."

Hatcher nodded sympathetically. "She was younger, right?"

"Yeah."

"A lot?"

"She was twenty-three when we got married," Zielinski admitted. "Halfway through college and never had anything but entry-level jobs. Once we got married, she quit work and school."

"Why?"

"We wanted to start a family, but that didn't happen."

"Not for lack of trying, I assume."

Zielinski smiled at that. "No, ma'am." His smile faded. "Anyway, that's why the judge gave her the ruling on the alimony. Now that the two-year window is closing, she's threatening to take me back for an extension."

"I'm sorry. Do you have a good lawyer?"

"Is there such a thing?"

It was her turn to smile. "Do you have an *effective* lawyer?"

"Not really. I can't afford it. The guy I've got would have a problem arguing that the world isn't flat, you know?" He shook his head. "Now I know how those mopes we arrest feel when they get the public defender. Except I didn't do anything wrong."

Hatcher considered for a moment. "I could ask around for a better family law attorney, Ray. Someone who will take payments, or—"

"That's not why I'm here."

"Okay. Then what?"

"I can cover the expenses, but only because I've been working a lot of extra details. My seniority lets me pick up most anything I want, so I use my days off to earn some extra money." He paused, then shrugged. "I work some evenings, too. That's part of why I came to day shift, so I could catch those early evening gigs."

"Sounds tough."

"It'd be a lot easier if I was a fireman, working once every three days, but I'm making it work. It's tight, but I'm scraping by."

"Be careful not to overextend yourself," Hatcher said. "You know what Sergeant McGee used to say."

"A distracted cop is a dead cop," Zielinski dutifully repeated. "I know, but I'm being careful."

"I hope so."

"The problem is that I got this chippy demeanor complaint a couple weeks ago, and it's hanging over my head."

"A shift-level complaint?" Hatcher had handled plenty of those as a sergeant, resolving a majority of them to everyone's satisfaction without involving Internal Affairs. Most of the time, the person complaining just wanted to be heard, and if she could endure thirty minutes of listening to a citizen gripe about one of her officers and save them an official complaint, she considered that time well spent.

"No," Zielinski said. "Full-on IA."

"Over what?"

He sighed. "I mouthed off a bit. Nothing that would have made a difference on power shift, but it's a different breed of citizen out and about on day shift. You know what I mean."

She did, without a doubt. "Have you talked to Dale Thomas?"

Zielinski snorted. "El Presidente? He's a tool."

Hatcher didn't respond to that, though she generally shared the sentiment about the union president. Instead, she told him, "I haven't seen the complaint yet, but I won't until IA finishes their investigation and forwards it through the chain of command."

"Who decides on a demeanor complaint? Is it the chief, or…?"

"All IA complaints are decided by the chief," she said. "But for less serious complaints, he tends to go with the recommendation from the chain." She tilted her head at him. "Are you here trying to sway the jury, Ray?"

"No," he said. "Honestly, I just want to know where the thing is at. IA isn't telling me squat. Thomas will turn it into a federal case if I ask him about it. I have no idea how long this is going to take, or if it looks like I'll get tagged with a founded complaint, or what. It's stressful."

"That's understandable."

Zielinski leaned forward. "Here's the biggest stress for me. If it ends up being founded, then that comes with an automatic three-month suspension from the extra duty list. If I can't work extra details, I can't pay my bills. The alimony, the child support, my rent…I'm upside down without the extra work."

Hatcher nodded in understanding. "Can you downsize at all?"

He let out a desperate chuckle. "I'm already living in a tiny apartment. No cable or internet. My only real luxury is my phone, and that's a pay-as-you-go plan."

"I didn't know it was so bad."

Zielinski frowned. "I thought it would only be temporary, but now who knows? I…I just need to know so I can be prepared for the financial fallout, that's all."

She leaned forward. "I'll see what I can find out, Ray. All right?"

"That'd be helpful." He looked relieved. "Thanks, Sarge…er, Cap."

Hatcher smiled at the term. Officer Dana-gerous to Sarge to El-Tee to Cap. Her career progression in nicknames.

He stood. "I should get back on the street. I'm sure the calls are stacking up like cord wood, making you look bad."

"Then go clear the screen, Ray. My career rests in your hands."

"You got it." Zielinski reached for the door handle, then paused. "Thanks again."

"You're welcome."

Something must have occurred to Zielinski, because he chuckled suddenly for no reason.

"What is it?" she asked.

He pointed to the closed door. "People are going to start talking again, like old times."

Hatcher smirked. "People always have something to say. You know where I stand."

"Pound sand, right?"

Zielinski's reply reminded her of Patterson's same attitude at the bar last night. "Exactly," she said. "If those people spent more time doing their jobs than gossiping like a bunch of old hens, there'd be no crime in this city."

"In my experience, the roosters gossip worse than the hens," he said.

"It's all clucking to me, and it gives me the same headache."

Zielinski pulled open the door. "Watch out for yourself, Cap. You're with the brass now, and that's through the looking glass."

"I know."

"You should've stayed a sergeant."

"I should've been a firefighter."

Zielinski laughed. "That's *my* line." He gave her a short wave and left the office.

Hatcher finished her coffee, which was now tepid. She jotted down a note to call Internal Affairs so she wouldn't forget. She'd call after her headache was gone. Meanwhile, she pulled out her notes for the strike team idea she'd told Farrell about, and got to work buffing out the rough edges.

Chapter 15

His wife waited on the doorstep as Tyler Garrett walked up with the kids. She wore yoga pants, a Lululemon sweatshirt, and a WSU baseball hat. Her hands were on her hips and her lips were pursed. She made no attempt to hide her irritation.

Garrett leaned down to his daughter and said, "Go hug Mommy."

Molly ran ahead of him, her little legs churning wildly as she laughed.

Jake, his son, looked up at him. "I told you she would be mad."

"It's all right," Garrett said.

As he got within speaking distance, he could hear Angie Garrett say, "Go inside, Molly, I need to speak with your father."

Jake reached up and put his hand in his father's.

"Jake," Angie said. "Inside."

"I wanna stay with dad for some more."

"Now!" Angie yelled.

Garrett leaned over and hugged his son. "Go inside. It's okay."

When they broke their embrace, Jake hurried inside. Angie reached back and closed the door. "Where the hell have you been, Tyler?"

"I was with the kids. You know that."

"You were supposed to have them back before four."

"So, I'm a little late. What's the big deal?"

"It's four-thirty. That's more than a little late."

"C'mon, Angie. We were having fun. Where's the harm?"

"The harm? Really? The harm is that you're not following the plan. I'm trying to work around your crazy schedule, but you never pay attention to what we've agreed to. You do what you want, when you want, and who pays the price? Me and the kids. We pay the price. Not you. No, not Tyler Garrett. You never pay the price."

"I took the kids to McDonald's. You said I could do that. They were having fun."

Angie looked away and shook her head.

"I'm trying, Ang. I'm really trying. I just wanted to see them having a good time."

She faced her husband. "Did they eat all their food?"

"Yeah. They ate good."

"Next time, would you text or something? Let me know you're going to be late?"

Garrett nodded. "Yeah, I will."

She lowered her head and looked at her running shoes.

"Angie."

"Don't."

"Why? You know how I feel."

"I don't feel that way anymore. Not ever again."

"What would it take? What would it take to for us to be like we were?"

"It's not happening, Ty. Just agree to the divorce and let's move on with our lives."

"But I still love you, Angie."

She turned and opened the front door. "Text next time you're going to be late." Then she stepped inside and closed the door, leaving Garrett alone on the sidewalk.

He wasn't supposed to start work for a couple hours. He had asked for some personal time before his shift started. Not feeling the need to hurry home nor to head into the department to start his shift, Garrett drove toward downtown. He quickly found a spot in a parking lot. The building was open to the public and he took the elevator up to the sixth floor where he rang the doorbell.

Tiana Kennedy opened the door, a look of surprise on her face. "Officer Garrett?"

"Yes, ma'am."

She wore a cream-colored sweater, green pants, and green hiking boots.

"What are you doing here?" she asked.

"Your insurance card," he said, holding it up. "I must have dropped it in my car after I stopped you."

Tiana smiled. "You dropped it?"

Garrett nodded. "Yeah, I dropped it."

"I think that has my work address on it." She grabbed the card. "Yeah, that's the work address, but you came here."

"Your driver's license shows here."

"You wrote down my address?"

"Yeah."

"Officer Garrett, did you keep that insurance card so you would have a reason to come here?"

He smiled. "What if I did?"

Tiana pushed the door open. "Well, then, don't stand out there."

Chapter 16

His day had been a total loss.

The lack of sleep coupled with the early morning meeting with the chief had sent it on an awkward trajectory. Stone hid out in his office most of the day. No one had called him from the department and he didn't receive any mail that required immediate follow-up. He had other duties beyond those at city hall, but Stone decided what he needed most was to be left alone, to reset his attitude.

The only bright spot was when Jean Carter stopped by to talk and laugh for a few minutes about her recent blind date. The two friends had reached an unspoken agreement to pretend their exchange in the lobby had never happened. That was the beauty of a long friendship—easy forgiveness. On a day like today, Stone was glad for such gifts. Other than Jean's visit, though, nothing was accomplished except pretending to work. Now that it was almost five, Stone powered down his computer and prepared to leave. He couldn't wait to get home, maybe go for a run, and get to bed early.

As he walked by the seventh-floor receptionist desk, he heard Mayor Sikes call out, "Gary! Hey, Gary!"

Stone stopped and turned, his stomach roiling.

Sikes walked over. His tie was crooked, and his hair mussed. It was the normal end-of-day appearance for the mayor.

He put his hand on Stone's shoulder. "You look like death on a cracker."

"Bad night of sleep, sir."

"Been there. You married? Girlfriend?"

"No, sir."

"Get yourself a girl. That'll take care of the sleeplessness." Sikes winked at him. "Know what I mean?"

The mayor looked around, then wrapped his arm around Stone's shoulders. He guided him behind the receptionist desk, out of sight of most passersby. He leaned in and asked, "What did you find?"

Stone stepped back from the mayor. "About what?"

"About the letter, of course."

"What letter?"

"Gary, don't play dumb with me."

Stone nodded. "Right. Yeah. The letter. The threatening one to Councilman Hahn, right? Yeah, well, we investigated it. The guy was your classic one-oh-five, that's department jargon for crazy person. Nothing to be concerned with, your honor."

Sikes grinned. "You sneaky bastard."

Stone's eyes widened. "Sir?"

"You think you can shine me on, don't you? That you're some kind of special."

"I don't know what you're talking about, sir."

"Of course, you don't. Just keep shining me on, then."

Stone remained silent.

"Gary, you like it here, don't you? I mean, in city hall."

He didn't like the smile on the mayor's face. It was no longer jovial, and his eyes were hard. Stone opened his mouth to answer, but the mayor cut him off.

"It's fun and exciting to be around everything going on, isn't it? Trust me, I love it. That's why I ran for a second term. I can't get enough of it. You like being near the action. I can see it in your eyes."

Stone didn't try to answer this time as he now had trouble swallowing. It was just like college again.

"You know you're in city hall at my pleasure, don't you? *My* pleasure. You're smart enough to have figured that out on your own, right? I didn't need to tell you that."

The mayor's smile wasn't right, Gary decided. Normal people don't smile like that.

"The chief serves at my pleasure, too. You serve at his. Everything rolls downhill. Get it?"

"Yes, sir."

"Here's my problem. I see you getting a lot of benefit from being inside city hall, but I don't see any bump from having you here."

Stone's eyes searched for an escape. There was none. No one else was coming to his rescue.

"I'm sure the chief gets a bump having you here. You know what I mean by that, right? *Bump*."

He focused on that ugly smile and nodded.

"So you give the chief his bump. Maybe you can give me a bump? What do you say? That sounds fair, right?"

Stone tried to swallow but he couldn't.

"You get something. Baumgartner gets something. I should get something. That way we all get a bump. Nod if you agree."

Stone nodded again.

"So, Gary, does Baumgartner got you working on any special projects?"

"What do you mean, sir?"

"Back to shining me on, Gary? I thought I just explained how that wasn't going to help you."

"Well—"

"I know about the letter, dumbass."

"Sir?"

"The Hahn letter. Not the threat, the one from the girl. Don't be so obtuse, Gary. You know it came to my office and I gave it to the chief. Not telling me what you know just makes you out to be a dumbass who doesn't understand how things work. Are you a dumbass, Gary?"

Stone winced.

"You see how easy it would have been for us to build trust here? Instead, you lied and avoided telling me what I needed to know. You wimped out."

Stone opened his mouth to speak but realized there was really nothing to say. He closed his mouth and stared at the mayor.

"Next time, man up, Gary. Choose your path and own it. You want to be the politician's best friend, then start acting like it. Understand?"

"Yes, sir," Stone whispered. "I understand."

"Then, by God, grow a pair," Sikes said before stalking back to his office.

Chapter 17

Tyler Garrett leaned his head back against his car seat and closed his eyes. He thought he could still smell Tiana's lotion on him. He knew it was a trick of his mind since he'd taken a shower once he'd gotten to the department.

The police radio chattered, but Garrett paid it little attention. His mind was on Tiana.

He'd gone there hoping to start something, but not expecting it to be what it became. The images played through his mind and a smile touched his lips.

He had some other things to take care of on his shift tonight, but maybe if things broke right, he could go back and see her again. If not, well, there was always tomorrow. She had even asked him as much.

"Charlie three sixteen."

Garrett's smile faded, and he opened his eyes. He was parked behind an industrial building on East Sprague Avenue.

He lifted the microphone from its cradle. "Three sixteen."

"Three sixteen," the dispatcher called back, "please see the call I just sent to your screen."

Garrett's eyes shifted to his mobile data computer. The screen lit up and he saw the call heading. Suicide. The address was far north, though, and he was a south unit.

"Three sixteen," he called.

"Sixteen," the dispatcher acknowledged. "Go ahead."

"Confirm, you're sending me north."

"Sixteen, that's confirmed." The dispatcher sounded slightly irritated. "All north units are currently engaged."

"Copy," he said and returned the microphone to its cradle.

He quickly read the initial incident report. A young woman in the Indian Trails neighborhood had been found unresponsive. The fire department had already responded and pronounced her dead.

Seventeen years old, Garrett thought, as he dropped his car into gear.

Bethany Rabe lay in her bed. She was cold to the touch. Her lifeless eyes stared up at the ceiling where a *Twilight* movie poster hung. Garrett craned his neck and looked at the poster. Vampires, he thought, and sniffed dismissively.

The girl wore a black T-shirt that said, *Baby Metal*. Her miniskirt was a green-and-black plaid. She wore holey black leggings underneath with black Converse tennis shoes.

An empty bottle of sleeping pills sat on the nightstand. A plastic bag that she had tied around her head was on the table. It had been removed by the responding paramedics.

Garrett moved the plastic bag with his pen to read the title of the book underneath. *Thirteen Reasons Why* by Jay Asher. Wasn't that a book about suicide? Garrett wondered. He made a note to research it further.

A marker stuck out from the middle of the book which caught his attention. Garrett leaned down to examine it closer. On its corner was a little blue badge. It was a symbol he was very familiar with as he had the same graphic on his own business card. Garrett slowly slid the card from the book, read the officer's name on the card, then tucked it into his notebook.

His eyes continued to scan the room but didn't see a suicide note. He walked back into the living room where Bethany's parents sat, each on an opposite end of the couch.

Lorraine Rabe's bob haircut, knit sweater, and polyester pants made her appear older than she was. She crossed her legs and fiddled with an unlit cigarette. Mascara streaked down from her eyes.

Donald Rabe wore blue jeans and a flannel shirt. His salt-and-pepper hair was shaggy for a man of his age. He was hunched over with his head in his hands.

They both looked up expectantly when Garrett entered the room. He had offered to call a chaplain to sit with them during their time of grief. Both declined the offer. Lorraine cited something about God not being there when she needed him and Donald replied, "It's not going to help now." Garrett didn't try to convince them that it would help. He wanted to get past this call and on with his night. He had other things to do, one of them being getting back to Tiana.

"Was there a note?" he asked.

"A note?" Lorraine said. "What kind of note?"

"No," Donald said, with a look disbelief toward his wife. "She didn't leave a note and we don't know why she did it. We loved our daughter."

Lorraine nodded in agreement.

"Had she tried something like this before?" Garrett asked.

"God, no," Donald said. He glanced at Lorraine.

Lorraine turned her hands up slightly. "Not that we ever saw."

"Did she have a history of mental illness?"

Donald whispered, "No," while Lorraine muttered, "None."

"Was she having any problems at school?"

The parents looked at each other, then shook their heads.

"What about a boyfriend? Did she have one?"

"I don't think so," Donald said.

"She might have been gay," Lorraine said.

"She wasn't gay," the father said, exasperated.

"How do you know?" Lorraine bawled. "Maybe that's why she did this. Maybe she was hurting inside because we hadn't accepted her."

"She did this because, well, honestly, I don't know why she would do this." Donald bent over and put his head back into his hands.

"So," Garrett said, "girlfriend?"

Lorraine put the unlit cigarette in her mouth but took it quickly out. "She has a friend," she said. "Little Oriental girl."

"Asian," Donald said, his head still in his hands. "The girl is Asian."

"You're correcting me *now*, Donny? Really? Now?"

Donald lifted his head, his face covered in tears. He looked at his wife and lifted his hands in defeat. "What the hell do you want from me, Lori?"

"This girl," Garrett said, directing their attention back to him. "The Asian one. Where does she live?"

Lorraine thumbed toward the east. "Three doors down. Her name is Ikuko. You can't miss her. She's the only Oriental in the neighborhood."

Garrett waited inside the house until a corporal arrived to photograph the scene, documenting everything.

He requested a detective but had no idea how long a response would take. Radio advised that one had been called out and was supposedly on the way.

The natural death of an elderly person, or even a middle-aged man with questionable health, would not need the response of a detective. However, the suicide of teenaged girl demanded it. Any suicide did.

Regardless, waiting around irritated Garrett, especially having to listen to Rabe's dysfunctional parents.

While the corporal worked, Garrett stepped out onto the porch, into the darkness of the night. He needed some fresh air and privacy to make a phone call or two. On the sidewalk, in a red ski parka that seemed overkill for a spring night, stood a small teenager. He looked closer and could determine her ethnicity. His phone calls would have to wait.

As he walked down the front stairs, the girl turned to leave.

"Hey," Garrett yelled. "Are you Ikuko?"

The girl stopped and looked back. "Who wants to know?"

"Officer Garrett. Spokane Police Department."

She turned fully toward Garrett now, her hands still in her pockets. Normally, he would ask someone he was talking with to remove their hands from their pockets, but he didn't fear the girl. By the look on her face, it was clear she feared him, though. She remained perfectly still as he approached.

When he was close, he could see she had a circular barbell nose ring and her left eyebrow was pieced with two rings.

"Ikuko, right?"

"What happened in there?" she asked, looking around him toward the house.

"Are you friends with Bethany Rabe?"

"Betty."

"Betty? Is that what she went by?"

Ikuko nodded.

"You were friends through, what, school?"

"And the neighborhood. I live over there." She pointed at her house. "We're in some of the same classes. She okay?"

Garrett looked back toward the house. "No. No, she's not."

"What happened?"

He studied the small girl. "Was she having problems at school?"

"Same as everyone. Why won't you tell me what's going on?"

"Was she seeing anyone?"

Ikuko's eyes widened. "I should go."

"Why was Betty talking with the cops?"

The girl turned and started walking. Garrett fell into step with her.

"I'm not going to let this go, Ikuko. You need to talk with me."

"Leave me alone. I can't be seen talking with you."

"Why not? If you keep walking, I'll follow you up to your house and talk with your parents."

She spun around. "You wouldn't."

"I would. I'm that kind of guy."

She pointed at Betty's house. "Tell me what happened to Betty!"

"She killed herself."

Ikuko's face widened. "Oh my God. She didn't."

"Yeah, she did."

"Oh, man." Ikuko spun in a circle. "Oh, man."

"Talk to me."

"I didn't think she would really do it."

"She talked about it?"

Ikuko lifted her hands to her head. "This is my fault. I should have said something. Oh God, I should have done something."

"It's not your fault. She did it to herself."

"How do you know?" Ikuko said, stepping toward Garrett. She moved her hands wildly as she spoke. "How do you *really* know? Maybe someone did it to make it look like a suicide. That happens, right?"

"Not very often."

"But sometimes it does." Ikuko's gaze was frantic.

"Why would you say that?"

"Because that's what *they* do."

"That's what who does? Who is *they*?"

"Men in power."

"What men? What men in power did Betty know?"

Ikuko suddenly looked frightened.

"Was that why she was talking with the cops? Was someone threatening her?"

She pointed to Betty's house again. "That could happen to me."

"Nothing is going to happen to you, Ikuko. Tell me what I need to know."

Ikuko started to turn, but Garrett grabbed her by the coat sleeve. Her eyes locked onto his hand. She tried to pull free, but Garrett held her in place.

"They'll kill me if I talk with you. I know it. I've seen the TV shows. That's what happens. It always happens."

"Enough!" Garrett snapped. "Your friend is dead. Tell me what was going on."

She again tried to yank free, but Garrett jerked her arm which caused her to stumble into him.

"Tell me," he said, his voice low and menacing. "I'm not screwing around."

Ikuko blinked several times. "You can't talk to me like that."

"I just did."

She stared at Garrett.

"Tell me or I make a big stink about you knowing Betty. I'll tell everyone how you helped me. I'll write your name in big letters on my reports. Everyone will know who you are and where you live."

"You can't!"

"You want to stay out of it?"

"Yes, please."

"Then tell me what was going on with Betty." Garrett tugged on the sleeve of her coat. "Now."

"She was messing around with some politician."

"A politician?"

"Yeah. A congressman."

Garrett straightened. "A congressman?"

"You know, the city congress. The guys that work with the mayor."

"You mean the city council?"

"Sure, that's what it was."

"Your friend was hooking up with a councilman?"

"Yeah."

Garrett studied Ikuko's face. "She was seventeen."

"So? That doesn't mean she can't have sex."

"Who? Who was she seeing?"

Ikuko looked around, her eyes scared. Tears streamed down her face now. "She never told me his name."

Garrett yanked Ikuko's sleeve, jerking her closer to him. "Quit messing around, kid. This is serious."

Ikuko looked up and down the street. "If they're watching, I'm already dead."

"Don't be stupid. No one is going to hurt you. Just gimme a name." Garrett wrapped his fingers around her wrist for emphasis.

"She only called him Denny. That's all I know. I swear."

He nodded. There was only one councilman who could fit that nickname. *Dennis Hahn.*

"Can I go now? Please!"

Garrett released her wrist. Ikuko immediately flipped up the hood on the parka and sprinted toward her house. She ran around the side of the house and disappeared.

He walked back toward the Rabe home but stopped before getting there. Garrett pulled the business card from his notebook and stared at it.

What did Officer Gary Stone and Councilman Dennis Hahn have in common? A dead seventeen-year-old.

He was going to have to do some additional work on this case.

THURSDAY

The essence of lying is in deception, not in words.
—John Ruskin, English writer and artist

Chapter 18

"Is the chief in?"

Marilyn looked up from her computer. "You're not on his schedule. Is he expecting you?"

Stone rubbed his face in frustration. "No, but he'll want to see me."

"He has a meeting with Captain Farrell in five minutes. He doesn't have time for you, Officer Stone. Set an appointment."

"Tell him it's about the report he asked me to handwrite. Be specific about that. He'll want to see me then."

Marilyn studied him for a moment before lifting her telephone and buzzing the chief. Stone couldn't hear whatever Baumgartner was saying but Marilyn didn't try to hide her side of the conversation.

"Chief, Officer Stone is here to see you. Yes. Uh-huh. I told him you were busy. That's right. Yes. Well, he said it was about the report you asked him to handwrite. Yes, sir. Right away."

She hung up the phone and turned to Stone, curiosity now in her eyes. "You can go in."

Stone hurried past her desk, through the little waiting room, and into the chief's office. He shut the door behind him.

Chief Baumgartner sat in his chair with only his socks on. His shoes were on his desk sitting on a couple pieces of white paper. He was in the process of shining them.

"Make it fast, Gary. I've got a meeting scheduled."

The chief picked up a shoe and buffed a brush across the toe.

"The mayor was all over me last night about the Hahn investigation. He was pushing hard to know what was going on."

The chief turned the shoe and continued buffing, not bothering to look at Stone. "And?"

"I wanted to let you know. I mean, he was pushing pretty hard."

"What did you tell him?"

"Nothing."

Baumgartner dropped the shoe on the desk and lifted the other. He immediately began buffing it. "How did he take it when you didn't spill?"

"Fine," Stone lied. As soon as the word tumbled out of his mouth, he wondered why he said it.

The chief stopped buffing and looked at Stone. "He took it fine?"

"Yes, sir."

Damn it, Stone thought. The first lie had already led to a second.

"I would have thought for sure he would have been angry. Or at least irritated." Baumgartner leaned back in his chair, one shoo-in his left hand and the buffing brush in his right. His stocking feet moved back and forth on the carpet as he thought. "He's up to something. He's slow-playing this. Be careful, Gary. Sooner or later, he's going to come to you and ask that you keep tabs on things here in the department. When he does that, you let me know, okay?"

Stone remained silent, because he was afraid anything he said would be another lie.

"Yeah," Baumgartner muttered, swiping the brush across the shoe leather, "that slippery son of a bitch is up to something."

"I won't say anything, Chief."

Baumgartner pointed his shoe at Stone. "That's good, Gary. Keep it that way. Don't tell him squat. I'll tell him what he needs to know."

Chapter 19

The morning rain pelted Margaret Patterson's car as she packed her things, readying herself for the run from the parking lot to the lobby of city hall.

She took a final swig of coffee and put the cup back in its holder. Her phone, car keys, and reading glasses were tossed inside her purse. She grabbed the newspaper and reread the headline: *Councilman Armstrong Accused of Kickbacks, Peddling Influence.*

It keeps getting better. Another councilman, Patrick Armstrong, was being called out for unprofessional conduct; this time outright illegal actions.

She opened her car door, slung her purse over her shoulder, and slipped out. Using the newspaper as an improvised umbrella, she held it above her head. She pushed her door closed with her hip, then hurried to the front entrance of the building.

A young man, a worker she'd seen somewhere before in the building, held the door open as she approached.

"Thank you," she said as she hurried past him.

She stopped just inside the building and flung water off the newspaper. It was probably ruined but she didn't want to toss the paper until she could make a copy of the Armstrong article.

On the sixth floor, she quickly walked to her assistant, Devan Bollman, who sat outside her office. She handed him the wet newspaper. Devan's lip curled as he held the dripping paper away from him. Just out of college, Devan was a slight man with gelled hair and a small hoop in each earlobe.

"Don't be a wuss, Devan. It's only water," she said and flicked the paper with her finger. "Make a copy of that article. Then throw it away. Put the copy on my desk. Got it?"

"You can just go on the internet and read it there."

Patterson blinked several times before saying, "What did you say?"

"You can—"

"Oh, I heard you, Devan," Patterson said. "I'm wondering why you think you could say that to me?"

"Well, I didn't—"

"I know you're not foolish enough to talk to me that way because I'm a woman."

Devan's eyes widened. "No, ma'am. I would never."

"Then is it because you think I'm stupid?"

"No, ma'am."

"Is it because you're stupid? I'm running out of options here."

"No, what I was saying is that the paper is wet," Devan said, crinkling his nose. "You can just as easily get it off the internet."

"Who sits in there?" Patterson asked, pointing to her office.

"You do," Devan said.

"And your job is what?"

Devan stared at her.

She pointed at her office a second time. "I sit in there and you sit out here. You're supposed to do what, Devan?" Her voice was raising, and Devan was noticeably uncomfortable.

"Assist you."

"You're supposed to assist me. Huh. You think you're doing that? Me neither. Okay, let's start again. What did I ask you to do?"

Devan looked down. "Make a copy of this article."

"And?"

"Put it on your desk when I'm done."

"Now, you're learning."

Patterson stepped into her office and set her purse on the desk, then spun around and left, without looking at Devan. She hurried toward Councilman Hahn's office. His office door was shut, but she could see him through the glass. He was on the phone. Patterson paused at the desk of his assistant, Jean Carter.

"Who's he on the phone with?"

Jean looked up at her. "I don't know, ma'am. Maybe a personal call."

Patterson stepped to the door and made eye contact with Hahn through the small window. He lifted a finger in a *just a minute* signal. She looked at the clock on the wall in his office. It was half past eight. The morning was quickly slipping away.

She opened the door and stepped into the office.

"Hold on," Hahn said, slightly irritated, and covered the telephone's receiver. "What is it, Maggie?"

"Did you see the article on Patrick?"

Hahn rolled his eyes. "Yeah."

"Then get off the phone. We need to game plan."

"This is my wife. She's planning a parent-teacher conference."

Patterson put a hand on her hip. "Are you kidding? She doesn't need *you* to plan it. We've got more important things to do."

Hahn watched Patterson for a moment further, then said into the phone. "Go ahead and pick a date. Then text me what you chose, and I'll have Jean put it on my schedule. Uh-huh. Yeah. I've got to go. Okay. Bye." When he hung up the phone, he turned to Patterson, "Okay, what's so—"

"Seriously, Denny? How are you not freaking out about this?"

Hahn leaned back in his chair. "It's an accusation. Nothing has been proven yet."

"According to the paper, HR has been actively investigating Patrick for months. Depending on what they find, we might have the police crawling around down here. Did you know about this? Because I sure as hell didn't."

"No, of course I didn't know."

"Who do you think the leaker was?" Patterson turned to look out the window of Hahn's office. She surveyed the other council members and their assistants. "Think it might have been Buckner? That sneaky prick might have leaked it to throw the press off his trail."

"If Buckner knew about it, we would have known about it."

Patterson looked over her shoulder to meet Hahn's gaze. "Good point." She turned her attention back out the office window. "What about the assistants? Think one of them could have heard about the investigation and spilled it to the papers?"

"Not Jean. If she knew something, she would have told me, and she would have kept it quiet. She's a professional."

Patterson eyed Jean. "Yeah, she's good." Then her gaze slid over to Devan who stood at the photo copier. "I can't say the same for boy blunder."

"You don't like your new assistant?"

She turned around and crossed her arms. "You're missing the point. If what the paper is saying is true, Patrick's got a serious problem."

"Let's wait and see what happens."

"No, let's strike. Now!" She clapped her hands in emphasis. "Listen. He's an asshole. He's always been one. Now he's an elected asshole who's taking money under the table and selling his vote. It's corrupt, and it makes us all look bad. That's why I want my pound of flesh now."

"I think maybe we should let things run their course."

"And waste this opportunity?" She shook her head. "No way. Justin's part of it, too. Both of those knuckleheads need to be taken down and we should lead the charge. If there's blood in the water, let's join the feeding frenzy." Patterson rubbed her hands together and laughed theatrically.

It was then she noticed how red Hahn's face had become.

"What's wrong, Denny?"

"Nothing?"

"You look like, something, I don't know. Did I make you mad? You gonna get sick?"

"No, I'm fine."

"Oh, shit. It's the cursing, isn't it? I'm sorry, Denny. I'll watch it next time. You know me. That's just how I was raised. Even my grandmother swore when she got excited."

He waved it off. "It's okay. Really."

"Regardless, I'm sorry for cursing around you. I'll watch it next time. Okay?"

Hahn nodded. "I'd appreciate it."

"So, here's what I'm going to do," Patterson said. "As soon as I leave here, I'm going to the mayor's office and try to get some face time with the mad king. Then I'm going to get some intel from Human Resources. If I can't, I want to use Jean to talk to the HR assistants."

"Jean?"

"Yeah, Jean."

"Why my assistant and not yours?"

They looked over to Devan who still stood at the copy machine. The wet newspaper in his hands was disintegrating. He looked up at the ceiling and lifted his arms in frustration.

"Do I need to say more?" Patterson said.

"Fine. I'll authorize her to work with you."

"You sure you're okay? Maybe you're coming down with something."

Hahn inhaled deeply. "Yeah, maybe."

"Well, stay back then. I don't want to catch what you've got."

Hahn's smile was weak.

"So, it's settled. We're going to get what we can on Patrick. Then we make a plan and go after him and Justin."

Hahn nodded. "Armstrong and Buckner."

"Should have been a cleaning brand," she said. "Anyway, we take those guys down, we'll establish ourselves as the

'Keep City Hall Clean' reformers, know what I mean?" She spread her arms wide across the air to accentuate the idea.

"Yeah," Hahn said. "It could work."

"Hell, yeah, it'll work. And if we don't do it, people are going to start looking sideways at us, wondering if we're into the same illegal dealings Armstrong is."

"Allegedly," Hahn corrected.

Patterson waved her hand dismissively. "Allegedly, my ass. I knew as soon as I read it that it had to be true. The guy is slime. That's why we have to take him down, and get the credit for cleaning house. Then when council president rolls around, you run for that position and I throw my support behind you."

"Council president?" Hahn said.

"Yeah, sure, Denny. You're a good guy. You're smart. You're a family man. That plays great on TV. If you run for council president, you'll be a natural."

"Council president," Hahn mumbled.

"Then maybe I'll run for mayor in three years. What do you think? You'd be council president, and if you throw your support behind me, I'd be a shoe in as mayor."

"Council president," Hahn whispered and looked up at the ceiling.

"Don't you see it? It's sitting there for our taking. All we have to do is build our brand. Let that brand be reformation. That's who we are. We're the reformers and we'll start with Armstrong and Buckner. Saying it like that makes them sound strong, but they're not. One's a thief and the other's a pervert. We'll take them down. We'll take their souls. They'll be crying like little bitches when we're done with them."

"Like bitches," Hahn whispered, still staring at the ceiling.

Chapter 20

Officer Ray Zielinski brushed the sandwich crumbs from his uniform shirt while looking at the empty baggie. It looked clean enough to use again, and it wasn't like he'd had mayonnaise on the sandwich. He didn't think he'd get botulism from any residual peanut butter.

He folded the baggie and put it back inside his lunch sack. Twin stabs of shame and anger hit him at the same time. Here he was, a veteran cop making a good living with great benefits, worried about whether he could get another day out of a two-cent plastic sandwich baggie. It was pitiful.

You did it to yourself.

The sentiment rang true in his ears, but that did little to alleviate his anger about it. His life right now was crap piled upon worse crap, and he refused to accept that all of it was his fault. Maybe some, but not all.

Early in his career, eating alone in his patrol car was something he'd done on graveyard, when there weren't many restaurants open. On day shift, however, the ritual was for cops to meet for lunch in threes and fours. There were plenty of dining choices, and Zielinski's platoon had more than a few foodies who were out trying new places every day.

Not him. He couldn't afford it.

He figured some of his new mates thought his habit of eating alone in his car was antisocial, the actions of a grumpy veteran, and he let them think so. Better that they think he'd become an old grinder than to know he was reusing sandwich baggies.

He scanned the pending calls for service on his mobile data computer (MDC). All were normal or low priority, so police radio didn't dispatch any of them over the air like they did with high priority or emergency calls. Officers were left to pluck the holding call of their choice off the screen.

Zielinski went call shopping. He rejected a couple of obvious report calls. He'd already been tagged with two today, and it was early yet. Let someone else catch the paper. Instead, he looked for something he could clear without paperwork. He landed on an Assist Other Agency call, which rarely led to a report.

When he pulled up the details, the address jumped out at him. It only took a moment for him to realize why. It was the house he'd gone to a couple of days ago with ol' Charlie Bravo, the Chief's Bitch. They'd gone to see the crazy letter writer in the wheelchair.

The agency assist request on his screen came from social services. A case worker was standing by, asking for police presence before making contact. It was a pretty common request from social workers with potentially violent clients.

Zielinski put himself on the call. His MDC beeped confirmation at him as he put the car in gear and headed toward Lyle Bunney's house. As he drove, he wondered what brought the social worker to Lyle's house. Did it have to do with physical issues, or was it a mental one? He glanced over at his MDC, and used his middle finger to tap the screen, bringing up the call. His eyes flicked back and forth between the road and traffic to the screen. According to policy, he was supposed to pull off the roadway or be at a stop in order to operate his MDC. Zielinski, along with every other patrol cop, ignored the impractical rule. Time was too limited to adhere to it.

Besides, the stop-and-go traffic on the arterial afforded him plenty of opportunity to read through the details of the call.

The social worker was Lindsay Wagner, and she worked for Mental Health Division (MHD). Zielinski grinned at that. That was the name of the actress who had played *The Bionic Woman* on TV back in the seventies. His older brother, Neal, who was nine years his senior, had had a poster of her on his bedroom wall. Zielinski had a little boy crush on her.

What was the character's name? Zielinski frowned for a second, surprised he couldn't remember. Steve Austin was *The Six Million Dollar Man*'s name, but what was hers?

Zielinski smoothed his mustache, unable to come up with the name despite his fleeting childhood affection. He glanced back at the MDC instead.

According to the text of the call, the visit was essentially a welfare check on Lyle Bunney. He imagined that consisted of making sure the guy had food in the place, that things were sanitary, and that he wasn't going all cuckoo for Cocoa Puffs in whatever special way his crazy worked. Recalling his visit to the house with Stone, Zielinski expected that Lindsay Wagner would be satisfied with the food and cleanliness situation, but maybe not so much with the crazy part.

Jamie Summers!

Zielinski snapped his fingers. That was it. Lindsay Wagner played Jamie Summers, *The Bionic—*

At that moment, he suddenly noticed that the car in front of him had stopped for traffic. Zielinski stomped on his brakes. The police cruiser lurched to a stop, but he felt and heard the unmistakable sound of the push bar on the front of his vehicle striking the rear bumper of the car in front of him.

"Damn!" Zielinski hollered. He restrained himself from slapping his palm on the steering wheel in frustration. The other driver was already looking at him through the rearview mirror in wide-eyed surprise.

He activated the emergency flashers and got out of the car. As he approached the space between the two cars, he could see a black mark on the white bumper of the Saturn.

The driver of the vehicle was already out of his own car.

"You okay?" Zielinski asked.

The man was tall and slender, wearing a pair of slacks and a dress shirt open at the collar. "I'm fine," he said, his expression worried.

"Wait here a second," Zielinski directed.

He walked to the front of the Saturn. There was an older Honda Accord ahead of them both, and the driver wasn't moving, even though traffic in front of the fender bender had started forward. Zielinski motioned for the driver to roll down his window. The man, a twenty-something with a baseball cap askew on his head, complied.

"Did you get bumped by this car?" Zielinski asked, pointing to the white Saturn.

"Nope."

"You sure?"

"Positive," the driver answered. "Can I go?"

Probably has a suspended license, Zielinski thought. Or a warrant.

"Take off," he said. *Today's your lucky day*.

He returned to the driver of the Saturn. "You're sure you're not hurt, sir?"

The man nodded. "I'm fine. You barely hit me."

Zielinski almost cringed at the words *hit me*. Big or small, a crash was a crash, and this one was on him.

"Do you have your driver's license, sir?" Zielinski asked.

"Sure." The driver took out his wallet and fished out his license, handing it to Zielinski. "Am I in trouble or something? I mean, I was stopped for traffic, and—"

"You didn't do anything wrong. I just need the information for my report."

"Oh. Okay."

The man wandered over to look at his bumper while Zielinski jotted down the information from the license into his notebook. The driver's first name was Neil, same as his brother's, but spelled differently. When he'd finished writing, he joined Neil at the point of the collision.

The guy glanced up at him and shrugged. "I don't see any damage."

Zielinski examined the bumper. To his eye, there weren't any cracks or creases in it. He ran a finger across the black mark, and some of the discoloration came off. He spit on his finger and rubbed a little harder. With some effort, the black cleared up where he rubbed, leaving a clean streak through the mark.

"See?" Neil said. "No damage. I can clean that off with a sponge when I get home."

Zielinski considered. Technically, this was a collision, and every collision required a supervisor response and a completed report. In addition, his sergeant would have to initiate an internal review of what occurred. No doubt how this review finding would come back. This was an entirely preventable crash and would end up in his internal affairs file. While he doubted he'd be disciplined due to the light damage, it would still be considered as part of his record when other complaints were reviewed.

Like the demeanor complaint hanging over his head now.

What if he didn't call this in? Since there was no damage and no injury, it was arguably not a reportable collision. At least, that's what he could say if he ever got called out on it.

The idea was risky. If it came back on him later, either because Neil called it in, reporting an injury or unseen damage to his vehicle, there'd be repercussions. He'd likely get both a preventable collision *and* a policy violation for not reporting it. The cheese eaters in IA might try to push an ethics charge, to boot.

"Hey, do you know Tyler Garrett?" Neil asked him.

Zielinski broke out of his reverie. "What?"

"Officer Tyler Garrett," Neil repeated. "You know him?"

He nodded slowly. "I worked with him on power shift for a few years. Why?"

"I ran track against him in high school," Neil said. "And I knew him some out at Eastern, too. Great guy."

Zielinski nodded again.

Neil lowered his voice a little. "I thought it was pretty terrible what the city tried to do to him. I mean, do you think they would have treated him that way if he was white?"

"Maybe," he said, cautiously. "I don't know for sure."

Neil's expression scrunched briefly in thought. "Yeah, maybe not all of it was him being black. It seemed like at least some of it was about him being a cop, too."

"You're probably right." Zielinski wondered where this was going. He felt the urge to wrap things up. The longer he stood here in traffic with his patrol car lights flashing, the faster the window closed on him having any choice on how to handle this.

"My cousin's a cop in San Jose," Neil said. "I don't talk to him all that often, but whenever we have a few beers…" He shook his head. "I mean, the stuff you guys have to deal with is intense."

"Sometimes."

Neil motioned toward the bumper. "I don't know if this'd cause you any hassle or not, but as far as I'm concerned, it's no harm, no foul. I'm not hurt, you're not hurt. All we got is a little mark on my bumper. I'll buff that out with a towel when I get home, and it'll be like it never happened."

Zielinski considered. Neil seemed sincere, and what he said was true. Why should he suffer a preventable collision that only amped up whatever discipline he might get from a founded complaint later on? Besides, if this were a collision between two civilians, all he would do is facilitate an exchange of information and send the drivers on their way. No report, no ticket.

Neil watched him, waiting. Zielinski made his decision. He removed a business card from his shirt pocket. After a moment's thought, he wrote his personal cell phone number on the back, then handed it to Neil.

"If anything changes, give me a call," he said.

Neil took the card. "Nothing will change. You barely touched me."

"Even so."

"I'll be fine, Officer…" Neil glanced at the card for a moment, then looked up sheepishly. "Zee…?"

"Zielinski."

Neil nodded, repeating the name. Then he stuck out his hand. "Nice to meet you."

He shook Neil's hand. "Likewise."

When Neil returned to his car, Zielinski slid behind the wheel of his patrol car. He waited for Neil to pull away before turning off his flashers and following.

That could have gone much worse.

As he drove, he felt increasingly uneasy at not reporting the collision. Yeah, he'd been lucky that there'd been no damage or injury. He was rolling the dice that it would remain unreported, and if he crapped out, there'd be hell to pay. He hadn't even told dispatch he was out on a contact. That wasn't even a One-David stop. It was a black hole stop, the type certain officers did when they knew they were on the edge of the law or pushing the boundaries of policy. Zielinski had never conducted one in his entire career.

He dug in his patrol bag while driving, fishing out some antacids. He tossed three in his mouth and chewed.

Hell to pay, but at this point, it was risk worth taking. He figured it had to be, since he'd just taken it.

Damn. Instead of climbing out of the hole he was in, he was digging it deeper. Now he had one more variable to worry about.

He wondered how much of Neil's attitude had to do with his cousin in San Jose versus his association with Tyler Garrett. He suspected it was at least fifty-fifty, perhaps even more heavily weighted in Garrett's favor.

Thinking about Garrett made his stomach gurgle, despite the antacids. Zielinski had always liked and respected Garrett. He'd been a hard worker and was tactically sound, even serving on the SWAT team for a period. When the shooting happened the summer before last, Zielinski had been the first backup officer to arrive on scene. The events that followed cast Garrett in a bad light, at least for a while, but what stuck with Zielinski was how his own first reaction had also been one of uncertainty and doubt. Even though he wanted to believe Garrett, there were a couple of things that bothered him from the beginning. A missing gun and a suspect shot in the back, for starters. Garrett's later behavior and his eventual arrest added more to his concerns. Garrett was eventually cleared officially, but the whole thing had a stink to it. He still wasn't sure whether to doubt Garrett or doubt the department.

Was Garrett dirty, or was he set up? And if he was set up, was it Detectives Talbott and Pomeroy that did it? They'd been the ones who supposedly found the drugs in Garrett's house, after all. Then again, the reaction of city hall and the department made Zielinski wonder if they had a hand in it, too.

Even though Zielinski had been grappling with his own issues since the shooting, the Garrett question never left him. Part of the reason he left power shift was because he was no longer sure about his fellow officer. If he was right about him being dirty, then he simply couldn't work with the guy. But if he was wrong, then he'd be too ashamed to work with him after having doubted him. Moving to day shift solved both possibilities, along with the more important advantage of affording him the opportunity to snag extra work in the evenings.

Changing shifts didn't answer his questions, though. The question still burned in him.

Zielinski turned onto Lyle Bunney's street, and immediately spotted a Ford Tempo parked in front of the house in virtually the same place where Officer Gary Stone had parked two days ago. Even at this distance, he could see someone waiting behind the wheel.

"Idiots," he muttered. "The world is full of idiots. Hopefully, she's at least a beautiful idiot."

He parked a couple of houses away and walked toward the Ford. A pudgy man with a thick, full beard got out of the car and approached him, sticking out his hand.

"I'm Lindsay Wagner," he said. "MHD."

Great. A man. With a beard.

Zielinski gave him a perfunctory handshake, eyeing the spiky wooden earring Wagner wore and the bristly beard that obscured the top half of his tie. *The guy looks like he should be working in a brewpub in Seattle, not getting a government paycheck.* "Why am I here?"

Wagner smiled. "Well…let's just say Lyle can get a little excitable sometimes. Deep down, he's got a kind heart, but he has a couple of mental health issues. I never know what I'm going to get when I talk to him, so my supervisor says I need to have you guys with me whenever I check on him."

"How often is that?"

"Monthly."

"And that's what this is? A welfare check?"

Wagner nodded. "That's it. I'll check on his mental state, for enough food in the—"

"I know what a welfare check is," Zielinski said shortly.

"Oh. Of course." Wagner cleared his throat. "Well, then, let's go talk to Lyle."

He followed the social worker to the door. Wagner stood in front of the door, like he was there to visit a friend, apparently oblivious to the danger. Zielinski scowled, and stood off to the side opposite the hinges.

Wagner knocked the same kind of polite knock that Stone had used a couple of days before. Zielinski wondered if he'd have to apply some power shift pounding to get Lyle to come to the door, but the man surprised him by answering on the second time.

"Hello, Lyle," Wagner said. "How are you doing today?"

"What the hell kind of question is that?" Lyle answered him. "Do you know what is going on in the world?"

"Some of it," Wagner said.

"Even some of it ought to scare the hell out of you."

"Can we come in and talk, Lyle?"

"We?"

Wagner glanced over at Zielinski. "I have an officer with me. After last time—"

"Does he have a warrant? Because the last cops that came didn't have a warrant, but they touched my stuff anyway."

"No one will touch your things," Wagner promised. "But after our last visit together, my supervisor is making me bring the police along."

"Why?"

"You don't remember throwing that book at me?"

Lyle didn't answer for a moment. Finally, he said, "I don't want the cops in here again."

Wagner spread his hands. "You know how this works, Lyle. For me to come inside, the officer has to come with me. And I can't complete my visit without coming inside. If I don't complete my visit, I can't sign off on your compliance with our plan, and if I don't sign off, you could lose some of your benefits."

"Okay, dammit. Come in and get your business done."

Wagner smiled. "Thank you, Lyle."

He stepped inside and Zielinski followed. Lyle wheeled away, his back to them.

"All right," Wagner began. "Shall we start with a walkthrough, or do you want to talk first?"

Lyle spun his chair around to face them. "Do your walk—" He stopped, staring at Zielinski. "You!"

Zielinski didn't respond.

Wagner looked back and forth between Lyle and Zielinski. "What is it?"

Lyle pointed. "He's the one who touched my stuff. He threatened to take me to jail for exercising my First Amendment right as an independent journalist!"

Zielinski rolled his eyes. "Again with the journalist thing, Lyle?"

"I have a blog!"

"My sister's kid has a blog. It's about snakes. He's nine."

"That's not the same thing," Lyle yelled. "Not the same at all."

"Pretty much."

"Not the same!"

"Okay, okay," Wagner interjected, stepping between them. "Let's bring it down a bit, gents."

Lyle waved the finger he was pointing. "I don't want that jack-booted thug in my private residence!"

"Easy, Lyle," Wagner said.

"I have Fourth Amendment rights!"

"I know you do and we're not going to violate them, or any of your rights."

"*We?* You're with *them* now, Lindsay?"

Wagner shook his head. "No. I meant *we* in the sense that both of us are here. That's all."

Lyle looked at him suspiciously, saying nothing, his finger still directed at Zielinski. The officer crossed his arms, and leaned back against the wall.

"You know me," Wagner continued. "I'm trying to help you, like always."

"Then why bring the military branch of city government here?" Lyle's voice rose.

"I told you," Wagner said. "My boss is making me."

"Your boss is in on it, too?"

Wagner hesitated. "How about this, Lyle? The officer will stand right there. He won't touch anything. He won't say anything. He'll just stand there like my boss requires while you and I take care of our business together. I'll make sure everything is good here. If you need anything, we'll figure it out. That way, I'll know you're all right, and you'll be sure to get your full check next month. Does that sound okay?"

Lyle seemed to consider the idea. Finally, he lowered his finger. "Fine, but he stands there, says nothing, and touches nothing."

Wagner held up two fingers. "Scout's honor."

Lyle's eyes narrowed. "The Boy Scouts are an arm of the Catholic Church and a recruitment pool for the Templars."

"Good thing I was never actually a scout, then. But I do promise, okay?"

Lyle watched him for a moment, then agreed.

"Great," Wagner said. "Now, I'm going to do a quick walkthrough, all right? Then we'll talk."

"Fine."

Wagner left the living room for the kitchen. Both Lyle and Zielinski watched as the social worker checked the cupboards and the refrigerator. "Is Marcy still doing your grocery shopping for you?"

"She's the only one I can trust."

"Well, she's doing a good job." Wagner left the kitchen and headed down the hall.

As soon as he was out of sight, Lyle's gaze snapped to Zielinski. "I know what you're up to," he said in a hushed voice.

"Six-one," Zielinski said. "Since high school."

Lyle frowned in confusion. "Is that some kind of code?"

"Yeah. It's called the standard measurement system."

Lyle scowled. "That's what you say."

"It is."

"I'm going to write a story about you and that other cop."

Zielinski raised his eyebrows and gave him a sarcastic look. "What, like a love story? I don't go that way, Lyle."

"No!" Lyle said through clenched teeth. "A journalistic blog entry, detailing the number and exact details of all of the constitutional violations you both committed two days ago. I made notes!" He grabbed a composition book from the coffee table and held it up.

Zielinski nodded. He supposed a blog post on crazy dot com was better than a demeanor complaint to IA.

"Once the citizens of Spokane read what kind of abuses are being perpetrated by the police in their name, you guys are finished."

"Yeah? Think they'll disband the department?"

"Yes!" Lyle hissed. "The Department of Justice will come in and put you under a Consent Decree and root out all the bad cops."

"All of us?"

Lyle pointed again. "All of you! You, and that college boy that came with you, and Chief Baumgartner, who I know for a *fact* is a Freemason, and that murderer Tyler Garrett, for starters."

Zielinski fell silent, surprised.

"You're all a bunch of murdering thugs conspiring to turn this town into the fascist capital of…"

Zielinski tuned him out, his mind spinning around how Lyle had just lumped him in with Tyler Garrett. He was nothing like Garrett. At best, Garrett won the lawsuit lottery and got money he didn't deserve. At worst, he was a murderer, just like Lyle claimed. All Zielinski did was work his ass off every day, scratching by while guys like this got free money from the government.

"Are you even listening to me?" Lyle snapped. "You have to listen to me. I pay your salary."

A bevy of comebacks to the oft-repeated phrase flashed through Zielinski's mind.

Here's your nickel back.

Or *I want a raise. I deal with difficult people too often.*

Or his personal favorite, *Since you're on government assistance, it's more like I pay your salary.*

He knew he shouldn't say anything, that he was pushing his luck, but he couldn't help it. He lowered his voice to a growl. "You write any more of those stupid letters, Lyle?"

"Screw you!" Lyle screamed. "I can write as many freakin' letters to as many freakin' people as I freakin' want! First Amendment!"

Wagner reappeared in the living room, an expression of concern painted on his face. "What's going on?"

"Screw you, Lindsay!"

Wagner held up his hands. "Whoa, Lyle. What's—"

"Screw you!" Lyle repeated. "Screw you and your beard!"

Zielinski watched the scene unfold, torn between enjoying the show and wondering what the hell he'd been thinking. Like he needed any more trouble. When Wagner glanced askance at him, he gave him an innocent shrug.

Wagner turned back to the man in the wheelchair. "Lyle…"

"Get out of my house! I'm blogging about this! Get out!"

Wagner hesitated. "I need to finish my visit."

"Get out, get out, get out!" Lyle screeched.

"All right." Wagner moved to the door. Zielinski followed. Once they were outside, Wagner pulled it shut. Then he looked at Zielinski. "What was that all about?"

"He seems angry," Zielinski said, turning and heading down the walkway.

Wagner followed. "I know, but…I haven't seen him like this since before we got him on his medication."

"Maybe he's off his meds."

"Maybe," Wagner said doubtfully. "But I checked his prescription bottles, and the pill count is right."

"He could be flushing the pills down the john."

"I suppose so. He's never been resistant to taking medication before, though." Wagner looked more closely at Zielinski. "Did you say anything to him to set him off?"

Zielinski stopped at the social worker's car. He met Wagner's gaze. "Let me ask you this. How exactly am I supposed to know what will set off a crazy person?"

Wagner frowned at the word *crazy*. "You weren't supposed to say a word. I promised him."

"Yeah, well, he engaged me in conversation. Not answering might have set him off, for all I know."

Wagner watched him for a moment, considering. "Are you going to write a report about this, Officer…" Wagner stared at Zielinski's silver nametag. "Zee…Zil…"

Zielinski sighed. He wanted to clear the call One-David, but he realized he needed to cut paper, even if the report was just to cover his own ass. "Yeah, I guess I will, since he's either crazy or off his meds. Or both." An idea occurred to him to keep from having to return to Lyle's house again. "I'll flag

Officer Stone in Special Police Problems on the report. He knows the situation."

Wagner scrunched his eyebrows. "How?"

"Some letters Lyle sent."

"More letters?" Wagner sighed. Finally, he said, "I guess I'll try again tomorrow when he's hopefully calmer."

"Perfect," Zielinski said. "Tomorrow's my day off."

Wagner gave him an incredulous look.

Hell with it. What's done is done.

He turned and walked back to the patrol car, leaving Lindsay Wagner behind.

Chapter 21

Chief Robert Baumgartner parked in the *Emergency Vehicles Only* spot near city hall. He drove a black, unmarked SUV, a model only K-9 and SWAT drove. Most of patrol was outfitted with Ford police interceptors while detectives and administrators drove the less expensive Chevy Impala.

Baumgartner wasn't elitist about his vehicle choice. Rather, it was practical. The new Taurus-based interceptor for patrol was smaller than its predecessor, the Crown Victoria, and the Chevy Impala that detectives and administrators drove was smaller yet. He'd ridden in both vehicles, and it was uncomfortable for any length of time. His large frame fit in an SUV, plain and simple. Driving one was a perk he allowed himself as chief.

He locked the car and walked toward city hall, strolling casually. An advantage of his six-foot-three frame was that his strides ate up a lot of ground. Even if he was in a hurry, he didn't appear to be. That was important. When people watched him, they needed to feel confident. How he carried himself, including how he walked, mattered.

At the entrance to city hall, the security guard waved him around the screening station. Baumgartner nodded in acknowledgement and headed for the elevators. He rode up to the seventh floor, exchanging brief pleasantries with people getting on and off. Those he knew, he called by name, sometimes reaching into his memory for conversations or events he'd shared with them in the past and then making references to those touchstones. It let people know he remembered them, and that made them feel important.

When the doors opened to the seventh floor, he made a beeline past the desk of Charlene Mapes toward Officer Gary Stone's small office. Stone was situated at the far end of the floor, about as far away from the mayor's office as he could possibly get. The door stood half closed. Baumgartner tapped on it and pushed it fully open at the same time.

Stone looked up from his computer. A nervous expression flashed across his face. He clambered to his feet. "Chief?"

Baumgartner waved at him, stepping the rest of the way into the small office. "Sit down, Gary."

Stone lowered himself into his chair, sitting with his back erect and his hands folded.

Baumgartner closed the door. "I have a question for you."

"Sir?"

"This thing with Councilman Armstrong…did you know anything about that?"

"No, sir."

"Not a peep?"

"No."

"What's his reputation?"

Stone swallowed, looking mildly uncomfortable. "I mean…there was talk that he was…unpredictable."

"He voted for the highest bidder, you mean?"

"I hadn't heard that specifically."

"What about kickbacks?"

Stone shrugged. "That part I don't know."

"I know about him being a little shady," Baumgartner said. "He was in the construction business before he got elected. But is this all smoke, or is there something more?"

"Chief, I…"

"As in outright criminal behavior, Gary. Any rumors of that?"

Stone shook his head. "I honestly don't know. You want me to look into it?"

"No," Baumgartner said. "Just keep your ears open."

"I will."

He looked around the bare office. "And hang a picture in here, for Christ's sake. Frame your academy certificate if you have to, but make it look like you're planning on staying for more than a week."

"Yes, sir."

Baumgartner nodded and reached for the door. "Keep up the good work, Gary. I've got you down here for a reason. You know what that is?"

Stone looked afflicted. "Yes. I mean, no. No, honestly, I don't know."

"Because you're you," Baumgartner said.

He left Stone to ponder that and walked as slowly as possible toward the mayor's office.

Along the way, he wondered why Stone seemed so nervous of late. Was it something going on in his personal life? Or had looking into the Hahn letter disturbed him that much? Baumgartner suspected the latter.

Not that he blamed the guy. He didn't like it, either. But sometimes things had to be handled a certain way to keep the whole structure from falling apart. It might not feel entirely right, but it wasn't entirely *wrong*, either. If it preserved the department or his officers, then that was an ambiguity Chief Robert Baumgartner was willing to endure.

Stone would get past it, just like he had once upon a time. He'd just have to make a point of helping the kid along.

Too soon, he stood at the desk of the mayor's receptionist. Charlene Mapes noticed him immediately but pretended she didn't for several long seconds. Then she feigned spotting him.

"Chief," she said, deadpanning. "I thought I recognized that cologne."

Baumgartner gave her a small but friendly smile. "If I knew you liked it, Charlene, I would have gone with a little extra this morning."

"Oh, I didn't say I liked it," Charlene said. She pushed a button and spoke into the mic on her headset. "Mister Mayor, the chief is here to see you." She hesitated, then glanced at her watch. "Yes, sir. About seven minutes late." She paused another minute, then surprised Baumgartner with an actual hint of a smile. "Yes, sir, he is. Okay, I'll send him in."

They were making fun of him, Baumgartner realized then.

You arrogant pieces of –

"The mayor will see you now," Charlene intoned, then turned back to her computer.

Baumgartner didn't bother thanking her. He headed toward the mayor's office. Bad enough he had to ruin two or three breakfasts a week spending them with the mayor, but now him and his stodgy assistant were cracking wise about him while he stood there?

He forced the anger down and opened the door.

Sikes was behind his desk, red-faced and with a small trickle of sweat on his brow.

A workout lunch, Baumgartner thought.

"Chief! Come in."

Baumgartner approached the desk and sat in the seat opposite it without being asked. Then he waited for whatever Sikes had planned.

The mayor held up the newspaper. "Did you see this?"

"It's a newspaper," Baumgartner said. "I've seen one before."

Normally, a sarcastic reply like that would elicit one of Sikes's famous mayoral scowls, but today, he only grinned. "It's not just *a* newspaper. It's *today's* newspaper. Filled with gifts from the political gods."

"Armstrong, you mean."

"Yes, Armstrong, the crooked fool. And Buckner, too, still giving interviews defending his right to bang the babysitter." Sikes slapped the newspaper down with satisfaction. "It's beautiful."

"You've got a serious case of *schadenfreude* going on there."

"Listen to you, with the big words. Aren't you the one chief left in the state without a college degree?"

Baumgartner shrugged. "I don't need a college degree to use my library card."

"Who goes to the library anymore? But I'll tell you what, Chief. You're right. I am enjoying the *hell* out of watching these idiots squirm in the public eye, all of their own doing."

"Hoisted on their own petard."

"What's that?"

"Nothing," Baumgartner said. "A little Shakespeare."

"Very little." Sikes's scowl returned briefly. "You're not glad to see all this?"

"I told you how I felt at breakfast the other morning."

"No," the mayor said. "Not the individual stuff. I mean all this chaos. Don't you just love it?"

Baumgartner blinked. As a career police officer, the very essence of his job was imposing some measure of order onto chaos. It was that way when he stumbled into his first patrol call and when he worked his first case as a detective. When he moved into leadership, nothing about that element of the job changed. His role was always to try to control bedlam, or at least mitigate it.

The mayor was staring at him, so he finally said, "I've always been more about re-establishing order."

"That's because you think like a cop," Sikes said.

"I am a cop."

"No, you're not. You're the chief of police. That's a politician, just like me."

I'm nothing like you.

"And," the mayor said, "every politician should appreciate and love chaos. You know why?"

Baumgartner knew why, but he shrugged anyway.

"Opportunity," Sikes said. "Chaos is opportunity."

Baumgartner had a flash of the schemer from *Game of Thrones* pronouncing *chaos is a laddah!* and tried not to smirk. He must have failed to completely suppress the expression, because Sikes gave him a curious look.

"You've never thought of it that way?"

"I've heard of never letting a good crisis go to waste," Baumgartner said. "I suppose I agree with that."

"This is the same thing. While these dick yankers are running around getting crucified in the media, you know who isn't? Me. Instead of dealing with the media, I can do the work I'm supposed to do."

"Armstrong and Buckner have tended to support you on most issues except public safety."

"True, but with both of them distracted by this media circus, I should be able to get some public safety measures passed that they would have fought me on." Sikes spread his hands. "You see? Opportunity."

Baumgartner saw his point. "It's preferable to the alternative," he allowed. Being in the center of a public storm with every media eye trained on him wasn't something he relished. It had been at the worst during the Garrett incident, and he wasn't eager to live through that again. If a couple of councilors wanted to take the heat for a while, that was fine by him. "Do you want me to send a detective down to work with Human Resources on the Armstrong investigation?"

The mayor shook his head. "No, let's give it a while. Let HR finish their part."

Baumgartner narrowed his eyes. "From what it sounds like, he could be guilty of trading in special influence, which is a felony."

"And if HR finds any evidence of something criminal along those lines, I'll have them report it."

"The problem is that they investigate personnel matters, not crimes. If they step all over the investigation, it makes it messier for my detectives when they try to follow-up and make a case out of it."

"You mean it might cause the entire thing to be drawn out longer?" Sikes asked, a gleam in his eye.

Baumgartner saw his meaning, but still didn't like it. "It muddies the waters and makes it difficult to successfully bring charges against the suspect."

"But it keeps the attention on the case, doesn't it? And we need to keep the spotlight shining where it is," Sikes said. "And the way to do that is to stay ahead of the game. Speaking of which, any more news on the Hahn letter?"

"Nothing yet," he said. "We're still working on it."

"Stone talked to the girl, though, right?"

"He did."

"And?"

"She's flaky."

"Meaning?"

Baumgartner took a breath and let it out. "Mister Mayor, let me put it this way. There are two kinds of sexual assault cases we encounter. One is the obvious kind, where there's physical assault, clear evidence, a credible victim, and a lying suspect."

Sikes nodded impatiently, waving for him to continue. "Of course. And the other is what? He said, she said?"

"Basically. It's hard to pin down whether there was consent when that's all you have to go on. It's even harder when the victim is…a little flighty."

"You know what that sounds like?" Sikes asked.

"What?"

"Like nothing I'd ever want to hear you say in public."

"Please," Baumgartner said. "I'm not that stupid."

Sikes didn't answer, but let the moment hang. Then he said, "She's flighty, huh?"

"Wouldn't commit to whether it was a sexual assault or not."

"He's finished either way," Sikes said. "She's seventeen."

"There's a big difference between sexually assaulting a seventeen-year-old girl," Baumgartner said, "and having an illicit affair with one."

"Not as far as the politics are concerned. He's toast." Sikes shook his head. "All the tail out there, and stupid Dennis couldn't get past his Britney Spears fantasy."

Baumgartner wondered if Hahn would even know who Britney Spears was, but it didn't matter. He got the point.

"Stay on top of this," Sikes told him. "I want to know what we've got so I can decide whether to stir up another political storm once this Armstrong circus fades from the front page. Or…" He thought about it for a few moments, a broad smile spreading across his face. "Or we put this in our pocket for a rainy day, when we really need Mister Straight and Narrow Dennis Hahn to go along on something."

Baumgartner didn't answer. He realized politics were necessary, but he never liked the taste.

"Bob?" the mayor pressed.

The chief shrugged. "Political storms seem to happen all on their own. And leverage is pretty good to have."

The mayor slapped his desk. "Now you're thinking like a politician!"

Sikes laughed, but Baumgartner didn't join in.

Chapter 22

Captain Dana Hatcher was already irritated by the time her patrol staff meeting got to the subject of her idea for a patrol strike team. For starters, she'd brought coffee and donuts. She thought it would be nice to treat her lieutenants, and the sugar and caffeine would help all of them stay alert during the meeting.

However, two of the lieutenants were fitness nuts who looked at both offerings as if Hatcher had offered them poison with a mucus chaser. The other four lieutenants were happy to slurp and munch the fare, but not one offered a thank you.

The thing was, not long ago, she'd been one of them. She served as a patrol lieutenant with four of the six before being promoted to captain. At least two of those had directly competed for the position against her, and although she didn't hold a grudge, it was clear both of them did. It was hard enough to command former peers, and harder yet when those peers felt passed over. She was fairly certain that they questioned whether her selection was based on merit or the perceived need to promote a woman. All in all, it was a tall order to connect with this group.

Unlike her predecessor, Hatcher led off her patrol staff meetings with a minimum of pronouncements from her or the chief's office. Only the highest priority items got any time on the agenda on the front end. Instead, she let her lieutenants go first, giving them the chance to get their ideas and issues out on the table while everyone was still fresh. In theory, this method should have demonstrated how much she valued them.

In practice, Hatcher thought their behavior showed they considered it a weakness—one of a feminine nature.

So when they finally got around to her agenda items, the attention level of several lieutenants was wavering. With this in mind, she rushed through her proposal for a patrol strike team. The body language on display told her it was not being well received. As she explained her idea, she saw crossed arms, backward leans, averted gazes, and even one less-than-subtle eye roll that passed between two of them.

"Excuse me, Captain?" Lieutenant Larry Keon interrupted.

Hatcher looked up. "Larry?"

"I'm just wondering, ma'am. Where are these extra bodies coming from? To form your team, I mean. New hires?"

"I covered that already."

"No, ma'am. You didn't."

Hatcher opened her mouth to argue but was suddenly unsure. It was in her proposal, but had she skipped over it while rushing through the details? Now she couldn't be certain.

"I'm taking one body from each sector. Days and nights."

Keon blinked and shook his head. "Adam, Baker, Charlie, David. Days and nights. So that's…*eight* bodies?"

"That's right. But we'll start with just four."

Keon sighed. "Captain, my guys are running from call to call as it is. You're talking about taking bodies, which leaves more calls for service for the remaining officers to handle. They're already slammed. Not to mention, I've had to direct my sergeants to deny vacation requests to maintain minimum staffing levels. The men won't accept this."

Hatcher leaned forward. "The *officers* will accept it," she corrected.

He sighed. "You know what I meant."

"I know what you said."

Keon glanced across the table at another lieutenant. Hatcher could read his sentiment in that look, but she didn't care.

"I've considered the point you bring up, Larry," she tried to explain. "Because on the surface, you're absolutely right. Fewer bodies means more work for those that remain. But there are two considerations that will keep that from being the case." She looked around the room, seeing a mixture of disdain and boredom on several faces. "First, when this team starts addressing these high-profile targets, all of the crimes that those targets commit will come off the table. There will be fewer crimes, thus fewer calls for your officers to respond to."

"*If* they do that," Keon muttered.

"They will. That's their purpose. Second, if we have to raise the threshold for which calls we respond to or how long some calls hold before a response, we will. In case you forgot, dispatch falls under my command, too."

"So my guys who are running call to call will still be allowed to grab a quick lunch, even if there are calls holding?"

"As long as they're not high priority or emergency calls, yes."

Keon looked doubtful, and he wasn't the only one in the room. "That sounds great in theory," he said, in a voice that suggested nothing of the sort. "But you know as well as I do that the first time some citizen who goes to church with the mayor or bowls with a city council member has to wait for a cop to show up for two hours, and then drives by a sandwich shop and sees my guys getting that quick lunch, they'll chirp to their pal, and we'll be right back to clearing the screen being the priority."

"That's not going to happen."

"That most certainly will happen," Keon argued. "It's inevitable. If you think it won't, you're dreaming."

Hatcher gritted her teeth. "I *mean* that when it does happen, we're not changing anything. I will stand by my decision."

"Stand by it all you want, but when the mayor orders the chief and chief orders you, everyone knows that you'll order one of us, and it'll be just like I said." Keon held up his hands. "Running call to call." He shook his head. "We can't spare the bodies, Captain."

Hatcher kept her frustration in check. "I hear your concern." She glanced around the room. "Are there any other suggestions about this plan? Other critiques?"

No one answered.

"Come on, guys. I want your input on this."

Keon shook his head. "Without enough manpower to support something like this, it just isn't feasible. Pointing out all the other flaws in the plan is a waste of time when the whole thing is a nonstarter."

Hatcher's frustration kicked up another notch. *All the other flaws?* Her first instinct was to snap back at Keon and put him in his place. She didn't need him man-splaining staffing issues to her. She needed him to professionally critique her plan so she could perfect it. If he was so fixated on the staffing issue that he couldn't do that, he should feel free to shut the hell up and let his colleagues do the heavy lifting for him.

Maybe she should have said exactly that, but she knew that if she did, the response from those colleagues wouldn't be compliant, or sympathetic. They'd think one word: *bitch.* In her experience, any time she exhibited a strong opinion or used her proper authority, that was how she was seen.

Of course, if she said nothing, then she had just let her lieutenant shut her down, and that made her weak. Essentially, she couldn't win.

"Everyone here has a copy of the NIBRS report," she said, struggling to keep the anger from her voice and failing. "You have the updated numbers from our own crime analysis unit. Unless you're really bad at math, it's obvious we are getting our collective asses kicked. Now, we *are* going to do something about it. If you don't like my plan, I suggest you come up with a better alternative in the next twenty-four hours, because I'm not going to the next command staff meeting without an answer for the chief when he asks what I'm going to do about these lousy numbers."

Keon frowned. "Twenty-four hours? That's not enough time, Captain."

"You've had this report as long as I have, Lieutenant."

He didn't respond.

"Does anyone else have anything?" Hatcher asked.

No one said a word.

"Then we're finished," she said.

The lieutenants exchanged a few glances, before standing and leaving almost as a group.

Hatcher sat in the conference room chair, thinking over the meeting. She was losing this group. There seemed to be so many dynamics playing at once. Hard feelings over the promotional process. The call for service demands. All the regular law enforcement and political pressures. And she had no doubt that one woman leading six men played a role, too.

She stood and started collecting the empty coffee cups. In her haste, she knocked over one that still had some coffee in the bottom. The cold brown liquid splashed out over the conference table.

Hatcher sighed. She used a couple of paper napkins to wipe up the spilled coffee, and then to sweep donut crumbs into an empty cup. Halfway through the process, she stopped.

Why am I on clean up duty?

Damn it, she brought the coffee and donuts. Not only did no one think to say thank you, but no one volunteered to clean up, either?

Besides that, she was the captain. They were lieutenants. If common politeness or gratitude didn't motivate them, then the police rank structure ought to have.

Hatcher dropped the napkin onto the table and left the conference room.

Back in her office, she alternated over stewing about what seemed more and more to be obvious sexism and trying to be pragmatic about how to win her team over. She'd never encountered this much coldness from a group of her followers before. As a sergeant, she experienced great loyalty and appreciation from her officers. Even as a lieutenant, her shift sergeants seemed to genuinely like and respect her. What was different here?

Was it her? The lieutenants? Something else?

Hatcher remembered when she made lieutenant, and how it was really the first time that she felt like she was part of the politics of the department. As a sergeant and an officer, she'd been impacted by department politics, but once she hit lieutenant, it changed. Being part of the politics felt altogether different.

Had she ever been close to any of her fellow lieutenants? She wanted to say yes, but she knew it wasn't entirely true. At least not to the same degree as other positions earlier in her career. The patrol teams that she led as a sergeant felt like family. Her fellow lieutenants felt like colleagues, at best.

She turned this over in her mind, trying to decide if she was right or not, and if she was, what she could do about it. Every so often, she'd replay an exchange from her meeting, and then get mad all over again.

Eventually, she felt bad for leaving the conference room a mess, so she started down the hall to take care of it. Chief Baumgartner came out of the bathroom and headed her direction.

"Dana," he said, smiling a little. "How's it going?"

"Good, sir. Thanks."

"Did you have patrol staff today?" the chief asked.

Hatcher froze. Had one of her lieutenants gone to the chief behind her back, telling him about her plan so it could get torpedoed before she even had a chance to present it? "Yes, sir. A while ago."

"I thought so," Baumgartner said. "You left a disaster of a mess."

"Me?" Hatcher replied, her stomach burning.

"You know what I mean. Your team."

"Sorry. I'll take care of it."

"Or get one of those lazy lieutenants to do it," Baumgartner said. He gave her a wink and headed toward his office.

Hatcher made her way to conference room and finished cleaning up. There were half a dozen Krispy Kreme's left in the donut box. She thought about taking them down to the detectives' division and putting them next to the big coffee pot there. Instead, she pushed the box into the garbage with the rest of the remains from her meeting.

Chapter 23

It was the bottom of the eighth inning and the Seattle Mariners were down four runs against the Texas Rangers. The season had only recently started and it already felt like the M's were in for another year of futility. It was a feeling he'd known often as a lifelong fan. At least the Mariners had hung around and not bolted for another state like the SuperSonics.

The game was on the TV with the sound off. Stone had his laptop open, surfing the internet. He might be a diehard fan, but that was no reason to suffer through another thirty minutes of agony until the final out.

He had started out doing something productive by reading the latest news. Then he got distracted by some gossip on the M's relief pitcher. Now, he was on YouTube watching the twenty-five greatest trick plays ever pulled off in a Major League Baseball game. The video was halfway through when there was a knock at his front door.

Stone put the laptop on the coffee table and climbed out of his chair. Checking the peephole first, he was surprised to see the man on the other side of the door. He hurriedly opened it.

Officer Tyler Garrett smiled at him. "What's up, Stoney?"

During his probationary period, he had spent a month on Garrett's power shift team, the group that straddled swing-shift and graveyard. It was the best team rotation he had as a rookie. Not only did he have a particularly great training officer, but Garrett went out of his way to make him feel like a regular officer and part of the team.

Stone registered Garrett's uniform which, as always, looked sharp on the man. "Is everything okay, Ty?"

"Yeah, sure, I was in the neighborhood and thought I would stop in to say hi."

"How did you know where I live?"

"Really? I checked your name on the MDC. Aren't you going to invite me in?"

Stone stepped back. "Yeah. C'mon in."

Garrett's eyes quickly swept the apartment. "Nice digs, Stoney. How come you've never had me here before?"

Stone's face flushed. "Well, I—"

Garrett turned and grinned. "Relax, man, I'm busting your chops. Mind if I sit?"

Without waiting for an answer, he sat on the edge of the couch. Stone returned to his chair.

"How are things at city hall? Liking it?"

"It's okay."

Garrett's eyes went to the TV. The Rangers' batter hit a line drive to the Mariners' third baseman which quickly turned into a double play. When he looked back to Stone he said, "City hall seems like a sweet gig, especially for a young buck such as yourself."

"Yeah. It's pretty cool."

"Allows you to avoid those rookie years of graveyard, huh?"

"Graveyard wasn't so bad."

Garrett chuckled. "Graveyard sucks. Power shift is where the action is. When you get done playing footsy with the politicos, you should come run-and-gun with us again."

Stone smiled, surprised that Garrett would encourage him to join his team. "Thanks."

Garrett's eyes traveled around the apartment once more.

"How about you, Ty? How are things since, well, you know."

Garrett's gaze returned to him. "Things are good, they're good. Got my footing back. Took some time, but that's how it goes."

Stone nodded. His first training officer had suggested he find men in the department to model himself after, to help acclimate himself to the culture and life of a police officer. It took Stone a while to settle on one, but Tyler Garrett was the guy he thought embodied the best about the police. He was smart and confident, neither emotional nor impulsive. He always appeared in control. To Stone, Garrett seemed like a guy who reached out to those who weren't as strong as him and helped them become better. He was the kind of man Stone wanted to be. Garrett might be more hard-charging than Stone was, but he could still model himself after his character and integrity.

"Hey, so we know someone in common," Garrett said.

"Yeah," Stone said, his face lighting up. "Who's that?"

"Betty Rabe."

Stone's face quickly darkened.

"You know her, then?"

"Yeah."

"I figured as much. It's a shame, though."

Stone leaned forward. "A shame?"

"She's dead. Killed herself."

"Oh God," Stone said. "How? When?"

"Couple nights ago. Pills and asphyxiation. She tied a bag around her head. Gruesome, man, it was a gruesome way to go. Ugh."

Stone's eyes drifted to the floor.

"She had this on her person." Garrett reached into his shirt pocket and pulled out a business card. He tossed it on the coffee table. Stone could read his own name on it. He immediately looked up to Garrett but didn't say anything.

"I didn't tell the responding detective that I found that card. I figured I'd wait until I talked with you."

"Why would you do that? That's tampering with a crime scene, isn't it?"

"You're a brother in blue, but if you want me to call the detective and hand the card over, I can do it. I'll do it as soon as I leave here, if that's really what you want."

"No," he whispered.

"Okay, Stoney, I won't, at least not yet. But you've got to help me understand some things."

His eyes hopped around his apartment for several moments before they settled back on Garrett. "Like what?"

"Like why there was no incident report for your contact with the girl. I searched. There's no report of you ever contacting her. Not even a CAD entry."

Stone blinked a couple of times. *I can do this.*

I can lie to Tyler Garrett.

"It wasn't that type of contact," he said with a shrug. "It was just some friendly conversation, you know, just checking on her. I gave her the card to call me if she ever needed something."

"Some friendly conversation, huh?"

"Yeah, exactly. Friendly conversation."

Garrett leaned forward and gave Stone a sly smile. "Were you hitting on her? Is that what you were doing? Were you trying to ball a seventeen-year-old?"

"What? God, no!" His face flushed again.

How could Garrett think I would do such a thing?

"I mean, she might have been cute if it wasn't for all that black makeup. Plus, it's hard to tell with her being dead. She looked waxy and all, but she was a tiny little thing. Maybe you go for that vampire look. Is that what you go for?"

"No, man, that's not what this was about."

Garrett spread his arms out on the back of the couch and crossed his ankles. "Then what was it about, Stoney? Regale me with your story."

Stone stood and ran his fingers through his hair.

"Having trouble with your tale?" Garrett's tone was calm and confident. "How about I help get you started? Use this for inspiration. Councilman Dennis Hahn…had a thing…for young Bethany Rabe."

"What?"

"Hard to believe, huh? But the councilman *was* sticking it to her. I figure that's why you were talking with her."

Stone turned around, putting his back to Garrett. He had nowhere to flee. He was inside his own house.

"So Betty had a friend, and this friend, she talked with me. Told me everything."

Stone glanced back at Garrett. "A friend knew?"

"Newsflash, man. A seventeen-year-old is dead. She had no history of mental illness. She killed herself because of a sexual relationship she had with a councilman. This story is getting out sooner or later. Maybe it makes national news. Doesn't take much to make national news. I should know."

"Wait. Did she leave a note saying that about Hahn? That she killed herself because of him?"

"That would have been something if she did, huh? No, there wasn't a note, but how hard was it for me to paint that picture? Not hard at all, was it? People are going to want to know why you're protecting a councilman. What answer are you going to give them?"

"I swear, it's not like that," Stone said, facing Garrett again. "It wasn't my choice to interview her that way."

Garrett clapped his hands once and dropped them in his lap. "Whose choice if not yours?"

"It was above our pay grade."

"Don't make me guess, Stoney. I want it straight. I've only got a few minutes before I have to get back on patrol. If I don't get your side of the story, I'm going to be forced to write an addendum to my report saying that I found a witness. I'll drop what I know about Hahn and you. Then you can deal with the detective. After that, I'm sure IA will come calling. That's a no brainer, now that I think about it. Have you dealt with IA?"

Stone gave Garrett a short shake of his head.

"I didn't think so. It's no fun, let me tell you that. And you'll probably get sued by the girl's parents. Oh no, her parents. I didn't tell you about them. They were distraught. Heartbreaking, man, just heartbreaking. They can't understand why their baby girl killed herself. They'll come after you for sure."

"The chief," Stone blurted. "The chief and the mayor. They tasked me with it."

"The chief *and* the mayor? They asked you to cover it up?"

"No, not cover it up. They didn't ask for that."

"Then what did they ask for?"

"They asked me to investigate."

"Investigate what? The relationship?"

Stone shook his head. "No. Didn't the friend tell you this? Betty sent a letter to the mayor's office claiming that Hahn assaulted her. Sikes and Baumgartner wanted me to look into it quietly."

"She sent a letter?"

"When I confronted her about it, she said she made most of it up to get even with Hahn because he broke it off with her."

"A letter."

"I swear, that's it. I was told to not tell anyone. Not even my sergeant."

"That's why you couldn't have an incident number show up, not even a One-David contact. Because there would be a record. They wanted you to interview the girl, determine what kind of damage was lurking out there, and come back and report, right?"

"Something like that."

"Hopefully, you wrote something to at least cover your ass? There's no record of you ever talking to her. I checked. You're way over the edge, man. You know that, right? Sikes and Baumgartner, they aren't out there with you. They stuck you out there, all by your lonesome. When cracks start to show—"

"I wrote a report," Stone said defensively. As soon as he said it, he knew he should have kept his mouth shut. But

Garrett was pointing out all the things he'd already thought, and it was upsetting to hear it out loud.

Garrett studied him as the words sunk in. "You wrote a report *outside* the system?"

"Yes."

"Ever do *that* before?"

"No," he admitted.

"Man, even I haven't done that. Still got a copy of it?"

Stone shook his head and looked down.

"You're telling me that an administrative badass such as yourself didn't keep a copy of a report that has such importance as this? No, I'm not buying it. You're smarter than that."

They stared at each other for several moments.

Finally, Garrett's eyes slanted, and he sternly ordered, "Go get your copy."

Stone slowly walked to the kitchen counter and picked up several sheets of paper. When he returned he handed them to Garrett. Along with the report was a copy of Betty Rabe's letter to the mayor.

Garrett scanned the documents. "You've got nice handwriting, Stoney."

"Thanks," he mumbled.

"Wait. You wrote this by hand?"

"I was directed to."

"By the chief?"

Stone nodded.

Garrett was quiet for some time while he read the report. When he was done, he went through a second time, much like the chief did when he reviewed it.

"I can't decide if this is a legitimate hashtag me too outing, or some outright fairy tale." He glanced up at Stone. "So, you think Hahn was clean when it comes to the assault?"

"Maybe."

"But you were leaning that way?"

"Yeah."

"And the girl? You believe her initial accusation was false, just a tale to get Hahn in trouble?"

"Not all of it. He took advantage, had sex with her. Maybe he assaulted her, maybe not. That's the gray area. The rest of it is pretty black-and-white."

Garrett set the papers on the coffee table in front of him. "What are you going to do about this?"

"This?" Stone said, pointing at the report. "Nothing. I'm doing nothing. I've already done my job. Now, I just want to keep my head down."

"They're setting you up. You see that, right?"

"I don't think so. They were trying to protect city hall."

Garrett smirked. "I know what they do when they try to protect city hall. Believe me. They're going to hang you out to dry."

"Not the chief. He wouldn't do that."

"The chief, huh?"

"He wouldn't do that," he repeated, then softly added, "to me."

Garrett looked at the palm of his hand for a moment. It was as if he was considering something. Finally, he said, "Know what the guys are calling you?"

Stone looked at him. "What guys?"

"The guys. Around the department. They're calling you Charlie Bravo."

"Yeah, so? I don't know what that means."

"It means you're the Chief's Bitch."

Charlie Bravo? That's what Ray Zielinski called him.

"Don't feel bad, man. There's always somebody hung with that label. You're just the latest in a long line of Charlie Bravos. After you're gone, there'll be another. Maybe in your job, maybe in some other position. But still the Chief's Bitch."

Without another word, Stone turned and went to the bathroom. He shut the door behind him. He started the cold water and splashed some in his face.

How could this be true?

He was doing his best to stand out, to make a name for himself. Were the other officers on the department really making fun of him? Were they really tearing him down for doing something they wouldn't, or couldn't, do?

He looked at his image in the mirror. The water running down his face looked like a waterfall of tears. He dried his face with a towel.

Screw them. I won't back down because of some name calling. Maybe Garrett was right. Maybe the city would hang him out to dry. Just like they had tried to do to Garrett.

When Stone stepped out of the bathroom, Garrett was standing over the coffee table. The pages of the report were spread out and he was tucking his cell phone into his back pocket.

Stone walked up. "Were you just—"

Garrett grabbed his shoulder microphone and said, "Charlie three sixteen. I'm clear and available for calls."

"Did you just take photos of my report, Ty?"

"Charlie three sixteen," dispatch called.

Garrett said to Stone, "Hold on." Then he pressed the button on his shoulder mic. "Sixteen, go ahead."

Stone bent and scooped up the various pages. "Did you take photos of Betty Rabe's letter? That was confidential."

"Charlie three sixteen, a report of a two-car collision at Twenty-ninth and Southeast Boulevard."

"Sixteen," Garrett said, "show me en route." He released the microphone. "Hey, man, it was nice catching up."

"I'm serious. Did you take pictures of my report?" Stone repeated.

"Y'know, Stoney, I always liked you. That's why I'm gonna look out for you," Garrett said as he opened the front door. "Why don't you give me a call sometime? Let's get a beer or something."

He turned and left, without waiting for Stone to reply.

Gary Stone stood in the middle of his living room, the various pages of his report clutched tight to his chest.

Should he tell the chief about this or should he keep it to himself? The chief would be angry, he knew. And there was nothing he could do to fix it.

Besides, what would Tyler Garrett do with some photos of his report? Maybe he was freaking himself out about nothing.

Chapter 24

Detective Wardell Clint sat in his car up the street from Officer Tyler Garrett's patrol cruiser. He'd watched Garrett go to a house mid-block. The Chevy Impala in the driveway had a license plate with five numbers and *D* at the end—a city police plate. So he wasn't surprised when he peered through his binoculars and saw Gary Stone answer the door.

Stone seemed surprised, though. Regardless, he let Garrett in.

Clint let the binoculars drop and hang from the strap around his neck. *What the hell kind of business did Garrett have with Stone?*

It couldn't be anything dirty.

Or could it?

What little Clint knew about Officer Gary Stone made that seem unlikely. He was more white collar than blue, a real cake-eater. He wasn't enough of a meat-eater to be dirty. Then again, most people would have never believed Tyler Garrett capable of the dirt he did, Clint included.

Clint jotted down the location and time Garrett entered the house. He waited, watching the front door.

What was Stone doing twenty-one months ago, he wondered. Was he already on this easy street city hall gig, or still in patrol? And if he was in patrol, what shift? Did he overlap with Garrett?

Clint wrote those questions down, carefully coding them so no one else would be able to read the notes but him. He'd have to find out the answers back at the station tomorrow. Maybe payroll could help him. They were always up on shift assignments so that officers' paystubs made it to the right place. Checking there might make the least amount of noise.

Time dragged past ten minutes, and still no Garrett. Clint gripped the steering wheel and squeezed, bleeding off some nervous energy. Then a thought occurred to him, and his jaw fell open.

What if Stone was the chief's go-between for dealing with Garrett?

Clint snapped his mouth shut and gave his head a shake. The question didn't go away, so he looked at it again. If the chief was dirty, he couldn't be seen in direct contact with Garrett. A chief of police meeting with a patrol officer would be odd in a single occasion and suspicious if it happened frequently. So the chief would need someone to act as an envoy.

But did that mean the chief was dirty? The truth of it would lie in Baumgartner's actions regarding Garrett. Had the chief actually penalized Garrett after the shooting? Clint had been assigned to shadow the county investigators, and everything he saw from the chief's office was supportive.

That's what you'd want, right?

"True enough," Clint mumbled.

It wasn't all roses, though. When Detective Talbott found drugs at Garrett's house, the chief suspended the officer until the matter was resolved. That was standard. The suspension was with pay, but that was also standard. The bigger question was, had the chief ever done anything detrimental to Garrett during that entire affair? Clint tried to remember, but every thought he had was something favorable the chief had done, including welcoming the son of a bitch back with open arms after the mayor's office forced the charges dropped and Clint's official investigation terminated.

How much of that was Baumgartner just doing what chiefs do, and how much of it was some kind of collusion?

Clint couldn't see any real evidence of malfeasance on the chief's part, but he had to be honest with himself about the fact he'd never really looked before. It was possible. He didn't trust the brass, who he imagined spent most of their time thinking of ways to screw over officers they didn't like. That was a far cry from criminal behavior, Clint supposed, but then again, it was also a far cry from good leadership. He should look into it. Maybe there was something there that just needed some light shined on it.

One thing was for sure. If the chief needed a go-between with Garrett, Stone was the perfect choice. He was the only patrol officer who had regular facetime with the man due to his position. No one would suspect him, and the milquetoast officer would do what he was told.

Garrett's voice came over his radio, all Denzel Washington smooth, announcing he was clear and available. Clint smiled a little when Garrett immediately got hit with a collision up on Twenty-Ninth Avenue. Then he realized he was going to be sitting off in his car, waiting while Garrett took care of the call, and his smile vanished.

A minute or so later, Garrett exited Stone's house and returned to his car. Clint wasn't sure, but it looked like Garrett had glanced in his direction. He couldn't tell for certain, but it only added to his suspicion that the cunning bastard knew he was being followed.

Clint considered sitting off on Stone's house for a while to see if he did anything or went somewhere in response to Garrett's visit. After a few seconds, he rejected the idea. Until he knew more about their connection, Garrett remained the better target to monitor.

He made his way to the collision scene, finding a nearby parking lot and monitoring the call from there. Garrett worked briskly, clearing the intersection and taking care of the paperwork. He even managed to make one of the drivers chuckle a little when he handed him the ticket.

Everybody loves Ty Garrett. He writes people tickets and they laugh about it. Clint tries talking to some people and they act like it's the inquisition. But Garrett gets away with it.

If they only knew.

He followed Garrett for the next several hours, but by midnight, he was yawning. The "hard crash" weariness that usually accompanied full-court press investigations at about the twenty-four-hour mark had settled into his bones, and he realized his night was done. When Garrett put himself out for a dinner break in his car, Clint decided it was time to call it quits.

Out of curiosity, though, he followed Garrett to see where he liked to eat his driver's seat meals. The officer drove downtown, parked in front of a condo, and headed upstairs. Clint frowned.

Barely separated and wasting no time.

He didn't know for sure, but he was willing to bet that one of the condos in that building had a sexy little chip living in it. Whether she was something new, or one Garrett was working before the separation, Clint didn't know.

He wrote down the time and the building address in his notebook, intending to look into it later. Then he turned his car north and headed home. He was tired, and no way was he going to sit outside and wait around while Garrett broke off a piece.

FRIDAY

It isn't the original scandal that gets people in the most trouble—it's the attempted cover-up.
—Tom Petri, former US Representative

Chapter 25

Chief Baumgartner stared at Gary Stone. The officer stood ramrod straight in front of the chief's desk, looking like a terrified, dutiful Marine about ready to fall on his sword. That's not what Baumgartner needed, though. He needed results, not sacrifice.

"Did you hear what I said, Gary?"

"Yes, Chief."

"Betty Rabe killed herself two nights ago," Baumgartner repeated anyway. "Two nights! Why am I only hearing out about this now?"

"I just found out last night, sir."

"How? Were you doing follow-up?"

Stone shook his head. "Officer Garrett stopped by my house to tell me."

"Garrett?" The chief sat back in his chair. "How the hell did he get involved?"

"He answered the suicide call. He saw my card at the scene, so—"

"Hold on. The girl had your *business* card?"

"Yes, sir. I gave it to her and asked her to call if she wanted to talk further."

"She didn't, though. Call you, I mean."

"No, sir."

"What happened to the business card?"

"Sir?"

"Think, Gary. Do you know if they left it at the scene or did someone pick it up? Did the parents ask why their daughter was talking to the police? For someone who was supposed to investigate this quietly, you left a trail of breadcrumbs."

"I'm sorry, sir."

"Don't apologize, Gary. Give me answers. Why was Garrett at your house?"

"He stopped by to ask about the card."

"That's not his job," Baumgartner pointed out. "That's the detective's job."

Stone shrugged.

The chief stared at the photograph of General Norman Schwarzkopf and himself framed on his desk, taken during one of the retired general's speeches on a book tour. He wondered what Garrett's game was, or if the man was just doing the follow-up for a lazy detective. It wasn't that out of the ordinary, especially if the detective actually *was* lazy. Baumgartner admired the initiative. It was something Baumgartner himself would have done way back when he was on patrol.

"What else did Garrett say?" Baumgartner asked.

"Nothing," Stone said. "He wanted to know why I'd contacted her."

"What did you say?"

Stone hesitated, then said, "I told him she'd made some threats against one of the council members."

"And he bought that?"

Stone nodded. "I mean, that's what I do, right?"

"I suppose it is." The chief mulled it over some more. "And this conversation happened last night?"

"Yes."

"Why didn't you call me, Gary?"

Stone blinked. "Sir?"

"Why didn't you pick up that department-issued Blackberry I gave you and call me? You've got my direct cell for a reason."

"Well…I didn't think…you know, I didn't want to bother you with it."

"But you thought it important enough to bring to me first thing this morning?"

"Yes."

Baumgartner leaned forward. "What the hell, Gary? Did your IQ leak out of your ears overnight or something?" He tapped a meaty finger on his desk. "This is the kind of information I need right away!"

"I'm sorry."

"Sorry does me no good." He shook his head. "I thought you had your arms wrapped around this."

"I…talked to her," Stone stammered. "And I gave you the report, just like you asked. What else was I supposed to do?"

"Handle it, that's what," Baumgartner snapped. "This is the kind of thing we have to stay ahead of. It could look bad if it goes public."

"Without the letter, how could that happen?"

Baumgartner clenched and unclenched his jaw. "Don't be naïve, Gary. There always seems to be a way. If not the letter, then some friend she talked to, or a diary tucked away in her nightstand. Hell, it could be lurking out there on social media. It's always something." He looked up at Stone. "You gave me the only copy of your report, right?"

"Yes."

"And the letter?"

Stone nodded uneasily. "I gave you the original."

"Good." Baumgartner took a deep breath and let it out. "Now I've got to call the mayor and tell him this just got a lot worse."

More chaos. Won't he be pleased?

Baumgartner picked up the phone, then glanced up at Stone. "You can go, Gary."

Relieved, Stone fled the office.

Baumgartner waited until the door was securely closed. Then he dialed.

Chapter 26

Councilwoman Margaret Patterson strode off the seventh-floor elevator, dismissively nodded at Charlene Mapes, and headed toward the mayor's office.

"Councilwoman," Charlene called.

Patterson stopped, but didn't bother facing her. She disliked the mayor's assistant.

"Ma'am," Charlene said, "he's on the phone. He's not to be disturbed."

Patterson turned around slowly then. "Really? Not to be disturbed? I just talked with the man. He told me to come right up."

"I'm sorry, ma'am, the chief called him."

Patterson rolled her eyes. "Are you kidding me? I'm being told to wait because of *the chief?*"

"I'm sorry, ma'am. I don't know how long they'll be."

Patterson headed toward the mayor's office.

"Ma'am!" Charlene called after her. "Councilwoman!"

She stood in the door of the mayor's office. He noticed her but immediately diverted his attention. His face was red and contorted with anger. Whatever he was discussing with Baumgartner was not a happy topic.

"Just find out," Sikes said and forcibly hung up the phone.

"Baumgartner?" Patterson asked.

"What?"

"Charlene said you were on with the chief."

"Tsk. She talks too much. I liked my last assistant better."

"Yeah, we know why you liked her." Patterson held her hands away from her chest, miming overly large breasts.

Sikes stared at Patterson for a moment. He then closed his eyes, took a deep breath, and let it out. When he opened them, he did so with a smile on his face. He pushed himself out of his chair and stepped around his desk.

His sudden change in demeanor shocked her. It was a trait Sikes was notorious for, but it was still unsettling to see it on display.

"Maggie, it's always nice to see you," he said, walking toward her. "You look lovely today."

She ignored his calling her by her nickname. "That's funny since I remember you referring to me as Butterface on your campaign trail."

Sikes waved her comment off. "Long forgotten."

"Not by me."

They shook hands and Patterson felt compelled to fake a smile.

The mayor pointed to the leather chair. "Grab a seat." With a toothy grin, he dropped into the couch opposite her. "So, what are we talking about this morning? Utilities? Parks budget? You name it, my time is your time."

"Are you serious?"

His eyes narrowed, and he loosened his tie slightly. "What's on your mind, Maggie?"

"Only my friends call me Maggie."

"I thought we were friends."

She kept her mouth closed but clicked her teeth together.

"We could be friends, you and me," Sikes said.

"I came up here to discuss the recent accusation against Patrick Armstrong."

"That's what you said on the phone, but that's not what you really want to talk about, is it?"

Patterson shook her head and continued. "Human Resources is investigating—"

"He probably did it."

"What?"

Sikes shrugged. "Armstrong is shady. You know it. The whole council suspects it. HR has been investigating him for months now."

"Did you know about this?"

"I know what I need to know."

"Was that a yes or a no?"

Sikes leaned forward and smiled. "I thought I just answered that."

"What's wrong with you? You avoided that question."

"I answered it."

Patterson pinched the bridge of her nose. "So, what's going to happen?"

"When?"

"When?" she repeated.

"Yes," he said, thoroughly enjoying himself.

Patterson glanced around, worried that this was some elaborate game to make her look foolish. "I don't understand."

"It's clear you don't, Maggie. What's going to happen *when*? That is the question. Understand?"

The mayor was normally arrogant and condescending, but this morning he was reaching new levels. She usually got the best results and learned the most about city hall when he was talkative, so she decided to play along. "What's going to happen when, Mister Mayor?"

"Right now, we're going to let the investigation continue as long as it takes." Sikes seemed very proud of himself.

"You said he probably did it, though. That Armstrong was receiving kickbacks or selling his vote. Why should the investigation take longer than necessary?"

"We want to do it by the book. Everybody deserves that. Then he will have his right to appeal. That takes time, too. You understand that, right? This is America. People have rights."

"What if there's enough for a criminal case? We're not going to allow him to sit in his seat, are we?"

The mayor opened his hands. "What can I do? I'm just the mayor. You as the council will need to vote. Can you get everybody to point in the same direction on this? Maybe censuring him would be a good first step."

"You're damn right we'll censure him. Can we get a copy of that HR report?"

Sikes covered his arms over his chest. "It's not official yet."

"That's bull. We should be able to see what your staff has done so far."

"You will," Sikes said, "but if you haven't figured it out yet, this is going to take some time."

"Are you telling me you want to delay action on this for some sort of political gain?"

The mayor feigned shocked and looked around his office. "Did I say that?"

"Yes, you did. You most certainly did."

"I think you misheard me. I didn't mean for it to come across that way." His chuckle was small at first, but then deepened.

Patterson rubbed her forehead. She'd come up to talk about the blood in the water surrounding Patrick Armstrong and Justin Buckner, but Sikes had somehow commandeered the conversation. He was mocking her because of the council's issues. He no longer saw the body as a balance to his power. She needed to assert herself, so she could push her agenda forward.

"Mister Mayor, the council is in disorder. Two of our members have found themselves in serious trouble. One of those is definitely facing a legal issue, and the other one has a political problem, based on public perception. But make no mistake, they are both vulnerable."

"Two members?"

"Yeah, Armstrong and Buckner."

"Oh, I thought there were three." Sikes was grinning.

"Three? No, there are only two."

"An honest mistake," the mayor said, "two and three sound so much alike." He was laughing again.

Patterson shook her head. "What are you talking about?"

The mayor's laugh died down. "What are you proposing, Maggie?"

She was off-kilter and she knew it. Whatever he was doing, it was working. He had thrown so many verbal jabs that she had turtled up, deflecting and defending instead of pushing forward with her ideas.

It was upsetting to watch the mayor behave in a manner that she could never pull off without someone questioning not only her sanity but her sobriety. Patterson decided to change tactics. She couldn't attack straight ahead, or he would see that coming. She had to sneak in from an oblique angle by trying to enlist him in a project she knew he would want to see succeed.

"The public safety meeting is coming up."

Sikes shrugged. "I know that."

"You've seen how we did in the NIBRS report?"

The mayor rolled his eyes. "The city looks like a crime disaster."

"Well, I'm going after the chief because of it."

All frivolity evaporated, and Sikes focused on her. She scored her first jab.

"Why are you going after Baumgartner?" he asked.

"Because he's the chief of police and the bad numbers are his fault. The weight should fall on his shoulders, not ours."

Sikes gave a slight shrug. "Agreed, but what's your *political* reason for going after him?"

"Because when you kill the king, you become the king."

The mayor's face reddened, and his lips turned into an ugly sneer. "*I'm* the king."

Now, she'd landed a punch. He was paying full attention now. A jolt of energy raced through her.

"Well, sure," Patterson said. "You're the king, but you're term-limited. You're out in, what, three years? What's the gain in me going after you? I'd waste a lot of time and energy going after what is essentially a lame-duck mayor. I've better things to do."

Anger flared in the mayor's eyes. The lame-duck comment had been an uppercut to his pride. Time to move in for the kill.

"You hate that fat bastard," Patterson said. "No matter how much you try to hide it, I know you hate him."

"I don't hate him," Sikes said, but it wasn't convincing.

Patterson chuckled. "Of course you do, Andy."

"*Mister* Mayor."

"Yes, *Mister* Mayor, but you hate him, and we all know it. His poll numbers are outstanding. Way better than yours."

"It's rigged," Sikes said. "Somehow."

"Sure, if that's what you want to think, but I need to be proactive. I'm going to be the next mayor."

Sikes stretched his jaw, then said, "I'm still mayor and I'll get those term limits removed, you watch. You won't stand a chance against me just like the last douche bag who thought he could take me down."

"Maybe," Patterson said. "Maybe not. I'm not Cody Lofton, though."

"That sounds like a threat."

Patterson shook her head. "Just a fact, but that's three years from now. Until then, the enemy of my enemy…"

"Is my friend?"

"You've been calling me Maggie. Only my friends call me Maggie, right?"

"As a councilwoman, you've got a good thing going, *Margaret*. Why would you poke the sleeping dragon?"

"Baumgartner's getting dangerous. Scratch that, he *is* dangerous. He's consolidated a lot of power. I think he's seen what the sheriff has done in the county and he wants to sit on a throne like that."

"He's never going to get a throne like that. The sheriff is elected. The chief is appointed. By me."

"That's all well and good, but you know just like I do that you can't fire the man, even if you wanted to."

Sikes looked hurt by her comment. "I *could* fire him."

"No, you couldn't. There would be serious public outcry. He's the most popular man in the city right now. More than you. More than the president."

Sikes yanked his tie to loosen it further.

"That's why I'll lay the crime stats at his feet," she continued. "He's responsible for the safety of this city. I'll paint him as an ineffectual defender of the public. Of course, you'll run to his defense. He's your guy after all. That's only right."

"Why should I do that?" the mayor asked, throwing his hands up. "It'll make me seem weak."

"You're only doing it until you turn and stab him in the back, just like they did to Caesar."

Sikes furrowed his brow. "Wouldn't I be Caesar in this example?"

Patterson waved his concern away. "You're overthinking it. Pick a different tale. It doesn't matter. You get the point."

"He'll argue it's the budget. They always do."

"Let him argue it. I want him to engage. If the big strong policeman stands up in front of the city and says he can't do his job because of the budget, you know what he's admitting to?"

"What?"

"That we're stronger than him. That we made his job tougher because of a spreadsheet."

For a long moment, Sikes considered what she had said. He then smiled and said, "So. Maggie. The enemy of my enemy, huh?"

Chapter 27

Ray Zielinski wandered into the detectives' division. He spotted the fabled coffee station right away. The rich aroma of some kind of expensive blend told him it was a cut above the convenience store swill he'd been drinking his entire career in patrol.

Good coffee and plain clothes. No wonder these guys never seem to leave the station.

Finding his way to Major Crimes wasn't as easy as discovering coffee Mecca, but after one wrong turn, he located the bullpen. Veteran Detective Marty Hill sat at his desk near the open doorway, his left leg propped up on a second chair. He saw Zielinski right away.

"Hey, Ray. Come to hang out on your day off?"

"How'd you know it was my day off?"

Hill gave him a knowing smile. "Come on." He pointed to Zielinski's jeans, shirt, and hiking boots. "Street clothes during day shift hours? Gotta be a day off."

Zielinski nodded. *Of course.* He motioned toward Hill's leg. "What's up with that?"

"Surgery," Hill said. "Just came back today for light duty."

"What happened?"

"Shot knee."

"You got shot in the knee?"

"No." Hill smiled. "My knees are shot. Doctor says the combination of football and all those years of SWAT runs—"

"Okay," Zielinski interrupted. "Listen, is Ward Clint around?"

Hill stopped, slightly surprised. Then he shrugged. "I'm not sure. I haven't seen him yet."

Zielinski stood there, glancing around, then looked back to Hill. "Where's his desk?"

"In the back."

He muttered a thank you and headed that way. Behind him, he heard Hill say, "Nice talking to you, Ray" in a mildly sarcastic tone.

He found Clint's desk tucked in a corner. The surly detective wrote furiously in a notebook as Zielinski approached. Clint's bushy hair was noticeably longer than the tight afro Zielinski had always seen him wear. The detective glanced up, registered who he was, and immediately closed the notebook.

"Officer Zielinski."

"Hey, Ward. I—"

"Don't call me that."

Zielinski hesitated. "Uh…"

Clint gave him a hard look, his eyes a little bleary. "My name is Wardell, not Ward. Maybe you didn't know that, so I'll give you a pass. But it doesn't matter, because as far as I know, we're not on a first-name basis, anyway."

Zielinski didn't respond immediately. How was it that he always tended to forget how abrupt Clint was? He'd only had a dozen or so interactions with him over the years, most of them at crime scenes. The man was always hyper-focused, so their exchanges were brief and professional.

Maybe he has a point. Maybe we don't know each other well enough for this conversation.

His next thought was that he should introduce Clint to Lyle Bunney. The two of them would have a lot to talk about.

"What is it?" Clint asked. "You're clearly on days off with time to burn, but I'm busy. What do you want?"

Zielinski glanced around for a chair. Another detective's nearby desk sat empty, so he reached for the chair. "Mind if I sit down?"

"Plan on being here that long?"

Zielinski let go of the chair. "Listen, I need to talk to you."

"So talk."

He looked around the nearly empty bullpen. He'd always figured detectives spent most of the day at their desks, but aside from Hill, only two others were there. They were well across the large room, but it was possible that they would overhear him.

"Maybe we could step into one of the interview rooms for a second?"

"Why? Are you investigating me for something?"

"No!" Zielinski lowered his voice. "I want to speak privately."

"Then you picked the worst place to do it. Between eavesdropping snitches out here and listening devices in the interview rooms, there's no such thing as a private conversation."

Zielinski thought about it for a minute. Clint was infamous for his conspiracy theories when it came to the machinations of the police department and city hall. Zielinski wasn't sure how much of it was department legend at this point and how much was true. He could see that Clint believed what he'd just said, though.

"I need to talk to you about Garrett," he said, keeping his voice low.

Clint leaned back in his chair, away from Zielinski. "Garrett who?"

Zielinski frowned. "Tyler Garrett. Come on, man."

"Why would I give a backwards dump about some patrol cop?" He tapped the badge on his belt. "See that? It says detective."

"You worked his shooting."

"I work a lot of shootings. World's a messed-up place and people try to kill each other all the time."

"I was there," Zielinski said, pressing on.

"I know."

"I was the first backup officer to arrive on scene."

"I know that, too. What's your point? You want a sticker or something?"

"Why are you being such a dick?" Zielinski growled.

"Why are you wasting my time?"

Zielinski gritted his teeth, fighting off the anger. "Something was wrong with that shooting. I knew it then, and I know it now."

Clint stared at him, saying nothing.

"Not just the shooting," Zielinski continued. "All the stuff that came after, too. Something's wrong. The whole thing reeks."

Clint's hard stare didn't relent. "You get promoted to Internal Affairs and I didn't hear about it?"

"No, damn it!" Zielinski kept his voice low but forceful. "This has been bothering me for a long time. Either Garrett was dirty somehow, or the department played him dirty. Or maybe the department covered up for him. I don't know. I just know something's dirty, and I'm trying to get my head around it."

"Why?"

"Because it's eating at me."

"No, why are you bothering me with this crap?"

Zielinski took a deep breath, reining in his frustration. He wanted to punch Clint right in the mouth but throwing fists with this man wasn't going to get him any answers. "You investigated the case."

"I shadowed. County investigated."

"The county couldn't find chocolate in a Hershey's factory," Zielinski said derisively.

Clint didn't smile, but his mouth twitched.

"You investigated, and even though you're such a prick, everyone knows you're good at what you do."

"*Prick?*" Clint repeated.

"Look," Zielinski said, keeping his voice as even as possible. "I know you had to see it. Something's dirty about it all. Tell me I'm not crazy. That's all I'm asking."

Clint shook his head. "I don't know anything more than what is reflected in my reports. I don't know if you're crazy or not, but your suspicions about this case are not accurate."

Zielinski stared at Clint, trying to decide if he believed the man. Conspiracy weaving aside, Clint's reputation as one of the best, if not *the* best, detective on the department was fairly universal. He wasn't going to win any popularity contests, but if a case could be solved, he'd solve it.

How could he not see the problems with Garrett and all that happened?

Zielinski glanced down to the notebook Clint had been writing in when he'd approached. "What's that?"

"A notebook."

"Doesn't look department issued."

"You work for the quartermaster now?" Clint snapped. "I use my own notebooks sometimes. What do you care?"

"I don't," Zielinski admitted.

"You got any more Oliver Stone conspiracy garbage you want to spin for me, Officer Zielinski, or can I get back to doing real police work?"

Zielinski sighed, defeated. "Yeah, fine. Sorry to bother you."

"Sorry doesn't bring back the five minutes I just lost."

That was finally too much for him. "Yeah, well, you can *bill me* for the time," he snarled. "There's a long line of guys trying to get into my pocket as it is, so you might as well join the party."

Clint didn't reply.

"Ah, forget it," Zielinski muttered, flicking his hand at Clint and turning away.

He walked out the way he'd come, through the bullpen. Detective Hill pointedly ignored him when he stalked past, making it clear to Zielinski that he was oh-for-two on the day.

Chapter 28

Gary Stone dropped into his office chair and turned to look at the empty back wall. He was still reeling from that morning's meeting with Chief Baumgartner. After getting his ass chewed for not immediately calling him about Betty Rabe's suicide, he returned to city hall and collected his interoffice mail. He was still trying to process where the chief got off treating him like he did.

He had always done exactly what the man asked. Whenever given a task, Stone completed it in a manner that was professional and unlikely to need follow-up by anyone else. It was a quality he took great pride in. It was also a trait that his former employers in the private sector appreciated. No one had ever talked to him the way that Baumgartner did earlier that morning.

It was uncalled for.

True, he'd never seen the chief in that way before so perhaps it was an anomaly. Maybe he was having a bad morning. If Baumgartner was experiencing any of the reservations that Stone had concerning not entering the Rabe report directly into the system, then he would be tense. He'd likely take it out on the only person he could, which would be Stone. Baumgartner couldn't take it out on the mayor. Trouble doesn't roll uphill.

Stone's thoughts returned to the previous night when Tyler Garrett visited his house. Garrett's comments now seemed to hold more weight. *They'll hang you out to dry.*

Tyler Garrett was the man Stone had always seen as the epitome of a police officer. If he was telling Stone to watch out, then he should probably do exactly that. But Garrett's outlook on the world was now jaded. How could it not be after all he'd been through? Shouldn't he take that into consideration when listening to Garrett's advice?

However, the guy had already protected him with his handling of the business card he found during his investigation into Rabe's suicide. Then Garrett came by to give him the heads-up on the action he'd taken. Tyler went out of his way to help Stone. Jaded or not, his advice should at least be taken for what it was—concern for a colleague.

But then Stone remembered Garrett standing over his report with a cell phone in his hand.

If he was worried about a coworker, a brother in blue, then why take pictures of his handwritten interview report? Stone was fairly certain that was what Garrett had done while he was in the bathroom. Even if he hadn't admitted to it, he didn't deny it. Stone wondered how Garrett could think that action was helping him out. How would him having a copy of the report benefit Stone?

He shook the thoughts from his mind and turned his attention to his interoffice mail. He quickly sorted through it. There were a couple pieces of junk mail. Then there was a report from Ray Zielinski about another contact with Lyle Bunney. Charlie Bravo, Stone thought angrily, and set the report to the side. He returned to his mail, quickly prioritizing what needed his attention and what didn't.

"Hey, boy-o," Jean Carter said.

Stone lifted his head to see her leaning around the corner of his office. She wore a light blue sweater and dark blue pants. He smiled.

"Got big plans for the weekend?" she asked.

"No. You?"

"Nope. Coffee or a drink? If you're not busy, that is."

"Definitely."

Jean glanced around. "Stay alert. Sikes is on the warpath this morning."

Stone's smile faded. "About what?"

"Who knows? But I gotta go. I'm in enemy territory. Bye."

He paused for a moment and looked out his window for any sign of the mayor. Not hearing him either, Stone grabbed the Lyle Bunney report. It was a single page write-up on an assist agency call. He wanted to rip on Ray for the short write-up, but it had been a simple call and wouldn't need more than that. Zielinski's writing was tight and economical. Stone noted the report number. Since this was an informational copy, he didn't need to take further action.

He tossed the report in the recycle bin and dismissively muttered, "Charlie Bravo."

"Who's Charlie Bravo?" the mayor asked, stepping into his office. His voice was low and demanding. His light brown suit looked fresh and his tie was in its proper place. It was still early, and the day had yet to take its full toll on his appearance.

"Sir?"

"Charlie Bravo," the mayor said, closing the office door. "Who is that? I heard you say it."

When the mayor repeated Charlie Bravo, a part of Stone really wanted to punch Ray Zielinski in his mustache.

"It's a band," Stone lied.

"A band?"

"Jazz fusion."

The mayor's face scrunched. "Of course. Sounds like your type."

"What?"

"Some kind of wimpy music. You'd like that stuff, wouldn't you? So tell me, Gary, why didn't you give me the heads-up about the girl killing herself?"

Stone stared at the mayor, partly because he was caught off guard by his abruptness, and partly due to the insult over his favorite type of music.

"Don't just sit there like some sort of turd on a log. Tell me why you dropped the ball on this. I had to hear the news from Baumgartner."

"Yes, sir, she killed herself."

The mayor threw his hands in the air. "No kidding, Gary, I just told you that. Are you just parroting what I say? I've got an idiot chief of staff to do that for me. Why do I need two parrots?"

"You don't, sir."

"That's right, I don't. I already talked to you about this. Help me and I can help you, but all I see is you sitting here in this, this, what the hell is wrong with your office, Gary? Why don't you have any pictures in here? Looks like a prison cell. Do you think being here is a jail sentence?"

"No, sir."

"I can make it feel that way, if you want."

Stone remained silent.

Sikes wiped a finger under his nose. "Who else knows about the girl's letter?"

"The chief and me." *And Garrett.*

"No one else?"

"No one else," Stone repeated. There was a pause and he knew he should have kept his mouth shut, but he said, "Except maybe your staff."

"My staff?" Anger flared in the mayor's eyes. "My staff has nothing to do with this."

"Well, someone saw the letter, right? Someone directed it to you before it got to the chief. I'm just saying."

The mayor's face reddened. "Listen, smartass, my people know how to do their job, which is more than I can say for you."

Stone stood, pushing his chair back. "I know how to do my job, *sir.*"

The mayor smiled, and his head began to bounce side to side, like a boxer preparing to enter the ring. "Growing a pair now. Nice."

Stone stared at him. Sikes was enjoying the conflict and Stone knew that he'd gone too far by challenging him.

"Maybe you can get a little hair on them, too, huh?" Sikes wriggled his fingers in front of his own crotch.

"Excuse me?" Stone said.

"That's right. Get them all swelled up with your pride." Sikes jabbed a finger at him. "Lemme see the report on the girl."

"I don't have it."

"Why not?"

"I gave the only copy to the chief. You'll have to get it from him."

The mayor began to bob his head again as he thought.

Stone stood stock-still. He knew better than to say anything that might provoke the incident further.

Sikes stopped moving and smiled. "Better be careful now, Gary."

They stared at each for a moment. Stone knew the mayor wanted him to ask why but he forced himself to remain quiet.

Finally, Sikes shrugged. "Now that I know you've actually got a pair of jimmies, I'm going to come by and kick them occasionally, just to remind you who's in charge."

Stone's eyes widened.

The mayor opened the office door and looked back. "Enjoy your day, Officer Stone."

Chapter 29

"You had lunch yet, Tom?" the chief asked.

Captain Tom Farrell nodded. They were sitting in the chief's office. Farrell wasn't sure why, but he wasn't surprised at being summoned. Baumgartner always seemed to like and respect him, and since the Garrett incident, the chief had relied upon his counsel more frequently.

Which makes it that much harder to keep lying to him.

"I ate earlier," he answered.

"Damn," Baumgartner muttered. "I was hoping we could grab a cheesesteak or something."

Farrell thought that Baumgartner could do with a few more salads instead of cheesesteaks, but he didn't say anything. He liked the chief and wanted him to stick around for a long time, but giving dietary advice wasn't why he was there, and he knew it.

Baumgartner shrugged and lifted his phone. "Marilyn? Call over to The High Nooner for a soup and sandwich. The usual. Thanks."

He hung up and turned his attention to Farrell.

"It's probably better that we talk out of the public eye anyway," he said. "We have a problem, and I want your thoughts on it."

"Yes, sir," Farrell said.

Baumgartner gave him a strange look. "All these years working together, Tom, and even behind closed doors, you never call me Bob. Why is that?"

Farrell thought for a moment. Baumgartner came on the department a few years ahead of him, and he was already a bit of an emerging legend by the time Farrell got out of the academy. He'd been one of Farrell's training officers, probably his best. Then Baumgartner became a sergeant, and Farrell was on his squad. *Baumgartner's Battalion* was the proud nickname they'd emblazoned on some black T-shirts to wear under their patrol vests. The trend of following the future chief up the promotional ladder continued to the present. Farrell was always just a rung or two behind.

"It's a matter of respect," he said. "You're the chief. This is the chief's office."

"So if we go golfing on a Saturday, off duty, I can pry a 'Bob' out of you?"

Farrell smiled a little. "Golfing is still pretty close to work. Maybe if we went fishing."

"Fair enough." Baumgartner took a deep breath, and let it out, all business again. "Here's the deal."

Farrell sat and listened while the chief laid out the details about Bethany Rabe. It was tragic, but at first, Farrell didn't see the problem for the police department. For Dennis Hahn, sure. But how did this cause the chief any concern?

Then he got it. "Stone's visit. He cleared it One-David, didn't he?"

Baumgartner shook his head. "No, he wrote a report." The chief slid a packet of papers across the desk to him.

Farrell picked up the report. The first thing he noticed was that it was one of the old forms. He shrugged that off. Maybe Stone didn't have the report writing software on his computer at city hall. Then he saw that the officer had written the report by hand, which was odd. An envelope and a short letter was attached to the end of the report.

He read through the officer's narrative. Stone's writing was clear and concise. He addressed everything Farrell would have thought to ask, even though Betty Rabe refused to be explicit and wavered in her allegations regarding the assault. He wondered if she was afraid because the man she was accusing was powerful. If so, it would be a valid concern.

When he finished the report, he thought about it for a few seconds longer. There was no way he could solve the riddle as to what really happened simply by reading a police report, no matter how well written it was. He felt bad for Betty Rabe, especially after reading through her letter.

"Seventeen years old," he said. "It's a shame."

"Under any circumstances, it's a tragedy." Baumgartner took another heavy breath. "And now it's a tragedy that might become a public storm."

"How so?"

"You're holding the only copy of the report, Tom."

"What?"

The chief just stared at him, letting it sink in.

Farrell looked down at the report again and realized what was missing. There was no report number. "This is a black hole report?"

The chief nodded.

Farrell considered it, surprised. "Stone did this?"

"For me, but yeah."

"He knew what he was being asked to do?"

"I made it clear." The chief studied Farrell. "Why do you ask, Tom?"

Farrell spread his hands a little and shook his head slowly. "I just never...he seemed like a straight-laced guy. A little vanilla, a real Melvin Milquetoast sort."

"He's a bit of a cake-eater, but he knows the score. He's more businessman than cop, and a businessman is closer to a politician than most people think."

Farrell didn't answer. Instead, he scanned through the report again, noting the level of detail in light of what the chief had told him about Stone.

Interesting.

"Look, Tom, it was the mayor who asked me to look into this. I didn't realize it right away, but it's clear to me now that he wanted to control the information and use it against Hahn if it panned out to be criminal. If it was a consensual affair—"

"Consensual? Hahn's what? In his forties? And a councilman. She's a seventeen-year-old girl. I have a bit of a problem calling that relationship consensual."

"Sixteen is the age of consent in Washington," Baumgartner pointed out.

"He's in a position of power, though. If she interned for him or was in some kind of a mentorship capacity, the law looks at that differently."

"It'll be your detectives that figure out that part when this hurricane makes landfall. Which I think it will, because the mayor will leak it eventually. The best-case scenario for Hahn when the people hear the details is that he dies a political death. Worst case for him, it's deemed criminal." Baumgartner leaned forward. "But for the mayor, and for us, the problem is this report. I think I misplayed this one."

Farrell set the packet of papers back on the chief's desk. "What are you going to do?"

"I see two choices." He lifted the report and set it on the corner of his desk. "One is to shred this."

Farrell frowned. "That might be illegal," he said. "Besides, we're not the CIA."

"I don't like it, either, but it's the cleanest option. This is the only written evidence of the event. There's no entry in the CAD system, either. Unless someone saw Stone interview her, or she told someone…" he trailed off.

"Or she sent an email," Farrell added. "Or she put it on some form of social media somewhere old guys like us never even heard of." He shook his head emphatically. "Chief, not only is that the wrong thing to do, it's a bad idea. Look at history. It's never the crime that gets people in the most trouble. It's the cover-up that follows that sinks them. You shred that report, and the public finds out, you lose the one thing you have with the people of this city that will keep you in that chair no matter who the mayor is or what the crime stats are. *Trust*."

Baumgartner nodded. "I just had to look at all my options, that's all."

"Well, I can't agree to that one."

"You're right, Tom. I'm not going to do it." He fingered the edge of the report. "The alternative is ugly, though. This report isn't in the system."

"Yet."

Baumgartner looked up at him. "There's a way to input it now? Or is it too late?"

"It's never too late. But the report number, and the date the number is generated, will both be after Stone's interview and the girl's suicide. Anyone who looks closely will see the discrepancy and point it out. It still looks bad and will cause questions."

The chief pressed his lips together. "How am I supposed to answer that question without lying? Because I can't do that, any more than I can shred this letter."

Farrell thought about it. "If you enter the report into the system and assign it to my division for follow-up, then you can honestly say the case is active. By policy, we limit public discussion on active cases, and you've always been consistent about that."

"If I were a reporter," Baumgartner said, "and I was asking about the timing of the events versus the timing of when the report was entered into the system, I wouldn't be satisfied with 'this is an active case, so we're not discussing it.'"

"Screw the reporters. They don't have to like it."

"When the media doesn't like something, they focus on it. And if they don't have facts, they speculate. They may do it from behind the safety of rhetorical questions and *allegedly*, but the message gets across all the same. And that doesn't even factor in someone from city hall leaking information." He shook his head. "How am I supposed to argue that commenting on this timing issue would somehow compromise the investigation? It sounds like a political dodge."

"That's because it is."

"How about some advice here instead of being Captain Obvious?"

Farrell hadn't seen the chief like this since the Garrett incident. It was disconcerting. "Then just answer the question," he said. "Call it an administrative delay. Or a routing error."

"Lie, you mean."

Farrell gave him a look of mild rebuke. "You were talking about shredding a black hole report two minutes ago. Now coloring the facts a little is too much?"

Baumgartner considered. "I guess it *was* an administrative delay, when you really look at it. Due to a routing error. Stone should have entered the report and had it cc'd to me, but the whole thing happened backwards."

"And Stone is solid enough for that? Even though you told him to do it in the first place?"

"He's a stand-up guy," the chief said. "I trust him."

A stand-up guy. The description irked Farrell. It was one of those terms that both cops and mobsters used to mean the exact same thing.

"There's your answer," he said. "It's still not strictly above board, but it won't turn into Watergate."

Baumgartner nodded slowly, seeming to let the idea sink in. "I think this is the best option," he finally said. Then he sighed again. "You know, when I came on this job, everything was so black-and-white. There were the good guys—and that was us—and the bad guys who were out there doing harm. We went out and caught the bad guys, and that was it. It was good-versus-evil. Simpler times."

"I don't think it was ever that simple," Farrell said quietly. "We had our illusions then, that's all."

"Illusions." Baumgartner repeated the word, seeming to muse over it. "Illusions about the right thing to do and the wrong thing to do, huh? Only no one ever tells you about all those cracks in between. All the gray. When is telling a small lie beneficial for the greater good? How much of the truth can you omit before what you're saying is a lie?"

Farrell didn't know what to say. At some point during their career, he supposed every cop went through the same thing the chief was describing. The nature of the job resided in the gray. For some officers, this conflict might come early. For others, it could end up being a rude awakening later on. Either way, it was a question every cop faced. He imagined that the chief faced it more frequently and with higher stakes. He was responsible for the fate of the entire department, not just his own career. If there was one thing he knew about Robert Baumgartner, it was where his loyalty lay. It rested firmly with the men and women of the department. He felt sure that if it came down to his career or the agency, Baumgartner would fall on his sword.

And all the while, I just keep up pretenses, knowing the real truth about Garrett. He was in no position to be judging anyone on degrees of truth.

"Thanks, Tom," Baumgartner broke into his reverie. "I needed a clear head to bounce this thing off of."

"Sure."

"Switching gears, will you do me a favor?"

"Of course."

"Check into how Tyler Garrett is doing."

Farrell's radar pinged loudly. Did Baumgartner know more than he let on? Was he aware of how he and Clint had been monitoring Garrett since the shooting?

He cleared his throat. "Why?"

"He responded to the suicide call. He saw Stone's card there, so he followed up with him about it. I want to make sure it's not a loose end, and that he's still tracking smoothly. It was a rough go there a while back, you know?"

Farrell nodded, watching Baumgartner as he spoke. He looked for any sort of tell, but Baumgartner would have made an excellent poker player, because he saw nothing. Or perhaps there was nothing to see. He couldn't be sure.

For a moment, he considered telling the chief everything. Just laying out the entire mess of what he knew, and what he'd done. What he and Clint were still doing. It was Baumgartner's department. He deserved to know, and maybe he could help.

Farrell glanced at the shredder next to Baumgartner's desk. Then he said, "Why not ask Dana? She's the patrol captain. Garrett's under her command."

Baumgartner frowned. "I'm asking you. You can look into it with these other considerations in mind, and I'd like to keep the loop tight on this one. Understood?"

"Got it."

"Besides, Hatcher has always been too soft on her own troops. You know that. When she was a sergeant, they used to call her Mother Hen."

"She takes care of her people," Farrell admitted. "That's not a bad trait."

"Unless the benefit to her people is detrimental to another team. Or to the officer. Not holding people accountable may seem like protection, Tom, but it hurts everyone in the long run."

Farrell didn't answer. All he could think of was Betty Rabe. Who was being held accountable for everything surrounding her death? And what about Tyler Garrett? When was he going to be held accountable?

"Anyway, check up on him for me, okay?" the chief asked.

Farrell nodded woodenly. "I will."

Chapter 30

"You wanted to see me, Cap?"

Hatcher saw Officer Ray Zielinski standing in her open doorway. She pushed aside her paperwork and motioned toward the door. "Close that."

Zielinski's face looked stricken, but he swung the door shut. When he turned back around, he remained standing.

"Go ahead and have a seat, Ray."

His eyes flicked to the empty chair in front of her desk, then up to her. "Do I need a union rep for this, Captain?"

"A union rep?" Hatcher was surprised at the thought. "No, why?"

Zielinski motioned toward the closed door. "The captain calls me on my day off, then has me close the door? Now, I'm wondering if this is a Sarge and Ray talk or a captain to patrolman talk."

Hatcher thought about it for a second. "I guess it's more of an unofficial captain to patrol officer talk, Ray, but nothing that requires a union rep."

Zielinski hesitated, then took the seat. He didn't say anything, only waited.

She decided to get straight to the point. "I asked IA about your demeanor complaint. The lieutenant over there, Sutherland, didn't want to talk about it. But I worked on him a bit and found out that it probably isn't going anywhere."

"No?" Zielinski looked suddenly hopeful.

"Probably not. After making the initial complaint, the complainant hasn't been cooperative with the investigators. He's canceled several interviews, claiming to be too busy."

Zielinski nodded. "I believe it. He was a self-important douche bag."

Hatcher frowned at the term but didn't bother to address it. "He sounds like the kind of guy who figures he already did his part by making the initial complaint and they should just do their job and figure out the rest."

"That fits."

"Sutherland said they were doing their due diligence, but he expects this one to die on the vine."

"That's great news."

"It's not a done deal, just a possibility."

"At this point, I'll take it."

"Don't get too excited. There was something else he told me."

Zielinski's eyes widened and his nostrils flared. An expression of panic flashed across his face. "What is it?"

My God, he's really feeling the stress.

Hatcher wondered what she could do to help him. There wasn't much, but one thing an officer like Zielinski appreciated was honesty, so she gave it to him. "You've got another complaint coming."

"Another? What for?"

"It's for demeanor again."

She thought she saw his concern fade slightly, but she couldn't be sure. Maybe it was just the shock wearing off. "Did you go on an agency assist recently?"

Zielinski started to shrug but stopped. "Wait. It's Lyle Bunney, isn't it? Cap, he's crazy. He writes these wacked out letters to senators, councilmen, even the chief."

Hatcher glanced at her notes. "No, this complaint came from a woman. Lindsay Wagner?"

Zielinski slumped. "Damn."

"Who is she?"

"She's a he," Zielinski said. "A social worker with Mental Health."

Hatcher put it together. "You were there to assist him with the one-oh-five?"

Zielinski nodded.

"Were you being a smartass?"

He nodded again.

"What did you say?"

"Nothing much," Zielinski said slowly.

"Like what?"

"I sort of got the mental guy spun up. I'd been there before, so I knew his hot buttons. He ticked me off, so I pushed them."

"And Wagner saw you do this?"

"Just the result."

"Why would he file a demeanor complaint?" Such an action was a pretty big deal, in her experience. A formal complaint was a nuclear move for an agency that worked so closely with the police department. The only thing bigger would be to go public.

"I might have been a little rude with him, too," Zielinski admitted sourly.

"Might?"

He shifted in his seat. "He probably thought so."

Hatcher folded her hands. "You don't need this right now, Ray."

"Tell me about it."

"If Mister Self-Important ends up cooperating and that first complaint is sustained, then a sustained complaint on this new one gets us into progressive discipline territory."

"You think I'll take a rip for this? A day or something?"

She shook her head. "I think a suspension is a little harsh, but a verbal reprimand for the first complaint becomes a written reprimand in your file for the second complaint. That's why they call it progressive."

"I know."

"If you land in some kind of jackpot after that…"

The same pained expression covered Zielinski's features. "Boom," he whispered.

Hatcher didn't respond right away. A couple of sustained complaints like the ones Zielinski was facing provided one hell of a springboard. If there was a following offense big enough, the sustained complaints on his record could mean the difference between a thirty-day suspension and being fired. She didn't want anything like that to happen to Zielinski. He was a good cop.

"Ray, what's going on with you?"

"It's…all the stuff I told you about before."

"I get it," Hatcher said, trying to strike a balance in her tone somewhere between firm and sympathetic. "But you're a good officer. You've got to put these distractions aside when you're on the clock."

"I know."

"Get your head back in the game."

"Okay, Sarge. I will." He dipped his chin in assent. "Thanks for the heads-up."

As much as getting a complaint sucked for him, Hatcher knew that knowing was better than it being a surprise from IA. She gave him a long look. "What can I do to help you with the outside stuff?"

Zielinski thought about it, then shrugged. "Nothing I can think of. I need to keep working the extra gigs until Amber's alimony ends. Then I can cut back a little."

"I think that'd be good for you."

"Yeah, as long as I don't spend the time drinking instead," he said.

"Is that something I should worry about?" Hatcher asked.

"No."

"All right, then." She waited a moment, then said, "If there's nothing else—"

Zielinski opened his mouth to speak, then closed it.

"What?" Hatcher asked. "Is there another complaint coming?"

Zielinski looked pained but shook his head. "No, Cap. Just something else that's bothering me."

"What is it?"

"Tyler Garrett."

Hatcher sat back, slightly surprised. "He's still on power shift."

"I know."

"What does he have to do with you?"

"I worked with him…when everything happened."

Hatcher nodded. She'd been the north side evening lieutenant at the time, but she had watched the events unfold from afar. "You think the department is trying to do you over like the city tried with Garrett?"

Zielinski clenched his jaw. "No, no, I'm not saying that."

"What, then?"

"I'm…I'm not so sure about Garrett anymore and it bothers me."

Hatcher thought about his words. Garrett had never been on any of her teams when she was a sergeant, and she didn't recall him being on her shifts when she'd served as a patrol lieutenant, either. But now she was the patrol captain, and everyone in a uniform was her responsibility now.

"Ray," she began carefully, "I think you've got more than enough on your own plate right now. Probably too much. Worrying about a fellow officer is admirable, but I think you should focus on your own situation. Let me take care of Garrett."

His face twisted into barely disguised anger, but he said nothing.

"You okay? You look upset."

"No, ma'am. I'm good."

"I'll check on him for you," Hatcher promised. "He's a good officer, and seems to have bounced back well, but I'll make sure he's fine. What is it that made you so concerned?"

Zielinski swallowed hard, his expression still dark. He gave his head a short shake. "Just worried," he grunted out.

Hatcher took that with a grain of salt. The gold bars on her collar sometimes kept even her longtime troops at a distance.

Zielinski obviously felt more loyalty to Garrett than to her at the moment. It made sense, even though she felt a bittersweet pang of sadness when she realized what had just happened.

"I'll check on him," she repeated. "But promise me you'll put a muzzle on the smart remarks, okay?"

"Yes, ma'am," came Zielinski's clipped answer.

He's definitely mad. Hatcher didn't let it bother her. Sometimes people had to hear hard truths, and they didn't necessarily like it. He would feel differently about it later.

"Okay," she said. "That's all I had to say. You?"

Zielinski shook his head. Then he stood and opened the door to leave.

"Ray?"

He stopped in the doorway and looked over his shoulder at her.

"Stay safe, all right?"

"Thank you, Captain," he said stiffly, then left her office, striding purposefully away.

Hatcher listened to his footfalls for a few seconds. She was glad he was on his weekend. A couple of days to clear his head, and then a Sunday shift for his first day back, which was usually slow, was exactly what he needed to get his feet under him.

That is, unless he works extra duty details all weekend.

She let out a small sigh, then turned back to her notes.

Chapter 31

Clint didn't like being summoned. It smacked of the power imbalance he'd endured his entire career. Not to mention what his people had suffered for four hundred years. The fact it was Captain Tom Farrell who did the summoning did little to assuage his annoyance.

He lurched his patrol car to a stop in the deserted parking lot of the Spokane Arena, his driver's window beside Farrell's, a classic police roadside position. "What is it?" he demanded. "You pulled me off a follow-up interview I was headed toward."

"About Garrett?" Farrell asked.

"No, Captain. I'm carrying a caseload, too, or did you forget that?"

"I'm well aware. I was just asking."

Clint thought about pointing out the disparity between how many cases he had versus his colleagues but didn't. For one thing, he hadn't seen a new file that morning, which was rare. Plus, Marty Hill was back on light duty, making phone calls with his busted knee propped up off to the side of his desk, and that helped. But mostly, he kept this gripe to himself because despite everything, he believed in the chain of command, and right now his case load disparity was between him and Lieutenant Flowers. The Garrett situation was a special one, though, and that one was between him and Farrell, because they were about the only two people who knew the truth.

"Can we make this quick?" he asked pointedly.

"Sure." Farrell gave him a long look. "You look a little ragged, Wardell. Everything okay?"

"Ragged? What's that supposed to mean?"

Farrell pointed at Clint's hair. "You usually keep a tight cut. It's getting a little shaggy. And there's a stain on your collar. Is that barbecue sauce?"

Clint stared at him, grinding his teeth.

My hair? *A spot of sauce on my shirt? Is this guy serious?*

"I'm fine, Captain," he gritted out between clenched teeth.

Farrell eyed him for another few seconds, then let out a small sigh. "I want to be sure you're okay, that's all."

"I haven't been okay since you happy assholes decided that since I'm black, I should shadow Garrett's shooting. That's what landed me in the middle of this mess. So spare me the concerned leader bit, Captain. Let's do our business so I can get back to mine."

Irritation flickered across Farrell's face.

Oh, you think you're irritated? How many hours of sleep you getting most nights?

"Fine," Farrell said. "What's going on with Garrett?"

"Not a damn thing worth reporting, or I would have come to your office on my own," Clint said.

"He seems fine to you?"

"That's the image he wants to present, so that's what everybody sees. And everyone seems to be buying it." Clint thought for a moment, then added, "Except maybe for his wife. She seems to have him figured out."

"They're still separated?"

"Near as I can tell. He has the kids often enough, but the pickups and drop-offs I've seen all happen at the front door. He stays outside, and she looks about as cold as a woman can get. I don't think he'll be charming his way back into that house. She's a smart woman."

"Maybe she knows something we can use."

"I'm sure she does," Clint says, "but there's no way she's going to tell me or anyone else about it."

"You don't think so?"

"Not a chance. She knows or suspects enough to kick his ass to the curb, but she isn't going to give him up to the police. She's got kids to think about."

"I thought she worked."

"She does," Clint said. He knew all about Angela Garrett's career, but none of it was relevant to this conversation. Instead, he explained, "Do you really think any mother is going to give up on the child support and the medical and dental that comes with Garrett's job? If I'm her, I'm wondering what good it does me to send the father of my children to prison and cut off the supply line to those kids. The answer is no good whatsoever."

"Except that it's the right thing to do."

Clint scoffed. "Right for who?"

"So there's nothing." Farrell frowned. "He's being a perfect citizen and model cop?"

"I didn't say that. He's got a couple of chips I'm sure he's banging, but since he's separated, and I'm not the morality police, I didn't see fit to report that."

"You know," Farrell mused quietly, "we might have enough already."

"To arrest him?" Disbelief was pasted across Clint's face.

"There's enough," Farrell persisted. "Think about it. We've got two scenes. They're both connected to Garrett."

"We went over this when it happened, Captain. It's too weak."

"An eyeball witness puts him at the Ocampo homicide."

"An *elderly* eyewitness," Clint corrected. "I doubt she's gotten more convincing in the last twenty-one months."

Farrell ignored him and continued. "There were witnesses at Talbott's shooting that saw a black male, and Garrett's buddy lives right there."

"Derek Tillman," Clint said.

"Exactly."

"Problem is, none of them identified Garrett as the male. And even if it was Garrett, the way they described it, he acted in self-defense."

"But Tillman—"

"Isn't saying squat," Clint snapped. "He's Garrett's boy, and that's that."

Farrell sighed. "It's still evidence."

"You're right. But most of it is circumstantial, and it's weak. It goes toward probable cause, but it's not enough."

Farrell muttered a curse in frustration.

Clint scratched the stubble on his cheek. "There is one thing we've got going for us, though." He glanced at Farrell, whose expression turned hopeful. "The bullet comparison. That could link the scenes."

Farrell shook his head. "I don't get it."

"We know Garrett killed Ocampo and his crew, right? And we know he shot Talbott. If we can match the bullets from both scenes to the same gun, it ties it all together. You see it?"

Farrell thought about it, nodding excitedly. "That's great. It proves it was Garrett."

"No, it doesn't. But it's physical evidence, which doesn't lie. And it adds to all the circumstantial evidence we already have. You have to ask yourself, what are the chances that all of this is a coincidence? The shooting outside Garrett's buddy's apartment, with a black male being described as the other party, along with an eyewitness identifying Garrett at the scene where the same gun was used in a murder?" Clint shook his head. "The sheer weight of the coincidence tips the scales."

"Sounds like probable cause to me."

"If the bullets match, I agree. Not enough to convict, but probable cause. *If* the ballistics line up."

Farrell knitted his brow. "Do they?"

"I don't know. Ocampo was Marty Hill's case, and the Talbott shooting was investigated by Liberty Lake, with help from the State Patrol. I'm not sure if the lab results on the ballistics are back yet in either case, or if anyone has requested a comparison."

"Well, find out."

Clint clenched his jaw. "Sure, Captain. I'll just go raid another detective's case file. Then I'll drive over to Liberty Lake, break into their police station, and do the same. And when they ask why, I'll tell them I've been running a secret investigation along with my captain for the past twenty-one months. I'm sure they'll understand."

"I didn't mean that."

"Maybe you can use some of your captain magic to get some information for once."

Farrell's expression darkened. "I'm sure you'll figure something out."

"I'm sure *I* will. *I* always do."

Farrell ignored the dig. "While we wait on that, keep on Garrett, even if there's nothing happening there."

Clint unclenched his jaw, working the muscles for a moment. Then he looked directly at Farrell. "The biggest development with Garrett is that I'm pretty sure he knows he's being followed."

Farrell looked alarmed. "He's seen you?"

"I don't know for certain. It's nothing I can prove, just a sense I have."

"Damn it," Farrell muttered. "That's probably why he's been flying so straight."

"Maybe. Or maybe he's clever and is taking no chances. It's not like he needs money. He got the settlement from the city, and this job pays well enough."

"What about his visit with Gary Stone?" Farrell asked. "Did you see that?"

Clint's eyes narrowed. "How'd you know about that?"

"Then you saw it?"

Clint nodded slowly, his mind whirring. Did the captain have a source he wasn't sharing? Since the Garrett incident, he'd always believed he could trust Farrell, if for no other reason than if one of them went down, they both did. Did he need to reconsider? "He stopped by Stone's house for about fifteen minutes last night. How did you know about it?"

"The chief told me earlier today," Farrell said. "Stone told him about it this morning."

"Huh," Clint grunted noncommittally.

"According to Stone, Garrett was there to talk about the suicide call he'd been on right before that. Seventeen-year-old—"

"Bethany Rabe," Clint said. "I know. I was on him that night. So?"

"So Garrett was following up with Stone."

"What does Stone have to do with it?"

"Rabe was connected to city hall." Farrell spread his hands. "What do you think Garrett is up to? Why is he doing follow-up that a detective should be doing?"

"I have no idea, but he's got an angle, believe me."

Farrell tapped his fingers on the steering wheel. "We can't take a direct approach and just have his sergeant ask him about it. Then he'd know we're watching him."

"If he doesn't already," Clint said.

And don't you mean he'd know I'm *watching him?*

"We've got to find a way to hem him in," Farrell said. "Narrow his field."

Clint grunted. He wished there was a way to do that, but if there was, he didn't see it.

"The patrol captain mentioned an idea to me a few days ago. I'd like your take on it."

He sat perfectly still, staring at the captain.

Farrell cleared his throat. "It's sort of a street crimes unit. A couple of small strike teams drawn from patrol. They wouldn't be responding to radio calls but targeting prolific offenders."

Clint continued staring, saying nothing.

"They might have a detective attached, too. You know, to work up search warrants, do follow-up, that sort of thing."

Clint stared.

"What do you think?" Farrell asked.

"I think it's a typical brass idea."

"Typical?"

"As in stupid."

Farrell leaned back. "What's stupid about it? It's not like it's a brand-new concept. Agencies all over the country do it."

Clint shook his head. People used to joke about the department dishing out lobotomies at promotions to go along with the gold bars, and he was starting to think they had a point. "Do you people ever pay attention to history?" he asked. "All kinds of departments put out little units like what you're describing and they get great results, for a little while. Then you know what they get?"

Farrell shook his head. "What?"

"They get Rampart scandal. Or the Chicago SOS mess. First, it's planted evidence, phantom informants, and tampered reports. Before long, you get people beat, stolen money, cops turning into criminals. All kinds of noble cause corruption, every time."

"This isn't Los Angeles," Farrell argued. "Or Chicago. It's different here."

"It's the same." Clint pointed at the captain. "You create an autonomous squad of patrol officers like that and turn them loose, you'll regret it." When Farrell didn't respond immediately, Clint added, "If you don't believe me, trust your own experience. You don't have to look any further than Tyler Garrett."

Farrell's neck reddened slightly. "He's the reason I think it's a good idea."

Clint squinted at him. "How does *that* make any sense?"

"A team like this with Garrett on it solves the problem of narrowing his field." Farrell seemed a little too pleased with himself. "We create a small team around Garrett and catch him in our trap."

"It's still a dumb idea," Clint said.

"Why?"

"For all the reasons I just said. You put Garrett on a team like that, it's like taking him to the buffet. He'll feast on that opportunity. Plus, I can't follow a team like that as easily as I can follow an officer on patrol. But none of that matters, because Garrett is too smart to fall for this. He'll see you coming a mile away."

"Not if we're careful. Not if we do it right."

"You're not putting *me* on that team," Clint said. "I'll tell you *what*."

"I agree. That'd be too obvious. But…"

Clint looked at him, suspicious. "What?"

Farrell shifted uncomfortably in his seat. "Maybe it's time to widen our circle on this."

He looked away abruptly and dropped his car into gear.

"What's wrong?" Farrell asked.

"You're talking stupid," Clint said. "So I'm leaving."

"Stand down," Farrell said forcefully. "That's an order, *Detective*."

Clint glared at him. The captain was testing the bounds of his respect for the chain of command now. He made no move to put the car back into park. "Do you really think you can throw your bars around at this point, *Captain*? Because you ask me, we are way beyond the veil where that's concerned. This is a whole different thing we got going on."

And I don't call you massah.

Farrell stared back at him for a few moments, then his gaze softened. "You're right, Wardell."

"I know I'm right."

"Look, I'm sorry. But at least hear me out, okay? These are thoughts for discussion. Not decisions."

Clint continued to stare, mulling it over. He was unmoved by Farrell's retreat. At the same time, he needed to assess how reliable the captain still was, and how much he could trust the man. There was only one way to do that.

He slammed the car into Park and let his foot fall away from the brake pedal. "Spin your web," he said, crossing his arms.

"I'm wondering if now might be a good time to bring the chief up to speed. Get him on board so that when we—"

"You bring Baumgartner on board, and there is no longer any *we*," Clint said. "He will torch this little operation in a nanosecond. You'll be forced to retire, and I'll probably end up in jail."

"Why do you say that? The chief is old school. He isn't going to want to see this stand. And he could bring some more assets to bear."

Clint snorted. "He's part of the brass, like you. The only thing you can trust less than the brass is a politician, and the chief is both. Him and all the other politicians put this Garrett mess behind them almost two years ago. They don't want to see it come back around." Clint shook his head deliberately. "Do not trust him with this."

"I…" Farrell trailed off, and appeared lost in thought, as if he was contemplating Clint's words.

"There's something else I should tell you," Clint said. "We're not the only ones interested in Garrett. Ray Zielinski came by my desk, asking about him."

Farrell looked surprised. "Zielinski? How could he know anything?"

"He worked with Garrett. He was first to respond to the shooting."

"How much do you think he knows?" Farrell looked worried.

"I don't think he *knows* anything. I believe he *suspects* a lot. But there's no way he has any inside information, or he'd have shared it with me. He seemed to want to see Garrett taken down."

Farrell pointed. "See? There's a guy we could bring onto the strike team. Have him watching Garrett and working with you. It could work."

"It won't work. Like I said, the man is cunning. He'll see Zielinski coming from the jump."

"Maybe not."

"He will. Besides, you really want to be telling someone about everything we know? Everything we did? Because that list ain't pretty, and I don't have any reason to trust Ray Zielinski other than maybe he hates Tyler Garrett."

"We're going to have to come clean eventually."

"I'm fine with full disclosure once we've got Garrett dead to rights. If we can prove all that he did before, and catch him at the same old tricks again, nobody is going to be too worried about what we knew and when, or how we conducted this investigation. Nobody that matters, anyway. Absent that trump card, it's a risk bringing someone else in on what we know. Even if I agreed to doing it, it wouldn't be for Ray Zielinski."

"Who, then?"

"Right now?"

"Yeah."

"Nobody. Right now, I'm starting to wish you didn't know about this, Captain."

A flash of anger crossed Farrell's face. "You don't have to worry about me, Wardell. I'm solid."

Clint didn't answer. He wondered suddenly if the captain had already told the chief and was floating the idea this way to see how he'd react. He watched Farrell's expression to see if he could pry out an answer, but Farrell seemed sincere.

"I know you don't trust anyone," Farrell said. "And I understand why. But that's the problem with you, Wardell. You've got one brilliant foot squarely set in reality, and the other one in the muck and mire of conspiracy theories and distrust. What scares me is that I don't think you realize this or know the difference."

Clint let out a small chuckle. "You're *scared*?"

"I'm concerned, yeah. It doesn't help that you look like you haven't—"

"Maybe you should be scared," Clint interrupted. "We're the last two standing. Everyone else who got in Garrett's way is dead."

Farrell stared at him, slack-jawed.

Chew on that for a while. He put his car in gear and, with a chirp of his tires, accelerated away.

SATURDAY

Fear and lies fester in darkness.
The truth may wound, but it cuts clean.
—Jacqueline Carey, *Kushiel's Avatar*

Chapter 32

Ray Zielinski was drunk by the time he realized he was still partially in uniform. He'd draped his gun belt and vest over the two hooks on the back of his bedroom door and hung his long sleeve shirt in the small closet, but he still wore the black mock turtleneck with the SPD insignia on the throat, his uniform pants, and duty boots.

Meanwhile the bottle of Jameson looked more empty than full, and considering he'd only just cracked the seal after getting home from an extra duty gig, that was no small feat.

The job had been presence detail at one of the local credit unions. They'd been robbed twice in the span of a month, and management decided they needed some extra police attention to reassure customers and employees. He stood around the lobby for six hours, being visible. A half-trained monkey could have done it. It was the most boring way to spend a day that he could imagine, but at least it paid.

The fact it was a Saturday wasn't lost on him. When he asked one of the employees what the hell ever happened to banker's hours, she told him, "We are not a bank and our customers' needs come first."

Zielinski hadn't replied to her, mostly because the first three things that came to his mind would have landed him in Internal Affairs with another demeanor complaint. The teller had that tight-mouthed snooty look that he recognized. She'd never have let his comments pass.

He raised his glass and toasted his own restraint. Then he blurted out all three responses, one after another, laughing darkly as he snapped them out into his tiny, empty apartment.

The toast left his glass drained. He briefly considered capping the bottle. He had a Sunday detail scheduled, after all. But he poured himself another two fingers of Jameson anyway and sat in the only chair in the living room. Even crazy Lyle had a bigger place than he did.

"Can you freakin' believe that?" he said, remembering the man's outburst. "I don't even have a couch. My apartment is so freakin' small and I'm so freakin' broke that I don't even have…" He paused and belched. "…a freakin' loveseat."

This wasn't who he wanted to be. Not some poor schlub without a couch.

It wouldn't be for much longer, he hoped. As long as Amber gave up on her ali*money* extension, he'd start to recover financially. If not, he was screwed. Jody's orthodontic bill was only the start of more expenses for the kids as they became teenagers. And even though he was paying through the nose, neither of them wanted anything to do with him. Sure, some of that was typical teenage angst. But it was also them still being angry over the divorce, and then him marrying Amber. Now that they were getting old enough to have some say in when and how often they visited him, that say was usually *Not today, Dad. I'm busy.*

That he didn't have many windows of opportunity to see them didn't make it any easier. He was either working patrol or working extra duty details. He missed a gymnastics meet a few weeks ago to stand guard at a car show, and you'd think he'd forgotten a birthday *and* Christmas. Besides, he thought it was another gymnastics practice, not a competition.

"Ray, my friend," he told himself in a voice of mock solemnity, "you are hanging on by a very thin thread."

The news from Captain Hatcher yesterday hadn't helped. Another demeanor complaint, this one from Lindsay Wagner. No way that guy wasn't going to follow through, unlike Mr. Big Shot from his previous complaint. He guessed it was about a hundred percent chance this one came back founded, starting the progressive discipline express, and worse yet, getting him suspended from the extra details that were his financial lifeline.

At least it hadn't been the black hole collision.

His mind flashed to the fender bender he didn't report, and his stomach instantly hurt. That's what he initially thought Hatcher was going to bring up when she said he had a new complaint. What was he thinking? Even though he was hammered now, he still realized it had been a bad decision. Trust your future to a *civilian*? Trust one of the people who thought they knew everything about police work and actually knew almost nothing?

"Not smart," he muttered, and took another sip.

At least Neil, the driver, hadn't complained. Even so, it galled him that the whole reason the guy even decided to cut Zielinski a break was because he'd been buddies with Garrett in high school. Or was it college? He couldn't remember, but the two of them played some sport together, and that made Neil think cops were okay people.

"Some of us are, pal," Zielinski said, lifting his glass in a mock toast that nearly sloshed his drink out. "And some of us aren't."

Garrett. Even if all the newspaper said about him wasn't true, and Zielinski was starting to think it might've been, he still didn't like the way Garrett acted like royalty around the department. Yeah, he'd been a good cop before the shooting, or at least seemed like it. But either he pulled some dirty crap, which made him no better than the people they both put in jail, or…what?

Zielinski concentrated on the thought. Or…even if the city tried to screw him over, he still didn't have to act all self-righteous and holier-than-thou about it.

He wished he knew which it was. Knowing might make him feel worse about either Garrett or his own police department, but it wouldn't eat at him like not knowing did.

And Dana, what was her problem? When she'd been a sergeant, she'd been intuitive as hell. During his first divorce, they got coffee frequently, and she always seemed to be able to tell when he needed to talk about what was happening, and when he needed to talk about anything but that. But yesterday, he tried to confide in her about Garrett and all he got was more of the party line. How Garrett was a model officer, and Zielinski shouldn't worry his little mind about it.

He was sure that she'd finally succumbed to the brass infection. He'd seen it many times before. People changed when they got promoted. Most turned into brassholes. Only one in twenty changed for the better or stayed true to their roots. He honestly thought she'd be that one, but he was wrong. She was one of them now.

Which left only one person he could talk to: Detective Ward Clint. Heaven forbid, he actually called the man that.

"Ward!" he yelled into the silence of his apartment.

Where did he get off being so pretentious about his name? At least people could pronounce his name. Try walking around the world with a last name like Zielinski for a while. Still, Clint was good at what he did. For a while now, he'd been sure Clint knew something. His skill as a detective was only over-shadowed by his reputation as *the* Honey Badger.

"He don't give a shit," Zielinski said in a slight falsetto, remembering the YouTube video featuring Clint's namesake. And Clint *didn't* give one, either. In a way, Zielinski respected that. He wondered if it made life easier, or harder.

Clint was a damn good detective. If anyone could figure out if Garrett was the victim or the bad guy, it was Clint. But he said he didn't know a damn thing. He was a typical honey badger son of a bitch, who said…what did he say again?

Zielinski took another sip of the Jameson, even though he knew that wasn't going to help cut through all the booze haze he was floating in. He tried to focus on his conversation with Clint, pulling it from his memory banks, running it through his mind.

He'd practically begged the detective to answer his questions. To tell him he wasn't crazy. Clint had to be able to see how much this was tearing him apart. Instead of helping a brother out, he said…

Zielinski focused.

He said…

Clint's direct tone brayed at him in his mind. *I don't know if you're crazy or not, but your suspicions about this case are not accurate.*

That was it. That was it, word for word. He could sit on the witness stand and testify to it. No compassion, no willingness to help. Just a condescending and dismissive *your suspicions about this case are not accurate…*

Zielinski stopped. Blinked.

He ran the words through his mind again.

Your suspicions about this case are not accurate.

About this case…

One of the things that made Clint a great detective was how precise he was. Every time Zielinski came across him, Clint impressed him with that precision. He was precise across the board, and that included language.

About this *case.*

No way would the man put it that way unless it was an active case for him. He'd say *that* case but not *this* case.

Clint knew. That hard-headed, elitist, anti-social conspiracy nut *knew.*

Zielinski thought on it some more while he sipped. He felt sure about his conclusion, but the skeptical part of his mind kept whispering that it was pretty thin, that he was making something out of nothing, that it was good old Detective Jameson solving this one, and it was all bull.

Maybe. But maybe not.

One thing was for sure. It didn't make his life any easier. It only added another person to the list of people he could no longer trust.

Or could he? Clint was probably keeping his cards close to his chest because he didn't want anyone, including him, to muck up whatever he was working on. Maybe if he had another talk with the man…

Zielinski's chin drooped to his chest, and he almost fell asleep right there. When he jerked back awake, he put down the empty glass, and staggered to the bedroom. He struggled out of his clothing and flopped onto the bed.

As a drunken sleep took him, his last thought was, *I can help you, Honey Badger.*

Chapter 33

Tyler Garrett parked down the block and exited his car. Even though he wasn't on shift, it was still a good operational habit. His eyes scanned the neighborhood as he approached the house.

He'd been by there earlier in the day, but no one had been home. It was his day off, so he was in no hurry to make contact. Truth be told, he didn't know what kind of outcome he was hoping for. This was more of an exploratory meeting. If something came from it, great. If not, he was out nothing but some time.

However, there was nothing gained if he didn't at least try. That's what he was always telling his son, Jake.

Councilman Dennis Hahn lived in a mid-century modern home on the South Hill. It was a pretentious dwelling as far as Garrett was concerned. The yard was professionally groomed. The garden was picture-perfect. And the house looked like it belonged on a magazine cover.

The spring sun had set a couple of hours ago and the house was lit up. Inside, a family moved about. They seemed to be in a good mood as they were laughing. Garrett saw the councilman and a woman he deemed age appropriate for his wife. There were two girls who appeared to be in their late teens. They were giggling and jumping with each other in front of the living room window.

Garrett took the whole scene in as he approached the house. As he got closer, he could see a television on in the living room, but some music drifted outside.

He bounded the stairs to the front of the house and rang the doorbell.

"I'll get it," a female called from inside.

The front door opened, and a teenage girl stood there behind the screen door. She was in black volleyball shorts and a T-shirt. He couldn't put his finger on the song, but it was a popular dance song he'd heard recently in the clubs.

"Hi," the girl said with a bright smile.

"Well, you're not in season," Garrett said.

"Huh?"

"Volleyball. It's a fall sport."

"Oh." Her smile broadened. "I like the shorts."

"Is your dad home?"

"Who should I say is here?"

"Tyler Garrett."

"Be right back," she said, keeping her eyes on him as she walked away.

Garrett waved to her as she left. She giggled then and hurried away. He stepped back and looked into the living room. The television show went to commercial. A blurb for the eleven o'clock news came on highlighting an in-depth investigation into the accusations facing Councilman Patrick Armstrong.

He turned his attention back to the front of the house as Dennis Hahn approached. "Officer Garrett," he said as he pushed the screen door open. "It's good to see you again." Hahn smiled and stuck his hand out which Garrett shook. "Everything okay?"

Garrett was in black slacks and a thin gray sweater. "Yeah, I'm off duty."

"Well, that's a relief. What can I do for you, Ty?"

"You have a nice-looking family, Councilman."

Hahn's smile faded slightly. "Thank you," he said, a hint of suspicion in his voice.

Garrett stepped back on the porch to watch Hahn's wife and daughters through the window, laughing and dancing with each other. The other Hahn daughter wore yoga pants and a tight long-sleeve T-shirt.

"Bad news about Armstrong and Buckner, huh?" Garrett asked.

"Yes," Hahn said, stepping next to Garrett to see what he was watching inside the house.

"They say bad news travels in threes. What do you say to that, *Denny*?"

Hahn glanced at Garrett, to the window, then back to Garrett. Hahn pulled the front door closed, muting most of the dance music. "I've already talked with Officer Stone."

"About what?" Garrett asked, still paying attention to the Hahn women as they laughed and played. "Your wife is very attractive. You did well, Denny. I can see where your daughters get their looks."

The councilman remained silent.

"Say, how old are those girls?"

Hahn pulled back from him. "What?"

"They look about the same age as Betty Rabe. What do you think?" Garrett glanced at the councilman then. "Was she a surrogate for one of them? Maybe both?"

Hahn's eyes snapped to the window then back to Garrett. "No!" The councilman moved away from the window. "It's not what you think."

"I know what it *was*. You were dicking a seventeen-year-old. Doesn't have to be more complicated than that to bring you down. Betty probably reminded you of the one in the yoga pants, right? Although, I think I'm partial to the one in the shorts. That's okay for me to say that, right, Denny? I mean, since you were hooking up with Betty and all."

Hahn's face flushed and his left eye blinked repeatedly.

"You know Betty killed herself, right?"

His face fell. "What? Oh, my God."

Hahn's wife came to the front door then. "Dennis, is everything all right?"

The councilman stared at her. Not saying anything.

Garrett smiled and stepped forward. "I'm Officer Garrett from the police department."

"Leah Hahn," she said and stepped out on the porch. A light sheen of sweat covered her face. She wore faded blue jeans and a thin, light blue sweater. Her teeth were unnaturally white and her lips full. "It's nice to meet you, Officer. Is everything okay?"

"Oh, yes, ma'am, definitely. Everything's fine. There was an issue at city hall earlier today and I'm just getting your husband up to speed on it."

Hahn and Garrett stood silently then, waiting for Leah to either ask another question or leave. She chose the latter.

"Okay, boys, whatever you're cooking up, I'll leave you alone. Dennis, the girls and I are waiting for you to pick the next song."

Leah stepped inside and closed the door.

Garrett glanced to the front window and Hahn's daughters were now watching their interaction. He smiled at them and they giggled.

The councilman turned to him and growled, "Knock it off."

"They're the same age as her, aren't they?"

Hahn leaned toward Garrett and lowered his voice. "Did she really kill herself?"

"How do you think I found out about you?"

The councilman's eyes lowered as he thought. "A note? She left a note?"

Garrett shrugged, but kept his eyes on the Hahn girls.

Hahn spun around to look at his daughters in the window. He shooed them away, then turned back to Garrett. "Do we have to do this now?"

"We can do this whenever you like. Betty will still be dead tomorrow."

Hahn winced. "Can we do it at my office?"

"Fine, Denny, that'll be fine," Garrett said. "I'll see you Monday. Enjoy the rest of the night with your family."

The councilman walked inside and closed the door. Garrett waited for the two girls to return to the window. When they did, he smiled and waved. He whistled softly to himself as he walked down the sidewalk.

Chapter 34

That son of a bitch. He lost me.

Clint knew that tailing someone without being noticed was difficult enough under the best of circumstances. Those included a team of several cars, communicating by radio, and driving nondescript vehicles which blended into the surrounding traffic. Preferably in the daytime. With an unsuspecting target.

Clint was driving his unmarked Crown Victoria, a beast of a police cruiser that was all but extinct. One glance was all it took to make it as police. He was following Garrett alone, at night, and he was pretty sure the slippery bastard knew Clint was there.

While tailing him, they ran into Saturday evening traffic on Division Street. Garrett made the light at Cataldo Avenue, right before the bridge that crossed the Spokane River into downtown, and Clint didn't. He watched Garrett's taillights until they disappeared around the bend. He knew that Garrett had only two options once he made the bend. West on Spokane Falls Boulevard, or south on Browne. Both took him deeper into downtown, although Browne would be the quicker route if he was headed toward the South Hill.

Clint accelerated when the light turned green. He weaved his way through traffic as best he could. When he made the bend, the lights for westbound and southbound traffic were both green. He saw no sign of Garrett's personal vehicle.

Time to choose.

Where's he going?

Clint ran through people Garrett knew and had contacted before. The most likely one that popped up was the little number he'd started seeing recently. All it had taken to find the name of the woman he'd stopped earlier in the week was to check Garrett's unit history. Her name was Tiana Madison Kennedy. A quick cross-reference confirmed her address at a downtown condominium. He'd seen Garrett going into the building on more than one occasion, presumably for a booty call.

And it *was* Saturday night, so…

Clint made his decision, taking Spokane Falls Boulevard. He wended his way through traffic, watching for Garrett's car somewhere ahead of him, but didn't see it. When he reached the block where Miss Kennedy lived, he slowed and trolled along the nearby streets, searching for Garrett's car.

It was nowhere to be found.

He kept looking for another twenty minutes, but after crisscrossing the three-block radius multiple times, he came up empty.

Clint pulled into a vacant metered slot. He didn't bother to put any coins in the meter. No one would ticket a police car, at least not with him sitting in it.

He stared at the condo building up the street. Tiana Kennedy lived on the sixth floor. Clint counted upward and then tried to imagine the layout of the floor. Did she have a city view or a river view? He saw four sets of windows facing the city side. Two were darkened. One was dimly lit with a television. The fourth was bright. Was one of those hers? Or was he looking at the wrong side of the building? He'd have to pull up the building plans tomorrow when he was at his desk and find out.

Then he realized tomorrow was Sunday.

Monday, then.

Down at the street level, the condo had a gated entry to a small parking lot. He wondered for a moment if the gate was accessed via code or a card. If it was a numbered code, it was possible she gave Garrett the code so he could park off-street.

Clint fished out his binoculars and scanned the vehicles inside the condo lot through the lenses. None of them resembled Garrett's.

He lowered the binoculars, admitting the truth.

He'd lost him.

Clint rubbed his tired eyes in frustration.

Garrett must have taken Browne southbound instead of heading east like Clint thought. He'd guessed wrong and Garrett could be anywhere on the South Hill. Or maybe he jumped on the freeway and headed east or west, out of town.

So what now?

He thought for a while, running through all the people Garrett might go visit on a Saturday night. Maybe he was keeping up the good son image and was seeing his mother. But he'd been driving an odd route if that were his destination. Where else? His mentor and friend Oakley was dead and gone. Garrett didn't seem to have any close friends. Clint had only seen him attend group settings, and those were a rarity. Despite being mister popular, outside of his assignations with the occasional woman, Garrett's social life wasn't much more robust than Clint's own.

Maybe that's where he should start. Garrett had a side piece or two around town. He could be with one of them instead of Miss Kennedy, despite her being the current favorite.

Again, though, none of those residences seemed to have been in his flight path.

So where did he go?

After a few minutes, Clint realized his best bet was to try to reacquire Garrett at his home. It was either that or go home himself.

Clint pulled out of the metered slot and headed toward Garrett's residence. He detoured along the way to check the small house that belonged to one of Garrett's older chips, but the house was dark and there was no sign of Garrett's car out front.

Once he reached Garrett's street, he slid into the familiar spot behind the big Ford F-150 up the block. The rig partially hid Clint's unmarked cruiser, and it was at the opposite end of the block from Garrett's usual ingress to his home.

He waited.

Dozens of simultaneous trains of thought whirred through his mind while he sat. It was always that way for him. His brain never tired of zipping around, chasing ideas and questions. Clint was able to somehow hover above the maelstrom, like an observer, monitoring the progress of all the different streams of speculation. Only when he purposefully focused did his concentration narrow to just one topic, and then it was laser-like.

At the moment, he tried to relax and hear all the different thoughts.

The loudest thought was a question—what was taking the lab so long on the Ocampo ballistics results? When he'd gone into Major Crimes that morning, he found the place was empty—detectives didn't work the weekend unless called out for an active crime scene.

Marty Hill's file cabinet was locked, but the desk was old. It didn't take much work for him to jimmy the lock and get a look at the Ocampo file. The status in the computer system when he checked had been Susp-PF, which meant suspended pending further. In this case, the *further* included a return on the ballistics from the state lab. Considering that the lab was currently over four hundred days behind on requests, Clint wasn't surprised to find that the tests were not yet completed. He would have thought a quadruple homicide merited jumping to the front of the line but figured that Hill's lack of an identified suspect or a murder weapon probably negated that advantage.

Speaking of Garrett, why was Ray Zielinski suddenly so interested in him?

And how long was this old Crown Vic going to last? His was the last of the road-worthy Crown Victorias in the fleet.

How many more miles did it have in it before it gave up the ghost and he was forced to accept one of the new Impalas that all the other detectives drove? He was sure those cars had GPS in them, and maybe other surveillance devices so that the brass could check up on him in real time. He figured this old girl had another six or seven months before the garage manager put his foot down on the expenses to keep it on the road. She already burned a little too much oil.

The boyfriend in the Ainsley case was definitely lying about the two black males forcing their way into the house. Now that Clint had the man's story locked in, he needed to figure out the right piece of evidence to use as a lever to pry the truth out of him. Wrapping that one up would make Lieutenant Flowers happy.

No way was he going to notify any next of kin on the Nylander suicide, though. Let the chaplain earn his pay.

Where the *hell* was Garrett?

Farrell was wavering and had been for a while. Clint had known this, but the Baumgartner suggestion was the proof he needed. Was he going to end up flying solo on this? Could he still trust the captain?

What was the one dollar forty-seven cent deduction from his latest paycheck to some vague entry called VSF? He suspected it was a sneaky way to siphon funds for some sort of off book operation, but was it local or federal? No one ever thought to check on such a small amount, which was how they got away with things like that. He made a note to stop by payroll at work tomorrow.

No. Monday.

He rubbed his head, feeling the afro shift under his fingers. Damn, maybe Farrell was right. His cut was getting long. He needed to see the barber tomorrow. Fighting the Sunday church crowd was less than ideal, but he couldn't spare the time on Monday.

The minutes slid past, reaching close to an hour. Every time a pair of headlights appeared on the residential street, Clint focused on the vehicle. Finally, one of them slowed and turned into Garrett's driveway. He could see from the outline that it was Garrett's car. The garage door went up and the vehicle slid inside.

Clint waited, watching the different lights go on throughout Garrett's house. Living room. Bathroom on, then off. Bedroom on, then off. Finally, he saw the telltale flicker of the television behind the blinds of the living room window.

He checked his watch. If Garrett was in now, he was likely in for the night. And Clint needed sleep.

He glanced back up at the living room window, imagining Garrett lounging on his couch, a beer in his hand, watching a movie or some sports. Probably baseball, this time of year.

Where did you go?

Clint let the question sit for a few moments. He knew there'd be no answer, at least not tonight.

He pulled out of his half-hidden spot and cruised up the street, giving Garrett's house one last look as he passed by, then headed home.

Chapter 35

Gary Stone thought it was only supposed to be dinner, something they did often as friends. Rarely had it ever rolled into a night of drinking. That wasn't the type of thing they normally did when alone nor would they seek to do when together. Going to clubs was what they did in college while in the company of other people.

They were at The Hot Box, the latest in a series of nightclubs that would open for a couple years, garner a lot of attention, then flame out.

The beat pulsating from the large, hanging speakers above the dance floor was loud and fast. The dim club was lit by neon lights and flashing bulbs. The dance floor was full of bodies, jumping, jiggling, and jerking, both in and out of rhythm to the beat.

Jean Carter leaned over to Stone. "Check her out," she said and nodded to a blonde girl dancing with a brunette. The two women were obviously enjoying the company of each other.

Stone watched the blonde, his hand wrapped around his drink.

"I think she's Eastern European," Jean said. "Probably Russian, just the way you like them."

Stone said, "You can't tell that from here." He squinted, though, and tried harder to see the girl in the dim light of the club.

"Sure I can," she answered, confident as ever.

Jean Carter and he had been friends since college, when he was dating her best friend and she was dating his brother. Neither of those relationships worked out, but they learned they liked each other as friends. They shared mutual interests such as books and music, although the genres in those categories were wildly apart. He preferred nonfiction and jazz, while she enjoyed science fiction and electronica. Both were open to reading or listening to the other's recommendation. They shared other interests such as baseball and exotic coffee.

The club tonight was Jean's idea and the choice of music was definitely her style. He would have chosen some place quieter. She seemed to be upset and wanted to go out for a late dinner and a drink.

As the two girls danced with each other, Stone realized how much he also needed a night out to blow off some steam. The two girls rubbed against each other as they danced. They're pretty, Stone thought.

I wonder if she's really Russian?

"Let's go," Jean said, tapping his shoulder.

"What? Where to?"

"Outside. You're getting that goofy stare. You know the one I'm talking about. Let's get some air."

He lifted his drink, but Jean covered it with her hand. "After we go outside."

"All right," he said and let Jean pull him out the front door and past the bouncers.

When Stone was offered the assignment at city hall, he jumped at it partly because of the opportunity it presented, but also the proximity it would put him to his friend. Jean had worked as an assistant for years. At times, he'd encouraged her to move on, to take something more challenging, but Jean liked where she was. It suited both her ambitions and her personality. She had no desire to climb a ladder but wanted to be where interesting things happened. Now that he was stationed within the building, he no longer suggested she look for something else.

Outside the club, they were met with the shock of a cool spring night. They walked away from the entrance and Jean aided Stone as he leaned against the brick building.

"You okay, boy-o?"

Stone nodded. "I'm good."

"You're hitting it pretty hard and here I was the one who wanted the night out."

"Been awhile," Stone said, his words heavy and slow. Even so, he was careful not to drag Jean into the Betty Rabe drama. "You're not exactly drinking like a nun, either."

"Drinking like a nun? What kind of analogy is that?"

Stone's smile was crooked. He laughed. "A drinking nun. That's stupid."

She joined in his laughter.

For dinner, they'd eaten pho at Viet Dong and the conversation was careful never to get around work. It focused on their interests and the friends they shared. Whenever work did come up, both quickly steered the topic back to a safe haven.

"So what's going on with you?" Stone asked. "Everything okay?"

Jean turned and leaned against the wall next to him. "No. Not at all."

"What's up?"

"Hahn's acting all weird."

Stone faced her. "Weird, how?"

Jean shook her head. "I shouldn't say."

Stone smiled. "Is okay. You can tell me. 'Sides, I won't remember tomorrow, anyway."

Her eyes met his and she seemed to be considering something before she spoke. "He lent me out to Patterson."

"That sounds kinky."

Jean hit him with the back of her hand. "Don't be gross. She wants me to ask around HR about the Armstrong investigation. See what I can find. I think they're scheming something, and I don't like it."

"Huh." Stone wondered if the Armstrong mess had been what she'd meant earlier in the week when she said something about things getting worse. He tried to focus on the thought, but his mind couldn't grab on firmly.

"I don't like being used that way," Jean said, her voice hardening. "Makes me feel…dirty, you know?"

He fought through the haze of alcohol. "I understand."

"There's also a rumor circling around that Hahn is somehow involved with the death of a girl. You know anything about that?"

He studied his friend before answering, but it was probably too long, he realized. "No, I don't."

"It's probably not true, but if you know something, Gary, you need to tell me."

Stone slowly blinked several times, but he didn't say anything.

"Because if it was Shelley Mason, I can confirm that she was an intern he was fooling around with last year. It didn't last long before she was asked to leave. If something happened to her, I don't know what I would do."

"Shelley Mason?"

Jean nodded.

"She was asked to go?"

"It was wrong, but HR wasn't involved. Holy crap, can you imagine if they knew about that with all this other drama going on?"

"Who asked her to go?"

Jean looked away, so he immediately knew the answer.

"You?"

"He asked me to, and I did it."

"Why?"

"Because I thought he was a good boss who made a single mistake. Now, I'm not so sure. I mean, having me do that stuff for Patterson, that really, you know, it made me mad. I didn't want him to get into trouble with Shelley, though. Do you understand? And I didn't want her to get dragged through the mud."

"Did she go?"

Jean suddenly looked sad. "Yeah. She was…, she was a nice girl. She was sad, too, but, you know, she saw the writing on the wall. She didn't want to be there any longer either."

"No one else knew?"

"Just Hahn and me, I think."

Stone leaned his head back against the brick wall. "Damn."

"Yeah. Damn."

The club's music continued to pulsate as people passed by, ignoring them. Stone turned to her. "Jean, why didn't you tell me about this when it happened?"

"I wasn't proud that I did it. Have you ever done something you're not proud of? You don't go tell the world about it. You just shut up, keep it to yourself, and do your job."

Stone stared straight ahead, her words ringing in his ears.

"Boy-o," Jean said, patting his shoulder, "I think I'm done. Call me tomorrow."

She left without another word, leaving him with his thoughts.

After exiting his Uber ride home, Stone stumbled to his front door. Once inside, he locked his house and put his back against the door. He inhaled and exhaled, working hard to regain control over the alcohol in his system.

Shelley Mason.

Stone repeated the name again, not wanting to forget it. She was another girl that Hahn had used and discarded. Had her dreams of being in city hall been dashed by her proximity to the councilman?

His eyes locked on to the report sitting on his kitchen counter. He walked heavily over to the counter and stared at it. His face twisted in anger as he snatched the report. With both hands, he applied tension in opposite directions. The papers began to tear, but he stopped.

Jean's words haunted him then.

Have you ever done something you're not proud of?

He dropped the papers back on the counter and sprinted to the bathroom. He flipped open the toilet lid, dropped to his knees, and vomited.

SUNDAY

*Worry never robs tomorrow of its sorrow,
it only saps today of its joy.*
—Felice Leonardo "Leo" Buscaglia,
author and motivational speaker

Chapter 36

Dana Hatcher allowed herself to sleep in. She and Maggie Patterson had gone out for a few drinks last night, and while she wouldn't have said she was drunk, she definitely had been feeling the vodka. Maggie seemed to be able to drink incessantly and hardly be affected, other than becoming a little more…well, a little more Maggie.

They'd met a couple of guys about halfway through the night and spent an hour or two dancing and drinking. She actually got to laugh last night, and that felt good.

When they left the bar, they tried to take a walk through Riverfront Park, but it was after midnight and she knew the park was closed. Security roamed around on bikes, shooing out stragglers and people who wandered in unaware of the park curfew.

Even though Hatcher knew this, she didn't say a word when the group decision came about. She wasn't sure why, other than that for one night, she didn't want to be a cop. Just a woman out for drinks and dancing and some fun. So she held her tongue while they made the short walk to the park.

Luckily, another couple was walking out as they approached and warned them about the curfew.

"The park Nazis are booting everyone out," one guy said.

"Closing the park is ridiculous," his drunk boyfriend added. "It's public land."

Maggie looked at her with a raised brow to confirm the park hours. Hatcher nodded, ending their big adventure.

As the group split up, Maggie offered her date a ride. Since both of the men had used Lyft to get to the bar, there was little pretense in the offer, and he immediately accepted. They said their goodbyes, Maggie hugging Hatcher and whispering lurid suggestions in her ear, until Hatcher laughed and pushed her away. The new couple walked away, arm in arm.

The other man, an art teacher name Kailer, stood watching them go, before turning awkwardly toward her. "So…?"

Hatcher took out her phone. "You need an Uber?"

He was disappointed but took it well. That was part of the reason why she'd said yes when he asked if he could call her sometime. They exchanged numbers and easy conversation while they waited for his ride. He gave her a short goodbye kiss, but it had been a good one, and made her glad that she might see him again.

She wished at times that she was as fearless as Maggie, but her days of going to bed with a man two hours after meeting him were long past. The truth was, those days had been fleeting enough, not fitting with her other life choices. As much as she wished she could forget about being a police officer for a short time, deep down she knew she could never completely *not* be a cop. She would always be careful. It was her nature, and her nature led her to this profession. The profession, in turn, reinforced her nature.

Lying alone in the warmth of her bed, she replayed all of this in her mind. She felt a tinge of regret, and maybe a little sadness, but mostly the whole night made her happy.

Ray Zielinski wasn't happy. His head throbbed. His mouth was dry and tacky. His stomach did flip-flops, and any thought of food or another drink almost sent him into the bathroom.

I could probably make the toilet from here. If I just got a little arc on it, I could puke right into the bowl from here.

He lay in his bed for a long while, unable to think of anything except how bad he felt. When he finally looked at his clock, he groaned.

He sat up. Cymbals crashed in his head.

Coffee.

And aspirin. Some antacids for the road.

He looked at the clock again. No time for a shower. His extra duty detail awaited him, and he was going to be lucky if he made it there on time.

Zielinski forced himself to stand and slowly pulled on his police uniform.

Margaret Patterson sat at her kitchen table and watched her children play outside.

The two seemed to be happy, chasing each other around in the backyard. She wouldn't admit it to most people, but motherhood wasn't her deal. She'd had the children for her husband, because she thought that's what a loving wife was supposed to do.

As the children grew, Patterson had an uneasy feeling that something was broken inside her. She just didn't connect with either of them the way that her husband did. It didn't matter whether it was the boy or the girl, she looked at them both like miniature aliens living in her house. The maternal instinct that so many others prattled on about was a mystery to her. She could pretend she had it when she needed to, but most of the time, the kids were little roommates who made messes that she was required to clean up.

Regardless, that didn't mean she was going to roll over at the divorce proceedings and let her husband have them. Quite the opposite. She fought for everything she could get, including custody. Besides, he was the one who wanted the legal separation, not her. Of course, she'd come back over the top to demand the actual divorce. She had thought their marriage was working just fine, thank you very much. He was the one who suddenly developed a need to search for meaning in his life, not her.

He claimed it was because he was unhappy, and the universe was pushing him in a new direction. It sounded like new age woo-woo to her. More than likely, he had a girlfriend stashed somewhere. She never found evidence of such, but it didn't mean she would ever stop believing that was the reason he wanted out. Why else would a man throw away seven years of a perfectly good marriage?

The kids continued to run around the backyard. Patterson tried to understand what they were doing. It looked like they were playing some weird game with a wiffleball bat, a deflated football, and a naked Barbie doll. She rolled her eyes. As long as the two of them stayed outside, it was fine with her. She didn't need to know the rules to that game.

She sipped her cup of coffee and thought about last night. Dana was always fun to hang out with, even if she was a bit uptight. Patterson figured that was the cop in her. It was good to have her around, though. It balanced out her wild side which she struggled to control following her divorce. Getting older hadn't helped.

Which was evidenced by her offering to drive Tanner home. It must have been his longish hair that did it for her. It definitely wasn't the stupid earring. And what kind of grown man owns a boutique guitar shop? Talk about arrested development. But he was cute and that was enough for a moment's distraction.

Thank God she didn't go up to his apartment with him. That would have been too much shame to bear. The hand job she gave him reminded her of a high school rendezvous and it seemed to make him happy. She would like to blame the moment on the vodka tonics, but she knew exactly what she was doing. He hadn't been forceful or even coercive. In fact, it was her idea. She just didn't want to go home after dropping him off, but she didn't want to go upstairs with him either. And, there was absolutely no way she would go down on him. She wasn't *that* kind of woman.

As he slid out of the car, he'd asked if he could see her again. Of course, she lied and told him he could.

Outside, her son hit the Barbie doll across the yard with the bat and her daughter ran away with the deflated football, holding it over her head as a trophy. She wanted to say that there was a metaphor for life in there, but the two of them were giggling wildly.

She sipped her coffee. *Nobody has that much fun in their adult lives.*

Captain Tom Farrell ate brunch with his wife, Karen. They'd been together since his first year of college. That had actually been his *only* year of college for a long time, as he'd left school to join the police force. He and Karen had been together for almost eight months at that point, and when she told him she was pregnant, the decision to become a cop was an easy one.

The pregnancy failed, with their unborn daughter inexplicably dying in the womb at the six-month mark. One terrible procedure later, the whole idea of their new little family was gone. They'd tried again, but nothing ever came of it. At some point, they both came to terms with their fate, and moved on. Karen went back to college and coaxed him to do the same once he'd made sergeant. He had her to thank for his bachelor's degree as much as anything he'd done to earn it.

And yet, she was one more person he lied to, that he kept from telling this huge secret he'd been hiding for almost two years.

It was exhausting.

"You want to try my eggs Benedict?" Karen asked.

Farrell shook his head.

Karen looked at him with concern. "You love eggs Benedict."

"I'm full," he told her.

She glanced at his half-eaten plate, then back to him. "Tom, is everything all right?"

"Everything's fine."

A slight look of hurt crossed her face. Most people might have missed it, but Farrell knew her expressions. She knew he was lying, and he'd wounded her.

"Is it work?" she asked. "You know you can talk to me about it. Maybe I can help."

I wish I could.

He forced a smile. "It's just some logistical crap I have to work out for the chief's command staff meeting tomorrow. Honestly, I should have stayed a sergeant." He motioned toward her plate. "Here, let me try a bite of that."

Clint slid into the barber's chair. He'd managed to come at the perfect time. The pre-church crowd had cleared out and the post-church crowd hadn't yet arrived. He even ended up with Abe, who was his favorite of the three barbers. Abe understood that most things aren't right in the world.

"Damn," Abe muttered, as he shook out the hair apron and spread it over Clint. "You're overdue, son."

"I've been busy."

Abe fastened the apron's collar. "A man can't ever be too busy to take care of his own hair. People judge you by your 'do."

"I hear that."

"And by *what* you do." Abe grinned at his own joke. "What you want, Wardell?"

"Tight," Clint said. "I want it tight."

Abe set at getting him correct.

Tyler Garrett pulled to the curb outside the small convenience store at Market Street and Rowan Avenue. The area had seen hard times over the past several decades and had not experienced the recent gentrification that other parts of the city had. The bright afternoon sun highlighted the ugliness the neighborhood did not bother to hide.

He rolled his window down and made eye contact with the Native American man leaning against the bus stop sign. He wore a red sweat suit and a dirty, white baseball cap turned backwards. The man slowly looked both directions then returned his attention to Garrett. He nodded once, a barely perceptible movement to anyone not watching.

Garrett pressed the accelerator, swung back into the lane of traffic before turning into the parking lot. The car stopped in the middle of the lot.

A tall, white man in a dirty, yellow windbreaker and a black beanie exited the convenience store and approached Garrett's car. He walked around the front to the driver's side. The gaunt man leaned on the open window and smiled, revealing a missing front tooth.

"How's business?"

"You tell me," Garrett said, not bothering to look directly at the man.

"Things is picking up. You know, you know. Making some headways into new neighborhoods. You know how it is, right?"

"I know how it is, Skunk," Garrett said, his eyes continually scanning the street. A couple of young kids rode their bikes southbound on the sidewalk.

Skunk looked up and over the roof of the car. Garrett's eyes flashed to his rearview mirror and saw the Indian at the bus stop nod.

The gaunt man bent back down and smiled, revealing the hole in his mouth again. "We good?"

"We're good."

Skunk reached into the car and shook Garrett's hand. When he was done, he turned and strolled back into the convenience store. Garrett opened his glove box and tossed a roll of uncounted twenty-dollar bills into it. There would be time to count it later.

He then dropped the car into gear and left the parking lot.

Chief Robert Baumgartner sat on the deck of his lake house, watching the sun dip in the sky. It had been a warm spring day, and a good one. He'd spent it with his girlfriend, Darla. She'd talked him into a short hike, which really meant a long one. Although he wasn't too excited about it initially, he felt good when they reached the summit of the small butte. They'd found a nice spot in the sun, spread a blanket and had a pleasant picnic, including some wine that she surprised him with, pulling it out of her backpack with a flourish. They ate and drank and laughed. If the little clearing wasn't so close to the path, and if he wasn't the chief of police, they might have risked going a little further than the few kisses they'd exchanged while chatting.

In a way, he was glad for the restriction. Darla was a smart woman, and she knew way more about a lot of things than he did. Politics, policing, guns, and football were all subjects in which he was the master and she the student. Everything else, it was her. He enjoyed learning new things from their conversations, and even the casual ones like during their picnic were revelatory for him.

Now, sitting on his deck with a cold beer in his hand while Darla napped on the couch, he was about ready to call this a perfect day. There was more to come, he imagined, but it had already been outstanding.

So why was he thinking about Mayor Sikes? And Councilman Hahn?

Why was he wondering how Gary Stone was doing, or what Officer Garrett was up to?

He almost called Tom Farrell. He reached for his department phone but stopped himself.

It's a perfect day.

Don't mess it up.

Gary Stone sat alone in his house. The TV was off, and his computer was powered down. There was no music playing. Reading a book held no interest to him.

Instead, he silently sat on the edge of his bed, staring at the picture on the wall. He'd taken the photograph several winters ago while visiting an uncle in Montana. It was of a snow-covered bison.

He wasn't sure why the moment appealed to him so much when he took the photo with his cell phone. It was a cold and windy day. The falling snow was heavy and had quickly accumulated. As he took the photo from the roadside, the bison stood there, eyeing him with something that Stone guessed was apathy. There seemed no curiosity nor fear in the animal's eyes. Stone was so proud of how the photo turned out that he had it blown up and professionally framed.

He also wasn't sure why it appealed to him in moments like this, but the lonely animal touched something stoic in him. The bison stood solid and unwavering while the elements beat down on him. His heavy exhale of breath plumed in the cold, winter air below his muzzle. Gary often wondered if he would be capable of being so resilient in his life, especially in trying times.

For the first time since he became a police officer, Stone didn't look forward to returning to work. It no longer held the promise of excitement nor the opportunity to experience something fresh.

Instead, it held an implied threat to his well-being. It was a new danger not from strangers or even criminals, but rather from those he worked with closely to protect and serve the community. During the academy, one of the instructors warned him that there would be more stress from within the department and city hall than he would ever experience out on the street. At the time, he hadn't been willing to believe it.

Those words now seemed prophetic.

MONDAY

For there is nothing hidden that will not be revealed, and nothing concealed that will not be known and illuminated.
—Luke 8:17

Chapter 37

Day shift roll call came early, something Ray Zielinski still wasn't used to, even this far into his tenure on this new assignment. Having to be in the drill hall, in uniform, and ready to go for a six a.m. roll call was nothing short of brutal.

Especially with the kind of weekend he'd had.

"Hey, Ray," Ben Varone greeted him. "You look like hell."

Zielinski grunted. Varone was always blunt, but that didn't bother him. Seeming way too alert this early in morning was another matter. He hated him for that.

"Let's get coffee right after roll call," Varone said. "We'll get you fueled up."

Zielinski grunted again.

Varone settled into his chair and checked his watch. "Only five fifty-four. I could have slept another six minutes this morning."

"Don't act like you weren't up at three," Zielinski croaked. Man, his voice sounded horrible. His throat was still raw from the puking he did that morning. A first-thing vomit sucked, but he had to get the poison out.

"Three thirty," Varone admitted. "I hit the gym, but I don't think I'm going to be going there anymore."

"You giving up on working out?" Varone was a fitness nut, so Zielinski doubted that was the case.

"No. I'll just have to find another gym. Bummer, too, because their collection of free weights is great."

"I don't get it," Zielinski said. "Why a new gym?"

Varone frowned. "I had a beef with a guy there last week. After I lifted, I checked out the racquetball challenge court. Some dude was there, so we played. He played dirty but was one of those pussies who whines when you dish it back. You know the type. I bumped him a little, he started a yelling match, and it got…physical."

"You fought?"

"He started it."

"Did he know you're on the job?"

"No," Varone said. "And after everything broke up, we talked it out. I even bought him a protein shake at the bar while we cooled down."

"So what's the problem? The gym management?"

Varone shook his head. "Some other civilian saw it all, and then heard from someone else that I might be a cop. He called in a complaint to Internal Affairs. It didn't take much detective work for them to run through the membership lists to figure out it was me. Hell, we get a law enforcement discount at the gym, so even Sutherland's cheese-eaters can follow that trail of breadcrumbs."

Zielinski froze, staring at him. The idea of another civilian seeing him tap Neil's car and calling 911 never occurred to him. He imagined a concerned citizen reporting how they'd just seen a police officer hit another car. Dispatch would check for any units currently out on a collision and see none. The supervisor would forward the anomaly to Internal Affairs.

"I'm sure it'll end up a founded demeanor complaint," Varone continued. "But who cares? My file is clean. All of my complaints are old and have timed out of my active file. Besides, I'm in the KMA club, as of February. They come down too hard on me and I'll just say 'kiss my ass,' and retire."

How long would it take for Internal Affairs to figure out who was in that collision, Zielinski wondered. There were only so many officers on day shift. Many of them would have been out on calls at the time. Some were on days off. The field of possibles would be small enough to call them all in for an interview. The question would be straightforward enough. "Were you in a crash at this approximate location on this date?" He couldn't lie to IA. That was a death sentence. So they'd find it was him. Then things would get nasty.

"You okay, Ray?" Varone asked. "Your stomach take a trip south?"

"Rough weekend," Zielinski said quietly.

"I bet." Varone clapped him on the shoulder. "We'll get some eggs and coffee in you in about…" he checked his watch again, muttering, "Two minutes to roll call, seven minutes of blah, blah, blah from the lieutenant, five minutes to get a car, three-minute drive to Waffles 'n More…what's that? Less than twenty minutes?"

Zielinski gave him a weak smile.

Varone chuckled at him. "You definitely need a cup, brother. After that, things'll be better."

Chapter 38

It was only a few minutes after eight and Councilman Dennis Hahn was already waiting outside Gary Stone's office. Hahn hadn't noticed him yet and, for a moment, Stone thought about turning around and leaving the seventh floor. Maybe he could run down the stairs, slip out the side entrance, and spend the day at the police department. There were plenty of other assignments that Stone had beyond city hall. He could keep himself busy and easily avoid Hahn. That would take care of today, but there would always be tomorrow. Whatever Hahn wanted, he knew it would somehow involve Betty Rabe. He could not escape moments like this forever.

Then he remembered the photo of the bison standing in the snow and it gave him a strange calm. Stone continued walking toward the councilman. He recalled standing outside The Hot Box with Jean on Saturday.

What was the girl's name that Jean said?

When Hahn recognized Stone, he forced a smile, but it did little to hide the anger seething underneath. He was dressed stylishly, and his short hair was gelled to perfection, but his eyes were panicked behind his tortoise-shell frames.

Stone nodded as he walked past Hahn and into his office. "Good morning, Councilman. Are you waiting for me?"

Hahn dropped the pretense of a smile. "Why else would I be outside your office?"

"I don't know," Stone said. "I hadn't thought about it."

The councilman swung the office door shut, causing it to slam. He scowled and looked through the window to see if his action had caught the attention of anyone in the outer office.

Stone dropped his interoffice mail onto his desk and sat in his chair. He envisioned the bison in the snowstorm.

Be the bison.

When the councilman turned back to look at him, he said, "Call Tyler Garrett."

"About what?"

"You know what."

Stone certainly did know, but he wasn't going to be bullied by Hahn. He didn't respect the man and he was trying to focus on developing the mindset of the bison this morning.

The cold does not affect the bison.

Stone remained silent and stared at the councilman.

"The hell is that?"

"What?"

"The stupid look you're giving me."

"I'm waiting for you to tell me what you want."

"I want you to run interference on Garrett. He came by my house on Saturday night and threatened me."

Stone leaned forward. "He threatened you?"

"Most definitely, he did. He came to my house and said he knew."

"Knew what?" Stone asked, refusing to play along.

"He knew about Beth Rabe, you simpleton."

Stone leaned back and crossed his arms. He worked to envision the bison again.

The falling snow does not bother the bison.

Hahn patted the air with his hands. "Hey, now, I'm sorry about calling you that. I'm under a lot of stress. You understand what that's like, right? I mean, this whole Beth thing has us all upset."

"She liked to be called Betty," he said.

"What? No. That's ridiculous. Her name was Beth. I always told her how pretty I thought that name was. She knew I liked it."

Stone watched Hahn, refusing to engage him further. He struggled to envision the photo, but he remembered the look in the bison's eyes.

The bison is apathetic to those smaller than him.

"So, anyway, Garrett asked me a bunch of questions about her. Did you tell him about her letter?"

"No," Stone said, realizing only after he'd spoken how easily the lie came.

"He said she killed herself. I tried to call her, but she didn't answer."

"Why didn't you call her parents?"

"Don't be a jerk, Stone."

Stone held his breath and thought about the picture. The bison seemed more obscured by the snow. His vision of the picture was not as he remembered it.

"Don't you go to the same church?" Stone asked.

"She was coming to church for a bit, but her parents don't believe. They didn't attend."

"You could have called her friends."

"Are you doing this to just needle me? I'm asking for your help and you say stupid stuff like that. No, I couldn't call her friends. Think about what you're saying here."

"Garrett is investigating her suicide. Tell him the truth."

"Have you lost your mind? You're supposed to work with us."

The bison seemed smaller in the picture than he remembered it. Stone's mind was now playing tricks on him. He concentrated harder to bring it in focus but was trying to stay engaged in the conversation with the councilman.

To control himself, Hahn looked up at the ceiling. "I can't talk to Garrett. He's like super cop."

Stone nodded. "Yeah, he's pretty good."

"He already knows what I did. He'll make me confess and I'll be ruined."

"You know, I didn't make those choices, you did."

Hahn's mouth opened. "You didn't just say that."

"What?"

"You're blaming her death on me?"

As hard as he tried to envision the photograph, the bison was completely obscured by the snow now.

"I didn't say it like that," Stone said. "I was only trying to say, you know, that you make your own choices. We all do. I'm not responsible to clean up your mistakes any more than you're responsible to clean up mine."

Hahn's mouth fell open.

"I want you out of city hall, Stone."

He felt his courage ebbing, so he stood to be on equal footing with Hahn. "I work where the chief tells me to work."

"Well, it's not going to be here any longer."

"This is the seventh floor," Stone said. "You don't have any authority here. You'll need to talk with the mayor."

Hahn pointed at Stone. "You just crossed a line, my friend. If it's the last thing I do, I'm going to ruin your career. And when I do, I want you to remember this moment."

Regardless of how much he struggled, Stone could no longer envision the bison in the snowstorm.

Chapter 39

Command staff meetings were never high on Captain Tom Farrell's list. In his opinion, they ruined Monday mornings. He liked Baumgartner well enough, but he often let the meetings go on much longer than needed. Everyone got a say, even if not everyone had something worth saying.

That morning, aside from a quick update on a couple of higher profile investigations, he had nothing for the good of the order. As usual, Barry, the administrative captain, blathered on about numerous things, most of which might have been worth discussing at the sergeant level, but weren't command-level concerns. Farrell guessed that looking important was more the point the man was going for, and quantity over quality was the approach he took.

Ellis, the civilian member who commanded crime analysis, records, and other civilian functions within the department, was even more concise than Farrell had been. He was grateful for that and made a mental note to take the guy to coffee later in the week.

When Ellis finished, Baumgartner turned to Dana Hatcher. She had her game face on this morning, so he had a pretty good idea what was coming. At least her idea would be worth spending some time on, unlike the thimble counting that Barry had been doing.

"Chief, we've all had a chance to see the NIBRS advance report," Hatcher said, "as well as the more recent statistics Ellis's crime analysts have put together."

"I haven't had a chance to review those yet," Barry said.

"None of it overlaps with your division," Farrell responded, unable to resist the not-so-subtle dig.

"The numbers are ugly," the chief said. "Let's leave it at that. Dana?"

"Sir, I believe we need to be proactive about this issue. We keep chasing our tails, taking calls, writing reports, doing follow-up, but we're constantly behind the curve."

"What do you suggest?" Baumgartner asked briskly. "And don't say you need more cops, because number one, there isn't any money in the budget, and number two, even if there was, I can't just go to the cop store and grab you a few off the shelf. Any new recruits are eighteen months out before they're trained up enough to help you."

"I realize that, sir," Hatcher said evenly. "I have a plan that will utilize existing resources from within patrol."

Baumgartner waved for her to continue.

"Historically, a large amount of our crimes are perpetrated by a small number of criminals. They—"

"I've always heard that," Barry said. "Is there statistical support for the claim, or is that just popular myth?"

Hatcher gave him a look that clearly said he should shut the hell up. Barry's small grin in reply was smug.

"It's anecdotally true," Baumgartner said. "But could we quantify that, Ellis? Could your whiz kids pull that data?"

"Yes," Ellis said, "but it would be a massive undertaking, the equivalent of a master's thesis or a doctoral dissertation. I can't spare the analyst time."

"Michelle Tremblay said the same thing when I asked her," Hatcher said. "And—"

"Who's Michelle Tremblay?" Barry asked.

"She's my senior crime analyst," Ellis answered. He turned back to Hatcher. "Sorry for the interruption."

Hatcher's gaze flicked to Barry. Farrell could see that her patience with him was waning. "No problem," she said. "She said it was too big a project, but she asked her other analysts for their best guess and made her own ballpark estimate, and collectively, they believe about five percent of the criminals are causing at least seventy percent of the crime."

"No way," Barry said. "I can't believe that."

Hatcher set her jaw. "Are you basing that on all your experience as a crime analyst, Barry?"

"No, but I am basing it on thirty-one years of law enforcement experience."

Farrell couldn't stop himself from rolling his eyes. Barry had managed to worm his way into specialty positions outside of operations for the majority of his career. What little time he was actually assigned to patrol was spent parked in his cruiser, tucked into safe little nooks all across the city, studying for promotional exams.

You're not a cop. You're an accountant.

"Well excuse me if I'm going to defer to the people who are actually reviewing police reports every day," Hatcher said, "not quartermaster invoices."

"Easy…" the chief rumbled. "We're all friends here. Dana, tell me your plan."

Hatcher met the chief's gaze. "If the estimate Michelle gave me is even close to accurate, it seems clear that we need to target these prolific offenders. If we can arrest them and get them out of circulation, it should reduce our crime rate substantially."

"How do you propose to do that?"

"I'm going to create a specialized team of patrol officers, drawn from existing manpower. To start with, it'll be a team of four. If successful, I'll add four more officers and we'll field two teams, working opposite shifts from each other to increase coverage."

"Doing what?"

"Targeting these offenders."

"What do you mean by 'targeting'?" Barry chimed in. "That sounds like profiling."

"We will target prolific criminals based upon their current criminal behavior. It isn't profiling. Not even close."

Barry, you're an idiot, Farrell thought. He liked how Hatcher put him in his place.

Hatcher glanced down at her notes. "As it stands, these criminals go on a mini-crime spree, doing damage to three, four, five victims in a row. These cases get reported a day later, maybe assigned for follow-up to different detectives, maybe not. Each event is treated separately, and by the time any heat from these crimes reach the perpetrator, they've already moved on to another six or eight victims. They probably don't remember the crime well enough to confess to it if they wanted to."

"It sounds like we're in a sorry state," Baumgartner said. Farrell caught the slightest bit of irritation in his tone. He hoped Hatcher did, too.

"We're always playing catch up," she explained. "We're like…" She paused, looking for the right analogy.

"Like Lucy and Ethel at the chocolate factory," Farrell supplied. "We can't wrap the candy quickly enough. The pieces just keep coming down the conveyor belt."

"Exactly."

"It's been this way, more or less, since 1960," Baumgartner grumbled.

"Sir?"

Baumgartner waved her question away. "Tell me the rest of your plan."

"That's the main thrust of it," Hatcher said, a little flummoxed. "Tom said he'd provide a single detective to the team, to handle search warrants and follow-up, as well as coordinate with the prosecutor."

"That's it?"

"I mean…" Hatcher paused before continuing, "Yes, sir. That's the broad strokes of it." She lifted a small packet of papers. "I have more details here. Logistics, scheduling, potential candidates."

Baumgartner seemed to think about it for all of six seconds. "I appreciate your efforts, Captain, but I'm going to deny your proposal."

"Proposal? Sir, it's a plan that I intend to—"

"Plan, proposal, whatever. It is denied."

Hatcher stared at the chief in what looked to Farrell like a cross between disbelief and anger. "May I ask why?"

Baumgartner took a deep breath and let it out. He glanced at his watch. "Yeah, all right. I'll tell you my reasons. But first, let me say that I appreciate your effort, and I agree with you that we have an obvious problem here. What you propose isn't a viable solution."

Hatcher stared at him, seeming to be waiting for his explanation.

"For starters, you don't have the staffing for this. Every body you pull off of patrol means more calls for service that the poor bastards left in the district have to answer."

"Sir, if the team targets the top offenders, those report calls will drop dramatically, and—"

"I heard your plan," the chief said tersely. "Do you want to know why I denied it?"

Hatcher pressed her lips together briefly, then gave him a short nod.

Careful, Dana. Baumgartner was generally fair, but he could get prickly at times. Especially if he was interrupted.

The chief held up one finger. "Insufficient staffing. Let's face it, that right there is a deal-killer, even if there weren't other considerations. How do you implement a plan with insufficient bodies to fill holes? You can't." He held up a second finger. "Direction. I assume you're going to select your hard chargers for this team? Real meat-eaters?"

Hatcher nodded, her face reddening. "Of course."

"I would, too. They'd be a perfect fit. Except that most of those guys are very headstrong and almost every one of them has their own particular thing that they are into. You cut them loose in a small group, untethered from answering calls for service, they're going to chase whichever rabbits interest them the most. Whatever crimes are the sexiest to them. That's what they'll focus on, whether it's part of your five percent or not."

"Sir, that's why I'd tell them what I want them to focus on. They'd be directed—"

"What? From your office?" Baumgartner shook his head. "No, once those kind of cops get out into the field, your directives won't mean much, if anything. They'll be pounding away at dope or gangs or stolen autos or whatever flips their switch. And that tendency brings up the other big reason why I'm saying no to this." He gave Hatcher a meaningful look. "Teams like this with a great deal of autonomy and a mandate to aggressively attack crime almost always end up making stupid mistakes. I'm thinking Rampart, or that gang emphasis patrol in Seattle last year. We don't need the scandal. Find another plan, Dana."

Hatcher looked deflated and angry at the same time. "Yes, sir."

Farrell lifted his fingers to get the chief's attention. Baumgartner nodded to him to proceed.

"Chief, I think Dana's one hundred percent right on the need to be proactive, and I'm more than willing to provide the detective she mentioned." He caught Hatcher's eye and saw a flicker of hopeful gratitude there. "Can I make a couple of suggestions about the plan?"

"Tom, I already denied it. We're burning daylight here."

"You might not be as inclined to deny her plan with a couple of changes," Farrell assured him.

Baumgartner frowned, but waved for him to continue.

"I want to say first that I agree with her estimate on the high frequency offenders, and the rough proportion of crime they are responsible for. I know staffing is tight on patrol, but if she lets a few low priority calls drop off the bottom of the call response, at least temporarily, that will ease the burden on the patrol cops who lose a body for the team."

"Those changes to the call response threshold come with a cost," Baumgartner said. "Unhappy citizens."

"That's why the changes are temporary, just in place long enough to get the first few arrests. Those arrests will reduce the crime rate, without a doubt. Then she can return the threshold to its previous levels, and the call load on the patrol teams will be roughly the same."

Baumgartner didn't appear to like the idea, but he didn't stop Farrell either, so the captain continued.

"The tendency to chase their favorite quarry is a potential problem, but one we can overcome by assigning a sergeant to the team as well."

"Full time?"

"Completely dedicated, yes."

"And where does he come from?"

"Patrol," Farrell said. "There are several teams that could run without their sergeant for a six-month period. These teams have strong corporals and mature officers. You can take a sergeant for Dana's team, and the patrol team that loses him will be fine. If the strike team is a success, you should be able to get city hall to fund a full-time sergeant. If it isn't, he goes back to his original team."

"Fat chance of those stingy bastards funding another sergeant's position." Baumgartner groused. He glanced at Barry. "Is there somewhere in the budget we could shake loose enough for one sergeant slot?"

Barry grinned at the chief. "Your wish is my command, my liege."

Baumgartner frowned, then turned his attention back to Farrell. "So this sergeant would be directing their activities?"

"Yes, right there on the ground with them. And I'd have the sergeant report directly to the captain for strategic direction. Maybe Ellis can assign a dedicated crime analyst to help the sergeant determine the best targets."

"I could probably make that work," Ellis said, his focus directed toward Farrell. "I can give you one analyst for about an hour a day. More, if the team shows results."

"That's perfect," Farrell said. "The sergeant gets fresh intel from crime analysis and directs the team's activity in person.

That close supervision solves your hot-dogging concern, and your corruption concern."

Baumgartner scratched his chin. "Yeah, I guess I could see that working. Maybe. With the right sergeant." He thought some more, then nodded. "When you put it that way, I like it. Write it up and get it to me by close of business today, Tom."

Farrell blinked at him. "Write it up?"

"Yeah, I want to see your plan on my desk by close of business. Is that a problem?"

"Sir, it was Dana's…" Farrell trailed off, looking over at Hatcher, who stared at him in shocked anger. He turned back to Baumgartner. The chief's glare cut into him.

"Get it done, Tom," the chief said. "We need this."

"Yes, sir," he answered. "I'll do that."

"Moving on," Baumgartner said, turning his attention to Barry again. "The budget. Take us through the numbers as of today."

Farrell tried to find a way to both listen to Barry drone on about the minutiae of the police budget, and to block him out at the same time. After an interminable review of the financial situation which essentially boiled down to, the budget was okay but would probably get worse next fiscal year, Barry finally surrendered the floor.

"Anything else?" the chief asked. When no one answered, he dismissed the group. He rose and walked toward the door that led to the short hallway connecting to his office. Barry scrambled to his feet and walked out with the chief, reminding Farrell of a remora fish with a shark. Ellis gathered his notes and headed out the opposite door, into the main corridor.

Farrell glanced over at Hatcher, who was openly glaring at him. He shifted uncomfortably in his seat. "Well, it looks like you got your plan implemented."

"*My* plan?"

"Everyone knows it was your plan. All I did was tweak it a little and—"

"Call it your own."

He stopped, surprised. "I never did that."

Hatcher stood, her angry gaze remaining fixed on Farrell. "Screw you, Tom," she said, then stormed out of the meeting room, leaving him behind to regret how things had played out.

Chapter 40

The knock on his door caused Gary Stone to look up from his computer.

"Checking out some porn, Stoney?" Tyler Garrett asked as he settled into the chair opposite him.

"What? No way. I would never."

"You know they can track that stuff, right?" He smiled.

Stone relaxed. "What are you doing here?"

Garrett shifted in his chair and crossed his legs. He wore gray slacks and a blue buttoned-down shirt. "I'm gonna talk with your boy, Hahn."

Stone's eyebrows raised. "He was already down here this morning telling me I had to get you to back off."

"Funny how that works."

"How what works?"

"They think they own you, don't they?"

Stone thought about it.

"They think because you're in their house, they can have you jump when they say jump. Fetch when they say fetch, like some kind of cake-eater. Do you feel like doing that?"

"Not so much. In fact, I want to get that guy."

"Oh, yeah? Why is that?"

"Because of how he thinks he did nothing wrong with Betty Rabe."

"He didn't, though, right? That's what your report said. And he didn't kill her. She killed herself."

"The relationship was wrong. Period. Regardless of what happened after."

Garrett waggled his hand. "Maybe, maybe not."

"Whatever. Hahn's smug about it, like he gets away with it no matter what. He says that he didn't have any effect on her, but I can tell you he did. I saw her. I talked with her. She was hurt by what happened and probably felt guilty, too."

"Probably."

"I hate guys like him. Guys who get away with whatever they do. I sort of wish I could have found something to nail him with. I'd have loved to see the look on his face when the cuffs go on."

"Get some righteous payback, huh?"

"No, that's not what I mean."

"Relax, Stoney. Don't be so uptight. That's the power shift way. Someone steps to you, you step right back." Garrett looked around the office. "Are you not planning on staying here long?"

"Why do you ask?"

"Your place is sort of nice. This is stark, man. I wouldn't want to work here. I'd at least want a picture of my family. Or my girl."

"I don't have a girl."

Garrett studied Stone. The way he looked at him made Stone uncomfortable. It was the way a kid studied a fly before he plucked the wings off it.

"You're not gay, are you?"

"No."

"Saving yourself?"

"No," Stone said with a nervous chuckle.

"Then why no girlfriend?"

"I had one. We broke up. I haven't found one I like enough to be with."

"Seriously, Stoney? You don't have an intermediate girl?"

"What's an intermediate girl?"

"An in-between girl. One that you spend time with until you find the right girl."

Stone shook his head. "That's not me."

"You don't hook-up just to hook-up?"

"That's not me." Stone repeated.

"Okay, Stoney. I get it. I like you, man. You march to your own drummer." Garrett nodded then. "So keep on marchin'. Don't let me push you into something like that. Stay true to yourself."

Stone's chest swelled with pride. To hear admiration from Garrett, his patrolman role model, was a big deal. "So what are you going to talk with Hahn about? I thought Betty Rabe's suicide was already done. What more do you need to know?"

"Funny you should ask. I've been thinking about her suicide. Perhaps it was…something else."

"Something else?" Stone said, a sinking feeling in his stomach. "I don't understand."

"I'll know more after I talk with him. But a little forewarning, things could get ugly and I think you're going to have to make a decision about your report."

"My report?"

"You should either get a report number and turn it in to records or destroy it, leaving the only copy with the chief. If things break a certain way, you'll have to lay everything at his feet."

Stone blanched. "I can't turn it in. That would ruin my career."

Garrett shrugged. "I understand."

"Ty? What are you going to do?"

Garrett ignored the question. "Now, if it was *me*, I'd tear it up, burn it, and throw the ashes into the river. You don't need that kind of weight hanging over you. Trust me."

"What are you going to do?" Stone asked again.

Garrett stood and smoothed his pants. "Wish me luck," he said and left the office.

Stone considered Garrett's warning as he watched him leave.

Chapter 41

Tyler Garrett walked off the elevator onto the sixth floor and the offices of the city council members. He'd been there a few times before, but it had been some time. He scanned the offices that ringed the outer wall, ignoring the desks in the bullpen area where the assistants sat.

Garrett headed toward Dennis Hahn's office. He stopped to talk with the assistant who sat in front. Her name plate read *J. Carter*.

She looked up at him with surprise. "Oh," she said.

"I need to speak with the councilman."

"Do you have an appointment?"

"It's not on your calendar. We met this weekend." The woman was about to ask another question, but Garrett said, "You should ask him," and nodded in the direction of Hahn.

The woman glanced over her shoulder at the councilman who stared directly at the man next to her.

"Uh, I guess you can—"

Garrett didn't wait for her permission and walked into the councilman's office. He shut the door behind him.

"What are you doing here?" Hahn asked.

"We were to finish my interview in your office," Garrett said, dropping into a chair. "I thought that's what you wanted."

Hahn's eyes glanced to his assistant, then back to Garrett. "People can see you."

"I'm not worried."

"Well, I *am*. I don't want to be seen with you."

"All right," Garrett said. He stood then and put his hand on the doorknob. "Let's go to the station. We'll finish the interview there." He twisted the knob.

"Officer, you will wait!" Hahn said emphatically as he stood. His face twisted in anger.

Garrett's hand remained on the knob. "Officer? Really? And what am I supposed to wait for? For you to jerk my chain?"

"You work for the city," Hahn said, his voice wavering. "I *lead* the city. Therefore, you work for me."

He chuckled. "Oh, I see. You think you have some leverage here. Well, screw you, man." He lifted his cell phone and waggled it. "How about I call for a uniform to escort you down to the station?"

Garrett yanked open the door and stepped out of the councilman's office.

Hahn ran around his desk. "Garrett," he called. "Garrett! Hey, now, I'm sorry."

He stopped near the receptionist's desk. She looked at them both with curiosity. Hahn smiled sheepishly at her.

"It's okay, Jean. I got my wires crossed, is all. Off—I mean, *Mister* Garrett, would you step back into my office?"

Garrett ran his thumb under his nose, like a fighter preparing to enter the ring. "*You* asked me to meet with you today," Garrett said. "Am I remembering that correctly?"

Hahn stared at him.

"Is that a hard question? I mean, if you forgot, you forgot. You can tell the truth, right?"

Hahn looked nervously around at the various assistants and the other council members. Several were looking in his direction. "Yes, yes, that's what happened. I forgot. That's it. I didn't put it on my calendar. It wasn't on my calendar, was it, Jean?"

Jean stared at Hahn for a moment then turned slowly to Garrett. She shook her head. "It wasn't on his calendar."

"See?" Hahn said, snapping his fingers. "The meeting wasn't there. I apologize for my oversight, Mr. Garrett. Can we start over?"

Jean furrowed her brow as she watched the exchange.

Garrett smiled. "Since you apologized so nicely, Councilman, sure, let's start over."

Hahn's face flattened, and he glanced to Jean. She quickly turned her attention back to her computer. The councilman spun on his heel and walked into his office. Garrett followed, closing the door behind him.

The councilman dropped heavily into his chair and rubbed his face several times. When he opened his eyes, he studied Garrett. "Thank you for not coming in uniform."

"Small favors, right?"

"Now that you've kicked me in the balls, can we get this thing over with?"

"That's up to you," Garrett said, taking a seat. "Where'd we leave off on Saturday night?"

Hahn raised his hands in frustration. "You said she left a note."

"Right, a note." Garrett's eyes narrowed as he thought. "About that. She didn't leave a note."

"What!" Hahn barked, leaning forward. He looked outside his office to see if anyone heard his outburst. When he faced Garrett, he lowered his voice. "I've been in a panic all weekend thinking that she left a note." His face had completely reddened. "Why would you tell me such a thing?"

"I didn't tell you she left a note. You just believed she did."

"But you let me believe it. Why would you do that?"

"To show you how bad things really are."

Hahn shook his head. "But you said—"

"What's out there is just as bad." Garrett opened his phone and showed him a picture. "That, councilman, is the letter Betty Rabe sent to the mayor accusing you of sexually assaulting her, but you already knew that letter existed, didn't you?"

Hahn's face slackened and the color slowly drained.

"You see what's happening right now? The truth is slowly leaking out."

The councilman bowed his head.

"Check this one out." Garrett turned his phone to show Hahn another picture. "This one is Officer Gary Stone's report regarding his interviews with both Betty Rabe and you. You'll notice he handwrote it."

"That sneak wrote a report?"

"And a good one, too. I'll credit him that."

"Oh, God," Hahn said. "I went down there and insulted him."

"I know," Garrett said with a chuckle. "He told me. Now, he's working on a way to bring you down."

Hahn's eyes widened. "Oh God."

Garrett smiled. "You really shouldn't dump on Stoney. Especially since he's here to keep an eye on you and the others."

"The others?"

"Council members," Garrett said, waving his finger in a circular motion as if to encompass the entire floor.

"What?"

"C'mon, man, you had to know that. It can't come as a complete surprise. The mayor and Baumgartner set this thing up. They put him inside city hall under the guise of threat assessment, but he's keeping a watch on what the council does. He reports directly to the chief and the mayor. You've seen it, right?"

Hahn squinted, thinking. "I think so. Yes."

"Have you ever asked him to do something?"

"Yeah and the little turd refused, saying he works only for the chief."

"He's not stupid. He knows the rules of the game."

"So I'm screwed, is what you're saying. They're going to use this Beth thing to take me down."

"Maybe, but there's a silver lining."

"What's that?"

"Me," Garrett said, tapping his chest. "I'll make it go away."

"How's that?"

"Stoney and me. We're friends. I'll get his copy of the report and destroy it. Then you'll only have to worry about the mayor and the chief. I can tell you this much, the report isn't in the system yet. That's why he handwrote it."

"What's that mean, if it isn't in the system?"

"They wanted it kept quiet for a reason. My guess, they want leverage over you. That's why I'd keep it quiet."

Hahn considered what Garrett said. "This isn't an interview, is it?"

"Sure it is. I'm interviewing you and you're interviewing me. We're checking each other out to see if we can work together."

"Work together?"

"You need someone on the inside, Councilman. Someone who can look out for your interests. Provide you with some protection at times like this."

"What do you get out of this…this arrangement?"

"Plain and simple, you'll owe me."

"Owe you what?" Hahn's voice was full of suspicion.

"That I don't know yet, but my mom always told me I'd need friends in the right places. I'm going to start with you."

"This sounds like you're blackmailing me."

"I'm helping you, Councilman. Are you too myopic to see that?"

"You know what they say, if it sounds too good to be true."

"This isn't too good, Denny. Trust me, I'm going to want favors and you're going to pay up. But I'll help you out of this jam."

Councilman Hahn leaned back and clasped his hands together as if he was praying. Finally, he said. "What do we do now? Do we shake on it?"

"What you do now is come clean. You tell me every piece of dirt that Stone might find that can hurt you. I need to know how to keep you out of trouble."

Chapter 42

Mayor Sikes studied Chief Baumgartner with a mixture of doubt and disdain. "So it's a bunch of patrol officers running around causing havoc?"

Baumgartner clenched his jaw. He wondered if the mayor was really as dense as he sometimes seemed, or if it was a calculated act that he put on to gain some kind of advantage.

Like what? A medal in the Special Olympics?

"The only havoc they'll be causing," he told the mayor, "is in the lives of career criminals who are victimizing our citizens…*your* voters. If you still care about them now that you're in your second term, that is."

Sikes's eyes narrowed. "Watch yourself, Bob. This isn't a free-fire zone."

Baumgartner ignored his warning. "My job is to do something about the crime in this city. That's what you told me last week. This is what I'm doing. A well-supervised, directed patrol strike team, supplied with real-time criminal intelligence."

"Don't call it that."

Baumgartner gave him a questioning look.

"Strike team," Sikes repeated. "Don't call it that. It sounds terrible."

"We don't have a name yet, but it won't be strike team."

"You should name it the Bad Idea Team. Every city I've seen do something like this ends up with a scandal."

"No," Baumgartner said. "Every time there's been a scandal regarding a team like this, you've seen it."

"You're playing semantics now."

"No, I'm not. The distinction is important. There are numerous agencies who employ some form of a team like this. You just don't hear about them because they don't make national news. I assure you, they're making local news because they're putting guns, drugs, and money on the table."

"I thought you were targeting property crimes. Burglars, vehicle thieves, that sort of thing."

"It's an expression," Baumgartner said. "Besides, it's all inter-related. They're stealing to fuel their drug habit."

Sikes shook his head. "I'm not in favor of this course of action. It seems like too much risk, no matter the reward."

"You'll change your mind in six months when the crime stats are golden."

Sikes gave him a Machiavellian smile. "If that happens, I'll be happy to share in the credit, Bob. But if this fails, it's all on you. The angry citizens whose calls you're not answering so you can staff this team, if the stats remain stagnant or get worse, and any trouble your team gets into…all yours. Get me?"

You devious bastard. He'd boxed Baumgartner into a corner. Now he either accepted these terms, or trashed Farrell's idea.

He considered a moment. Then he said, "I've always been careful not to take too much credit for the crime rate going down, because I figured that would mean I'd need to take the blame when it went up. It sounds like you've figured out how to beat that particular problem."

Sikes kept grinning at him, waiting.

"Yeah," Baumgartner finally said. "I get it."

After he left the mayor's office, Baumgartner stopped by to see Stone. The partially open door was an invitation to knock, so he did, but swung the door the rest of the way open in the process.

Stone looked up, concern flashing in his eyes. When he saw the chief, the expression didn't change.

"How're you doing, Gary?"

"Fine, sir."

"You don't look fine. You looked worried."

Stone took a deep breath and let it out. "I suppose I am."

"About what?"

Stone motioned for the chief to close his door. Baumgartner did, then waited for him to speak.

It took him a few seconds. Finally, he said, "Things around here are crazy, sir. First there was the whole Betty Rabe letter and the report you had me do…"

Baumgartner was glad Stone had the sense to ask him to close the door before talking about such a sensitive matter. He wished he also had the sense to not talk about it in the first place.

"…and then her suicide. I've got the mayor leaning on me every day. He acts like I'm a spy…"

Because you are.

"…he wants to turn into a double agent…"

Which I predicted.

"…and now Hahn is mad at me because of how we've handled his case. He's threatening to destroy my career—"

"Wait. Why is Hahn upset?"

"He thinks we were supposed to be helping him," Stone said. "Now he thinks we screwed him."

Damn it. I need to get that report entered into the system.

"How? Did you say something? Or do something?"

"No," Stone said hurriedly. "Garrett interviewed him."

Garrett again. The chief burrowed his brow. "Why is Garrett talking to him?"

"Her suicide. He's following up."

"Did I make Tyler Garrett a homicide detective and forget I did it?" Baumgartner growled.

He shook his head. "Gary, if Hahn needed to be interviewed, it should have been you. That's why I've got you down here. To take care of it. Not to let it unravel."

Stone looked stricken. "I wasn't part of that case, sir. I'm doing the best I can. There's…there's a lot of threads to follow."

"No. There's one. *You*," Baumgartner jabbed a finger toward Stone, "do what *I* tell you to do. You take care of business. You get results. Do your job, Gary."

He left Stone sitting at his desk, stalking out of the office. By the time he reached the elevators, he got his gait back under control, projected his trademark easy confidence. But inside, he was seething. As soon as he got back to his office, he was going to call Tom Farrell.

Christ, he was hungry.

Chapter 43

Hatcher picked at her sandwich, only half listening to Maggie Patterson's story about how her Saturday night went after they separated.

Patterson noticed. "What's wrong, Dana?"

Hatcher shook her head. "Work."

"Okay…so spill."

"We're playing hooky," Hatcher said. "It's supposed to be fun. We promised no work talk."

"Consider it a campaign promise, easily broken. What's going on?"

Hatcher told her the entire story. All the work she'd put in regarding the details of the plan, large and small. How she'd presented it to the chief and he shot it down. Then Farrell made a couple of minor adjustments to her plan and passed it off as his own.

"Ugh," Patterson. "Typical man. I'm telling you, a man comes across the Mona Lisa, he pees all over it, and then decides he was the one that painted the damn thing in the first place."

Hatcher didn't laugh, but only because it felt that way.

"Fat Boy is still going to implement it, though?"

"Yes."

"There you go. It will be under your command, right? So it will be your baby." She popped a roasted baby carrot in her mouth and chewed. "Sometimes you have to fight for credit, sometimes you have to fight for results. Be happy."

"It's not going to be under my command," Hatcher said mournfully.

"What?"

"They're moving it under investigations because there's a detective in the unit."

"What?" Patterson repeated. "The whole team is a bunch of patrol cops, right?"

Hatcher nodded. "Because it has an investigative function, they're pulling it out of patrol and giving it to investigations. It's completely bogus."

"And investigations is Farrell's unit," Patterson said.

"Yeah."

"So he gets the credit *and* the results."

Hatcher nodded.

"For stealing your idea?" Patterson's voice had an edge to it.

"Pretty much."

"You want me to burn it down?"

Hatcher shook her head. "You couldn't stop it."

"Want to make a bet?" Patterson said in a hard voice. "I can't stop it from happening. That's all within the chief's purview, but I sit on the Public Safety Committee. I'll make sure the reporting of it is a miserable affair and I'll call out every hitch and stumble along the way. After a while, Fat Boy will never want to mention it again, or even hear about it. He'll shelve the concept and blame Farrell for bringing it up to him in the first place."

Patterson grinned, her eyes aglow with the concept of battle.

"It'll be beautiful," she said.

Hatcher hesitated. "It was a good idea," she said. "It'll work."

"It is a great idea," Patterson agreed, "but it was *your* idea. So it can't work. Not for them."

Hatcher reached for her glass of wine, stalling. She'd seen Maggie wound up before, but never quite this vindictive.

She swallowed her wine and dabbed her lips with her napkin. Patterson waited patiently When she could delay no further, Hatcher said, "I'm angry, Maggie. It's complete garbage."

"It is."

"But if I have to choose between someone else getting credit for knocking down our property crime problem, or seeing the crime rate continue to rise, I have to go with taking care of the bigger problem here. I can't put my career before the mission."

"Why not? The chief put his good old boy's career before yours."

Hatcher felt that same stab of anger she'd experienced in the command staff meeting again. "I know," she said in a low voice. "But that doesn't make it right."

Patterson shrugged. "It's not about right and wrong. It's about results."

"That's what I'm saying."

"Well, the result is going to be that some man is getting credit for your work. You sure you can live with that?"

Hatcher nodded, though she could feel her resolution wavering in the face of the inequity. "If I have to."

Patterson took a sip of her wine. Then she gave Hatcher a look of pure certainty. "You'll change your mind about that," she pronounced.

Chapter 44

"That mayor," Baumgartner complained to Farrell. "He's a piece of work."

Farrell glanced around The High Nooner diner to make sure no one heard the chief. "What's the problem?"

"He doesn't know the first thing about police work, but I'll give him this. He's a wily bastard when it comes to politics. If I could think politics one hundred percent of the time, I could beat him, but I've got to think about running this department, so he's got me at a disadvantage."

"What happened?"

Baumgartner waved away his question. "What have you done so far on this strike team?"

Farrell paused. The idea hadn't been his, and although he knew his modifications were what got it over the hump with the chief, the bulk of the plan was Hatcher's. He decided to try one more time to make that clear. "Sir, the idea for this plan was Captain Hatcher's. And it uses mostly patrol officers. Don't you think—"

"What I think, Tom, is that her plan was half formed. You made it workable. And it doesn't matter who the personnel are, their function is more investigative than patrol. They belong under your command."

"I get what you're saying, but since it was her plan originally…" he trailed off in the face of Baumgartner's level glare.

"Look," the chief said, "Dana's a good leader. That's why I promoted her, but she still thinks like a lieutenant, and she hasn't learned the ropes yet at the command level. She needs a little seasoning."

"This could help her gain that experience," Farrell offered.

"It could, but her inexperience could also mess it up, and I can't risk that." He reached out and put his hand on Farrell's shoulder. "I need my best man on this, Tom, and that's you. All right?"

Farrell felt a surge of pride at the chief's words. He nodded. "Yes, sir."

"Good." Baumgartner picked up his sandwich and took a bite. "And come up with a name," he said around his food. "Something catchy that doesn't include strike team."

"I will."

Deep inside, Farrell was relieved. He'd said what he needed to in good conscience, but he was glad this new team would be under his control. It was going to be his Garrett trap, the doubts of Wardell Clint be damned.

"Now," Baumgartner said, still chewing. "Tell me why Tyler Garrett is talking with Councilman Dennis Hahn."

Farrell was surprised by the question. "I...I don't know offhand. He's patrol. Why don't you check with Hatcher?"

"I asked you to look into Garrett, so I'm checking with you." Baumgartner swallowed, and then gave Farrell a pointed look. "Plus, it sounds like he's doing investigative work, not patrol work. What the hell is going on?"

"I imagine he's following up on the Rabe suicide."

"He definitely is. I got that from Stone. But *why* is he? Shouldn't one of your detectives be doing that?"

Farrell considered. "There was nothing at the crime scene to connect Hahn to her death. There'd be no way my detective would even consider that conversation."

"But Garrett did."

"He had Stone's card," Farrell said, connecting the dots easily enough. "And Stone had his interview with Betty Rabe. He must have told Garrett enough for Garrett to make the connection."

"Did you check on that card like I asked?" Baumgartner said.

"I did. It wasn't listed as evidence. My detective never found it."

"Which means Garrett kept it. That's awful ballsy for a patrolman."

It's dirty. That's what it is.

He once again felt tempted to bring the chief in on what he knew. Clint's warnings clanged in his ears, though, and he hesitated. The chief seemed to be souring on Garrett, which could make this a good time to lay out the case for him.

But it was Clint's voice that won out, and he held his tongue.

Instead, he said, "He's a hard charger. Ex-SWAT, all of that. Maybe he wants to wrap everything up himself in case there's any glory involved."

"Maybe," Baumgartner said doubtfully.

"Has Hahn contacted you about it?"

"No. And the mayor didn't know about it, either."

"Then I'd say let it slide," Farrell said. "Maybe Garrett is onto something and Hahn really is dirty. If that's the case, everybody wins."

"Except Hahn."

"Screw him. He was taking advantage of an impressionable seventeen-year-old. He made his choice already."

Baumgartner eyed him with mild surprise. "You're getting ruthless, Tom. That's a part of you I haven't seen before."

Farrell didn't answer. There was a lot the chief didn't know about him.

TUESDAY

When a man lies, he murders some part of the world.
—Paul Gerhardt, German theologian and poet

Chapter 45

Zombie houses were a chronic problem following the market crash. There were hundreds, if not thousands, around Spokane County. The homes were abandoned by their owners when they found themselves financially underwater, making mortgage payments on houses that no longer held a fraction of their pre-crash value. These properties soon ended up in the foreclosure process and, due to state laws, bank regulations, and other bureaucratic snafus, they remained in limbo for months, sometimes years.

They were often symbolized by boarded up windows, graffiti, and the ever-present "No Trespassing" warnings posted on the front doors.

Drug users and drug dealers were the first to understand the value a zombie home provided. It was a free place to ply their trade or use their drugs and one they could abandon without more than a moment's regret.

Even though the economy had recovered, zombie houses remained scattered about the county.

Ezekiel "Skunk" Hetzel sat against the living room wall of an abandoned home near the corner of Haven Street and Everett Avenue. Several days before, he'd removed the No Trespassing warning off the front of the house before going around back and kicking in the rear door. He wasn't worried about anyone seeing him.

Across the alley was the back of The Red Dragon restaurant. At the end of the block was a little convenience store and the Northern Rail Pub. It was a great neighborhood to conduct business in. There were hardly any nosy neighbors to be concerned about. As long as he kept a low profile and didn't make too much of a scene, he would be good for a few days. If not a few weeks.

Skunk didn't live in the little house. Instead, he was living in the basement of his mom's house. That arrangement was only temporary, though, until he saved up a nut to get his own place again. Things had been tight since he got out of jail, but everything was looking up now. The little house he'd broken into was only for conducting business.

"Hey, Skunk?"

"Yo, T, in here."

Wanting to impress his new business associate, he quickly got to his feet. Skunk heard him walking through the house before he saw him.

Tyler Garrett was an impressive man. He was always dressed sharp, but today he was extra tight. Black slacks, black mock turtleneck, and gray Columbia windbreaker which hung open revealing the gun tucked into the waistband. It was raining slightly outside, and the jacket glistened in the low light of the house. The brim of Garrett's gray baseball hat was rolled so it touched the edges of his eyes. He looked like a man not to be trifled with. Skunk knew that instinctively.

"No trouble finding the place?" Skunk asked, sounding like his late father.

Garrett shook his head. He was about to say something when his nose crinkled. "Smells like your ass in here."

Skunk flinched in embarrassment. "There's no running water."

"You took a dump in the bathroom? What'd you wipe with?"

"I brought toilet paper. There's a store around the corner. I'm not an animal."

"Man, next time you get one of these houses, don't use the toilet in it, okay?"

"Right. Okay," Skunk said. "I'm sorry, man."

Garrett pinched his nose for a second then blinked away his reaction to the smell. "Nasty."

"So, T, what did you want to meet for? Got us another hookup?"

"Not yet. I need a favor."

"You got it, you got it, just name it."

Garrett moved to the hallway where light shone in from the back door. There was an open door that led down to the basement. He pushed it closed completely to let more light in the hallway. He pulled out two pieces of paper and handed them to Skunk.

"This," Garrett said, tapping the handwritten note, "is a girl you need to see. That's her address. You talk to her about this guy." He tapped the other piece of paper which was a photograph cut from a newspaper. No text accompanied the photo.

"Who's the guy?"

"You don't need to know."

"Right," Skunk said. "Don't need to know."

Garrett tapped the photo again. "Ask the girl about this guy. Ask her if she knows him. She will. If she says doesn't, she's lying."

Skunk met Garrett's gaze. "If she says she doesn't, she's lying."

"That's right." Garrett tapped the handwritten note again. "This girl knows that man. You need to tell her that the cops or a reporter or someone is going to come talk with her soon about that man. She needs to keep quiet. Don't say anything. Got it?"

Skunk's brow furrowed.

"Hey, are you following all this?"

Skunk nodded. "But why aren't you telling her all this? Why me?"

Garrett stepped back. "How many people know me?"

He had now offended Garrett twice. First with the unflushed dump and now this stupid question. "I don't know," he said.

"Take a guess."

"A lot, probably."

"That's right, Skunk, a lot of people know me. My face has been all over the news. That's why I need you. You're my emissary."

"Emissary?" Skunk repeated, liking the sound of the word.

"Yeah, emissary. You need to carry a special message for me."

Skunk repeated the words Garrett had told him. "So what happens if she doesn't want to remain quiet?"

Garrett was thoughtful for a moment before saying, "Then tell her she'll end up dead."

Ezekiel Hetzel's eyes widened. "Really? We'd have to kill her?"

"C'mon, man, what do you think? Use your best judgment when you're talking with her. You'll do fine. I trust you."

With that, Garrett turned and left him alone in the house.

Chapter 46

"Dana?"

Hatcher was stepping through the threshold into her office with a fresh cup of coffee when she heard Farrell call her name.

She ignored him and sat at her desk, picking up the first piece of paper within reach and studying it intently.

Farrell appeared in her doorway. "Hey, Dana, can I talk to you for a second?"

Hatcher looked up. "I'm kind of busy, Tom. I have to figure out what calls we're not going to answer so you can have your strike team. You know, the team *you* came up with?"

"You're still mad."

"Why should I be mad? I didn't put in hours of work on a plan that one of my supposedly trustworthy colleagues hijacked in front of my boss. At least, I'm pretty sure that wasn't me."

"Dana…"

"Wait." She cocked her head. "Was that me? I don't know. I'm just a dumb girl." Hatcher gave him a mock pout.

Farrell looked wounded. He started to sit, but Hatcher held up her hand, stopping him.

"I'm busy, Tom. Seriously. What do you want?"

"I wanted to apologize. I didn't—"

"Apology accepted."

"Really?"

"No. I don't need your apology. I'd like my team back, though."

Farrell frowned. "I can't do that. The chief is fixed on this being under investigations."

"Your division, you mean?"

"Look," Farrell said, "I tried to tell him whose idea it was at the meeting. You were there. You saw. And when we talked again yesterday, I made sure he heard it again, but he's not listening. You know how he can be."

"Male?"

Farrell shrugged. "Chiefly."

If he was a woman, the word would be bitchy.

"I looked for you yesterday afternoon," Farrell continued, "but you weren't in your office."

"I took some time off. So?"

"Nothing. But I wanted to coordinate with you on this. It might be assigned to my command now, but there's no reason we can't work together. Bounce some ideas around, work some strategies. I'll make sure the chief knows, so the credit gets shared."

A part of her wanted to take him up on it, if only to be involved in what she had created. But another part heard only condescension.

"If you're here to assuage your guilt, I really don't have time for that," Hatcher said. "I've got a patrol division to run."

Farrell nodded. "I understand."

Do you?

She doubted it.

He turned to go. At the doorway, he looked back. "It's a good idea, Dana. I'll make sure to keep you in the loop."

He left.

Keep this *in the loop.* She flipped the bird at his back.

Chapter 47

"He was sort of…rough a couple times, I guess, but he never really hurt me."

For nineteen, she had a young face. Officer Gary Stone thought she could have easily passed for sixteen, which was odd when most girls her age were trying to pass for older.

Shelley Mason crossed her arms and waited for his next question. She had fake eye lashes and glasses that Stone suspected were cosmetic only. Her red, long sleeve T-shirt read *Gonzaga Bulldogs* and was a size too small for her. It left little to the imagination.

"So Dennis Hahn never assaulted you?"

"No."

That morning, while getting coffee with Jean, Stone had to ask her about the girl she mentioned on Saturday night. He hadn't written her name down and had forgotten it. Jean was reluctant to say the girl's name, afraid it could somehow blow back on her. She said she regretted having told him, that the alcohol had lowered her inhibitions. Stone pleaded with her until Jean finally said the girl's name. She then walked away in a huff, leaving Stone alone in the line for coffee.

"You said he was rough. What does that mean?"

"He has issues. I mean, we all do, probably, right?"

They were standing outside the entrance to the campus library. Stone had suggested they go someplace quiet, but Shelley said it was fine conducting the interview there in the open. She said no one was going to stand around and watch them, plus she had a report she had to finish so she didn't want to spend too much time walking around trying to find a place to talk.

Stone had managed to track her down, first through DOL, then through social media. She agreed to meet with him here. He thought she would be reluctant to meet since he was vague about what he was investigating, but after he said he was with the police department, she checked his online and social media presence. She told him he seemed okay and agreed to meet on the condition she kept her name out of whatever "thing" he was following up on.

"What issues are those?"

Shelley's face scrunched, "Really?"

"If you want to tell me, I'll listen. I'm trying to learn about Dennis. He's been accused of assaulting another girl."

"Oh," she said, pulling at the bottom of her shirt. "He was never mean. It wasn't that way. He liked to put me over his lap before we did it was all."

"Over his lap? To spank?"

"It was sort of, well, weird. I think he liked to play daddy."

"Oh."

"I mean, I was cool with it the first time, you know, him being all *Fifty Shades* and what not. But it sorta stung and it didn't do anything for me, not even a little bit. For him, it did something, though. It was pretty hot after that." Her face reddened at the revelation.

Stone shook his head. "He stopped when you asked him to?"

"Sure. I mean, he wanted to do it again, the spanking thing, but I wasn't into it. I'm not effed up that way."

"Is that why you broke up?"

Shelley looked at Stone as if he were simple. "We were never really together so there was no reason to break up."

"Ah."

"We hooked up. You know, had some laughs. Messed around. He was pretty fun for an older guy."

"That pretty fun older guy asked you to leave the office where you were employed."

"It happens. I mean, I knew what I was getting into. I'm not stupid."

"I didn't say you were."

"Anyways, I was just interning there for some school credit. Not the end of the world. My parents weren't even mad because it was a credit they didn't pay for."

"Did they know about him?"

"Of course not. Do you tell your parents about your sex life?"

"No," Stone said, feeling slightly flushed. "So you're cool with how he treated you?"

"Not really cool, no. But I know how the world works. I also didn't want my name dragged through the mud. I plan on being someone someday, so I don't need some stupid hassle."

Stone took a moment to review his notes.

"Someone really accused him of assault?"

He nodded.

"I wouldn't have taken him for that type. You can never tell, you know."

He remained silent.

"You know who you should talk to? There was this other girl we partied with once. Sonya. She let him spank her. Hard, by the way. Much harder than me, but that girl, she liked it. I mean, a lot. She had some real daddy issues. I stood by and let them do their thing until they were done. Then we all played."

"The three of you?"

"Don't be a prude. Everybody does it."

"Not everybody."

"Well, most everybody I know has tried it. Although we really didn't do it together, together. We basically watched each other. Dennis liked it that way. That part was…well, you can imagine."

Stone ignored responding to her and made an entry into his notebook. When he looked up, he asked, "Sonya. What's her last name?"

"Meyer, I think. After her, I was old news pretty quick. We never hooked up again."

"Did that make you mad?"

"Not really. It happens. Sometimes you're the flavor of the month, sometimes your last month's special. Next to Sonya, I was last month. She's really pretty. He liked looking at her. I did, too, I guess."

"Do you know where I can find her?"

"Not really. I think he met her at some coffee shop."

"Some coffee shop? Which one?"

"I couldn't tell you. What can I say? The guy was charming when he poured it on."

"Did you friend her on any social media? Maybe I can find her that way."

Shelley tilted her head. "Why would I do that? I saw her naked. I didn't need to be her friend on Facebook to get to know her better."

"How old do you think she was?"

"My age."

He then studied her and thought. He wondered if he was missing any questions.

"Is there anything else? I need to get back inside so I can finish my project."

"No, nothing else. Thank you for your time."

"Remember our deal." She turned and trotted to the door. He watched her vanish into the building.

Councilman Hahn has a thing for young women.

It sounded like he also had a way of charming them when he talked with them. He wondered what it was about the man that those young women found so appealing. He snapped his fingers, realizing that was a question he should have asked Shelley. He took a step toward the library but stopped. He'd already taken enough of her time and the question wasn't going to affect the outcome of anything. It wasn't worth further bothering the young woman.

He jotted the question in his notebook. He would ask Sonya Meyer that when he found her.

Chapter 48

"That's Dennis."

"Dennis?"

"Yeah, Dennis Hahn," the olive-skinned girl whispered.

Ezekiel "Skunk" Hetzel tapped the black-and-white newspaper photo. "Somebody is gonna come ask about this man."

Sonya Meyer pulled back slightly and rubbed the side of her face where he had slapped her earlier. "Why? Why would they come to talk with me?"

Skunk waved his hand. "None of that matters. What does matter is you need to keep your mouth shut. Got it?"

She put her hands to her head. "No, no, I don't get it," her voice returning to its normal volume. "Why are you doing this? Why are you here?"

"Because the cops or…or…*damn!* The cops are gonna be coming."

Sonya stared at him. "Why are the cops coming here? What did I do?"

"I don't know," Skunk said and stomped his foot. He wished he'd gotten some more information from Garrett. He felt like a fool telling this woman to keep her mouth shut when he didn't know why she had to do so.

When he had first arrived at the small house near Deaconess Hospital, she opened the front door and looked slightly confused at the man standing there. She was a pretty young woman in yoga pants and matching sweatshirt. "Yes?"

"Are you Sonya Meyer?"

"Yes."

"Is anyone else here with you?"

"What?"

He shoved his way into the house then. He didn't know why he did it, but he thought it was better to conduct their business inside. It was his best judgment, as Garrett had said. He was lucky no one was home with her.

She had screamed, but he slapped her to stop it. Then she reached for her cell phone which he took away. She lashed at him, scratching his forearm, so he slapped her a second time. Skunk felt a swell of pride that he controlled the situation so fast.

But that pride had ebbed away as she asked questions that he didn't know how to answer.

"I didn't do anything!" she yelled.

"This isn't about you!" Skunk hollered over her, stamping his foot several times. "It's about him," he said, tapping the photo.

"What did he do?" she screamed. "I want to—"

Skunk slapped her hard. Her eyes widened with fear, and she stopped talking.

He stuck his finger in her face. "Keep your mouth shut when the cops show up. It's that simple."

Sonya backed away from Skunk until she ran into a wall. Her hand touched the side of her face where Skunk had hit her.

"It's simple, lady. Why can't you get it?"

"I didn't do anything," Sonya whispered.

Skunk dropped his hands. "Listen. I'm sorry I scared you. I don't normally do this type of thing. It's my first time. You understand?"

"I didn't do anything," she repeated.

"I heard. Now, shut up, will ya? Or you're gonna make me hit you again."

Sonya stared at Skunk.

"All you need to do is be quiet when the cops show up. It'll be that easy. Simple, right?"

She shook her head.

Why was this stupid woman not getting it?

"What's your problem?" Skunk said and stomped his foot. His anger was spiraling out of control.

"I didn't do anything!" she screamed.

Skunk stepped across the room. Sonya brought her hands up to her face to protect herself so he punched her in the stomach. She collapsed to the floor.

"I heard you the first time," he yelled.

She was on her hands and knees, sucking for air. The punch felt good. It made him feel powerful. More than that, though, it just felt *right*.

At that moment, he knew he was on the right course.

He was using his best judgment.

Chapter 49

Officer Gary Stone pulled to the curb alongside Bishop Court. He was a couple hundred feet away from her house.

He initially found Sonya Meyer listed in DOL and went to the address where it showed she was living. Unfortunately, she no longer lived there. The apartment manager was cleaning the unit she had vacated but he was happy to provide Stone with her forwarding address. He gave Sonya a glowing review, along with several unsolicited comments about how pretty she was and how he'd miss having her around the apartment community. Stone wondered if that was one of the reasons why she moved to the little bungalow on Bishop Court.

Directly in front of the house was a silver Honda CRX. He ran the plate and it quickly returned showing as registered to Sonya Meyer. With her car sitting out front, he expected her to be home.

The little brown house was rundown and the trees on the property were overgrown. It gave off a haunted vibe. *It would be a great house around Halloween.*

He walked up the crumbling sidewalk, ascended the steps to the small concrete porch, and knocked on the door. He didn't hear any noise from inside. His second attempt was more forceful as he recalled Ray Zielinski's powerful knock from a few days prior.

Charlie Bravo.

Screw Ray.

No, that wasn't right. He shouldn't think like that. He needed to be positive regardless of how people like Ray treated him. For a brief second, he wished he could take back his negative thought. *I should be like the bison in the snowstorm.*

The bison didn't worry about what others thought of him. He tried to picture the scene again but still couldn't.

Sonya Meyer hadn't come to the door. Stone pounded once more. He then stood on his tiptoes and looked through the little window at the top of the door.

There was a body lying on the floor in the living room. His heart suddenly began racing and he reached for his police radio, a response that would have been normal while he was on patrol. Unfortunately, he didn't have his radio with him.

He took a step back and kicked the door. It didn't budge.

Another attempt and the same result.

No way Stone was going to call for backup to come and kick the door open for him. He was a cop, for Christ's sake, and he needed to get in that door.

He set himself again and kicked near the doorknob. The door started to give. The movement energized Stone and he quickly returned to his starting position.

The next attempt worked, and the door swung open and banged loudly into a wall.

He ran into the house and checked on the woman. Her face was bloodied, and he felt for a pulse. There was none.

He pulled his cell phone from his pocket and dialed dispatch.

Chapter 50

Clint stopped in front of the bungalow. He noticed a pair of uniformed officers, one standing at the door, one at the sidewalk. Officer Gary Stone, with his blue slacks, checkered shirt, and solid yellow tie, stood next to the door as well.

Prior to arrival, Clint had been interviewing a peripheral witness to close out a weak-ass robbery case that Lieutenant Flowers laid on him at the end of shift yesterday. The lieutenant obviously hadn't deemed it difficult enough to budge Clint from being next up on the wheel, because he'd gotten called to this homicide. It was further evidence Flowers didn't run the case assignment system fairly.

The officer at the end of the walkway looked barely out of the training car. Her dark hair was pulled back into a short ponytail. She was of some Asian descent, but Clint refused to speculate on the exact origin. Her face showed a look of mild trepidation when he approached. Clint was fully aware that he had a reputation. He even knew that some people called him the Honey Badger, but he didn't care. All he wanted was for people to do their jobs with some degree of skill and alacrity.

"Why is there no crime scene tape up yet?" he barked at the female officer.

She glanced toward the front door. "Sir?"

"String some tape," Clint ordered. Since the rookie probably didn't know what she was doing, the detective pointed to a couple of anchor points. "From there to there."

"Yes, sir."

"Then get out your notebook and start a log."

The rookie stared at him, blinking nervously. "A log?"

"Didn't your FTOs teach you anything?"

"Yes, sir. They did."

"Well then, string some tape," Clint told her brusquely. "No one gets past you without checking with me first."

"Yes, sir." The rookie ran to the nearby police cruiser.

Clint stayed where he was. Someone had to hold the outer perimeter. Besides, he always liked to stand back and take in the whole scene, working his way slowly toward the victim.

The bungalow was old, probably built close to a century ago. He could see signs of modern updates, but they did little to counterbalance the wear and tear on the place. Maintenance of the vegetation was overdue. The walkway was cracked and crumbling, but for that matter, so was the city sidewalk on this block.

The place had a dark and foreboding look to it, but Clint noticed that a cheery shade of yellow curtains hung in one small window. The curtains in the other window, nearest the door, were open. His eyes went back to the curtains then to Officer Stone's yellow tie.

His observations were cut short as the other patrol officer walked over. Clint didn't recognize the man, so he glanced down to the silver nametag above his breast pocket. *K. Norton.* A SWAT pin resided just above the nametag.

"Why are you yelling at my rookie?" Officer Norton asked him, his voice challenging.

"I wasn't yelling. I was instructing."

"I'm her FTO. Instructing her is my job."

"You didn't do your job, so I had to."

Norton scowled. "Look, don't think just because you're—"

"I don't have time for this, Officer Norton. This is a crime scene. There should be an inner and outer perimeter already established, with those lines of demarcation clearly indicated with crime scene tape. That's your job as a patrol officer on scene, and it's your job to teach that to your probationer."

Norton hesitated. "We're holding those perimeters. But I didn't think there was any rush."

"No rush?" Clint asked. "Dispatch said there's a dead white girl in there. You don't think the news and the lookie-loos are going to start showing up soon? I'm surprised I beat them here."

The officer looked uncomfortable. Then he said, "She's never been to a homicide scene before. I wanted to see how'd she would do."

Clint stared at him, a common tactic he used in these situations.

"You know," Norton said, "to see if she remembered her training from the academy and her other FTOs. This is her last week in the training car. She's got to get her wires straight."

The detective continued to stare, waiting for Norton to fill the silence.

"I didn't forget," Norton told him. "It was supposed to be a teaching moment, and you blew it."

Clint looked over to where the rookie was rummaging through the trunk of the patrol car, looking for crime scene tape. Even from this distance, he could see the bright yellow roll attached to the trunk lid in a netting pouch. "She's never strung tape for a crime scene before so she needs guidance," he said. "That's why you're here. To train her."

"Don't tell me how to do my job."

"Then *do* your job," Clint snapped. "Amateur hour is over. Get an inner and outer perimeter set, and *you* start a crime scene log. Anyone wants to enter the scene, send your rookie to find me and get permission. Got it?"

"Don't talk to me like you're my boss," Norton said, his voice low. He puffed out his chest and took a step closer to Clint.

"This is *my* crime scene, and you're assigned to it. I *am* your boss right now, and if you don't get your ass moving, I'm going to put you on it in front of your rookie. And then I'll be sure to detail your little screw up here to your sergeant. You get me?"

Norton thought about it for second. Clint wasn't sure which threat would get him to back down, but he was confident one of them would.

After a few moments, Norton shook his head in disgust, and started walking toward the patrol car, muttering to himself. "Homicide, step aside, huh? Or in this case, make way for the Honey Badger."

Clint remained in his position until the two patrol officers strung the outer perimeter tape. Then he walked to the front door, where Officer Stone stood guard.

"You first on the scene?" Clint asked him without greeting.

Stone nodded. He looked a little nauseous.

"Got an ID on her?"

"Sonya Meyer," Stone said. "Her name is Sonya Meyer."

Clint looked at the door jamb, which was broken inward. Multiple black scuff marks were on the door near the knob, with one in the center of the door as well.

"Was this already kicked in when you got here?"

"No," Stone said. "I did it."

Clint pointed at the marks on the door, making a circular motion with his pen. "All of them?"

"Yeah. It…took a few kicks to get it open."

"Uh-huh. Why'd you kick the door?"

Stone took a deep breath and let it out. "No one answered when I knocked, even though I gave it a power shift knock. Her car's here, so—"

"Which is hers?"

Stone pointed. "The silver Honda there."

Clint made a note. "No one answered and…"

"I looked through the window. That's when I saw her on the ground, so I booted the door."

The detective pushed the door open with the tip of his pen. The victim's body lay inside. He saw signs of head trauma.

"I checked her pulse, but there wasn't one. Then I called it in."

"Was she warm to the touch?" Clint asked.

"What?"

He didn't repeat the question, just waited.

Stone seemed to process the words, then considered the question. "Yeah," he finally said. "I mean, she wasn't cold or anything."

"Did you move her?"

"No, I only touched her throat."

"No one else was here, I take it?"

"That's right. Norton and I swept the house when he arrived, but it was empty. Hey, what was going on with you and him?"

"Education," Clint said. "Did you see any sign of forced entry when you got here?"

"No, none."

"Why were you here in the first place?"

Stone shifted uncomfortably. "To interview her."

"Why?"

"It's…complicated."

"Then use small words."

Stone hesitated, then sighed. "What a mess."

"Details, please."

"I was here to talk to Sonya about her personal relationship with a councilman."

"Which councilman?"

"I…I don't know if I should say."

Clint peered closely at him. "You're at a homicide, son. Talking to a homicide investigator. You really think you want to withhold information?"

"No," Stone said slowly. "But I don't know if it's relevant."

"Relevancy is my job. Yours is to tell me what you know. Considering there's a dead girl in there, and people are frequently killed by people they know, I'm going to say it's relevant. Now, which councilman?"

Stone swallowed, not answering.

"There's only six male councilmen, Officer Stone. One is openly gay, another is in the closet. That leaves four possibles.

Now, are you really going to make me play a game of city hall *Clue* to figure out what you can tell me right now?"

"No," Stone said. "I guess not. It's Dennis Hahn."

"It figures. And?"

"He was fooling around with Sonya Meyer. And Shelly Mason before that. She's the one who gave me Sonya's name."

Clint made notes. "How did you get Mason's name?"

Stone paused. "A friend tipped me off."

The detective didn't like how Stone was hanging onto his secrets, but he could see in the man's demeanor that this one seemed to matter more than outing the councilman. He decided not to push the issue, for now.

"Why are you investigating the councilman? Is this some kind of secret police political activity, or was there a crime?"

"There was an allegation," Stone said. "A letter to the mayor's office that hinted Hahn may have sexually assaulted a girl."

"Sexual assault?" Clint gave him a dubious look. "That should have gone to the Sex Crimes Unit for detectives to investigate. You're not qualified."

Stone hesitated before answering. "The chief wanted to be sure there was something to investigate first. So he asked me to look into it."

Clint wrote that down, feeling a small surge of adrenaline. This was proof of the collusion he'd long suspected between city hall and the leadership of the police department. Either the chief and the mayor were looking to protect Hahn, or they were looking to have something to blackmail him with. He was sure of it. It was typical politics around this town, and probably only the tip of the iceberg.

"Who else was involved?" he asked quickly. "Captain Farrell?"

"No," Stone said.

"Captain Hatcher?"

"No. No one else."

"What about at city hall? The mayor's chief of staff?"

"No." Stone shook his head. "The mayor got the letter and gave it to the chief. The chief asked me to check into it. That's it."

That was never it, but he let the matter slide to the back burner.

"Was there anything to the sexual assault allegation?" he asked Stone.

"Honestly, I couldn't tell. She was a little flaky. First, she said it was consensual, then she acted like maybe it wasn't. It was confusing."

"What's the report number?"

Stone froze. "The…what?"

"I'm assuming you wrote a report," Clint said. "What's the report number?"

"I…I don't have it."

"What's wrong with you? You didn't clear it One-David, did you?"

"No, I wrote a report."

"Well, get the report number to me." Clint glanced down at Meyer. His mind clicked on something. Sonya Meyer. Shelly Mason. Both had the initials S.M. Was this a coincidence? "The girl who wrote the letter," he asked Stone. "What was her name?"

"Bethany Rabe."

B.R., not S.M. So nothing there…wait!

"Bethany Rabe committed suicide last week," Clint said coldly, his jaw clenching. His car-side conversation with Captain Farrell rang in his ears now, and the missing pieces fell into place.

"I know." Stone look remorseful.

Clint ground his teeth. "And Tyler Garrett responded to the scene."

Stone nodded, then gave the detective a questioning look. "How'd you know that?"

"I'm a detective, that's how!" he snapped. "Now, what do you know about the Rabe suicide?"

"Just that it happened. You should talk to Ty. He's the one following it up."

Ty, huh? You two are on a first name basis now? Clint looked hard at Stone, appraising him. Was this white bread weasel in league with Garrett? Or in love with the man's image like most of the department?

Stone squirmed under Clint's scrutiny. "What?" he asked.

"Give me Shelley Mason's contact information," Clint demanded.

Stone paused, then fumbled to remove his pocket notebook. He read off her phone number. "I promised I'd keep her name out of it," he said, a pleading tone in his voice.

"That was a stupid thing to say. We're the police, not some newspaper."

Stone gaped at him, looking chagrined.

Norton's rookie approached with a roll of crime scene tape in her hands. Clint took a quick look at her nametag. *J. Yang.*

He pointed. "Run the tape from here to there, Officer Yang."

"Yes, sir." Her voice seemed less rattled than before.

Clint watched while she attached one end of the crime scene tape and strung it across the front of the house. He didn't need to monitor her work, but it gave him a chance to think. His mind was whirring. Garrett's fingerprints were all over this. He wouldn't be surprised if it had been Garrett that killed Sonya Meyer.

But why?

Clint shook off the question. *Why* was almost always the last answer an investigator got, if ever. But one idea already sprang to mind. Maybe Garrett had gone from the drug trade to some modern form of pimping. Clint didn't know if his objective was money or blackmail material, but either one was a possibility. Or both.

For now, he'd focus on the evidence. He'd comb the scene for the physical variety, but he would need to backtrack Stone's investigation, too.

He wanted to leave this scene once it was secured and go interview Shelley Mason. He knew he could do a better job than whatever feeble attempt Stone managed. The temptation was strong, but he resisted. Mason wasn't going anywhere.

Then a thought struck him.

Unless Garrett kills her, too.

The man was capable of it, Clint knew. But why kill either of them? The detective let his mind tackle the question. Maybe Garrett was running these girls. One of them, maybe Meyer, decided she wanted out, and her death was Garrett's answer. Or Garrett could be blackmailing the councilman…but if that was the case, why kill Meyer?

He chewed on that. If the councilman submitted to the blackmail, that made Meyer dangerous. And expendable.

Garrett didn't leave loose ends dangling. The son of a bitch had been thorough twenty-one months ago, and he'd been careful since. There was no reason to believe he wouldn't be again.

Clint couldn't be in two places at once. It was either the crime scene or Shelley Mason. And if Mason was somehow involved with Garrett, then she might be able to give him up.

The detective tapped his pen on his notepad, thinking.

Officer Yang tied off the crime scene tape, looking to him for approval.

Clint nodded and she looked relieved.

The crime scene or Mason?

He glanced at the doorway that led to Meyer's dead body. That was real, he reminded himself. She was dead, and someone killed her. Maybe it was Garrett. That was just as likely as Shelley Mason being involved with him, maybe more so. And you only got one shot at a crime scene. One shot to get it right. If Garrett killed Meyer, then this was the chance Clint had been waiting for. His best chance to bury Garrett.

That decided it for him.

At the same moment, a news van pulled up, stopping in the middle of the street, just outside the outer perimeter tape.

"Get me some more cops," Clint told Stone. "We need to secure the alley and keep these hyenas at bay."

"Will do," Stone said, and trotted toward his car.

"Mind the outer perimeter," Clint said to Yang. "And absolutely no details to the media. Tell them nothing, got it?"

Yang nodded. "Got it." She headed back toward the yellow tape at the sidewalk.

Clint stepped inside Sonya Meyer's house, closing the door behind him. He ran his hand over his fresh haircut as he examined the scene.

Shelley Mason would have to wait.

Chapter 51

He entered the house as before and called out, "Skunk, where you at?"

When the man didn't answer back, Tyler Garrett froze and listened. Something wasn't right. The man had texted him to meet yet he wasn't responding.

Garrett pulled the Glock from the back of his pants and tucked it into his chest. He didn't push it away from his body like they did in the movies. That was a sucker's play, just asking for someone to reach out around a corner and try to take it away. Keeping the gun pulled tight to his body reduced the chance someone could take it from him and would require them to get close to do any harm. By that time, it would be too late for them.

He moved slowly through the kitchen, past the restroom that still reeked of feces, the stairwell to the basement, and then into the living room.

Skunk stood in the corner of the darkened room, his hands in his pockets. His yellow windbreaker stood out, but it was hard to see his features especially with the hood up over his head.

"Hey, Skunk."

"Yo, T."

"What are you doing over there?"

"Just chillin'. You know, lyin' low, lyin' low." His words were slow and rhythmic.

"Why didn't you answer me?"

Skunk didn't reply.

"Are you high?"

Skunk chuckled. "Yeah, man. Maybe. A little."

"Step into the light."

He took a hesitant step forward. Garrett kept the gun pointed at his chest.

"You gonna shoot me, T?" he asked, his voice still rhythmic.

"Take your hands outta your pockets, buddy. Let me see what you've got in there."

He removed his hands and opened them. When Skunk saw his palms, it was as if he was seeing them for the first time.

Garrett lowered the gun. "You got me worried, man. What happened with the girl?"

"She din't lissen."

"What's that mean?"

"I tol' her to keep her mouth shut, but she woon't lissen."

Garrett tucked the gun into the back of his pants. "Why wasn't she listening?"

"I don't know, T. I tol' her what you tol' me. That the cops was coming, and she need to keep her mouth shut."

It wasn't exactly what he'd told Skunk, but it was close enough.

"What happened when you told her that?"

"She started lipping, man."

"Lipping?"

"You know. Talking smack, talking big."

"The girl did that?"

"Yeah," Skunk said, his head bobbing several times as he nodded. "She was…a bitch."

"How old you think she was?"

"Wha, man?"

"Humor me."

"I dunno."

"Was she like eighteen or nineteen?"

Skunk's head bobbed. "Prolly. Yeah."

Garrett stepped to him. "So a young girl was talking smack to you?"

He slowly blinked. "Yeah."

Garett slapped him.

The smaller man spun to the floor. He pushed the yellow hood from his head and got back to his feet.

"The hell, T?"

"Get your head right, Skunk. This is important."

"Yeah, man. Okay."

"Tell me exactly what went down."

"Yeah, man, right, okay. The girl, she was unbelievable."

"Unbelievable?"

"Yeah, you understand? She just yammered."

"Yammered?"

"Like a little barky dog. Like a chihuahua. Yap, yap, yap. That's what she sounded like. A little bitchy chihuahua."

"Right," Garrett said.

"Chihuahua," Skunk said in a sing-song pattern.

"Focus, man. What happened then?"

Skunk's head bobbed. "I tol her if she din't stop talkin', she'd end up dead. Jus like you tol me to say."

Garrett knew what happened then and he grimaced. "Tell me you didn't kill her."

"You tol me to use my best judgment. You tol me to! The girl wouldn't stop, Garrett. She wouldn't stop! I had to do something. She was gonna call the cops."

"Was she really?"

Skunk stared at him.

"Was she really!" Garrett yelled into his face.

The smaller man in the yellow windbreaker flinched. After a moment, he shrugged. "I dunno."

Garrett closed his eyes and thought. He looked for every angle that it could come back on him.

"I'm sorry, T."

When Garrett opened his eyes, he asked, "Where are the papers I gave you?"

"What?"

"The papers?" he asked with a snap of his fingers.

Skunk reached into his pocket and pulled out a single, crumbled piece of paper. It was the photograph of Dennis Hahn. He handed it to Garrett.

"Where's the note? The one with my writing?"

The smaller man shoved his hands back into his pants, then he tried the pockets of his jacket. Finally, he shrugged. "I dunno."

"Did you have it at her house?"

"Yeah, man, that's how I found her."

"But you're not sure you had it when you got here?"

"No."

"Could you have dropped it while you were at the house?"

Skunk grew quiet as the thought.

Garrett watched him think. Finally, he grew impatient and repeated, "Could you have dropped—"

"Maybe, man, maybe. I dunno. It happened so fast."

Garrett snatched him then, yanking him by the jacket and turning him around. He shoved Skunk's head into the wall, but the smaller man didn't go down.

Instead, he just stood there, staring ahead, trying to understand what had happened. Garrett shoved his face into the wall again, this time harder.

Skunk lost consciousness then and began to collapse. Garrett snaked his right arm around the man's neck, making sure his forearm remained on the throat. With his left hand, Garrett grabbed his right wrist and applied pressure to Skunk's windpipe until he crushed it.

He let him collapse to the ground then. Garrett stepped back as Skunk flailed about, gurgling on his own blood. When the smaller man finally fell silent, Garett nudged him with his foot. Skunk didn't move.

Now, he needed to find the note with his handwriting on it. It was a piece of evidence floating out there that pointed back to him.

Garrett needed to go to Sonya Meyer's house before someone found her.

Chapter 52

Officer Ray Zielinski wadded up the hamburger wrapper and pushed it into the paper bag. He'd just finished wolfing down two greasy burgers. It was "2 for $2 Tuesday" at the local fast food restaurant, and he'd taken advantage of the price. Brown-bagging it got old.

He wiped off his fingers and checked the waiting calls on his MDC. The list appeared on the screen, and he frowned. There were more now than when he'd cleared the neighborhood dispute and hit the drive-through just a short time ago. Was he the only one taking calls today?

Through the power of the MDC, he could check on the rest of his lazy platoon. In the old days, he had to keep it straight in his head where everyone was, but now the information was a button away.

He couldn't resist the temptation to run a quick unit status check on the entire team, and saw that everyone was tied up on calls, including a couple of units loaned south to secure a homicide scene. Now, no one was available and calls were stacking up.

"That's the sergeant's problem," Zielinski grumbled. "Not mine." All he could do was take them one at a time.

He scrolled down, looking at the call types and locations. If he was the only one free, then he decided he'd earned the right to call shop. His gaze flicked down the list, until it stopped suddenly on an address he knew.

Agency Assist the call type read.

He put himself en route to the call, knowing it was a bad idea. He even knew how IA would frame it. Two trips to Lyle Bunney's house looked like a coincidence. Three times was definitely purposeful. How many other calls were available to him, but he chose this one?

Zielinski didn't care. He was tired of being pushed around. His exes, the strain of money problems, the constant worry about getting jammed up by complaints, the recent collision, the stuff with Garrett…he was sick of it all. Besides, maybe he'd get a chance to apologize, or tell Lindsay Wagner to eat a bag of dicks. He didn't know what he really wanted, except that he wasn't going to let any of it stop him from doing his job.

When he turned onto Lyle Bunney's street, he spotted Lindsay Wagner's car parked right in front of the house just like before. In keeping with the déjà vu theme, he pulled to the curb in the same spot he'd parked the two previous visits, several houses away. Then he exited his car and approached the social worker.

Wagner recognized him from a ways off. He scowled and put his hands on his hips. "What are you doing here?"

"You called the police," Zielinski said. "I'm the police."

"I didn't want *you*."

He stopped a couple of feet away from Wagner. Something was different, and he noticed it after a second. Wagner's long, thick beard was braided, Viking style.

Zielinski smirked. "This is the police department, not a buffet," he said. "You get who you get."

"I don't want you here," Wagner said.

"Everyone else is tied up. You get me, or you wait."

"How long?"

Zielinski shrugged. "I'm not a fortune teller. A while."

"That's unacceptable," Wagner said.

"Unacceptable?" he bristled. "Where do you get off dictating how we—"

A gunshot split the air, followed immediately by a bullet thunking into Wagner's car.

Wagner froze, his eyes widening.

Zielinski drew his pistol instinctively, moving toward cover and pointing his gun in the direction of Lyle Bunney's house, where the shot came from. "Get down!" he shouted at Wagner, reaching for his radio.

Wagner stared at him, unmoving.

Another shot rang out.

Wagner's eyes flared even wider in surprise, then slammed shut as he grimaced and howled in pain. His hands flew to his leg, and he crumpled to the ground.

"Damn it!" Zielinski yelled.

Another shot slapped into the side of the car. Zielinski's mind raced, even as everything slowed down. He remembered the .22 rifle inside Bunney's house. It had been a bolt action, not a semi-auto. Bunney would have to work the bolt for every shot and find his target again.

A shot buzzed over Zielinski's head, causing him to duck in response. Then, moving in a crouch, he pointed his pistol at the house and fired. He aimed for the windows but didn't worry about exactly where his shots landed. All he wanted was suppressing fire to buy him a few seconds.

Wagner stared down at his own bloody leg. When Zielinski reached him, he holstered his Glock, grabbed the screaming man by the belt and his braided beard, and dragged him behind the car. As he cleared the edge of the car, and let go of Wagner, a bullet skipped past him, whistling off the pavement.

Zielinski hunkered near the wheel of the car and drew his gun again. He slid his radio free and brought it up to his mouth.

"Shots fired!" he called. "Baker one twenty-three, shots fired!"

Chapter 53

Detective Clint stood in the living room, watching impatiently while the crime scene tech meticulously measured and photographed the crime scene. He'd begun his own career as a tech, and overseeing their work was something he usually took pleasure in, if only because these men and women knew how to professionally and efficiently do their tasks. But today, he wanted the job finished, and the results completed, as unreasonable as he knew that time frame to be.

So far, he'd seen no obvious evidence that pointed to a suspect, but that didn't surprise him. The tech would collect fibers, scrape under Meyer's nails, and search extensively for other forms of physical evidence. Clint had made it clear to her that this case required that she go the extra mile. The tech looked down at the deceased young woman and shook her head sadly.

"I have a daughter her age," she said in a quiet voice.

Clint was struck by how far removed from motherhood she'd looked in her dark blue coveralls, white hair net, goggles, and latex gloves. He didn't care, though. Whatever motivation she needed was fine with him.

Watching her work wasn't enough to bleed off his nervous energy, so he started to look through the house for any other evidence. He poked through belongings and paperwork, glancing at each, making a note if it seemed like it might somehow be relevant. Then he returned to check on the crime scene tech. She was still photographing and measuring near the victim's body.

"You get that small bit of spatter on the wall behind her?" he asked.

"Not my first rodeo, Wardell," she said, not stopping her work or looking at him.

Clint grunted. He glanced through the small open window out to the perimeter. The news cameras were pointed toward the house, but they'd already shot their stock footage, and now would only roll if there was a statement from the police or if the reporter went live. He glanced at his watch. They were in between the noon shows and the evening news, so he doubted that would happen. If nothing changed, he expected they'd pack up and leave soon, having collected enough to say whatever speculation they wanted on the news.

He saw someone in plain clothes talking to Officer Norton at the yellow crime scene tape.

More yellow. Curtains, crime scene tape, Stone's tie…

Clint blinked, recognized the man next to Norton. It was Garrett.

"What the hell?" he muttered.

The crime scene tech paused. "What is it?"

"Nothing," he told her. "Proceed."

She shook her head slightly and continued with her work.

Clint went to the front door and exited the house. By the time he stepped under the inner perimeter tape past Officer Yang, Garrett had done the same at the outer perimeter, smiling and bumping fists with Officer Norton as he did so.

"Hey!" Clint yelled. "Stop right there!"

Garrett turned toward him, still smiling easily, and kept walking up the concrete path toward the house.

The detective took long, purposeful strides, dropping his hand to his gun. "I said, *stop!*"

Garrett stopped, holding his hands up at shoulder level. "Whoa, easy there, big fella. We're on the same team."

Clint stopped a foot from him. "What the hell are you doing here?"

"Same thing you are. Checking on a dead girl." Garrett lowered his hands.

He forced himself to unclench his jaw. "You've got no standing here."

"I'm police, just like you."

Clint stared at him, trying to push aside his anger to think rationally. Why was he here? Was he fishing to find out if they'd discovered any evidence? Or taking some perverse pleasure in showing up on a murder scene he'd committed, just to rub Clint's nose in it?

"You're a patrol cop," Clint said. "Not a homicide detective."

"I'm a whole lot of things."

You got that one right, you dirty…

Then something clicked for him—Locard's law. The rule of transference at a crime scene. A suspect always brought evidence, even if it was microscopic, *to* the crime scene. He left evidence *at* the crime scene. And he took evidence with him *from* the crime scene when he left. Garrett was trying to defeat that law by coming to the scene in this context, so that if they found other evidence of his presence at the house, there'd be a plausible explanation for it.

Well, of course, you found one of my head hairs near the victim's body. I stood over the poor girl with Detective Clint when I came to help solve this tragic murder.

"You trying to O.J. my crime scene?" he growled.

"What?" Garrett asked.

"You heard me. You here to pull some kind of reverse Fuhrman?"

Garrett shook his head, looking confused. "Look, man, I'm here at the request of Councilman Hahn. They had a relationship."

"I know all about it."

A micro-flash of concern registered on Garrett's features, but it was gone immediately. "When I heard she was dead, I came running."

"How'd you hear?" Clint snapped. "You got an MDC in your personal car now?"

Garrett glanced over his shoulder and motioned at the assembled media. At least one of them was rolling film on their exchange, but Clint didn't care.

"It's all over the news," Garrett said, his tone making it clear that the answer was obvious.

"Not her name."

Clint stared at him, waiting.

Garrett hesitated a second before answering. "I recognized the house when I saw it on the TV. It's distinct, you know? Spooky-looking."

"You've been here before?"

"Nope, but I looked it up on Google Maps when the councilman told me about her."

"He told you about his extramarital affairs? Why would he do that?"

Garrett's eyes narrowed. "I probably shouldn't say any more."

"Why? Because you killed this girl?"

The officer shook his head in disgust. "You just can't let it go, brother."

"And I never will, *brother*." Clint spat the last word. "Don't play that card with me. Now answer my question."

"I shouldn't say any more."

"That's ridiculous. Tell me what you know."

"If I do, it'll jam up the chief, the department, and the councilman."

Clint thought about that. It fit with what he already knew about the scheming that was going on between city hall and the police department. He wondered again if Baumgartner was in league with Garrett. That would explain a lot. He couldn't imagine the chief trusting Officer Gary Stone to do any work on the dirty side.

Clint jabbed his finger emphatically toward Garrett. "You are *not* coming into this crime scene."

"That's not for you to say."

"The hell it's not. This is my scene." Clint whipped his finger toward the street. "You, get out."

"This is above your pay grade, Detective."

"Pay grade don't mean squat. I'm the lead. It's my scene." Garrett shrugged.

A sudden commotion drew Clint's attention. Several of the officers who had been securing the crime scene bolted for their patrol vehicles. One was already speeding away, lights and siren blaring. The news cameraman scrambled to get a shot of it.

"Stay right here!" Clint ordered Garrett. "We aren't done."

Garrett raised his hands, placating him. "You got it, man. I ain't moving."

Clint spun and hurried toward Norton, who was slamming his trunk lid shut and preparing to leave as well.

"What the hell do you think you're doing?" Clint asked. "This is an active homicide scene."

"Shots fired on a cop up northeast," Norton snapped. "We're leaving. Guard your own damn crime scene." He flung open the car door and jumped in.

"Leave Yang," Clint ordered. "I have to keep the scene secure."

"Fine!" He waved at Officer Yang, who was at the passenger door, reaching for the handle. "Stay here!"

Yang dropped her hand away from the door.

"You're on guard duty," Norton said, as he pulled his door shut. The car lurched forward. A moment later, his lights flashed and his siren screamed. Yang watched him go, her expression half confused, half angry.

"Don't worry about it," Clint told her. "He's a jerk."

Yang gave him a strange look. "I *know* he's a jerk, but he's my FTO."

"More jerk than FTO." Clint pointed to the crime scene tape. "Hold the perimeter. Keep the log."

Yang held up the clipboard with the crime scene log and nodded.

"No one in unless—"

"—they get your permission first," she finished. "I got it."

"Good. That means sergeants, brass, anyone."

"I understand."

Clint turned and headed back toward the house.

One of the news reporters hurried to intercept him. Her microphone dangled from her hand, so he knew she wasn't broadcasting live. "Detective, what was that about?"

It was about go screw yourself, Clint thought, and kept walking.

Then a thought struck him. They'd find out about the shooting soon enough. Someone would call from the TV station or they'd hear it themselves on a scanner in their van. Once that happened, the whole lot of them would flee his scene to get to something juicer. It was inevitable.

Would telling her now be that wrong?

Clint turned back to the reporter, who was still watching him.

"It's a shooting," he said. "Up north."

"A police shooting?" Her interest was piqued.

"Officers are involved," Clint said. "But I can't say any more than that."

"Where is it?"

Clint stared back at her and said nothing. He rarely told the media anything, leaving the brass to do it. Usually, releases were made over his objections, unless the reason was a request for information from the public. Clint had a reputation for being tight-lipped with the media, and he needed to maintain it. Besides, he'd already given her enough to get the response he wanted.

The reporter waited a moment, but when it became clear he wasn't going to say any more, she turned and hurried back toward her van. "Pack up!" she yelled to the camera man.

Clint turned on his radio and switched to the north channel while he watched the other reporters notice what she was doing and run over to her. He wondered if she'd share the information and was surprised that she did.

Since they probably all had police scanners in the van anyway, she was smart to tell them and bank a little favor for it. She played it the same way he had, albeit for different reasons.

Clint listened intently to the radio traffic, wondering for a moment who was involved in the shooting. When it was clear that sufficient units were responding to the scene, he clicked off his radio and continued to watch as the collected media scrambled to get all their gear into their respective vehicles. Tires chirped as they pulled away, and the sound gave Clint a small sense of satisfaction. He'd just manipulated the media. How was that for a turn of events?

Then he noticed that the front yard and the porch area were empty.

Garrett was nowhere to be seen.

Chapter 54

Lindsay Wagner stared right at Ray Zielinski. His expression was one of overwhelming fear, coupled with an odd vacancy. He held onto his leg where he'd been shot. Blood seeped through his fingers and pooled onto the concrete.

Another bullet pinged off the car, causing Zielinski to duck instinctively. This one struck something in the engine block before ricocheting.

Zielinski cursed. Pinned down by a guy in a wheelchair with a .22 while a social worker bled to death a few feet away. This was *not* how he saw this call going.

He cursed again, holstering his gun. Keeping low, he shifted toward Wagner. "Put more pressure on it," he said. "Push hard."

Wagner blinked at him, his expression unchanged. The strong smell of the man's musky cologne and his blood filled Zielinski's nostrils. He reached for Wagner's belt, unbuckling it and jerking it free through the loops. Wagner let out a surprised cry as he did so. He examined the belt. It wasn't leather, as he expected, but made of interwoven cloth.

It didn't matter. He wrapped it around Wagner's leg about six inches above the wound, cinching it down into a makeshift tourniquet.

Wagner screamed in pain.

Another shot rang out, zipping overhead.

Zielinski's radio crackled. "Several calls report that shots are continuing to be fired," the dispatcher said, her voice only slightly elevated. "All units proceed with caution. Baker one twenty-three, an update?"

He ignored it all, slipping the buckle pin into the cloth to help hold it in place. Then he grabbed Wagner's free hand and slapped the end of the belt into it. "Pull on this," he instructed him. "Keep it tight. Got it?"

Wagner didn't respond.

"Hey!" Zielinski barked and yanked on Wagner's beard. The social worker yelped. "You hear me? Keep this tight and you stay alive!"

Wagner nodded shakily. He closed his hand around the belt, keeping it taut.

Zielinski pulled out his radio and put it to his lips. "Baker one twenty-three, have medics standing ready to treat a gunshot wound to the leg. I've applied a tourniquet. Mark the time."

"Copy, twenty-three."

Another shot shattered the driver's side window of Wagner's car. Then Zielinski heard an outraged cry come from the house. "Shit!" yelled Bunney. "Bags of freakin' shit!"

His mind raced. He tried to count the number of shots Bunney had fired but couldn't. It had to have been at least ten, maybe more than twelve. If so, he was out of bullets. He'd have to reload, which would take him a while, unless he wanted to drop one right into the open chamber for each shot. Even that would be slower, though.

Training and common sense dictated that he stay behind cover with the injured Wagner. Keep the wounded man alive and hold down the fort until the cavalry arrived. Patrol cops first, and eventually SWAT. They'd surround the house and then figure out the best way to end the confrontation, whether it was an armed assault, or to gas him out, or get a negotiator to come in and try to talk him into surrendering.

But what if he could end it now, before Bunney could reload?

Zielinski glanced at Wagner. The man kept the tension on the makeshift tourniquet. Wagner would be fine without him.

In a moment, he made his decision. Keeping low, he bolted for a tree on the edge of Bunney's yard. Once he made it there, he drew his gun again. He took a second to recall the layout of the house. A quick look at the damage to the front windows told him Bunney was probably firing from the living room.

Now or never.

He crouched and ran up to the corner of the house. He ducked further as he slid along the front of the house toward the porch, staying below the shattered front window. Inside, behind the slightly parted curtains, Bunney rambled in frustration.

When he reached the porch, Zielinski hopped onto it. Without hesitating, he reared back and delivered a powerful kick to the front door. He planted his foot right beside the doorknob and followed through with all his weight. The doorjamb shattered. The door sprang backward into the house.

Zielinski followed, holding his gun at the ready.

He saw Bunney almost immediately, his wheelchair right where Zielinski had expected. Bunney was pushing rounds into a small magazine. When he saw Zielinski, he flung the rifle and magazine away before the officer could get a word out of his mouth.

"Drop it!" Zielinski shouted anyway.

"I did, I did, I did!"

"Don't move!" the officer bellowed.

Bunney lifted his hands in the air. "Don't murder me! I dropped the gun. I surrender!"

Zielinski stared at him. The crazy bastard had just shot at him. Tried to *kill* him. He deserved a bullet in the chest.

No.

He kept his gun trained on Bunney. "Don't move," he repeated. "And shut the hell up."

Lyle Bunney didn't move, and for once, he had nothing to say, either. He sat in his wheelchair, hands up and trembling, while Zielinski reached for his radio with his left hand.

"Baker one twenty-three," he said. "Code four. Slow 'em down."

"Copy, code four," the dispatcher repeated. "Baker one twenty-three is code four. Units can lower their response."

Zielinski put his radio back on his belt and listened to the approaching sirens.

Chapter 55

"Stay right here! We aren't done."

Clint was mad, and Tyler Garrett knew it. He had pushed his luck by walking into Clint's crime scene without the detective's authorization. Then he pushed it further by calling the man "brother." He knew the crazy bastard wouldn't buy it. Clint wasn't the type to nod to another man simply because they were the same race, let alone call him brother. But Garrett tossed the word out anyway, just to rub him the wrong way.

Clint had been following him since the shooting nearly two years ago. Due to that, Garrett was forced to live his life in a perpetual game of cat and mouse. Always looking over his shoulder, around corners, and under his bed for Detective Clint. It was a grind to live that way. He would do what he had to do to survive and thrive, but the opportunity to mess with Clint was too good to pass up.

Garrett raised his hands in mock surrender. "You got it, man. I ain't moving."

Something big was happening elsewhere. Garrett immediately knew it. Several officers ran to their patrol cars and raced away with lights and sirens activated.

The camera crews turned to film the action.

Clint trotted toward Officer Ken Norton, who looked like he was preparing to leave as well.

Garrett scanned the scene and realized everyone's attention was elsewhere. He turned and casually walked up the stairs toward Sonya Meyer's house.

An evidence technician stepped out. She wore blue booties over her shoes and a head cover hid her hair. Her eyes locked onto Garrett's as they passed each other.

"All done?" Garrett asked.

"Yes," she said, still waiting for him to say something additional to put her at ease.

"He asked me to take a look at her," Garrett said with nod toward Clint. "I'm working another case where her name came up."

The evidence technician shook her head. "Poor girl," she said and continued down the steps.

Garrett stole a final glance at Clint who actively engaged with Officer Norton, then stepped into the house and out of the detective's line of sight.

The woman's body was crumpled on the floor. It didn't take a thorough examination to determine that Skunk had done a real job on her. Her face was a mess. Blood was everywhere about her head and shoulders. That was what Skunk's best judgment looked like.

Garrett only had seconds to see if he could find the little orange note that he'd given Skunk. More than likely it had already been found. Officers had been in the house as well as the evidence technicians. Worse, Clint had been there. He would have homed in on a handwritten note immediately.

Regardless, Garrett needed to at least hope that it had been overlooked. His eyes scanned around her body. Nothing.

Then he searched the floor of the house. Again, nothing.

Tires chirped outside, and he looked around. He thought most of the officers had already left the scene.

He noticed a slight breeze blew in from the open door. Perhaps the note had fallen out of Skunk's pocket and had blown under a piece of furniture.

Garrett dropped to his hands and knees and quickly looked under the couch, the chair, the ottoman, the—

"What the hell are you doing!"

Clint stood in the doorway.

"Get out of there!"

Garrett sat up on his knees, his buttocks resting on his heels. "I was looking for a weapon."

"Get out of there," Clint repeated, this time controlling his anger.

Garrett stood slowly, then. "You know, I was only trying to help, Ward."

Clint's smile was crooked, as if unpracticed. "Normally, I'd get upset if another man misspoke my name."

"What?"

"I know what you're up to, *brother*. Better watch your step."

Garrett's ploy had failed, and his eyes narrowed for a moment, studying Clint. His face relaxed again, looking for another angle of attack. Clint had plenty of hang-ups, Garrett knew. He would keep poking at them until he found one that got a result he wanted.

He snapped his fingers and said. "Wardell. That's right. I'll remember that." Garrett walked toward the front door, but Clint held up his hand, stopping him.

"What now?"

"Show me your knuckles," Clint demanded.

"What?

"Your knuckles. Show them to me."

Garrett thumbed toward the girl. "You think I had something to do with this…Ward?"

Clint remained poker-faced.

Garrett was disappointed. Normally, a couple jabs at Clint's name were too much for the man to let slide. He held up his uninjured hands, showing the backs of them to Clint. They were standing very close. If Clint sensed the danger, he didn't let it show in his eyes.

The detective examined Garrett's knuckles, then frowned. "You're playing a game, Garrett."

He dropped his hands and stepped back. "I told you why I'm here."

"I'm not buying it."

"I don't care if you buy it."

Clint stepped into him. "You better care, Officer. Right now, I'm writing you into my report. It's going to look like you tried to interfere with a crime scene."

Garrett studied him for a moment, then said, "You might want to rethink that."

"Yeah?"

"Yeah."

"Pray tell."

"This story is right up your alley…Wardell."

Clint opened his mouth briefly to object but closed it slowly.

"There was a young woman—" Garrett began.

The detective's eyes flicked to Sonya Meyer.

"Try again."

Clint's eyes narrowed as he thought. "Betty Rabe."

Garrett nodded. "Who had a brief relationship with a handsome councilman."

"Hahn," Clint said.

"That relationship soured, and the young woman may have sent a letter to get the councilman in trouble."

"She sent a letter to the mayor. And?" There was no surprise in Clint's words.

This caught Garrett by surprise. He took a deep breath, steeling himself. If Clint knew more than he was letting on, he could be setting Garrett up. Clint was one of the best at suspect interrogation, it wasn't a department secret.

His best option now was to forge ahead. Lay out the cards that he had started to play. There was no one else in the room, in case he ever had to backtrack and deny what was said.

"Not understanding how city government works, the young woman thought the mayor would have some influence over the councilman."

"What did the letter say?" Clint's eyes flickered with interest.

Garrett relaxed slightly. The detective knew some, but not everything. He was back in control.

"It said she was seventeen, that she was in a relationship with the councilman, and that he had raped her."

"He raped her?"

Garrett nodded slowly.

"What happened to the letter?"

Clint's mild interest showed he had almost sunk the hook with the lie about the rape. He hadn't committed fully to Garrett's story yet.

"The mayor, seeing the opportunity this letter presented, gave it to the chief of police, who gave it to his personal lap dog to investigate."

"*Stone*," Clint said, nodding. He was swimming around the hook, considering it.

"Charlie Bravo," Garrett affirmed.

"The mayor and the chief, huh?"

"Stone investigated. He went to both the young woman and the councilman for their sides of the story."

"That's when the councilman called you?"

Garrett was about to agree, to take the opportunity that Clint gave him, but he saw that doing so would put him into a trap. Clint could easily knock down that story. Also, Garrett's investigation into Betty Rabe's suicide could be seen as opportunistic. He was walking a fine line now. The truth was still better than a lie.

"No," Garrett said. "I didn't know Hahn then."

Clint's brow furrowed.

"Dispatch sent me to Rabe's suicide."

"That was out of your district."

"They sent me to it," Garrett said. He wasn't sure if Clint had followed him that night. There were some nights he definitely knew he was being followed, others when he knew he'd lost the detective, and still others where he wasn't sure if the man was out there or not. He wasn't about to reveal that he knew he was occasionally followed but decided to hold that card for another moment. Instead, he said, "You can verify that."

"You know I will."

"I figured as much."

The game of cat and mouse continued even when they stood toe-to-toe. Garrett realized now that some of the story he was telling the detective was already old news, that Clint was letting him run his story until he caught a lie.

"While there, I met a friend of Rabe's who told me about her relationship to Hahn. When I interviewed the councilman, he told me how he was being squeezed by the mayor and the chief. I believed him. I've been squeezed by them before. I think you've been squeezed by them, too, right?"

Clint remained silent, considering what he said.

The line Garrett walked had become thinner. He had to be more careful now. Not saying enough would make him suspicious. Saying too much would make him more suspicious. To say anything wrong would give Clint ammo to shoot holes in his story. Instead, he needed to give Clint only enough for him to look elsewhere, but he also wanted the detective's conspiracies to wrap in on themselves.

"Stone investigated the initial case and wrote a report. He never entered it into the system."

Clint blinked a couple times, as if he was pulling himself back to the current moment.

"What?"

"Stone wrote a report."

"I know that."

"But he never entered it into the system. It never got a report number. As far as the department is concerned, Officer Stone never talked with Betty Rabe or Councilman Hahn."

"About a rape allegation? Why would he do that?"

Garrett knew he'd sunk the hook.

"Because that's what the chief told him to do."

As he thought, Clint made a sucking sound between his teeth. "How do you know this?"

"Stone told me."

The detective slowly nodded, as if he were putting pieces together inside his head.

"When I pressed him during my follow-up, Hahn also told me he had a couple of other relationships. Sonya Meyer was one."

Clint's gaze hardened. "So, you came running when you saw her house on TV."

Garrett met his gaze and didn't look away.

"Who was the other woman?"

"Shelley Mason."

"Shelley Mason," Clint repeated.

"Yeah, Shelley Mason."

Clint remained silent for several minutes as he thought. Garrett watched him with fascination. He would have loved to know how the man was putting together those pieces in his head.

When Clint refocused on him, he said, "Get out of my crime scene," and pushed Garrett out of the house.

Garrett did not resist this time. When he was outside, he hurried to his car, knowing full well that Wardell Clint had bitten the hook.

Chapter 56

"Get that media van out of the street," Captain Dana Hatcher told the nearest patrol officer. "Keep this roadway clear for emergency vehicles."

"Yes, ma'am," the uniform responded, and strode away to follow her orders.

Hatcher surveyed the scene and found nothing else that needed her attention, so she made her way toward the ambulance parked near Zielinski's patrol vehicle. She'd been told that another unit already transported the wounded social worker, but she saw that a medic was checking Zielinski at the back of the open ambulance. She noticed Dale Thomas, the union president, standing nearby.

Oh, joy.

As she walked, Captain Tom Farrell parked his car just across the street. When he saw her, he trotted over. "I've got detectives and crime scene techs on the way," he said. "I take it the scene is secure?"

Hatcher gestured toward the target house, where a pair of uniformed patrol officers guarded the front door. "There's two more in the back," she said without looking at him.

"Good," he said. "We can probably drop that to one on each door once the detectives and techs start their work."

"Fine," she said curtly, still walking.

The two of them reached the back of the ambulance together. The medic had been checking Zielinski's pupils, but snapped off her pen light.

"I told you, I'm fine," Zielinski said.

"Let the medic do her work, Ray," Hatcher said. She glanced at Thomas, giving him the barest of nods.

"I'm done, actually," said the medic, a woman with the edges of a flowery tattoo creeping up from her collar. She kept her attention focused on Zielinski. "You're still feeling the effect of the adrenaline. Don't be surprised if you crash hard, and either get really tired or extremely anxious. That's normal."

"Is drinking Jameson normal?"

The medic shrugged. "A little wouldn't hurt."

Zielinski looked at Hatcher. He even gave her a tiny grin. "My kind of doctor."

"I'm glad you're all right," Hatcher said.

He shook his head. "It was the craziest thing. We were just standing there, and all of the sudden—"

Hatcher raised her hands. "Ray, stop. Don't tell me anything. We'll talk after your interview."

Zielinski gave her a confused look.

"She's right," Thomas said. "I was about to stop you myself. Don't make any kind of statement until after the shooting is investigated and has a case finding."

"Shooting?" Zielinski repeated. "I didn't shoot him. They took him into custody without a scratch."

Farrell glanced at the shot-up car that now sat all alone on that section of the block. "Looks like a lot of ejected casings on the ground over there. So you definitely shot *at* him."

Zielinski's expression turned dark. "Is this being treated as an officer-involved shooting?"

"No," Farrell said. "We're investigating it as an assault with a deadly weapon. But…you should still listen to your union rep. If you want to talk to investigators, you'll get a chance, back at the station."

Zielinski frowned but didn't reply.

Hatcher reached out and squeezed his shoulder. "It's going to be okay, Ray. I'm just glad you're all right."

He looked away. "Okay. Thanks."

"If you need anything, let me know."

Zielinski didn't reply.

"I'll be sure to pass on any of my member's needs," Dale Thomas told her curtly.

She gave the worm another cool look but didn't bother to answer him. She turned and walked away.

Farrell fell in beside her. "Ever since they went with a full-time, for-hire president..." he muttered.

Hatcher stopped near the shot-up sedan. "The chief on his way?" she asked.

Farrell stared back at her. "He's already come and gone."

"What?" She looked at him in disbelief. "How long did he stay? Five seconds?"

"He checked on his guy," he said, defensively. "There's a homicide on the south side he needed to see about, too."

"One of his own guys is shot at and he can't bother to hang around at the scene for a few minutes?" She pointed toward the ambulance, where the medic was shutting the rear door, preparing to leave. Thomas and Zielinski had moved to the rear of Zielinski's patrol car. "They're taking Ray down to the station for an interview soon. Is he going to spend any time with him there? Will that be more convenient for him?"

"Dana..."

"This is bull."

"Come on," Farrell muttered. "Zielinski's fine. He didn't kill the guy."

Hatcher stared at him, not believing what she'd just heard.

"By policy, he doesn't even need to take the three days of admin leave," Farrell continued, "unless he wants to, or thinks he needs it."

"By *policy?*"

"I'm telling you what his options are. This situation doesn't meet the critical incident designation, so there's no mandatory admin leave."

"I'm glad you're so concerned about my officer," she said.

"Don't be that way."

"You're right. I should start spouting policy instead." Hatcher turned away from him and walked back toward

Zielinski. She wanted him to know she cared about him. Besides, at that moment, she'd rather endure the presence of Dale Thomas than spend any more time with Tom Farrell.

Chapter 57

Garrett jogged through the alley, looked both ways before he crossed Haven Street, then entered the alley on the other side of the street. He continued his pace, his eyes scanning for onlookers. At the last moment, he turned and ran into the backyard of the small, dilapidated house. He burst through the back door and closed it immediately behind him. He turned on his small flashlight.

The stench of feces assaulted his senses again. He hurried down the hallway, stepped over the body of Skunk, and searched the living room. Since the windows were boarded up with plywood, no light shone inside. Slowly and methodically, his flashlight covered every inch of the room.

He covered his mouth and nose with his gloved hand.

Garrett stepped into an empty bedroom. It took only a moment to verify that the little orange note was not there.

A few steps and he was into the second bedroom. Another sweep of the flashlight and still no sign of the small orange paper.

As he breathed through his fingers, he smelled the new leather gloves. They helped mute the smell of human waste but didn't fully cover it.

He passed the stairwell to the basement and the bathroom and checked the kitchen. No note.

One room left. He opened the bathroom door and almost retched immediately. The smell was overwhelming. The toilet was full of feces and toilet paper.

A nearly empty roll of toilet paper sat on the edge of the sink. Garrett swung the flashlight around the floor and saw the little piece of orange paper near the base of the toilet.

It must have fallen out of Skunk's pocket the last time he used the head. Garrett reached out with his foot and ended up kicking the note further behind the toilet.

He yelled into his gloved hand.

With an inhale of air through his fingers, Garrett bent down. He held on to the edge of the sink for support and reached behind the toilet. His fingers snatched the note and he scrambled back out of the bathroom.

He slammed the door behind him, bent over, and gagged for several moments. He fought to keep the contents of his stomach inside him.

At the rear of the house, he stopped and turned back. He walked down the hallway and opened the door to the basement. He shined the light down the steps for a moment, then clicked it off. The house went completely dark.

It took a few moments for him to feel comfortable in the darkness. When he did, Garrett lifted Skunk's body and held him at the top stair. With a shove, Garrett sent Ezekiel "Skunk" Hetzel tumbling into the basement. He turned his flashlight on again and saw Skunk's body lying in a contorted mess on the concrete floor.

He shut the door and walked to the back of the house. Even though he was wearing gloves, he wiped off his fingerprints from the doorknob. He was fairly certain that was the only surface he had touched during his visits to the house.

Garrett wondered how many times he'd been seen going in and out of the neighborhood. A couple times he was in uniform. A couple times he was in plain clothes. It was a dumpy house in a terrible block in the worst part of town.

Was anyone really going to pay attention to him?

He was betting that no one would.

Chapter 58

The media vans were long gone, so Clint and Farrell were able to stand in the front yard of Sonya Meyer's house and speak outside of Officer Yang's earshot. In hushed tones, Clint told Farrell about Garrett's visit to the crime scene. He left out Garrett's accusations against the chief and the mayor, not sure if he was ready to share those with Farrell yet. Garrett's presence at the crime scene was bad enough. As he spoke, he noticed the captain's brow furrow, but he didn't seem to grasp the magnitude of what had happened.

"He contaminated the crime scene," Clint said. "Now even if I find evidence of him being in the house, there's an explanation. Even a public defender could show reasonable doubt with a jury over that."

"You really think it was him?" Farrell asked. "Wouldn't the council member be the more likely suspect?"

"You ever meet Dennis Hahn? He seem to you like the type who could beat a girl to death?"

"No," Farrell admitted. "But a lot of people aren't what they seem."

"True enough, but I made a couple of calls since I've been here. I talked to Jean Carter, his personal assistant. She ran down his schedule and confirmed that he was present at all meetings and events. Based on a preliminary estimate on the time of death, that alibis him pretty solid."

"People lie."

"All the time. I'll have to follow-up and verify once the medical examiner narrows down the time of death. But Hahn is unlikely to have been the one to do this. Garrett, on the other hand, is on his day off." He gave Farrell a pointed look. "And he just happened to show up."

"That's not as strange as it sounds, actually."

"Why not?"

"He was working on something involving Hahn."

"He told me. So did Stone." Clint peered at Farrell, suddenly suspicious. "You knew about this? Hahn, Stone, Garrett, all this mess?"

"Not immediately, but yeah."

"Are you kidding me?"

"The chief told me about it."

"The chief," Clint repeated. Everything Garrett had told him was ringing true. He stared at Farrell.

Can I still trust you?

Farrell spread his hands apologetically. "He tells me things in confidence, Wardell. I give him advice."

"And keep his secrets."

"If it's appropriate. What business is it of yours?"

Clint shook his head, trying to break free of the anger he felt rising in his chest. "If Garrett and Baumgartner are in this together, doesn't that make it my business?"

Farrell gave him a doubtful look. "They're not. Baumgartner asked me to check on Garrett. That's why I talked to you."

"Maybe you got played. Maybe that was all about him wanting to find out if anyone is on to his boy."

"No, I don't believe it."

"You don't *want* to believe it."

"That's not it."

"The chief is dirty, or he's blind when it comes to Garrett. Either way is bad for us."

"He's not dirty."

"It sure sounds like it." Clint took a half step back and glared at Farrell. "Are you in it with the both of them? Is that it? Is that why you wanted to tell the chief everything, bring him into the loop?"

"No!" Farrell snapped. He glanced over at Officer Yang, who was staring straight ahead, doing her best not to notice the argument. Farrell lowered his voice another notch. "Look, that was a mistake, okay? You were right. We need to keep this contained."

Clint took a deep breath and let it out. Then he said, "Garrett is involved somehow in this woman's death."

"I can't believe he killed her."

The detective thought of Garrett's undamaged knuckles. "Maybe he didn't, but he's involved. I don't know exactly how, but he is."

"You're sure of that?"

"I'm positive. I don't know what his game is, but he's playing something."

Farrell nodded. "I can believe that."

"Well, ain't I just overjoyed." He leaned closer to Farrell. "You want this to stay contained, Captain? Keep me in the loop."

"I will."

Clint snorted, and brushed past him, heading back into the house.

Chapter 59

He yanked opened the door before she could knock a second time. She jumped slightly and her eyes widened in surprise. She wore a women's newsboy cap, a black jacket buckled around the waist, and knee-high boots.

"What the hell, boy-o?"

Gary Stone stepped back to let Jean Carter into his house. She dropped her purse upon entering, walked into the living room, and dropped onto the couch. She crossed her legs to the side of her. She had texted to say she was coming over because she needed to talk with him in person. He asked if she wanted to go out for something to eat, but she said that the conversation had to be done in private. Stone tried to get more out of her, but she quit replying to his text messages after that.

"What do you mean?"

"What's going on with you? With Councilman Hahn?"

Stone ignored her questions and pointed to the kitchen. "Want something to drink? To eat?"

"I want the truth, Gary."

He stood at the edge of the living room, hesitant to commit to this conversation.

"Listen, Gary. I know you sometimes have to keep secrets. I do, too."

"Like Armstrong? You knew about that long before the paper got hold of it."

"Of course I did. That's our jobs, right?"

"You didn't tell me."

"I didn't even tell my own boss!" she snapped. "And don't change the subject. Something's not right with Hahn. I got a call from a detective today."

"Which one?"

"Clint Wardell."

"You mean, Wardell Clint."

Jean's eyes rolled up as she thought, then she shook her head. "Okay, whatever. Clint, right? He called about Hahn's whereabouts today."

"And?"

"And!"

Stone stared at his friend.

"That's all you're going to give me, Gary? *And?* Clint asked if I ever heard of Sonya Meyer. I told him I hadn't. He was evasive when I asked who she was and why he was asking if the councilman had ever met with her. Who's Sonya Meyer, Gary?"

Stone looked around his apartment.

"Gary!"

"She's a woman who was murdered today."

"Why was the detective calling me then?"

Stone sat in the chair across from her. There was no avoiding this conversation. "I dunno. He was probably trying to get an alibi for Hahn."

"Why would he need an alibi?"

"Because he had a relationship with her."

"No, I said it was Shelley Mason he had a relationship with. I don't know who Sonya Meyer is."

"I talked to Shelley. She told me about Sonya. By the time I got to her house, she was dead."

Jean's hand lifted to her mouth. "Oh my God. You found her?"

Stone nodded.

"Oh, Gary. I'm sorry. Are you okay?"

"Yeah. I think so. Yeah."

They stared at each other for a few moments until Jean said, "So, this detective, Clint, he thinks Hahn killed this woman?"

"I don't know. Maybe. Probably not. He has to run everything down. Understand?"

"Sure. I get it. Like they do in the movies, right? So, there's another name I heard recently. Betty Rabe."

"Where did you hear it?"

"Does it matter?"

"This one does. No secrets, Jean. It's important."

"Charlene asked me about her."

Great. Charlene Mapes, the mayor's assistant. Just what he needed.

Jean continued, "She asked if I'd heard anything about her. I told her no, that I hadn't. She told me she saw a letter that this girl sent to the mayor about the councilman. Then she said the girl killed herself. She said the mayor and the chief are investigating it. Do you know anything about this?"

"I do."

"This is the thing I asked you about when we were at the club. Remember? You denied knowing anything about it."

"I was trying to protect you."

"I don't need protection, Gary! I need the truth. Am I working for some sort of monster?"

Stone stood then and walked as he spoke. "I dunno, Jean. I don't. He's a perv. That I do know."

"Most guys are," she said.

Stone stopped and stared at her.

"Don't get butt hurt now. Finish what you were going to say."

"Here's the deal," he said and then told her everything. He told her about Betty Rabe's letter, his interviews with her and the councilman, the backroom dealings with the mayor and the chief. When he was done explaining the situation, he said, "That's why I'm freaked out. If this thing comes out, they can throw me under the bus. I'm the fall guy for the whole incident if it turns bad."

"You didn't kill her."

"No, but I'll be the one everyone can point to and say he bungled the investigation. Everyone dances away, but me."

"Maybe this job isn't for you, Gary."

"Being a cop?"

"No, being a politician."

"I'm not a politician."

She gave him a knowing look.

"Whatever," he said.

Jean stood and grabbed Stone by the upper arms. "You need to tell someone about this. Go to Human Resources and tell them. They can help you."

"I'm not an employee of city hall."

"You're an employee of the *city*, Gary. They can help you. Don't be a dumbass."

"I can't. I gave my word to the chief."

"You're going to be loyal to a man who might throw you under the bus to protect himself? How does that make any sense?"

"I can't explain it, but it makes sense to me. When I joined the department, it felt special. You probably won't understand, but I was part of something bigger than I had ever been part of before."

"Don't say brotherhood."

"No, let's say family. I was part of a family."

"That family is going to disavow you if they get in trouble."

"They haven't yet."

"You're going to let that happen just to prove that your fears were correct? You're not going to protect yourself first?"

"Even if it all comes out and falls on me, I'll stand up until it happens."

"And if it does? Then what will you do?"

Stone thought about showing Jean the photo of the bison in the snow-covered field hanging in his bedroom. He thought it might help explain how he felt, but she had never seen his bedroom. They weren't those kinds of friends. Instead, he said, "I'll take it like a man."

"Whatever that means," Jean said.

Chapter 60

"I've read your name on some articles about me. Some good, some bad."

"I write the truth. Good or bad, that's a judgment call the reader makes, not me."

Reporter Kelly Davis leaned back in her chair. They were in the food court of River Park Square, the shopping mall in the heart of downtown. When Garrett called her, asking to meet, he tried to get her to go someplace quiet. Since she didn't know him, she insisted on meeting someplace public. This was the most public place he could think of and she reluctantly accepted.

Hundreds of people were in the food court. No one appeared to pay any attention to them.

"I've got some info for a story I think you will find very interesting."

"Of course you do."

Garrett frowned. "What's that mean?"

"You're not the first cop with some beef to come to me and try to get me to write his story."

"That's not what I'm doing."

"It's funny that you all complain about how unfair the media treats you, but you embrace us with open arms when you need us."

"Flip the coin, lady. You treat us the same way. You dump on us until you need us. Then you say things like 'never forget' until you do."

Davis glanced around the food court. Garrett watched her and waited. He liked this woman. Not only was she attractive, she was self-assured. She seemed the type to not put up with any crap. There was something in the way she carried herself that reminded him of his wife, Angie.

When her eyes returned to Garrett, Davis said, "Let me hear your story. I'll let you know if it's any good."

"I don't want my name anywhere near this article."

"That's not how it works."

"It does for this one."

"No, it doesn't." Davis stood and pushed her chair back.

"Hey, hold on a sec," Garrett said. "This involves the mayor and the chief."

"Doing what?"

"Covering up the sex crime of a councilman."

"Buckner? That's old news."

"Not Buckner."

Davis tilted her head. "What?" she whispered. "Not Armstrong. He's into more than kickbacks?"

"Not Armstrong. Wanna stick around and hear the story now?"

She slowly sat and pulled her chair back to her.

"Councilman Dennis Hahn has a history of inappropriate relationships with young women."

"No chance," Davis said. "Not Holy Hahn."

"One of which was underage." Garrett knew the age of consent was sixteen, however, saying a girl was underage was the type of bait a reporter couldn't help but chase.

Davis stared at him for a moment, then pulled out her notebook to take notes.

"Here are three names for you to research. Bethany Rabe. Shelley Mason. That's Shelley with an 'ey' by the way. And Sonya Meyer."

When Davis was done writing, she nodded.

"Bethany Rabe was seventeen years old and preferred to be called Betty, although her family and Hahn called her Beth. She sent a letter to the mayor's office alleging that Hahn assaulted her."

"There's proof of this letter?"

"The mayor's office staff saw it."

"Physical proof would be better."

"I figured." Garrett pulled out his phone and showed a picture of Betty Rabe's letter.

"Who has this letter now?" Davis asked.

"The chief of police. The mayor asked him to look into the matter, but he asked him to do so discreetly."

"Discreetly?"

Garrett nodded. "They assigned the Special Police Problems officer to do it."

"Special Police Problems? Is that a real thing?"

"Real as you and me. It's a stupid name but check it out if you don't believe me. Anyway, it's Officer Gary Stone. He's assigned to city hall. That's easy for you to find, right?"

"Gary Stone? Yeah. I've talked with him before. Nice guy."

"Right, everyone thinks so. Stone interviewed Betty Rabe and then Hahn about the alleged assault."

"What happened next?"

"Nothing."

"Nothing?"

"Stone handwrote a report."

Davis didn't react.

"Let me repeat," Garrett said, "he *handwrote* a report. Know what that means?"

She shook her head.

"It means it was never given an incident number. It was never entered in the system. This report about the alleged sexual assault of a minor by a city councilman never existed."

Davis's pen hovered over her notepad as she thought. When she looked up, she said, "They wouldn't do that. Not the chief. Maybe the mayor, but even he's not that stupid. That would destroy both of them."

Garrett showed her a picture of Stone's report. "Here's the report. Believe me now?"

"Email that to me."

"No. I don't want it traced back to me."

"Who has the original?"

"Baumgartner. I think Stone might have a copy, but I can't be sure. He may have destroyed it. He's freaked out about what they asked him to do."

"And there are no other copies of that report?"

"Besides my photographs?"

"Exactly."

Garrett looked over to another table where Tiana Kennedy sat intently watching him. "That woman over there has a copy for you. Along with a copy of Betty Rabe's letter. When we're done here, she'll walk over and drop that folder she's holding. Then what happens afterwards is up to you."

"This could blow up city hall."

"Don't stop with the letter," Garrett said.

"Why?"

"Because Betty Rabe killed herself when she didn't get the help she needed."

"Oh my God."

"Shelley Mason was also involved with Hahn. She was an intern in city hall and was fired because of her relationship. The termination was done quietly and didn't involve Human Resources."

"That's some underhanded maneuvers," Davis said.

"That's your tax dollars at work."

"What about Sonya Meyer?"

"She was murdered this morning."

"Really?"

"I wouldn't lie about a murdered eighteen-year-old."

Davis bent over her notebook and wrote frantically for several minutes. When she looked up, Garrett was in the process of standing.

"You've got everything you need," he said.

"I have more questions for you."

"No. My name stays out of this. I don't want to be anywhere near this. Not after all I've been through. Understand?"

"Yeah, of course," Davis said, and looked expectantly to the black woman.

He waved to Tiana who slowly walked over, a manila folder in her hand. When she was near the table, she dropped it in front of Davis.

Garrett stood and put his knuckles on the folder. "You want my recommendation? You don't reveal that you have these copies yet. Play it out that you have the story but you're looking for the proof. See what the administration does. If they destroy the report, they hang themselves. If they do come forward, you can verify that nothing was changed."

He tapped the report once, then wrapped his arm around Tiana's waist and pulled her into him.

The reporter put her hand on the folder and looked up at Garrett. "What do you get out of this?"

"Justice," he said. "I can't get them for what they did, but you can."

WEDNESDAY

The battlefield is a scene of constant chaos.
The winner will be the one who controls that chaos,
both his own and the enemy's.
—Napoleon Bonaparte, French statesman and military leader

Chapter 61

Captain Dana Hatcher tossed the folded newspaper onto her desk and set down her Starbucks coffee cup. She'd splurged on a fancy drink this morning after spending a restless night still angry at Farrell and the chief over how they handled the Zielinski shooting. The whole department seemed upside down to her.

It was early yet, so she closed her door and sat down to have her coffee in peace.

When she became a lieutenant, she had to attend a state-certified leadership course. It was an intensive three weeks with a lot of reading on behavioral science, and difficult, brutally honest classroom discussions. At its core, the emphasis of the course had been meeting the needs of your followers. Not long before her promotion to captain, the chief pegged her to attend a command college course. That was the first hint that she was likely to get the nod for the promotion. She spent three full months away from home at Northwestern University's School of Police Staff and Command, and the curriculum was remarkably similar to what she'd studied in the three-week course. Take care of your people, be honest with them, expect the best from them, and those people will be mostly happy and do great work. While she learned a number of new concepts and ways to approach problems, both courses served to validate what she had always believed and tried to do, even as a sergeant.

She knew Baumgartner and Farrell had been through command school and had some of the same training. So why did they seem to be doing things that were antithetical to everything she'd learned was good leadership?

Ray Zielinski might be a mess right now, but he was *their* mess. And no matter how tough or how experienced a cop might be, getting shot at was a scary experience. Baumgartner barely coming to the scene to check on him was a cardinal sin, as far as she was concerned. Sure, he dropped in to see Zielinski for a little longer at the station, but that was a weak gesture—too little, too late.

What could be more important than one of your officers being shot at?

The answer, she knew, was nothing. Absent a dying officer elsewhere, nothing was more important in that moment.

Hatcher sipped her frothy, sweet coffee, then leaned back and closed her eyes. Despite her frustration, she tried to see the situation from the chief's perspective. Zielinski had been shot at, and he'd returned fire, but no one was killed. Even the wounded social worker was in stable condition at the hospital. Chief Baumgartner, an old school cop if ever there was one, probably downgraded the priority based on that. Add to that, there was a homicide on the other side of town.

Her lip curled as she realized she'd probably hit on the truth of it. Although it explained the chief's behavior, it didn't excuse it, at least in her mind. This old school thinking was out of step with today's police officer. They weren't all rough and tumble ex-military, former football players like when Baumgartner came on. Or hell, when she did. Cops were smarter now, and better at talking to people. They were also allowed to be more human. It wasn't a donuts and black coffee world anymore. It was a world of bagels and…well, something special from Starbucks.

She hung around the station yesterday until Zielinski's interview was finished, checking on him before and after. While the union president guarded Zielinski from her like she was the enemy, she could tell Ray appreciated her being there. He seemed a little rattled by the turn of events, and knowing what else was going on in his life, she was sure he was feeling the stress. Even so, he'd acted admirably, saving the social worker's life and somehow avoiding a fatal shooting of the suspect. Really, he saved two lives.

Hatcher's eyes snapped open. How had that not occurred to her yet? She should put Zielinski in for a life-saving award, at the very least. He deserved that kind of recognition for his actions. Not only that, but an award like that might mitigate some of his other internal affairs issues.

She made a note on her to-do list. That made her feel a little better. She took another drink of the caramel latte and flipped open the newspaper. The banner blared at her.

Another Sex Scandal at City Hall!

Below that, the headline read:

Suicide and Murder Surround Councilman Hahn's Affairs; Rumors of Cover-Up by Mayor, Police Chief.

"You've got to be kidding me," Hatcher muttered, and started reading.

Chapter 62

The newspaper shook in Officer Gary Stone's hands.

There on the front page was the entire story of the Betty Rabe incident. He tried to read the article, but he kept coming back to the headline. He knew who the anonymous source for the article had to be. The only other guy who was involved as much as he was.

He'd gotten a call last night after Jean left. It was from a phone number he was unfamiliar with, so he let it go to voicemail. He wasn't in the mood for to deal with another problem, so he didn't check the message check until he got to his office. It was a reporter asking him to call her in reference to a story the newspaper planned to run the next morning—*this morning.*

His office phone rang but he refused to look at it. It had been ringing almost constantly since his arrival. He had also turned off both of his cell phones. There had been a barrage of text messages from guys on the department asking him what was going on. Everyone wanted to get in on the drama.

When he walked into city hall that morning, no one made eye contact with him. He didn't understand why until he saw the newspaper headline. Now, people walked by his office and peeked at him. If he caught them looking, they quickly averted their gaze.

He finally gave up trying to read the paper and folded it. He thought about throwing it away but decided he should keep it to reread it later when he was calm.

Garrett. He did this to me.

But, why? Why would he do this? He is supposed to be my friend.

Stone put his elbows on his desk and put his head in his hands. He tried to picture the bison in the snowstorm, but all he wanted to do was get up and leave. He thought about calling in sick but immediately rejected the idea. The chief would see that for sure. There was no way that would be approved.

He thought about his last conversation with Councilman Hahn. He had told Stone to remember that exact moment because the councilman threatened to ruin his career. Unfortunately, he was right. Hahn had now destroyed his career, but not by doing anything directly to Stone. Instead, he had done it to himself. He could have avoided all of this by standing up and doing what he thought was right in the first place.

His phone rang again, but he ignored it, not bothering to look up from his hands.

"Answer your phone, why don't you?"

Stone lifted his head to see Mayor Sikes standing in his doorway. "Sir?"

"I've been calling for you and you're ignoring me like I'm some chump."

"No, sir, I didn't know—"

"My office. Now!"

The mayor spun and stalked away. Stone scrambled from out behind his desk and fell into step behind him. Workers watched with fascination as Sikes paraded him through the seventh floor like a scolded puppy that had just peed on the carpet.

Two security guards waited near the mayor's office. They watched Stone with disappointment.

When they entered the mayor's office, Sikes said, "Shut the door."

Stone did as the mayor asked, latching it silently. When he turned around, Sikes was already in his chair, behind his desk, yanking at his tie.

"Where do you get off?" he yelled, his face tomato red.

Stone opened his mouth to speak, but the mayor cut him off.

"Why in the hell would you talk to the newspaper about that girl's letter?"

"I didn't do that."

"That's a lie." He repeatedly slapped his desk. "You're a liar!"

"No, sir. I didn't do that."

"Who else could have all that information? Hell, I didn't even know about the latest girl, what was her name?"

"Sonya Meyer."

"See!" Another slap of the desk. "That's what I mean. You knew *everything*. You're the only one who could have talked."

"Mr. Mayor—"

"Don't gimme that *Mister Mayor* crap, you mealy mouthed sonofabitch. You talked with the enemy of the people. Why would you do that? I was good to you. I was nice to you!"

"But I didn't talk with them."

"Then who did, Stone? Tell me who did."

Stone thought for a moment about the bison standing in the snow. The bison hadn't been betrayed by a friend. "It was Tyler Garrett."

"Garrett! What is wrong with you, Stone? Garrett is a hero and you blame your actions on him? He didn't even know about this."

"Let me explain, sir."

"No," Sikes said, standing. He pointed at Stone as he walked past him. "You are what is wrong with the police. We need ethical men in the department, not opportunistic spineless punks like you."

Stone saw it then. This was him getting thrown under the bus. It had started, and Sikes was sharpening his tongue, figuring out the best way to drive home the knife before he stood in front of the cameras.

The mayor threw open his door and waved. The two security guards appeared. "Escort this man out of the building."

"Sir?" Stone said.

"I no longer want you in *my* building."

"That's fine," Stone said, "but I don't need a couple guys to walk me out."

"You think that, huh? That's what you think? Well, *we* need them, because *we* don't trust you anymore. We escort anyone out that we deem a security risk and guess what, buddy, that's you."

Sikes turned to the seventh floor and yelled. "I don't want Baumgartner's spy in city hall anymore!"

When he looked back at Stone, he smiled. "Get the message?"

"Can I walk back to my office and get my stuff?"

"You know what, hotshot? Your stuff is already waiting for you downstairs. That's what they've been doing while we've been talking."

Stone shook his head and stepped out of the mayor's office then. One of the security guards reached for his arm.

"The hell, man?" Stone said, yanking his arm free.

"Sorry," the guard said, chagrined.

Stone walked to the elevator and waited. He turned around and saw the entirety of the seventh-floor staff watching him with a mixture of emotions—curiosity, anger, and disappointment were the easiest to read.

Jean Carter stood near the stairwell. She looked sad. Stone wondered how much of the mayor's tirade she had overheard.

He gave her a slight nod.

When the elevator dinged its arrival, he entered the cab. When Stone turned around, Jean had vanished into the stairwell, presumably running down to the sixth floor.

Chapter 63

Councilwoman Margaret Patterson leaned into her computer and watched the news coverage as it was coming in live. It was a bloodbath. And she loved every second of it.

Earlier, she'd read the article about Denny Hahn and couldn't believe it. He always seemed like a decent guy, a family man, a crusader for women's rights. Now, he was outed as some sort of pervert, perhaps a pedophile, maybe he was even involved in a woman's murder.

The whole thing was an ugly mess that involved the mayor and the chief of police. She might have to bide her time to take out the mad king, but she felt the prickling excitement around the idea of ruining Fat Boy's career.

Would the rest of the council get on board? She frowned. Who knew what the hell the rest of the council would do?

She replayed her recent conversation with Dennis Hahn about Councilmen Justin Buckner and Patrick Armstrong. No wonder he was reluctant to go after them. That's when she realized that three councilmen were in trouble.

That's right. Men.

Buckner was in trouble for sleeping with a babysitter. It was legally okay, but it looked bad. The guy was a moron.

Armstrong was jammed up for taking money for influence. That was illegal, and he should be removed from office and get some jail time.

Now, Hahn tossed his hat into the douchebag ring for a series of affairs with barely legal, maybe not even legal aged, young women. The murder accusation seemed muddy and reeked of fake news, but it was still there and would hurt Hahn.

The more she thought about the three men the more she came to one conclusion—why did she care if any of it was legal?

This is the kind of opportunity I've longed for.

She didn't need Hahn to be a reformer along with her; she could lead the charge all by herself. She worked better alone anyway and now she wouldn't need to share any credit. She could immediately make the call for the removal of all three men from their council seats on the grounds of violating their moral turpitude clause.

Patterson needed to call the city attorney and talk with her, make sure she clearly understood the moral turpitude clause before she made the announcement. She didn't want to announce it and then find herself in violation of it as well. She thought about the recent rendezvous with Tanner, the guitar shop owner, and wondered if that would be seen as a violation. She didn't see how, but better safe than sorry.

She couldn't remember if a council member had ever been removed from their seat in the history of the city. If it hadn't occurred, it could happen three times at once. Her name would be legend in local lore. She grabbed her office phone and dialed the city attorney's number.

While it rang, she saw motion in the bullpen and watched Jean Carter hurry back to her desk. She dropped into her chair. The poor woman. She was aces at what she did.

Her eyes slid to her own assistant, Devan Bollman. He had headphones in while he typed. His head bobbed happily to some music while he worked. He obviously didn't understand the gravity of today's events.

Patterson made a mental note to keep an eye on Carter. If things went south with Denny, and they certainly looked they were headed that way, she wanted to rescue Jean. She could use a smart, solid assistant like her.

Devan could be collateral damage for all she cared. The idiot probably wouldn't realize what was happening, anyway.

Chapter 64

Officer Ray Zielinski had always heard you had to hit rock bottom before things could get better. Sitting at a ritzy South Hill coffee shop with Union President Dale Thomas, he was sure he'd hit that point.

The scariest part of the whole thing for Zielinski was that Thomas seemed to be the only person who understood what he was going through right now. If that wasn't rock bottom, Zielinski didn't know what was.

"I really wish you'd taken advantage of the three days of paid administrative leave," Thomas was saying. "Expanding the parameters of what qualifies for that is a benefit we fought hard to get for the union members."

Zielinski grunted into his black coffee and took a drink. This was the downside to using an outside lawyer as union president instead of a rank-and-file cop. Thomas didn't seem to realize that if he took those three days voluntarily, without having been shot or otherwise injured, most cops would think him weak. Mandatory was one thing, but voluntary looked like he was either gaming the system or was a shrinking violet. Good cops hated both laziness and cowardice. Since Thomas had never worn a badge, Zielinski doubted he could make the union president understand.

Then Thomas surprised him. "You're worried that if you go on admin leave, people will think you're a wimp, right?"

Zielinski swallowed his coffee. "They would."

"Some might," Thomas admitted. "Mostly your old patrol bulls, but the majority of people would understand."

"No, they wouldn't. Cops are judgmental as hell. I'm already hearing whispers about what I did."

"What kind of whispers?"

"The officer safety kind," Zielinski said. "That what I did was reckless. Cowboy stuff."

Thomas sipped his frothy drink, considering. Then he said, "That kind of criticism is probably coming from a different crowd than the ones who might have a problem with you taking some time to recover from the shooting."

"See?" Zielinski raised his hands in frustration. "I can't win, either way."

"People are always going to talk. You're correct about police officers being judgmental, especially when it comes to Monday morning quarterbacking."

"Exactly." He shook his head in disgust. "Remember Tyler Garrett a couple of summers back? He did the exact same thing I did—charge the shooters. Everyone thought what he did was brave, even though his suspects got away. I arrested *my* shooter, without having to kill him, and yet people are gossiping that my officer safety sucks? It's bull."

Thomas nodded along in agreement.

"What's the difference?" Zielinski complained. "Is it because he's black and I'm white?"

"I don't think that's it," Thomas said, glancing around to see if anyone heard Zielinski's words.

"Then what? He's SWAT and I'm not? Or nobody died, is that it? Somebody has to die for me to be a hero? Otherwise, I'm just some kind of code-four cowboy."

Zielinski noticed a pair of women staring at him in disapproval from across the small coffee shop. They had the privileged look of women who might star in *Housewives of Spokane*, if the reality show ever deigned to come to someplace as low rent as the Lilac City. He should have known better than to agree to meet Thomas on the South Hill. He should have stayed north, in his own district, and made the union president sit down in a greasy spoon somewhere in the rough-and-tumble Hillyard neighborhood instead.

The women kept looking at him, so he stared back until both broke eye contact, and went back to talking quietly between themselves.

"Great," he muttered. "Everyone else in the world gets a coffee break and no one thinks twice about it. But let a cop in uniform take one, and everyone stares like he's lazy or something."

"They were looking over here because you were getting loud," Thomas said.

"Whatever. The way my luck is going, they'll probably file a complaint." He turned back to Thomas. "That's the other thing I'm concerned about. If this officer safety buzz reaches Internal Affairs, I could end up getting jammed up over it."

"I don't think that's likely."

Zielinski ignored his comment. "Plus, there's that social worker, Lindsay Wagner. They could blame me for him being shot, too."

"You saved his life."

"Like that will matter."

"Ray, take a breath."

"I am breathing."

"No," Thomas said. "Take a breath. A deep one. And tell me what song is playing right now."

Zielinski hesitated, but did as Thomas suggested. He drew in a deep breath and let it out. Then he concentrated on the music being piped throughout the coffee shop. A violin played what should be a guitar riff over the background of synthesizer chords. After a few seconds, he recognized the tune.

"It's a terrible elevator music version of 'Sunshine of Your Love.'"

"It is pretty bad."

"Ought to be illegal."

Thomas smiled. Then he said, "Look, Ray, I'm not going to try to tell you that progressive discipline isn't a potential problem for us if they start piling on complaints. But let's not start buttering the toast while the dough is still rising, huh?"

Zielinski raised an eyebrow. "What the hell is that supposed to mean?"

"It means that there isn't a problem yet. All you've got is two pending issues. One is likely going to be dumped because the complainant isn't interested enough to cooperate. And the other complainant is still alive because of you, so there's a good chance he changes his mind, too." Thomas spread his hands. "Then, *voila*. You're in the clear. No worries."

Zielinski thought about his unreported collision. "Things happen," he said. "You know they'd do me if they get the chance."

"Sure. Look what they tried to do to Garrett."

Garrett. The name made Zielinski's stomach hurt.

"You okay, Ray?"

Before Zielinski could answer, his radio chirped. "Baker one twenty-three, can you clear for a call?"

He brought the radio to his mouth. "Twenty-three, go ahead."

"Possible suicidal subject," the dispatcher said, reciting a nearby address. "Complainant is on scene with the victim, waiting for police arrival."

"Method?" Zielinski asked. The last thing he wanted was to walk into another shooting.

"Asphyxiation," the dispatcher answered. "Victim is calm, according to complainant."

"Copy," Zielinski said. *Asphyxiation? What the hell did that mean?* Then he looked at Thomas. "See? I get all the crazies."

"Stay safe," Thomas said. "We'll talk again tomorrow, okay?"

"Sure." Zielinski stood and walked out of the café to his car. The drive to the address took less than a minute, making it obvious to him why the dispatcher had tagged him for the call. Plus, he stuck out like a sore thumb with a Baker designator sitting in the middle of Charlie sector.

Serves me right.

When he turned onto the block, he was surprised to see a news van in front of the target address. Since when did a suicidal person merit a media response? The news reporter noticed his car and pointed. The camera man swung the lens in his direction.

Zielinski frowned. He punched a key on his MDC, putting himself on scene. Then he pressed another key, bringing up the call. He scanned the text and almost immediately saw what the dispatcher had avoided putting out over the air. The victim's name was Dennis Hahn, the councilman.

"Damn," he muttered. "Thanks for the warning." The dispatcher should have asked him to call in to radio for this additional information, instead of letting him fly in blind.

He took a moment to prepare himself, then exited his patrol car. As he approached the house, the news reporter angled to cut him off.

"Officer, are you here to arrest the councilman?" She thrust the microphone in his direction.

Zielinski didn't answer.

"Officer, can you answer the question?"

He kept walking, not even looking her way.

She kept pace with him, continuing to fire questions his way until they neared the porch.

Zielinski stopped and gave her a sharp look. "You're trespassing," he said. "And interfering with police business."

She gave him a sour look. "Have you heard of freedom of the press?"

"Have you heard of haul your asses back to the sidewalk?"

Her eyes widened slightly, then a sly grin spread across her face. She turned to the cameraman. "You get that?"

"Got it."

"Good. Let's go."

The two of them returned to the sidewalk, although the cameraman shuffled backward, keeping the lens trained on Zielinski. The officer found himself hoping the cameraman's heel caught a break in the walkway and sent him toppling over, but knew it was unlikely. He was in the rich part of town, where walkways were always smooth.

Once the news media was out of earshot, he knocked on the door. A man opened it immediately and held it open wider for him.

"Come in, please."

He stepped inside, and the man closed the door. He was a forty-ish-year-old black man, carefully groomed, wearing a dark blue Gonzaga Bulldogs sweatshirt that looked like he'd bought it five minutes ago.

"Thanks for coming so quickly." The man held out his hand. "I'm Anderson Simmonds."

Zielinski shook his hand. "What's going on?"

Simmonds shook his head sadly. "I came over to check on Dennis. I've done his taxes for years, and we're friends. When I read the paper this morning, I knew he might need someone to talk to. So I came by, and no one was home. I checked to see if his car was in the garage, and it was. When I looked a little closer, I saw that it was running and Dennis was in the driver's seat."

Ah. Asphyxiation.

"I pounded on the garage doors, but he either didn't hear me or was ignoring me," Simmonds continued. "So I ran around to the rear of the house, and thank God the sliding door was unlocked. I ran through the house to the garage, shut off the car engine, and got him into the living room."

"Was he conscious?"

Simmonds nodded. "A little woozy. He'd obviously been doing some drinking beforehand."

"Sounds like you saved his life," Zielinski said. "Where is he now?"

"This way."

Simmonds led him down a hallway toward what Zielinski expected would be the living room. He rested his hand on his pistol, just in case. If Hahn really wanted to die, he might try to salvage this failed attempt by doing something to force

Zielinski to shoot him. He hoped not, but he wasn't going to get killed by not being prepared for the worst.

The hallway led to the living room, just as he'd thought. Dennis Hahn sat on the expensive couch, his head buried in his hands. His usually perfect hair was in disarray. A bottle of scotch and a glass with two fingers of the amber liquid was on the table in front of him. The pungent smell of car exhaust hung in the air.

"Denny?" Simmonds said. "The police are here."

Hahn looked up. When he saw Zielinski, his lip curled. "The last thing I need is the cops, Andy. Thanks a lot."

"He's here to help you."

"Ha!" Hahn snorted. He reached for his drink. "I'm sure he is."

Zielinski stepped forward. "Can you put that glass down, sir?"

Hahn hesitated, glancing at the glass midway to his mouth. "I suppose I can," he said, his words slurring. Then he tossed back the entire balance of the scotch in the glass, swallowed hard, and slammed the glass down onto the dark wood coffee table. "Happy?"

He decided battling with him over a glass tumbler wasn't worth it. As weapons went, it wasn't the most dangerous. Instead, he focused on keeping his expression neutral, and asked, "What's going on here today?"

"I'm having a drink. You want one?" Hahn let out a rueful chuckle and reached for the bottle.

Simmonds moved quicker, snatching the bottle by the neck and pulling it away. "Let's lay off the booze for a little while, maybe?"

"Screw you, Andy. You're a terrible friend."

"It sounds to me like he's a pretty good friend," Zielinski said.

Hahn turned toward him, his expression venomous. "How would you know?"

"He saved your life."

"Like I said," Hahn sneered. "A terrible friend."

"What should he have done?"

"Let me be, that's what."

"If he'd done that, you'd be dead."

Hahn glared back up at him, saying nothing.

"Was that your intent, Mr. Hahn?" Zielinski asked. "To die?"

"That's *Councilman* Hahn," Hahn replied haughtily.

Not for much longer, I'm guessing.

"Was that your intent, Councilman? To die?"

Hahn shrugged. "You're so smart, you figure it out." He snapped his fingers. "Damn it, Anderson. Pour me a drink."

Simmonds shook his head and strode away toward the kitchen with the bottle of scotch.

The councilman sighed. "Oh, sure. Desert me, just like everyone else. My wife and daughters bailed this morning, as soon as they saw the article online. Now my supposed best friend is stealing my best scotch." He turned back to Zielinski. "You ever get the feeling everyone is looking to screw you over?"

"Sometimes," Zielinski admitted. "Look, Councilman, I'm going to be straight with you. Based on your actions this morning, I have to take you to Sacred Heart Hospital for a mental health evaluation."

"To hell with that," Hahn said. "I'm not going."

"Refusing is one option," Zielinski said, "but let me tell you what that looks like." He stepped closer to Hahn. "I don't have a choice in this situation. It's my duty. So if you refuse, I have to take you into custody for an involuntary mental health hold. That means handcuffs. It means walking you out the front door, past those news cameras, into the back of my police car, all of it. Then, at the hospital, you're on a mandatory seventy-two-hour hold. That's three days in the psych ward."

Hahn blanched. "Three days?"

Zielinski nodded.

Hahn reached for his glass, then noticed it was empty and set it down. "Those jackals have been out front since earlier this morning. They kept calling my cell phone to get me to come out and give a statement. I had to shut off my phone. I can't even call my daughters."

"Walking out in handcuffs certainly gives them a statement," Zielinski said.

The councilman shook his head. "I don't want that. I won't do it."

"If you refuse, that is exactly what will happen. But there is another option."

Hahn looked up, suspicious and hopeful in the same glance. "What is it?"

"You ask me to give you a ride to Sacred Heart for a voluntary mental health referral," Zielinski explained. "A self-referral. I drive you there, and once you see a doctor for an evaluation, you're free to decide how long you want to stay."

What he'd said wasn't entirely true, especially if the evaluating doctor decided he needed to be held longer, but it represented the best-case scenario. For Zielinski, it was true enough to get the job done.

Hahn stared at him. Zielinski could see he was considering. He didn't worry about being able to subdue Hahn if it came to it, and he doubted that Simmonds would intervene. That said, fighting with a councilman, even a disgraced soon-to-be former councilman, didn't seem like a great idea to him.

He tapped his handcuff case, sweetening the deal. "A voluntary referral means no handcuffs."

Hahn thought it over a little longer, but Zielinski could see he'd already decided and now was just making a show of it.

"All right," Hahn agreed. "That's what I'll do."

"Good decision," Zielinski said. "I need you to stand up."

"We're going *now*?"

Zielinski nodded.

"But I...I need to call my daughters. And—"

"You can figure all of that out from the hospital," Zielinski said. "We have to go now. Please stand up."

Hahn struggled to his feet. Zielinski reached out and helped him stand, then patted him down quickly. Hahn's pockets were empty.

"You want your wallet or something?"

Hahn nodded. "It's on my bedroom table."

"I'll get it," Simmonds said, and headed down the hallway.

"Do you have a coat?" Zielinski asked.

"By the door."

They walked down the hallway. By the time they reached the door, Simmonds joined them. He extended the wallet toward Hahn, but Zielinski took it.

"That's mine," Hahn objected.

"I'll give it to you at the hospital."

Hahn frowned.

"I'll lock up the house, Denny," Simmonds told him. "Don't worry."

Hahn didn't answer. He reached for a coat from the rack, but Zielinski took it first. He checked the pockets, then handed it to Hahn, who looked at him in disgust. "Jeez. Paranoid much?"

Zielinski ignored his comment. He gave Simmonds a nod and a muttered "thanks" before putting his hand on the door.

"I'd recommend saying nothing to the reporters," Zielinski said.

"Please," Hahn scoffed. "I know how to handle the media."

"Either way, we're not stopping. This is a courtesy transport, not a press conference. We keep on walking. You get me?"

"I understand, Officer. Let's get this over with."

Zielinski opened the door, and let Hahn step out first, following after. The councilman started down the walkway, and Zielinski stayed close. As he expected, the news reporter moved to intercept them.

"Officer, is the councilman under arrest? What's the charge?"

He ignored her and kept walking.

Hahn raised his hands up so that she could see his bare wrists. "Do you see any handcuffs, Serena?"

"No," the reporter answered. "Are you saying this isn't an arrest?"

"It's definitely not. I've done nothing to merit an arrest."

"Are you responsible for the deaths of Bethany Rabe and Sonya Meyer?" she shot back.

"I have no comment on those ugly accusations," Hahn said as he walked toward Zielinski's car.

"If you're not under arrest, why are the police here?"

"The mission of the police isn't just to arrest people," Hahn said. "They serve and protect. Right now, this officer is escorting me to a crucial meeting."

"That sounds like a personal taxi service, Councilman."

Zielinski clenched his jaw, wishing Hahn would shut up.

"You people have me under siege in my own home. This was the only option."

When they reached the police car, Hahn started toward the front passenger door. "Wait," Zielinski said. He opened the driver's door and popped open the door to the backseat.

"The *back* seat?" Hahn said, his voice low and disbelieving.

"My gear is in the front seat."

"So move it."

Zielinski shook his head.

Hahn stared at him, engaged in a brief battle of wills. If they'd still been in the councilman's living room, Zielinski had no doubt it would have taken handcuffs to end the situation. But out here, with cameras rolling, Hahn quickly relented. He came around to the rear door and slid into the back seat.

"Thanks a lot," he said sarcastically.

Zielinski closed the back door and got into the car. As he started the engine, he glanced into the rearview mirror and caught Hahn glaring at him. "Don't make me regret the no cuffs part," he warned. "You won't like it if you do."

Hahn looked away.

He waited for the MDC to boot up, then updated his status. He typed *One in Custody, voluntary MHD, en route SHMC.*

"Why are you just sitting here?" Hahn complained. "You're giving them more of a photo op."

Zielinski said nothing. He pressed SEND and waited until the system confirmed his message. Only then did he put the car in gear and headed toward Sacred Heart Medical Center.

The two of them rode in silence for over a minute, before Hahn muttered, "He was supposed to help me."

Zielinski stopped for a red light. He studied Hahn in the rearview mirror. The councilman was staring out the window, looking forlorn.

"Who?" Zielinski asked. "Who was supposed to help you?"

Hahn turned to meet Zielinski's gaze. Then he shook his head slowly. "You're all the same. You all protect each other."

"Who was supposed to protect you?"

"The thin blue line, right?"

"I don't know what you mean," Zielinski said.

"Sure you do."

"How can I help you if you won't tell me what I need to know?"

Hahn let out a short bark of dark laughter. "You know what? That's exactly what he said to me."

The light turned green, but Zielinski didn't move right away. "Who said that to you?"

Hahn shook his head and looked away. "Don't even talk to me anymore, man. You're all the same."

The car behind Zielinski gave a short, almost apologetic beep of its horn. After a moment, Zielinski let off the brake and drove toward the hospital.

To hell with him. I've got my own problems.

Chapter 65

"What is going on over at your department, Dana?" Maggie Patterson asked Hatcher, as soon as she closed the door to her office.

Hatcher sat in the chair in front of the councilwoman's desk, shaking her head in anger. "It's a good old boys' network. I thought it was bad when Baumgartner gave Farrell my strike team. I didn't realize it was even worse."

"It's been the status quo for a hundred years," Patterson agreed, her voice full of vitriol. She sat in the chair next to Hatcher instead of going behind her own desk. "They've had an absolute stranglehold on local politics ever since the city was founded."

"It's ridiculous."

"It's like the freakin' mafia," said Patterson.

"If that newspaper article is accurate, Baumgartner was protecting a sexual predator." Hatcher felt the same anger she'd been feeling all morning rise in her chest again. "I can't understand that, politics or no politics."

"His days are numbered," Patterson said.

"Obviously. No way Hahn survives this."

"I mean your boss. This will bring the Fat Boy down."

"It won't. He's too popular. People love his whole Gary Cooper, frontier justice approach. He's a damn character to them."

"It doesn't matter what the people think. The chief isn't elected, he's appointed."

Hatcher gave her a dubious look. "Do you really think Mayor Sikes has the guts to risk firing him? Especially since he was part of it."

"What do you think?"

"You're the politician, Maggie. You tell me."

Patterson leaned forward. "I honestly don't know what that guy will or won't do. But I'll tell you this. You work with me and we'll push Fat Boy out. Then I'll make sure *your* name is on a short list for chief."

"I just made captain," Hatcher said, surprised.

"Which makes you part of executive leadership. You're qualified."

Hatcher thought for a moment, processing the idea. "I'm the youngest captain," she said. "Both in time on the department and time in grade."

"That doesn't matter. What matters is what you've done in your career, and what you do from here on out."

"What do you mean?"

"I mean, do your officers like you?"

Hatcher considered. Ray Zielinski's face flashed in her mind's eye. "I think they do," she answered. "Most of them, anyway."

"So you'd have their support," Patterson assured her. "That matters, especially to the council. But what really matters is that you have access to what's going on within the chief's command staff."

"Are you talking about gaining experience?"

"No. I'm talking about gaining information."

Hatcher gave her a slightly confused look. "I don't follow."

"Dana, let me be as clear as possible. You get me an opportunity and I promise we'll take that fat bastard out."

"I—"

Patterson held up her hand. "Before you answer, hear me out on a couple of things."

"Maggie…I don't know if I can…I mean, you're talking about…"

"I'm your friend," Patterson said. "Trust me for a minute or two here, all right?"

Hatcher thought it over, then gave her a short nod. Maggie was right. They were friends. Besides, all they were doing now was talking. There was nothing insidious about that.

"For starters, take a look at the state of this council. Three men are on their way out. I've set it in motion. Hahn and Armstrong are slam dunks. Buckner may continue to fight it, but my guess is that he'll see the futility of it all and resign." Patterson held up three fingers. "That's three new positions."

Hatcher listened, letting Patterson's words roll over her.

"This is a revolution, Dana," Patterson continued. "One we win."

Hatcher frowned. "Why does it have to always be us versus them? Black versus white, men versus women. It's exhausting."

"It's the way of the world," Patterson said. "But if you want, look at it like this: the smart people versus the corrupt and the moronic."

Hatcher cocked her head. "We're the smart people, right?"

"Of course! The important thing is that we'll get at least two women in those three slots, maybe all three. No matter how you cut it, we'll have a majority. After that, some things will change around this town."

"For example?"

"How about a woman running the police department? Does Chief Hatcher sound nice to you?"

Hatcher smiled slightly in spite of herself. "It does, actually."

"Good. And that won't be all. Men have been running this place long enough. It's time for some fresh ideas, and that means us. We'll make changes to city government, *positive* changes."

"Like what?"

Patterson leaned forward, giving Hatcher an intense look. "Like changing who sits in the big chair up on the seventh floor," she said, her voice brimming with confidence.

Hatcher met Patterson's gaze. She could see the ambition in the councilwoman's eyes, and she wondered how much of her own reflected back. And what was wrong with that? Ambitious men have been celebrated for centuries. Why shouldn't she pursue her own ambition? As chief, she could have a positive influence on the entire department, as well as the community. She could be part of a change. Maggie was right about that—a change was overdue.

To make a change like this, she would need allies. That was what Patterson was proposing—an alliance for the greater good.

Patterson seemed to sense her thoughts. She reached out and took Hatcher's hands in her own. "This is the right thing to do. It's our duty. But I need your help, Dana. I need you with me on this. Are you?"

Hatcher squeezed Patterson's hands.

"I'm in."

Chapter 66

"This is your fault!" Mayor Sikes screamed at Baumgartner. "You let this happen!"

The chief stood in front of Sikes's desk, letting the mayor's tirade wash over him. After a few more expletive-filled accusations, Sikes brushed his hair from his eyes and crossed his arms, glaring at the chief.

"You're right," Baumgartner said. "I screwed up. I should have had the report entered directly into the system."

"That's right."

"I violated my own policy."

"That was a stupid decision."

"It was."

"A decision *you* made," Sikes pointed out.

"It was entirely my decision," Baumgartner agreed. "And it violated policy. You should discipline me for it."

"I should *fire* you for it."

Baumgartner didn't react, other than to tilt his head slightly at the threat. "If one of my officers committed a similar violation, basically failing to file a report, I'd suspend him for a day. Absent any kind of disciplinary history, I wouldn't fire him for it."

"You're the chief," Sikes argued. "You're held to a higher standard."

"Absolutely," Baumgartner agreed. "I should definitely receive more than a day."

"Like being fired. That's more than a day."

Baumgartner paused. He'd been standing in front of the mayor's desk to receive his ass-chewing but he decided that time was over, so he moved toward the chair opposite the mayor's desk.

"I didn't say you could sit," Sikes snapped.

Baumgartner ignored him and sat. Then he looked directly at the mayor. "The thing is, I'm going to take a few lumps over this. We both know I've got enough goodwill banked with the public to overcome that. The city council is a mess right now, so I don't see them being a problem for a while, and besides, they bow to the will of their constituents. That leaves you."

"Your boss, you mean?"

"My boss," Baumgartner repeated, "who gave me the letter and asked me to look into it quietly."

Sikes's eyes widened slightly, before his face collapsed into a dark scowl. He pointed a finger at Baumgartner. "Don't think you can scrape this crap off your shoe onto me, Bob. You made the decisions you made. That's on you."

"It's completely on me, but let's face it, *Andrew*…if this gets too big or too loud, you'll get pulled into it. Pretty early on, I'd guess. And then you'd have that same crap on your shoe, too."

Sikes continued to scowl, but he said nothing.

"I'm surprised," Baumgartner said, "that Kelly Davis didn't call you asking for a comment on the story."

The mayor shifted in his chair.

"If they ran that story without verification from an additional source, the paper could expose themselves to a hell of a lot of litigation."

Sikes looked away and rubbed his face.

There it is, Baumgartner thought. "So she called."

"Don't push me, Bob."

Baumgartner fell silent then. He now knew the reporter had called the mayor. Sikes must not have considered it worthy of dealing with at the moment. Now, it was going to bite them both in the ass.

"Three days," Sikes finally said. "I'm suspending you for three days for the policy violation."

The chief considered the punishment before saying, "That sounds equitable."

"And no burning vacation days in lieu of suspension days. Three full days, with loss of pay."

"I understand," Baumgartner said.

"Then it's settled."

"I'm glad we got that behind us."

Sikes sighed. "It doesn't solve the problem of the original report."

"I'll enter it today."

Sikes leaned back, steepling his fingers. "You could, but what if…I mean, is there a way to make it look like it was entered earlier?"

"No. The system is designed with safeguards. It has to be infallible, to hold up in court."

"No system is infallible," Sikes said. "Couldn't you swap it out with some earlier report? A nothing report that no one will miss?"

Baumgartner shook his head. "I thought about that, briefly. I don't believe it would hold up to scrutiny. Plus, it's a clear violation of state law. In the end, it'd only add to the problem if we were caught."

"Getting caught always adds to the problem," the mayor said wryly.

"True. But someone once said something to me that seems to apply here. It's never the crime or the initial mistake that gets people in the most trouble. It's the cover-up that follows."

"Great advice." The sarcasm in the mayor's voice was unmistakable. "We could have used that kind of wisdom before we were already in the middle of a cover-up."

Baumgartner frowned. Sikes just didn't get it. "A swap isn't a viable option," he said.

"Then what if we just shredded it? There's no way anyone can prove it existed, and we can let Hahn twist and burn in his own self-created hell."

Baumgartner shook his head. "I already considered that. Not only is it wrong, but it may be illegal. Besides, it's too risky."

"How is a nonexistent report risky?"

"It came to this office via letter," Baumgartner reminded him. "How many people saw it before you did? And then there's Gary Stone."

"Your little spy, you mean?"

"He was here to be a liaison, not a spy."

Sikes gave him a knowing look.

"Regardless," Baumgartner said, "I didn't authorize him to leak the information to the paper, *if* he is the leaker."

"You don't know?"

The chief shook his head.

"You've got a leaker in your department and you don't know who it is? You better get on top that that, Bob. Like *yesterday*."

"If the leak came from my department," Baumgartner said quietly.

"Don't try to pass the buck again!"

"I'm not, but it could have come from your staff, or the council staff. We don't know."

"Why don't you try talking to your little spy and see if he's the one?"

"I will."

"You should take his badge, the little traitor."

Baumgartner didn't answer. He could see the trajectory Sikes was on and that was to make Stone the scapegoat. He'd have to protect Stone, maybe find some low-profile position for the man, because he had no plans to fire him. He'd been a good soldier, if a flawed one. He followed orders, showed discretion when it counted, and remained loyal when he didn't have to.

That was a rare thing in a young officer.

Chapter 67

Detective Clint stopped writing his notes, rereading what he'd written. The notes were all coded, and it was a new cipher that he'd switched to after the Garrett shooting. As he read, he massaged the meaty part of his hand between his thumb and forefinger, which was sore from the furious writing he'd been doing.

On the surface, the Sonya Meyer case was going nowhere. The crime scene techs collected plenty of hair and fiber evidence, but there was no way of knowing who the hairs belonged to until a DNA analysis was conducted. That would take weeks, if not months, due to the eternal backlog at the state crime lab.

If Clint had his way, DNA requests would be screened for several factors before they were allowed to be submitted to the lab. A homicide case should be a given. Sexual assaults and serious physical assaults would also have priority. Crimes against children, too. Beyond that, the cost of the lab work for a DNA recovery and comparison run seemed to him to greatly outweigh the marginal damage the victim suffered. But thanks to stupid television shows, citizens had an expectation that there'd be DNA analysis for every lawn mower theft and window smash that occurred. Most cops bowed to that expectation and made the lab request, clogging the system. The result was a whole lot of wasted time while the lab technicians prioritized submissions, having to factor in how long a case had been waiting and dealing with cops calling to check on the status of their evidence.

It should be simple. Process the worthy crimes, reject the rest. But craven idiots were in charge of the world, so his homicide was going to take forever to return any DNA-based evidence.

Not that DNA was the magic bullet everyone thought it was. Even if the lab found DNA, there might not be a match in the database, so he'd have an UNSUB, an unknown subject. The DNA could end up belonging to some acquaintance of Sonya Meyer's, or even a previous tenant, since she was relatively new to living in that bungalow. Meyer's fingernail scrapings had been minimal, and it wasn't certain whether she got any of her attacker's DNA under them. But if she'd managed to scratch the killer in self-defense, the placement of that DNA under her nails would be strong evidence.

Outside of that, even if he got lucky and found DNA for a potential suspect somewhere on scene, it was largely useless if it belonged to Garrett. The officer had defeated the value of the evidence by slipping into the crime scene under quasi-legitimate circumstances. The memory of it still burned in Clint's gut. He could put together a case that overcame this obstacle, if he was able to develop other incontrovertible evidence, but knowing the weak-willed prosecutors, the case probably still wouldn't be filed. And if Garrett was being protected by the chief, the no-go on the case was a given.

Clint finished rereading his notes. He realized he was letting his suspicion of Garrett color his analysis of the actual evidence available. An objective view pointed to Hahn as the most likely suspect, but Clint had confirmed the councilman's whereabouts that Jean Carter had reported to him. Multiple unconnected witnesses had seen him engaged in typical political business during the time period of Meyer's murder. Even if Clint stretched the estimated time of death a little, Hahn still had a solid alibi.

So maybe he had someone do it for him. Men like Hahn don't do their own dirty work, they hire it done.

That brought him back to Garrett. He could be working for Hahn. But he'd seen Garrett's hands. Not a scratch on his manicured hands. And Sonya Meyer had clearly been beaten by someone's fists. The medical examiner found three perfectly spaced bruises on her face that were the telltale signs of knuckles. No one could hit a human head that many times without some sort of injury resulting from it. It wasn't possible.

Clint stopped, correcting himself.

It was possible. It just wasn't *likely*.

What if Garrett wasn't working alone? He'd worked with the drug dealer Ocampo before, and both Talbott and Pomeroy. Maybe he had assembled another crew, and one of those underlings killed Sonya Meyer.

Clint frowned. In all the time he'd followed Garrett, he'd not seen any evidence of collaboration. The dirty cop seemed all alone. But could he have missed Garrett's accomplices somehow?

He doubted it, but admitted it was possible. Especially given how careful the man was.

In the end, Garrett remained a suspect, but only in his coded notes. If Lieutenant Flowers found out he suspected the department's golden child, the company man wouldn't be able to run to the chief fast enough with the news. Then it'd be Clint's ass in a sling. He limited his mention of Garrett to describing his interference at the crime scene. In a perfect world, Internal Affairs would grab onto that and Garrett would get spanked, but Clint wasn't too optimistic about that happening.

He turned back to the case. If it was Garrett, why kill Sonya Meyer? To protect Hahn? What did Garrett get from that?

The newspaper article bothered Clint, too. Whoever leaked that story knew everything, or damn near. That made for a short list of suspects. Him, Farrell, Baumgartner, Stone, and Garrett. He didn't leak it. Baumgartner certainly wouldn't do it. He doubted Farrell would, either. The captain was too loyal to Baumgartner. Far too loyal, as Clint saw it, but that was a matter for him to dissect another time.

That left Stone or Garrett.

Probably not Stone, he decided. That cake-eater didn't have the balls, for one thing. Even if he was motivated to do it for some crazy reason—revenge, maybe?—leaking all the details seemed against his own self-interest.

So it was Garrett.

But that didn't make sense, either. Garrett had been working for Hahn. Or working the man somehow. Either way, going to the paper and outing him after putting in all that effort to pull his chestnuts out of the fire didn't make sense.

Unless Garrett simply brought the whole thing down as a "screw you" to the city and the police department.

Would he do that?

What good would that do? How did it serve his agenda?

Did Garrett even *have* an agenda, or was he freewheeling this?

Clint pinched the bridge of his nose, closing his eyes. He had too many questions, and too little data, too little evidence. He needed to start eliminating some possibilities. Finding out if Garrett was the leak would be a good start. That would tend to indicate that he wasn't working for Hahn but blackmailing him. If Hahn refused to give in, going to the newspaper would be Garrett's response. But was he doing this for his own purposes, or working for the chief?

What about Farrell? Was he in league with Baumgartner, or could Clint still trust him?

And what if—

"Hey, Wardell?" A voice broke into his thoughts.

Clint's eyes snapped open. Officer Ray Zielinski, in uniform, stood next to his desk. "What do you want? I'm busy."

Zielinski seemed unperturbed by his brusqueness. "You're working the dead girl, right? Sonya Meyer?"

Clint gave him a questioning look. "That's my case, yes. Why?"

"According to the news, Dennis Hahn's a suspect."

Clint didn't answer, waiting for Zielinski to continue.

"Is that true?" Zielinski asked. "About the councilman?"

"Sharing of investigative details is on a strict need-to-know basis," Clint said. "You don't qualify."

Zielinski shook his head. "Always the hard ass, huh? You know that no one likes you, Wardell, right? Some people, like me, *try* to like you but no one really does."

Clint shrugged. "I don't give a damn."

"Yeah, I know. Honey Badger, right? Only I don't buy it. I think you're just like the rest of us, Wardell. I think you do care."

"Why are you here?" Clint asked. "I've got work to do, and since you appear to be on shift, so do you."

"I *am* working," Zielinski said. "I'm trying to pass on some information to you, but you have to make everything hard."

Clint was tempted to tell the officer to put his information in an additional report and he'd read it when he got the opportunity, which might happen if people ever quit interrupting his work. But the prospect of something helpful on the Meyer case won out. "What's your information?"

"I took Hahn to Sacred Heart earlier this morning on an MHD hold."

Clint hadn't heard that yet. The news was interesting but hardly evidentiary. "Why?"

"He tried to off himself."

"How?"

"Carbon monoxide. Started up his car and never left the garage. A friend found him while he was still half conscious."

Clint considered the information. Then he asked, "Did he make some kind of admission to you about Sonya Meyer?"

"No," Zielinski said, "but on the way to the hospital, he talked about some cop who was supposed to help him."

"Who?"

"He wasn't specific. Mostly, he accused me of being in on it somehow. Code of silence stuff."

"Is that it?"

Zielinski looked slightly disappointed. "You don't think that's important? He was banging your victim, and now he's talking about some cop who was supposed help him out somehow?"

Clint didn't respond. He gave Zielinski a flat stare.

Zielinski waited several seconds. Then he shrugged. "It's your case. I figure the cop was Stone, and that you might want to know."

"Stone?"

"Yeah, you know, the Chief's Bitch?"

"I know who he is. Why do you think it was him? Did Hahn allude to him?"

"No," Zielinski said. "I figured since he was down at city hall, he'd be the one playing footsie with the politicians."

Clint fell silent, running the idea through his mind. Had he underestimated Stone? He didn't think so. Running interference for a councilman was one thing, but there was no way Stone would commit murder for him. Besides, it was Stone who discovered the body…

He frowned. Discovering the body meant getting his DNA all over the crime scene in a legitimate way, didn't it? Just like what Garrett did. Finding Stone's DNA now, or Garrett's, wouldn't prove anything other than they were both there, and both with a legitimate reason.

And he'd never examined Stone's hands like he had Garrett's.

Stone, Stone, Stone…was it possible?

Of course, it was. But was it *likely*?

Another possibility occurred to him. Zielinski had worked with Garrett for several years. They were friends. He'd been the backup officer on Garrett's shooting. He could be in collusion with Garrett right now. Or being manipulated by the officer, sent here to give Clint a red herring to chase down.

"Anyway," Zielinski said, "I did my part by telling you. I didn't mention any of this in my report about the mental health referral. You want me to write an additional report on what he said?"

Clint gave Zielinski a discerning look. Where did the veteran officer stand? He'd come to him recently with concerns about Garrett. Were those legitimate, or was he playing double agent, trying to get a read on how much Clint knew? And this information on Hahn, and his speculation about Stone, was he being straight about it, or was it designed to send Clint on a wild goose chase?

All of this could be easily Garrett throwing up chaff, trying to elude detection.

"Wardell?" Zielinski was looking at him askance. "You want me to cut you an additional report or what?"

Clint shook his head. "No. I'll put it in my notes."

"Okay."

Zielinski didn't leave immediately, and Clint realized he was expecting a thank you. Clint turned back to his notes without a word. After a few seconds, Zielinski let out a small, grunting sigh, and left.

I need to interview Hahn. Figure out what his relationship with Garrett truly was. Maybe the answer to Sonya Meyer's death lies with that.

Clint stared down at his notes, which were full of many more questions than answers.

Chapter 68

Captain Tom Farrell pulled up to a stop in front of the house. His conversation with Chief Baumgartner still rang in his ears.

"What the hell am I supposed to do with him?" the chief had asked. "I can't have him out on patrol. It's too much exposure. I can't risk firing him, and besides, he's been a good officer. He deserves some loyalty, but I have to tuck him away somewhere out of sight."

It was Farrell who gave him the answer. "Give him to me. I'll put him on my street crimes squad."

Baumgartner had looked at him in surprise. "You sure that's a fit?"

"It'll be a perfect fit. Trust me."

The chief thought it over, then agreed. "Street crimes, then. Is that what you're calling the unit?"

"No," Farrell told him. "I don't have a name yet."

"Make it something catchy," the chief said. "But stay away from military references."

"I'll figure it out," Farrell promised.

Now, sitting in front of the officer's house, he prepared himself for his pitch. Sure, he could just assign the man, if he wanted to. The chief had the authority to make special assignments at his discretion. But Farrell had a greater need than just the chief's directive to cut into the crime rate. He had a second, deeper purpose and that required commitment from the officers on the team, not merely involvement. There was a world of difference between the two, and Farrell knew it. One of his mentors had stressed how important it was, and that to understand the difference, he didn't have to look any further than a ham and egg omelet. The chicken was involved, but the pig? The pig was committed.

So how to get this officer to commit?

Farrell thought it over for a few more minutes, then got out of his car and went to the officer's door. He knocked and waited. After what seemed like a long while, the door opened. A disheveled version of Officer Gary Stone looked at Farrell in mild confusion.

"Captain?" Stone asked.

To Farrell's eye, Stone looked beaten, like chewed up bubble gum dragged across the floor of a cigarette factory. He wondered for a moment if that would work to his advantage or not.

"Hello, Gary," Farrell said, realizing that this was the first time he'd ever called Stone by his given name. "Can we talk?"

Stone swallowed hard, thinking about the request. "Do I need my union rep or something?"

Farrell gave him a smile he didn't entirely feel. "Nothing like that. I just want to talk to you for a minute."

The younger man hesitated a little longer, then opened the door to let him in.

The remains of a pizza and several empty beer bottles were on the kitchen counter, and a blanket was in disarray on the couch. The muted television showed some kind of romantic comedy Farrell vaguely remembered seeing with his wife.

Stone closed the door and snapped off the TV. "You want to sit down?"

"Sure."

He tossed the blanket to one end of the couch, where he plopped down. Farrell took the other end. They sat in awkward silence for a few seconds before Farrell spoke.

"I know this has been hard," he began, but Stone interrupted him with a bark of humorless laughter.

"Hard? My career is ruined."

"It's not ruined. This is just a setback."

"A *setback*?" Stone looked at him in disbelief. "Captain, I was kicked out of city hall. The mayor had security escort me out like some kind of trespasser. It was humiliating. And then the newspaper—"

"The newspaper is a rag. There's a reason people call it *The Socialist Review*."

"Cops and hardcore conservatives call it that," Stone said. "No one else does." He hung his head miserably. "Everyone I know has read that article. My name is worthless now."

"You're right," Farrell said.

Stone looked up. "Huh?"

"I said, you're right. At this very moment, your name isn't worth much. But like all things, that's temporary."

"It feels permanent."

"It feels that way, sure. But let me tell you a couple things I've learned in my long career, Gary. I've learned that the public is fickle, and that most people have the attention span of a gnat. Today, your name is worthless. Next week, no one will remember you. The week after that, they'll be singing your praises for some heroic action."

Stone seemed doubtful, but then a curious expression crossed his features. "Like how they treated Garrett, you mean?"

Farrell tried not to react. There'd be time to tell Stone everything he needed to know about Garrett later. Now, he just needed to get him to take a first step. To commit. "Like him and a hundred other cops over my career," he said. "You can't worry about what the newspaper says about you or what the public thinks on any given day. It's all transitory."

Stone took a deep breath and let it out in a whoosh. "Even if that's true, Captain, the chief is mad at me. And the mayor hates me. Neither one is going to forget about it. I know both of them well enough to be sure of that."

"You're right," Farrell conceded. "Neither one will forget. But the chief's not mad. He's proud of you."

"Proud?"

Farrell shrugged. "Proud…and a little mad. But I've worked with Chief Baumgartner my entire career. He doesn't hold a grudge against good cops."

Stone stared at him, soaking in the words.

"And the thing about mayors," Farrell continued, "is that they come and they go. Sikes is gone in three years, and someone new will be on the seventh floor. We'll all still be here. Even if this mayor tries to go after you before then, the chief can protect you."

"He shouldn't have to protect me," Stone said, lowering his gaze again."

"I know, Gary. Sometimes that's not enough. Sometimes we have to find the higher good."

"I don't think there is one," Stone said.

Farrell studied Stone. It was clear the man was trying to come to terms with something. "Is there something you want to ask me, Gary?"

Stone nodded. "Yeah. Why did he do this?"

"Who?"

"Garrett."

Farrell's mouth began to drop, so he quickly clenched his teeth and remained quiet.

"He said he was looking out for me. I mean, I thought we were friends, but I don't see how this helps. Maybe he wasn't the one who leaked everything to the press, but if not him, who?"

Farrell let the moment hang while he considered his reply. What could he say at that moment that would not be too much and reveal what Clint and he had been working on for going on two years? He couldn't take Stone into his confidence, not this soon. Not only would Clint blow a gasket, it was foolish. He didn't truly know how Stone would stand up in a pinch. He needed to bring him along slowly. However, knowing that he believed Garrett might be behind his removal from city hall was suddenly an ace up his sleeve that he didn't have before.

In the end, Farrell remained quiet and only shrugged in response to Stone's question.

Tears filled the younger man's eyes then. "I think I'm done."

"What does that mean?"

"I'm going to turn in my gun and quit. Go find something else that doesn't make me feel so…dirty. I thought this was something special, but it's not at all what I thought."

"Welcome to adulthood," Farrell said, his voice slightly stern. "The world is a much grayer place than most people realize."

"Not the whole world," Stone said. "Just this one. I don't think I can be a part of it anymore."

"Don't quit, at least not yet."

"It's for the best."

"Why'd you become a cop, Gary?" Farrell asked. "And I'm not asking for your hiring board answer that you want to help people. I want your real reason."

"I…I really did want to help people."

"And?"

"And make a difference," Stone said.

"And what else?"

Stone shrugged. "I don't know."

"You do know. You already said it." Farrell leaned forward slightly. "You wanted to be part of something special, something bigger than yourself. Am I right?"

"Yes," Stone admitted. "But it doesn't really matter now. It's over."

"No, it isn't over. I came here especially for you."

"What's that mean?"

"Gary, you're the best communicator we have in the department. Maybe it's that marketing background, it gives you something special. I need someone like that for what I'm envisioning."

"What's that?" Stone asked.

"It's a chance to do it all," Farrell said. "Help people, make a difference, and be part of something meaningful. A chance for you to stop being a politician, and to be a cop again."

Stone looked at him, his expression difficult to read. "What are you talking about?"

"I'm talking about a special team," Farrell said. "A special team, with a special purpose."

Chapter 69

Detective Clint found Kelly Davis at Atticus Coffee, her usual haunt. He'd known about her long-standing afternoon habit for years, and the piece of knowledge served him well on those few occasions he needed to speak to the veteran reporter.

She didn't notice him tucked away in a corner while she ordered her cappuccino. He waited until she had her small cup and moved outside before following her. She'd settled into a small table in the sunshine when she spotted Clint. To her credit, her expression barely changed.

"Detective," she greeted him, motioning to the chair across from her. "Care to join me?"

Clint knew this conversation could be handled briefly while he remained standing. But he also knew that social customs seemed to matter a lot to some people, and he believed Davis was one of those people.

He took a seat.

"What are you drinking?" she asked amiably.

"I'm fine," Clint said. "I need to talk to you."

"I assume that's why you're here." Davis sipped her cappuccino and waited for him to proceed.

"Your article on the Hahn conspiracy," Clint said. "I need to know—"

"Conspiracy?" Davis shook her head. "I don't think I used that word in my article."

"You intimated it."

"I reported it. It is up to the reader to form her own conclusions."

Clint ground his teeth. He didn't care about journalistic semantics. He just wanted an answer to a simple question.

With an effort, he kept his tone neutral. "You clearly had a source for the article."

"Did I?"

"Don't be coy," Clint said. "Isn't journalism supposed to be about the truth?"

"Fair statement," Davis said. "But whose truth?"

"I'm talking about objective facts."

"I haven't heard any yet."

Clint forced himself to remain focused on his purpose. He didn't want to spar with her, and he didn't want to tell her off and ruin any chance of her cooperation. "Your article refers to sources. That's a fact."

Davis shrugged, conceding the point. "I have a source who confirmed an unfiled report of a sexual assault. That is a fact."

"Confirmed?"

"And I attempted to interview the mayor, the chief, and Officer Stone but none have returned my calls yet. I'm expecting a call from the city attorney any time now."

"I'm conducting an investigation into Sonya Meyer's murder," Clint said. "I need to eliminate some suspects from consideration."

"Who are the suspects?"

Clint shook his head. "It's an ongoing investigation. I can share everything with you when it's resolved, but not before."

"Once it's resolved, I can get it all through a freedom of information request," Davis said. "I won't need you at that point."

Clint thought of his coded case notes. "You'll still need me. There's always stuff that doesn't make it into the official report."

"Are you suggesting there's corruption within the homicide unit?"

"No. I'm stating a fact. Not every fact or nuance makes it into the official report."

Davis took another sip of her cappuccino, watching Clint. Then she said, "On most days, I might enjoy playing this game of who's going to show who first, Detective. But I came over here to relax and soak in the sun. So how about you just get to the point?"

That was fine with Clint. "I need to know your source for the story."

"No, you don't. You *want* to know the source for my article."

Clint shrugged.

Davis shrugged back, miming him. "People in hell want ice water. That doesn't mean they get it."

"It's important to my investigation."

"I'm not sure if that's true, but it doesn't matter. There's no way I'm betraying my source."

"Not even to help solve a murder?"

Davis sat up straight. "Tell you what, Detective. You lay out your case for me and explain how knowing my source will solve the murder. If it really means bringing a killer to justice, I'll tell you. But you've got to show me."

"It's an open investigation," Clint said. "I can't."

"Well, that article is part of an open investigation, too. So I guess we're both stuck, unless we decide to trust each other."

Trust. If the English language made any sense, trust would be a four-letter word.

"I'm not asking for anything official," Clint said, trying a different tack. "I can find evidence through other means. I only need some indication, to narrow the field so I know where to focus."

Davis shifted back in her seat, crossing her arms.

"Was it Tyler Garrett?" he asked, watching her carefully.

Clint thought he saw a flicker—a micro-expression—but he couldn't be sure.

"Or was it Gary Stone?"

Davis's expression hardly changed, and he couldn't read the slight variations he saw with any certainty.

"Garrett?" she asked. "Stone? Are you telling me that you suspect these officers were involved in the murder of Sonya Meyer?"

Clint hesitated, considering his answer. "I...I'm not discussing that. I only want to know—"

"Detective," she interrupted, "I don't know exactly what is going on in your police department, but while I fully intend to report on it, I am not going to be dragged into the middle of it. I operate under a code of journalistic ethics that are nonnegotiable. You can't swoop in here and interrupt my coffee break with your broad pronouncements about what you need and expect me to betray those ethics. What did you think was going to happen? That I'd see your badge and be overwhelmed?"

Clint realized this was a lost cause. He stood up. "Journalistic ethics, huh? Sounds like a contradiction in terms to me."

"You mean like police integrity?"

Clint bit back his reply. He saw her true colors now, so at least the encounter wasn't a total loss. He knew her agenda. In a strange way, it aligned with his own, though she didn't see it yet. Even so, her refusal to help him today actually helped Garrett, regardless of who her source was.

You're all protecting him. Even the ones who don't know it.

The reporter was still watching him, so he gave her a short nod. "Ms. Davis," he said stiffly.

"Detective."

Clint turned and left the coffee shop.

EPILOGUE

In the midst of chaos, there is also opportunity.
—Sun Tzu, Chinese general, author, *The Art of War*

Chapter 70

Ray Zielinski stood outside the door to the hospital room, suddenly unsure. When he'd changed out of his uniform after shift, he'd had no plan to come to Holy Family Hospital. Tonight was rare in that he didn't have an extra duty gig, and he looked forward to the down time. But when he got into his personal car, the idea came to him, and he started driving until he was in the parking lot, and then walking into the hospital.

Maybe part of the reason had been the notification from IA that one of his demeanor complaints had been suspended as inconclusive. He'd learned that first thing in the morning, and while he'd have liked to have been exonerated, an inconclusive complaint was, for all practical purposes, just as good. The complaint was dead. His unreported collision still lurked out there, but for now, at least one less thing hung over his head.

Then, right after lunch, he got a call from his attorney, who informed him that the judge had denied Amber's motion requesting an alimony extension. She could still force the issue to trial, but due to the denied motion, the legal costs would be at her expense. His attorney didn't think she'd do that, and Zielinski thought he might be right. Maybe the guy wasn't quite the dumbass he'd thought.

So it was entirely possible that this trip to the hospital came to him out of the blue because he was feeling good, like things were breaking his way, and that he shouldn't let anything get in the way of doing what he thought was right.

This is probably still a bad idea.

He knocked, anyway.

"Come in," a weak voice called from within.

Zielinski eased open the door. He saw Lindsay Wagner sitting up in the bed nearest the door. The other bed was empty and made.

Wagner seemed surprised to see him, because he didn't say anything right away. The man's hair was flat and greasy, and his beard disheveled.

Zielinski moved closer to him, standing at the foot of the bed.

"I thought I'd see how you were doing," Zielinski said.

Wagner cleared his throat. "Yeah, huh?" He pointed next to where the blanket covered his single leg. "Still hurts, even though it's gone."

Zielinski had heard of that. Phantom pain, it was called.

"They've got you on meds?"

Wagner nodded. "Best the city can buy. But I try to take it easy on them. I've seen too many people get hooked, you know?"

He realized he was staring at the way the thin hospital blanket formed around the nub of Wagner's missing leg. How there was so much empty space below it, next to his remaining leg. It looked odd to him.

He glanced up, shaking his head a little. "I'm...I'm sorry they had to take it."

Wagner's eyes watered, and he looked away angrily. "It's not your fault. Infections happen, even in hospitals."

Zielinski didn't know how to answer that.

Wagner wiped at his tears, his jaw set. "They tell me that the bullet clipped my femoral artery. My doctor said the tourniquet you put on probably saved my life. So...thanks."

The words had an angry, hollow tone to them, but Zielinski muttered, "You're welcome."

They both fell silent for a long minute. Then Wagner turned toward him again. "I'm sorry. That was a pretty weak way to thank someone for such an important thing."

"It's fine."

"No, it's not. But it's…it's been hard. Sometimes I feel angry about what I've lost, other times I feel grateful to be alive. I'm all over the place emotionally, and the drugs don't exactly help keep me grounded."

"It's a good thing you work for Mental Health, right?"

Wagner gave him a strange look, then actually laughed. "Yeah, I guess so. I know all of the resources my department has to offer. Good point." He thought about it, then laughed a little more. "I can't believe you dragged me by my beard."

"I can't believe they let you wear a beard like that."

Wagner chuckled. "The benefits of a government job. You would if you could."

"I have a government job," Zielinski pointed out. "And I'd never grow a beard like that."

"And yet, they let you get away with that 'stache."

Zielinski grunted, disguising a laugh. *Score a point for the social worker.*

Another silence set in, this one a little easier. Wagner stared down at his hands, and Zielinski gazed out of the hospital window at the lights of the nearby houses. He imagined the people inside those houses, many of them sitting down to dinner, all going about their lives, never touched by the darker underside of their city.

"I heard it all, you know," Wagner said, after a while.

He looked back at him. "All?"

Wagner nodded. "I was pretty panicked at first, and I don't remember much. Just the shots and the pain and the blood, and then you grabbing me. But once you put that belt in my hand, things cleared up. I was still scared as hell, but I was aware. I heard Lyle yelling 'shit' right before you took off running toward the house."

Zielinski watched him speak, saying nothing.

"It's weird," Wagner said. "I mean, I was absolutely terrified that I was going to die. But when I heard you yell at Lyle not to move, I was just as afraid that you were going to shoot him. That you'd kill him."

He nodded slowly, not knowing what to say.

"Cops in this city don't exactly have a great track record when it comes to shooting people," Wagner said. "I've seen the national statistics. Maybe it's an aggressive philosophy, or maybe it's bad luck. I don't know. But I can tell you that I was afraid for Lyle." He paused, licking his lips before continuing. "That fear didn't go away when I heard Lyle yell that he'd dropped the gun. All I heard was the terror in his voice when he begged you not to murder him."

"I wouldn't do that," Zielinski whispered.

Wagner swallowed. "I wasn't sure. You'd been there before, and things didn't go well. And Lyle had been shooting at us…at you."

"I would never do that," Zielinski repeated.

"I know," Wagner said. "I know that now." Wagner smoothed the blanket in front of him and took a wavering breath. "I want to thank you for that. For…Lyle. People like him are the whole reason I went into this career. He can't help himself. Hell, he can't even get out of his own way. He needs me to help him. Maybe I can't save him from everything, but I can help him. That's all I want to do. Getting back to work is the only thing I'm focused on right now."

"You'll get there," Zielinski said quietly.

Wagner met his gaze. "I will." His expression was hopeful, even as tears sprang to his eyes again. "I *will*."

Zielinski swallowed and was surprised at the lump in his own throat. Despite the emotion, he felt strong. He nodded to Wagner.

"I know," he said.

Chapter 71

Captain Tom Farrell sat in his staff car, all alone in the nearly empty parking lot at the Spokane Arena, waiting. The spring sun was almost completely behind the mountains to the west, splashing a deep violet across the sky. The hum of passing cars on nearby Boone Avenue mixed with the steady chatter on the police radio, but despite the background noise, everything seemed still and quiet to Farrell.

He'd heard Garrett getting flagged down by a citizen reporting a suspicious circumstance of a possible dead body. He reported he was in Baker sector following up on a hit-and-run. Baker sector was outside his normal assigned patrol zone, but criminals didn't live and operate in neat zones the way the department deployed its teams. Regardless, he was sure Clint would have a theory or two why Garrett was really in Baker sector and it would have nothing to do with a collision investigation.

A couple minutes later, Garrett came over the radio. "Charlie three sixteen."

"Three sixteen," dispatch responded. "Go ahead."

"Sixteen," Garrett said, and then, for some reason, repeated his unit identifier, "Sixteen, confirming there is a dead white male at my location." The address he provided was up north.

"Three sixteen, do you need a medic?"

"Negative. He's been there some time. Start a supervisor and some additional units."

"Three sixteen, copy."

It sounded like a stinker and he'd smiled at that. Let the hotshot deal with an unpleasant call. It was a little karma, the first of what he hoped would be a slew of it coming around for Garrett.

His phone buzzed, and he checked the text. It was from Clint.

Seems a legit call. G probably did it, though. Headed to arena now.

Farrell chuckled slightly. He couldn't tell if Clint was being sarcastic or if he really thought this random event was Garrett's doing. That had become the default for the detective. To his eye, everything evil that happened in the city these days, Garrett was responsible for until proven otherwise.

He knew he had to manage Clint better. But how to do that? No one had ever really been able to accomplish it without resorting to pure hierarchal authority, and even then, Clint's compliance was grudging.

Besides, Clint was at his best when he followed his own way. He couldn't hold it too much in check or guide it with too firm a hand, especially since what they were doing was so far off book that he sometimes wondered if he was breaking any laws.

At least Gary Stone took direction well. He'd sent the officer to a two-week vehicle surveillance school in Seattle. Having a purpose seemed to brighten the young officer's morose attitude. Farrell counted on that continuing as he formed his team. He still needed to select a sergeant and the rest of the team members, but he had a few names on his short list, one in particular. They'd slow the upward crime trend, he knew. Maybe even reverse it.

That would make Baumgartner happy. After battling through the Rabe/Hahn incident, the chief was looking for a few wins to hold up to the public, and to the public safety committee. He'd confided to Farrell that Councilwoman Patterson was clearly gunning for him. Farrell didn't know Patterson well, but she seemed formidable. His bet was still on Baumgartner, though.

For his part, Farrell had been able to move things along. Hatcher remained cold to him, but he'd work on that by including her in the team's activities and successes. He understood why she was angry, and in another time and place, he would have stopped at nothing to kick the team back to her. It *had* been her idea. But he had another reason for commanding this team, a deeper purpose, and it was more important than anything.

He'd always heard that what goes around, comes around. But he'd also learned that sometimes you have to be the one to bring it around.

I'm coming for you, Garrett. We're *coming for you. And you will pay for the evil you've done.*

Farrell took a deep, cleansing breath. The day had been warm, and he could smell asphalt, but also the cool air coming off the Spokane River. It was a clean smell, and it gave him hope. Clint would be pulling up next to his car window soon, full of pragmatic pessimism and a thousand suspicions, but that was still a few minutes away. For now, he enjoyed the last light of the day, the smells and the sounds of the city, his city.

Chapter 72

Near the corner of Haven Street and Wellesley Avenue, Officer Tyler Garrett pulled his patrol car to the curb. He clicked off the local news channel and the political roundtable he'd been listening to on the radio.

He'd become a news junkie over the past several weeks since the story broke about Councilman Dennis Hahn and Betty Rabe. It was something he would never openly admit, but he liked watching how everyone danced to the music he played.

The resulting public outcry following the article was loud, and there was still an ongoing story today, although much of the initial anger and anguish had petered out.

At first, Mayor Sikes laid the blame entirely at the feet of Chief Robert Baumgartner. He tried to fault Officer Stone, but the chief cut that line of fire off, leaving the mayor to grumble openly about *his* police department, instead of a single officer. Garrett could not believe his good fortune that the two men who had screwed with his life following his shooting were openly sniping at each other in the news. Sharing the story with Kelly Davis had turned out better than he anticipated.

The potshots by the mayor and chief didn't last long, though.

Shortly after the story came out, the chief held a press conference and stated unequivocally that only he was to be held responsible for the screw up in reporting. Kelly Davis asked the chief directly if Officer Gary Stone had been instructed to keep the report out of the system. Baumgartner stated he had given poorly worded orders to Stone, but that was not his officer's fault.

To Garrett, Stone was a decent guy, but he was a poor cop. He was better suited for sipping lattes and creating PowerPoint presentations than kicking in doors and chasing down lowlifes. He was honestly surprised that Stone survived the incident. He wasn't sure where he'd been transferred to within the department, but he hadn't been terminated. It just reinforced the adage it wasn't what you knew, it was who you knew.

Baumgartner never wavered from his conviction that, ultimately, he was the one to be held responsible, not Stone. Garrett doubted the chief would ever do something like that for him, nor for many other guys on the department. Only his pets.

The chief also refused to call it a cover-up even when Kelly Davis continued to prod him in a subsequent interview. He stated she was bordering on the edge of fake news, a term that he borrowed from Mayor Sikes who himself had appropriated it from a recent presidential race. When supporters of Baumgartner began showing up outside city hall with *#fakenews* placards, Sikes soon championed the chief's position. That was a dog whistle for the mayor's diehards and before anyone knew it, there were daily crowds outside city hall in support of Sikes and Baumgartner. Garrett wondered if these were the same people who called for his firing following his shooting.

Councilwoman Margaret Patterson had immediately called for the chief's resignation which Baumgartner declined to even entertain. She then called on the mayor to fire him. In a display of rediscovered loyalty, Sikes stood behind his man, saying that he was sure Baumgartner had learned from the incident following his three-day suspension and would be clearer in his directions next time. Patterson threatened a council resolution of some sort, but with the current state the council was in, no one believed her capable of mounting a serious threat. She continued to bark, but there was no bite. Garrett liked the woman for her tenacity, but she was the type of person whose ambitions were too easily detected. Even he could see why she wanted to get rid of Baumgartner and it wasn't a good look in light of a young woman's suicide. It reeked of opportunism.

As for Dennis Hahn, his world collapsed after the story. A hospital employee leaked that he had been voluntarily committed to Sacred Heart following a suicide attempt. His wife and children went to her parents' where she was interviewed by a local news channel. It wasn't the flattering portrayal of a devoted spouse most politicians would enjoy. Patterson called for the council to remove Hahn, along with Patrick Armstrong and Justin Buckner, for violations of their moral turpitude clauses. When Hahn returned home, he packed a bag and fled Spokane. The man was weak. He should have stayed and fought like both Armstrong and Buckner. It was unlikely that those two would retain their seats, but at least they would go out fighting like men, not rolling over and curling up like Hahn.

Garrett exited his car and quietly shut the car door. The evening sun was setting, and he smiled. He might call in later and ask his supervisor for some comp time. He wanted to leave early tonight so he could spend some extra time with Tiana.

He studied the small house. For the past couple of workdays, he needed a viable reason to leave his sector. Tonight he finally got one with a hit-and-run suspect who lived in north Spokane.

He keyed his shoulder microphone. "Charlie three sixteen."

"Three sixteen, go ahead," a male dispatcher responded.

"Following up on a hit-an-run investigation in Baker sector. I was just flagged over at the corner of Wellesley and Haven. Also."

"Sixteen, go ahead." The dispatcher sounded bored.

"Female complainant stated there is a strange smell emanating from a nearby house where transients appear to be coming in and out."

"Sixteen, copy. Do you need an additional unit?"

"Not at this time. I'm code four," Garrett said. "Let me see what this is, and I'll advise."

"Charlie three sixteen, copy."

Garrett walked confidently around to the rear of the house. The smell wasn't strong, but if he focused, he could pick it up—the cloying smell of death. At the back, he pushed the door and it opened easily. He pulled his flashlight from his duty belt and yelled, "Spokane Police Department."

He felt foolish yelling into the house.

No one was going to answer him, but it was partly for show as much as it was for officer safety. Skunk hadn't been found yet. Garrett had been diligently watching for a call of a dead body, but no one had alerted the department. With each passing day, a worry grew in his gut that maybe someone had seen him in the neighborhood prior to killing the man. He'd learned to trust those nagging voices in his head. If someone had seen him near the house and the body was discovered by someone else, he would have a tough time explaining his presence in the neighborhood. However, if he was the one who found the body, and someone reported seeing him in the neighborhood, he would at least have some plausible deniability that they were mixing up their officers.

Garrett covered his mouth and nose with his gloved hand and walked inside. He quickly ensured that no one else was in the house. He doubted they would be, but he needed to be sure. Then he opened the door to the basement stairwell and saw Skunk, still lying in a heap.

He turned and exited the house. While he walked back to his car, he breathed the fresh air deeply through his nose. The stench of rotting flesh was hard to escape. It was then he realized he hadn't smelled the rancid feces coming from the bathroom. *Small blessings.* "Charlie three sixteen," Garrett said into his shoulder microphone.

"Three sixteen. Go ahead."

"Sixteen," Garrett said, then released the mic button as he stifled a yawn. "Sixteen," he repeated, "confirming there is a dead white male at my location." He read the numbers off the front of the little house.

"Three sixteen, do you need a medic?"

"Negative. He's been there some time. Start a supervisor and some additional units."

"Three sixteen, copy."

Garrett tuned out the dispatcher then and opened the passenger door to his car. He pulled out his nylon lunchbox and tossed it on the hood of his car. He proceeded to remove a ham and cheese sandwich.

As he ate, he watched the setting sun.

This homicide, Garrett mused, should be classified One-David—officer response, no report needed. No one would miss Skunk, not even his family. He was a waste of skin, an oxygen thief, a burden on society. Spending time on a homicide report was a waste of valuable resources, unless Wardell Clint caught the call. Then to hell with him. Let him spin his wheels on it. Waste his time. But for everyone else, Skunk didn't rate.

Which was too bad, because Garrett had hopes for the man. Unfortunately, he had turned out to be a moron, a guy with a soft head, and a weaker ability to reason. That cost him in the end. Hell, it cost Garrett, too, but he would overcome it. He always did.

And there would be more guys like Skunk out there. Garrett believed that. More than that, he knew it. There would always be more guys.

Because that was the first rule that he learned about building a drug crew.

Junkies and dealers are a renewable resource.

Acknowledgments

The authors wish to thank the following early readers for helping make this book what it is: Melanie Donaldson, Dave Mather, John Emery, Kristi Scalise, David Conway, Cheryl Counts, Judy Orchard, Bonnie Conway, and Carla Warren.

About the Authors

COLIN CONWAY is the author of the 509 Crime Stories, a series of novels set in Eastern Washington with revolving lead characters. They are standalone tales and can be read in any order. He served in the US Army and later was an officer of the Spokane Police Department. He's a commercial real estate broker/investor, owned a laundromat, invested in a bar, and ran a karate school. Colin lives with his beautiful life partner, their three wonderful children, and a crazy, codependent Vizsla that rules their world. Find out more about him at his official website: **ColinConway.com**.

FRANK ZAFIRO was a police officer in Spokane, Washington, from 1993 to 2013. He retired as a captain. He is the author of numerous crime novels, including the River City novels and the Stefan Kopriva series. He lives in Redmond, Oregon, with his wife Kristi, dogs Richie and Wiley, and a very self-assured cat named Pasta. He is an avid hockey fan and a tortured guitarist. You can keep up with Frank at **FrankZafiro.com**.

Are You Ready for the Next Book in
the Charlie-316 Series?

BADGE HEAVY

When the Spokane Police Anti-Crime Team (ACT) was formed, the expectation was that its efforts would make a dent in the city's rising crime rate. In only its first few weeks of existence, the team has done even better than hoped for, racking up arrests and seizures of guns, drugs, money, and stolen cars. Everyone from the mayor to the citizenry seems happy with ACT's swift results.

But there are darker agendas surrounding this team. Bonds of loyalty are being forged, secret schemes made, and suspicions are focused in all directions. In the midst of run-and-gun police work, officers will discover that not everything is as it seems. Who to trust becomes a life and death question for everyone involved.

In this third installment of the Officer Tyler Garrett saga, the stakes have risen even higher. Garrett seeks to solidify his position. Officer Gary Stone undergoes a surprising metamorphosis. Captain Farrell tries to bring the situation to a head. Rookie Jun Yang struggles to find her place, while Officer Ray Zielinski must repay a debt that threatens to land him in greater danger. Meanwhile, Detective Wardell Clint continues to gnaw at the bone of the case that has consumed him for almost two years.

Something has got to give.